Also by Anna Jacobs

BIRCH END SAGA
Daughter's Journey
Widow's Courage

ELLINDALE SAGA
One Quiet Woman
One Kind Man
One Special Village
One Perfect Family

RIVENSHAW SAGA
Time to Remember
A Time for Renewal
A Time to Rejoice
Gifts For Our Time

THE TRADERS
The Trader's Wife
The Trader's Sister
The Trader's Dream
The Trader's Gift
The Trader's Reward

E SWAN RIVER SAGA
Farewell to Lancashire
Beyond the Sunset
Destiny's Path

HE GIBSON FAMILY
Salem Street
High Street
Ridge Hill
Hallam Square
Spinners Lake

THE IRISH SISTERS
A Pennyworth of Sunshine
Twopenny Rainbows
Threepenny Dreams

THE STALEYS
Down Weavers Lane
Calico Road

THE KERSHAW SISTERS
Our Lizzie
Our Polly
Our Eva
Our Mary Ann

THE SETTLERS
Lancashire Lass
Lancashire Legacy

THE PRESTON FAMILY
Pride of Lancashire
Star of the North
Bright Day Dawning
Heart of the Town

LADY BINGRAM'S AIDES
Tomorrow's Promises
Yesterday's Girl

STANDALONE NOVELS
Jessie
Like No Other
Freedom's Land

A Woman's Pro

TH
A

TH

TH
A

TH

T

ANNA JACOBS

A Woman's Promise

Birch End Saga Book Three

First published in Great Britain in 2020 by Hodder & Stoughton
An Hachette UK company

1

A CIP catalogue record for this title is available from the British Library

Hardback ISBN 978 1 473 67786 9
eBook ISBN 978 1 473 67787 6

Typeset in Plantin Light by Palimpsest Book Production Limited, Falkirk, Stirlingshire

Printed and bound in Great Britain by Clays Ltd, Elcograf S.p.A.

Hodder & Stoughton policy is to use papers that are natural, renewable and recyclable products and made from wood grown in sustainable forests. The logging and manufacturing processes are expected to conform to the environmental regulations of the country of origin.

Hodder & Stoughton Ltd
Carmelite House
50 Victoria Embankment
London EC4Y 0DZ

www.hodder.co.uk

Dear Reader,

Here is the third story in the Birch End series. I hope you enjoy *A Woman's Promise*, which is set in 1935 and is about a woman who is not following a traditional path in life.

After that we'll be moving on to a new series set in Backshaw Moss which is 'near' Birch End in my imaginary valley. I keep having to remind myself that it's an imaginary place, it seems so real at times. I've 'seen' the heroine of the new story but I have no idea yet what she'll get up to. She'll show me once I start writing properly about her life.

Readers seem to have enjoyed my old photos, so I've added two more to the end of this book: at least, one is a photo, but the other is something a bit different.

The young couple in the photo are my parents just before they married, aged nineteen and seventeen in 1939. This was before my dad got called up into the army. He was sent to the Middle East in 1941 and spent the rest of the war there. They didn't see one another for over four years, but they wrote every single day. After he came back, they didn't let anything separate them, as you can imagine.

I still remember him returning after four years away. I was nearly five by then and not at all used to having a dad living with us. The family woke me up in the middle of the night and brought a big soldier in uniform into the bedroom I shared with my aunt. So of course I stuck my tongue out at him. I got teased about that for years.

I thought I'd show you something different instead of a second photo. This is a page from my great-aunt's autograph album from about 1905, with a pencil sketch done by one of her friends. The album has at least a dozen careful drawings, really good ones too. Without the distractions of TV and computers, people often entertained themselves by doing creative things. I've smiled at this man falling over on the ice a good few times over the years. It's a very feeble joke but a very careful drawing.

I hope you enjoy my new tale. There are more stories fighting one another at the back of my brain to be given their day in the sun. I'm not short of story ideas, just time to write them.

At least I don't waste my writing time by ironing! I haven't ironed anything for about ten years. My husband and I were wondering the other day where we've put the iron and if it still works. But neither of us tried to find it.

Happy reading!
Anna

A Woman's Promise

I

Lancashire: January 1935

Frankie Redfern sighed and pushed her hair out of her eyes, retying the piece of string she'd grabbed to hold her hair back as she bent over to apply a final coat of polish to the small bookcase she was working on.

It would have been more practical to have worn her hair short and more fashionable too, but her mother would have thrown a fit if she'd done that as well as going out of the house wearing 'those ghastly men's trousers'.

'Was your mother in one of her moods today, miss?' the foreman asked.

'How did you guess?'

'You've got that look on your face again.' He gave her shoulder a fatherly pat and left her to get on with the work she loved. She'd taken her brother's place in the family business during the Great War, but that was patriotic so her mother had had to put up with it. But to stay on working there after it ended was apparently shameful.

Her fiancé, Martin, had been killed in the last year of the war and then her twin brother Don a few weeks later. That had been the worst time of her whole life, the very worst. When others were out celebrating the end of the war, she'd locked herself in her bedroom and wept.

Frankie's father had told his daughter to do what she

truly wanted, and tried to stop her mother nagging. As if anyone could.

As a child, she'd often wondered why her mother didn't love her. She could tell, because she saw how her mother treated her brother.

Fortunately, she had known that her father loved her and Don equally, and that had helped so much. And when both young men had been killed, her father had helped her cope with her grief.

Oh well, no use going over that again. Sometimes in life you just had to carry on.

She stopped to stare at herself in a mirror as she moved to and fro, putting away her tools. She would turn thirty-eight in a few months. Where had all the years gone since the Great War? Sixteen years it was now. With well over a million young men killed there simply hadn't been enough men left to provide husbands for all her generation of young women, so she'd never married or had a family.

She shook her head, annoyed at herself. She had a satisfying and useful life, so must be content with that. At least she had work she loved to fill her days.

Her father came out of his office with a pleased look on his face. 'That was Mr Paulson on the telephone. We got that job doing the repairs on that Ravensworth Terrace house, the one where they had a fire in the back room last week.'

'Oh, good!'

'You'll enjoy the work because there's a fancy mantelpiece to redo as well as repairs to some furniture. I'll leave the delicate stuff to you while I supervise the rest.'

'I'll enjoy that.'

Sam nodded, picked up a chisel to get on with his work then put it down and looked round as if checking that no one was near. 'I'd better warn you: your mother was going on at me again last night after you went to bed for letting you carry on working here. She says we're not short of money now, which is true, and I should get a man in to do that work. She got hysterical and threatened to burn all your trousers.'

'I thought we'd sorted that out once and for all years ago. I can't work properly in skirts, anyway. It'd be dangerous and they'd get in the way. What started her off this time?'

'Her friend Lily's daughter has got engaged to a widower. Nora's about your age apparently, so it's raised Jane's hopes that you can still find a husband. She's saying it's not too late for us to have grandchildren, even if you are a disappointment to her.' He patted Frankie's shoulder. 'Eh, she never gives up, does she? And that cousin of hers seems to be egging her on. Lately it's as if Higgerson wants to get you out of the business. What's it got to do with him anyway?'

'I can't abide Higgerson. Thank goodness he's only a distant relative.'

Frankie let her own determination show. Her father hadn't been well lately and had given in to his wife on a few smaller things, as if he didn't have the energy to argue. 'I will *not* spend all day sitting in the office, or even worse, stop work completely, Dad. I'd go mad with boredom.'

She looked down at her hands, hard-working hands on a tall strong body. She had calluses on them here and there, earned by honest toil. She held them out to him pleadingly now. 'I'm good at working with these, you know I am, Dad.'

'Aye, you're as good as any man at the cabinetmaking side of our business, I admit, and better than most. But not everyone agrees that it's right for you to do such a job, however good you are. I've had people say to my face that you're taking work away from a man.'

She snorted in disgust. 'Show me the man in Ellin Valley who can do what I do!'

'I can't, because there isn't one. You're the best I know at what you do. Exceptional, old Bill used to say. And he was the best foreman I ever had, so no one could know better. Even so, you only got your trade papers because the authorities thought the Frankie who'd completed the apprenticeship was a man.'

'I was lucky there, wasn't I?' They'd been too embarrassed about the mistake to take her trade certificate away again, especially with Bill backing her.

He sighed. 'I worry about you, though, love. What will happen to you and the business if I die?'

'You're just going through a bad patch with your health,' she said soothingly.

'It's more than that. I'm not as strong as I used to be and I'll turn sixty next year. Sometimes men of my age drop dead unexpectedly. I've seen it happen more than once, lost a good pal last year like that.'

She felt sick at the mere thought of losing her father.

He paused, fiddled with a piece of wood and then burst out, 'Eh, Frankie love, you're still a fine-looking woman and you don't look your age at all. It *is* still possible that you could marry. I won't nag you like Jane does, but I hope you won't turn away the chance if a good man tries to court you.'

'It wasn't only my twin brother who was killed in 1918, but my fiancé, Dad.'

'Do you still think about him?'

'In a way. I remember how I loved Martin with all my heart. I couldn't marry anyone just to be able to call myself Missus. I'd have to care for him as well.'

'We all had young loves once. Not many folk get to marry them.'

'I know.' Her father married his first love. After the poor girl died, his parents had encouraged him to marry Frankie's mother even though she was older than him because Jane would bring him money. And he'd paid for it dearly.

No use dwelling on that. 'Working with you has given me more satisfaction than a loveless marriage and life as a housewife ever could, Dad.'

'I do understand how much you care about your work, but surely you wanted children?'

She didn't talk about that to anyone. Of course she had wanted children, still felt sad about the lack. She tried to distract him.

'I'm not cut out to be a housewife. You've heard Mother's view of my sewing many a time. As for playing the piano, which she's also been suggesting I try again, I was Mrs Fumble Fingers with that when I was younger. Remember?'

He grinned. 'I used to go out for a walk if I was at home while you did your daily half hour on the piano. You're definitely not musical.'

'No. I'm practical and what I love most is working with wood.' She picked up a piece of oak and ran her fingertips down the grain, a lover's caress. 'I was lucky. Bill was a wonderful teacher.'

'Aye, and after the war when there wasn't much work around, those pieces of furniture you and he made helped bring in much-needed money. People are still willing to pay more for your pieces.'

'I know. But even now they offer less if they know they've been made by a woman.'

'I don't take less, do I?'

She smiled at him. 'No, Dad.'

He sighed wearily. 'I'm fighting your mother all over again about you working with me, though. It's very wearing.'

'Yes. We've both suffered the sharp end of her tongue lately and she's getting worse.'

They were both silent for a moment or two, then she said briskly, 'Anyway, I'm set in my ways now. I couldn't stay meekly at home and let a man order me around. Why should I? I've got a good brain in my head as well as these hands.'

'Aye, you're right about that. But will you make me one promise, at least?'

She looked at him suspiciously. 'What about?'

'If you ever do meet a likely chap, you'll give him a chance.'

She couldn't see herself meeting anyone at her age, so shrugged. 'All right. I promise.'

'And if anything happens to me, you'll find someone to marry as quickly as you can.'

She looked at him anxiously. He must be feeling worse than he'd let on.

His voice grew harsh. 'Promise that, too.'

'All right. I promise.'

'I know you'll keep your word, my lass. You've never in your life broken a promise to me.'

'What happens to the business if you die?' He'd always refused to talk about that.

'It's time you knew. The business has to go to her. I signed a lawyer's paper about that when we married because her family supplied the money to set things up.'

'She wouldn't let me work here if she was in charge.'

'No. I'm afraid not. I've always hoped she'd change her mind when she saw how good you were at the work, but she won't.' He shook his head sadly. 'She's grown more unreasonable over the years, I'm afraid. I threatened to change my will the other day when we were arguing, and she turned very strange, said I'd regret it if I did and she still had family to look after her interests.'

He looked so worried Frankie waited a few moments to

let him calm down before she spoke again. 'If anything happened to you, I'd leave home and set up my own cabinet-making business, perhaps in another town. I have the money my brother and Martin left me. I've looked after it and it's grown quite nicely. If I were careful, there would be enough to start a small business.'

He frowned. 'You've got that much?'

Her voice thickened with tears. 'Yes. But I'd rather have had them alive still than have their money, far rather.'

She kept her bank book and a few other important papers in a locked strong box she'd bought. It was at the office where her mother couldn't break into it. She rummaged through Frankie's bedroom regularly.

Realising that her father was still talking, she forced herself to pay attention.

'I've never said anything to your mother about you dealing with the money yourself because it'd give her something else to get upset about.'

'Does she know you pay me the same wages as a man?'

'Good heavens, no! She'd throw a fit. Even the Bible disagrees with her on that: "the labourer is worthy of his hire".'

'Or *her* hire!'

'In your case well worth it, love.' He changed the subject then.

But their conversation left her feeling even more worried than before.

That evening her mother didn't stop talking about Lily's daughter Nora finding herself a man at last, all this interspersed with pointed remarks about *Frances* being so unnatural that she'd never made the slightest effort to attract one.

It was a relief when bedtime came and Frankie could take refuge in her bedroom.

One day she'd have a home of her own, where she could do what she wanted and didn't have to go to bed so early to get a bit of peace and quiet. She could have afforded to buy a little house, but it'd cause talk for her to leave her parents' house and live alone in the same town.

Over the next few days Frankie wished very strongly that Nora hadn't found herself a husband, because it had stirred up hope in her mother again. She started nagging Frankie about her appearance and would probably now go on the hunt for a husband for her daughter – and just about any man would do.

Ugh! Frankie hated the thought of being paraded around like a prize cow as her mother had done after the war.

And that horrible cousin of her mother's would no doubt join in the hunt this time. Why had Higgerson started paying more attention to her mother? It didn't make sense. He'd never seen her so often before and he always looked bored when he came to call on them.

After days of that haranguing, Frankie decided to go for a long walk across the tops at the weekend. She loved to stride out over the moors beyond Birch End and breathe in the clean, bracing air.

It was never as good going for walks here in Rivenshaw. Towns were smoky places and the only park was small and full of people who knew her mother and reported back on who Frankie spoke to, it always seemed.

She had to run a gauntlet of criticism and even disobey a direct order to go to church. As she left the house, her mother screeched down the hall after her, 'You'll be sorry, you cheeky young madam. I'll bring you to heel yet, see if I don't.'

Frankie sighed with relief as she hurried to catch the only Sunday morning bus up the hill towards the village of Birch

End. She'd walk on the moors nearby and then follow a country path she knew back down to Rivenshaw.

She needed to have a good long think about her life. She couldn't go on like this and would have to find some way to change things.

2

Jericho Harte woke in the basement bedroom he shared with his two younger brothers and looked up at the frost on the window at the top of the ventilation well next to his bed. He didn't like to lie around once he'd woken, so got up and crept up to the living room, leaving his brothers sleeping.

His mother was already up and dressed, sitting sipping a cup of tea. He waved to her and went into the bathroom to wash and dress. As he returned, he paused at the door to smile fondly at her. They'd moved recently from the slum at Backshaw Moss into this three-room dwelling with the luxury of its own bathroom, and she hadn't stopped smiling and looking happy since.

He was grateful to the Pollards for giving them this place in return for helping keep the house and its occupants safe. Wilf Pollard was a shining example of how far hard work could take you in life. He'd started from humble beginnings and managed to support his first wife and children through the hard times by going on the tramp to find work in nearby towns and villages. In the process he'd learned to do all sorts of jobs.

After her death he'd re-married and joined Roy Tyler as a junior partner in his building business, which was based in Birch End. They'd started giving work regularly to Jericho and casual jobs to his brothers sometimes.

Now that his family was starting to get on its feet again after his mother's long illness and expensive operation, Jericho wanted to do more than just make a living. He was determined to make a success of his life. He might not do as well as Wilf, but he could try, couldn't he?

He realised he was still standing like a fool, holding the teapot and doing nothing with it. After pouring himself a mug of nice strong tea he sat down at the table.

'You're looking well, Mam.'

'I am well now, thanks to you boys. But I'm sorry my appendix operation and recovery from it took all our money.'

'Your life was worth every penny. Look, I've got some really good news for you, Mam.' He paused and took a deep breath, hardly daring to say it out loud, 'Mr Tyler has offered me a regular job.'

'Oh, Jericho love, I'm that pleased for you. Maybe now you can make a more normal life for yourself in other ways.'

He looked at her warily, guessing what was coming. 'You're not talking about me finding a wife, are you?'

'Well, you're thirty-five and it'll be too late to start a family if you leave it much longer.'

'I'm not marrying just for the sake of it. I've not met anyone I *want* to marry and I've seen how unhappy some people are if they marry the wrong person. I'd rather stay single than risk that. Far rather.'

'Lots of people are happy together. I was with your dad.'

'I know, Mam. I remember. But you've been without him for ten years now. Why don't *you* find yourself another husband if you're so keen on married life?'

'Cheeky devil!' She pretended to swat him with the newspaper.

He changed the subject. 'I think I'll go for a tramp across the tops this morning.'

She looked out of the window. 'When I brought in today's milk bottles it felt as if there was damp in the air.'

'Well, even if it rains and I get wet, I won't melt.'

He got restless sometimes, couldn't just sit around doing nothing. Maybe once he was working full time, he'd not have that problem. But nothing ever really switched off his brain and stopped him thinking about the wider world, even if the newspapers he read for free at the library were usually several days old.

By nine o'clock the sun had melted most of the silver frost from the grass, so he put on his overcoat and wrapped his neck in the long multi-coloured scarf his mother had knitted for him. He wore it more to please her than because he would feel the cold. He put his cap on too, so that he would look respectable. It was what you did. But he'd take it off and stuff it in his pocket once he was away from the village. He loved to feel the wind in his hair.

He set off along a little-used path that twisted round the edge of the field next to their back garden and led up the hill behind the new houses in the posher part of Birch End. The council hadn't allowed Higgerson to block that ancient right of way when he built these, thank goodness, or everyone would have had to go a much longer way round to get up to the moors.

Higgerson! Jericho hated even the sound of that name. The fellow might be the biggest builder in the valley by far, but he was also the biggest cheat, building shoddy houses which looked nice but soon developed faults.

He'd been their landlord in Backshaw Moss, owned half that slum, and his agent had refused to do any repairs. When they kept asking he'd had the Hartes and all their possessions thrown out.

Jericho clicked his tongue in annoyance at himself. What was he thinking about that sod for? They had a lovely home now, thanks to Wilf, who did know how to build and repair houses properly.

He whistled tunelessly as he strode along. He hadn't even

suggested that his brothers join him. They thought him crazy going out walking for no reason, but he loved it. It felt good to be out on the tops, so very good! He breathed deeply, enjoying the bracing air.

He was looking forward to starting work full time at Tyler's tomorrow, but today was his own to enjoy as he pleased.

As he left the last buildings behind, Jericho saw a woman walking across the moors in the distance and stopped to shade his eyes. There was something familiar about her. Oh yes, it was Miss Redfern, who worked in her family business in Rivenshaw. Carpenters they were and had a good reputation.

She'd been pointed out to him a while back as an oddity because she did a man's job. The conversation had stuck in his mind, because the chap who'd told him about her had got very worked up about her taking men's work. When Jericho asked what exactly she did, his companion had scowled in her direction.

'Claims to do fancy cabinetmaking and inlay work. I'd like to see that! No woman can do such skilled work. But if your father's the boss, like hers is, you can say what you want, can't you, and no one will dare to contradict you?'

'There aren't many men in the valley who're trained cabinetmakers. Who is she taking jobs from? Who's there to do the work if she doesn't?'

'They'd come from elsewhere. Work's not plentiful anywhere in the north. A woman shouldn't be doing it at all, that's what I say, and I'm not the only one.'

Jericho didn't argue because he didn't care what this fool thought. Women had done men's work during the Great War, all sorts of jobs, and had helped win the war for their country. Why, his own mother had worked in a place making parts for army vehicles and left him and his brothers with her mother. No one had complained about her taking a man's job then, had they?

He reached the moors proper and carried on across them, knowing his path would join Miss Redfern's. There was only one way up to Hey Top from here and it had the best view across this part of the Pennines. He hoped the sight of a man going in the same direction wouldn't make her nervous because he'd set his heart on sitting on a sheltered rocky ledge he knew and simply drinking in the view.

She glanced in his direction a couple of times and paused once to shade her eyes and stare at him.

He carried on, striding as steadily as he could along the uneven ground of the narrow path. When he was a few paces away, they both stopped and he nodded to her. 'It's a lovely day, isn't it, Miss Redfern?'

'You know me?'

'I've seen you in town.'

'You look familiar to me, too, but I don't know your name.'

'I'm Jericho Harte. I'm starting a new job with Roy Tyler tomorrow. I was coming to sit on Hey Top and look at the world.'

After another searching glance she seemed to relax. 'I was going to do the same thing.'

'If you'd rather I leave you to do that alone, I'll walk on and find somewhere else to sit.'

'That'd be silly, wouldn't it? There's plenty of room for both of us. I love to look out across the tops to Yorkshire.'

He nodded and waited for her to move forward and choose a place to sit, then found himself a seat on the other side of a tumble of smaller rocks. She couldn't think he was waiting to pounce on her from there.

He saw that she was still watching him, smiling slightly as if she'd understood perfectly well what he was doing. Then she took a few deep breaths, clasped her arms around her knees and seemed to forget about him.

He didn't forget about her. She seemed to fit in here as if she was part of the landscape and by hell, she was a fine figure of a woman. He couldn't help noticing that because he was over six foot tall and found most women too small and childlike for his taste.

'I heard your family had moved into the back part of the cottage on Croft Street, Mr Harte,' she said suddenly. 'It's such a pretty building and I envy the Pollards living so close to the moors. His children must love having a big garden to play in as well.'

He was glad she'd spoken first, had wanted to chat to her, but hadn't liked to start a conversation.

'They do enjoy it. They're a grand pair of little 'uns.'

She stared into space again and when she spoke, he wasn't quite sure whether she was thinking aloud or continuing their conversation.

'I'd have given all my dolls and toys to be allowed to play wild out of doors as a child, but my mother didn't think it nice for little girls to get themselves dirty. I used to sneak out to play with my brother, though, and come back dirty anyway. It was worth a scolding.'

He decided it'd be all right to answer. 'It's normal for kids to get dirty. Me and my brothers all did.'

'Yes. But my mother still complains if I look less than neat, even now, though how she expects me to do my job without getting dirty sometimes, I don't understand.'

'Someone told me you're a cabinetmaker. You couldn't stay tidy while you're doing that sort of work.'

'No. My twin brother was given little tools and taught to use them as a boy but I had to throw a few tantrums to get my own hammer and saw, and be allowed to play with similar pieces of wood.' She looked at him as if expecting criticism.

'I envy you having a proper trade. I've had to pick up what skills I could along the way. I passed the exam for grammar school, mind, but my parents couldn't afford to send me there. Luckily for me Mr Tyler thinks I'm good with my hands, so he's taken me on and he's going to give me some more training. I shall enjoy that.'

'He's a good builder, everyone says so. Higgerson on the other hand—' She broke off and gave him a doubtful glance as if not sure whether to continue.

He finished it for her, '—cuts corners when he can. I'm not afraid to say that aloud, because he already hates me and my family.'

'He hates anyone else who's doing well, but he's left my father alone so far. That's partly because he's a distant relative of my mother's and partly because we only work in a small way, as well as making furniture. So that doesn't conflict with his building business.'

'He hates Mr Tyler. I worry that Higgerson will try to get at him and destroy his business. He must have thought it was going downhill without any help from him after Trevor Tyler was killed, but now Mr Tyler's bringing it to life again. The lads at work are all a bit worried for his safety. We need to—'

The brightness of the day suddenly dimmed and he didn't finish what he'd been going to say but looked up to see that while they'd been chatting a cloud had covered the sun and other clouds were racing across the sky to join it. 'I think it's going to rain soon. I was so lost in the pleasure of having someone to chat to that I didn't pay attention to the weather.'

He stood up and gestured towards the path. 'If we don't want to get soaked, I think we'd better start back towards Birch End.'

She stood up as nimbly as he had. 'I suppose so.'

'You don't sound as if you want to go back.'

'I don't. My mother has invited a gentleman to tea. She's trying to match-make. I don't want to marry.'

'Not ever?'

'No. Because it'd mean I'd have to stop working.'

'Why should it mean that?'

She looked at him as if surprised. 'Because men don't like their wives working outside the home. They just want domestic slaves.'

'That'd be a sad waste if you're as good at cabinetmaking as people say.' He noticed suddenly the calluses on her hands and enjoyed the way she was striding out as strongly as he was. She was different from other women but in ways he liked.

'Yes, it would. But my father is getting nagged because my mother's desperate to find me a husband. Any man will do. She's worn my father down about things before and he's not been very well lately so I worry, but she won't wear me down. I refuse to marry someone just for the sake of it.'

She sighed and her voice grew softer. 'I was engaged at the end of the war, but Martin was killed. He taught me what real love is like, though.'

She flushed and added, 'I'm sorry. I don't know what's got into me today. I don't usually talk to people about my feelings, but she's been going on and on at me all week worse than ever and I've had to bite my tongue till I felt the words would burst out of me.'

'I'm happy to lend an ear.'

'You're easy to talk to. Please don't tell anyone what I said, though. It's all just – you know, got on top of me lately. Which is why I came out here instead of going to church.'

'I promise I'll not say anything. And I wish you luck with your tea party.'

'With Mr Timson? I shall hate every minute of it.'

'Timson!' Jericho had been about to say something but

snapped his lips closed again. That man was famous for his lecherous ways but you couldn't say that to a lady.

'It's all right. I've heard about him. People whisper titbits of gossip behind my back but I have excellent hearing. Anyway, I met Timson once or twice while his poor wife was still alive. She looked unhappy and cowed, and even when she was in the room with us he still stared at me in a way I found offensive. There is no way on earth my mother could persuade me to have anything to do with him.'

She set off walking again and he followed suit, rather surprised at what she'd told him. Being comfortably off financially clearly didn't mean someone had an easy life. And what was her mother thinking of, inviting that lecherous scoundrel round to tea just because he was looking for a new wife to run his house and warm his bed?

As a few fat raindrops began to plop on his face and hands Jericho looked up at the sky. 'Look at those dark clouds. It's going to pelt down soon. There's a sort of cave just down that slope. I discovered it as a lad. We could shelter there and wait till the worst of the rain eases off. If you don't mind scrambling down the rough ground, that is.'

'I don't mind at all. You lead the way. I don't want to go back until I have to but if I turned up soaked to the skin, she'd not let it drop for days.'

When she stumbled and nearly fell, he grabbed her hand with a laugh and she smiled back. He kept hold of it till they got to shelter.

The place was barely big enough to be called a cave but it faced in the right direction to avoid the prevailing winds. He watched her take off her headscarf and try to shake off the raindrops, but one end caught in her hair and pulled some of it out of the bun. It tumbled down on her shoulders, a lovely rich brown with chestnut glints.

'Oh drat!' She began to fumble with the scarf and only made things worse. 'I can't find where the end is caught.'

'Keep your head still.' He leaned across and gently untangled the scarf from the hairpin that had snagged the end of it. 'There you go.'

'Thank you.' She sat on the rocky ledge, clasped her hands round her knees and stared out at the curtain of rain that had shut them into the cave. 'My goodness, it is a heavy downpour!'

'It'll ease off in a few minutes.'

He stared out too, or tried to, but his gaze kept going back to her. He hadn't realised how beautiful she could look with her hair spread over her shoulders and her face flushed and laughing. Did she hide her beauty on purpose? No, it wasn't beauty exactly, more a sort of vibrant womanhood. He doubted she'd ever gone hungry like most poorer women. Indeed she looked to be brimming with health and vitality. That was far more attractive to him than doll-like prettiness ever could be.

Who'd have thought? He hadn't found a woman attractive for years, nor had he tried to find one and start courting. What would have been the point? He couldn't afford to marry and he didn't want to get trapped into marriage and poverty by landing a woman in trouble. But Frankie Redfern was magnificent. Beyond his reach, of course, but if she hadn't been, he'd have loved to get to know her better.

She turned and saw him looking at her. His admiration must have shown because she flushed slightly. 'As you may guess, I'm a tomboy at heart. My mother says that sort of behaviour puts men off.'

'It wouldn't put me off. You're a lovely woman.'

The words seemed to echo and it was his turn to flush. 'Sorry. I didn't mean to be personal.'

She surprised him by chuckling. 'It's a long time since a

man gave me a sincere compliment, and I don't find what you said at all offensive. Thank you for making me feel good about my appearance. *She* says I look more like a man than a woman the way I dress.'

'She must be blind.'

They continued to sit there, not talking for the sake of it but occasionally exchanging remarks. He enjoyed the companionable silences in between too.

'It's easing off,' she said after a while.

'What a pity.'

She nodded, stole a glance at him and smiled rather shyly.

Another silence, then she looked at the little fob watch pinned to her shirt and stood up. 'I'd better get going or I'll be late for tea and she'll throw a fit. I've enjoyed your company, Mr Harte.'

'And I've enjoyed yours, Miss Redfern.'

After that they walked along, only chatting about the view or how to avoid a puddle covering a dip in the path. But he still enjoyed being with her. And couldn't stop admiring that beautiful hair.

3

When she got home, Frankie was greeted by her mother with, 'What on earth have you been doing to come home looking like . . . like a beggar woman?' She dragged her daughter into the sitting room and pointed to the mirror over the fireplace. 'Look at you! Not even a hat! Just a scruffy old headscarf. That's the last time you go out walking on the moors on your own, the very last.'

'Let go of my arm, please, Mother.'

Instead, Jane gave her daughter's arm another shake and tightened her grip. 'Not till I've brought you to your senses. Take a good, long look at yourself. I will *not* have you going out on the streets again looking like that.'

What Frankie saw in the mirror were two women who resembled one another slightly physically, but oh, not in character. Her mother was shorter and usually had a sour expression on her face, which seemed to mar her looks. Today she was furiously angry and it showed, turning her face into a warped, ugly mask.

Again Frankie tried to pull away but her mother took her by surprise, giving her a hard shake and dragging her round to face the mirror again. She tried to keep calm, because a lack of response usually defused the situation, but even that didn't work this time.

She couldn't understand this fury. Was it because of Nora finding a husband? Or was her mother's temper getting worse for some other reason?

'Just look at yourself. What on earth made you go out walking in such chancy weather anyway? And on the moors of all places. You could have been murdered out there and your body never found.'

'There's no one to harm me there. It's not as if I was in Backshaw Moss.'

'Well, when you come back with your hair all bedraggled, you look more suited to a slum like that, more like a factory girl than a young lady. How are we to get your hair dried and put up in a nice, flattering style before your guest arrives?'

As the grip on her arm relaxed a little, Frankie pulled away and took a quick step backwards. 'Timson isn't *my* guest. I can't stand the man and how can you not know that he has a terrible reputation as far as women are concerned?'

'You haven't even given him a chance. His wife must have made him unhappy at home to make him look elsewhere for comfort. I find him very pleasant and once you've had time to enjoy his company, you'll feel differently about him too. He isn't married now, so you can give him a chance – as your father told me you'd promised you would.'

'I promised my father to give a chance to a decent man, not to a . . . a lecherous one.'

'Watch your language!' Her mother slapped her across the face so hard Frankie stumbled back a couple of steps. Jane froze, looking worried for a few seconds, before tossing her head and scowling at her daughter again.

'How dare you hit me?' Her new position in the room let Frankie see in the mirror that her father had been standing in the hall eavesdropping and must have seen what happened. But even as she watched, he turned and walked away, making no attempt to tell his wife not to do that again. His avoidance of this confrontation hurt her far more than the slap had done.

She whirled round and tossed words at her mother like arrows. 'Don't you *ever–dare–*do that to me again!'

'You deserved it. You shouldn't have spoken to me like that. I'm your mother and I have the right to chastise you as long as you're living under my roof.'

'I see.' There was only one answer to that – she'd have to find another home. But she didn't say that yet because she didn't want to do anything rashly. Instead she contented herself with, 'You should be ashamed to throw me at a man like him. Any man would do for you, though, wouldn't he? As long as he was able to marry me and give you grandchildren to bully, like you're trying to bully me now. Well, you can entertain Timson on your own. I'm not going near him.'

She fingered her cheek, which was still stinging from the blow, and another glance in the mirror showed her how red it was. The words seemed to burst out of their own accord. 'If you ever lay a hand on me again, I shall leave this house and set up home on my own.'

'Oh yes? And how could you afford to do that? I'd make sure you didn't work for your father any longer, for a start. In fact, I may do that anyway. *He* won't take your side against me. He knows where his money comes from.'

She'd said that before and Frankie didn't believe her. Only something seemed to be stopping her father from intervening. She made no attempt to continue their argument, merely turned and walked swiftly past her mother up to her room.

'Get your clothes changed and hurry up about it.' Her mother yelled up the stairs after her. 'I want you down here in time to greet our guest.'

Frankie didn't answer. She locked her bedroom door on the world and went to stand by the window, breathing slowly and deeply. Once she touched her sore cheek, which felt hot. She pressed it against the cold windowpane as she tried to calm down.

All she could see through the window was their own backyard and rows of houses jostling one another in this sought-after position near Rivenshaw town centre. Large, comfortable houses, some of them, but she positively ached sometimes for the greenery and space they were lacking.

She swallowed hard but now that she was alone she couldn't stop a few tears from trickling down her cheeks. She didn't often let herself weep but this was too much and she wasn't going to put up with it any longer.

Her mother had crossed a line today. She would no doubt tell her husband she'd been driven to desperation by her daughter's unnatural behaviour. Well, Frankie was not going to be treated like that. This was the twentieth century not the nineteenth.

The role of women had changed during the Great War and though people had tried to send women back into the home after it ended, they hadn't succeeded with everyone. She'd read in the newspapers over the years about women who did new things like flying aeroplanes, driving cars anywhere they chose or travelling round the world on their own. And like her, some went out to work in jobs other than domestic service, either out of necessity or because they wanted a more stimulating life.

Was it time for her to buy a car of her own instead of using the family car when allowed? Like many people her mother didn't believe women could drive as well as men, and had only given in about her learning because their business needed Frankie to drive.

A few months ago she'd mentioned buying her own car and her father had begged her not to. He'd tried to make it easy for her to 'borrow' the big comfortable Morris Oxford, but her mother stopped her if she could. Anyway, she would prefer a smaller vehicle. Maybe she should think about it again. It'd give her a lot more freedom.

Someone knocked on the bedroom door. 'Miss Frances! Your mother says to hurry up.'

She didn't answer, was still trying to work out how long it would take to arrange to move out and where she should go.

Would her father really do as her mother had threatened and sack her if she left home? She doubted it but hated to make him have to choose between his daughter and his wife. And lately the wife always seemed to win.

Tomorrow, Frankie decided, she'd better make enquiries and find out what sort of house and workshop she could rent. Just to be prepared. She had a rough idea how much the whole thing would cost, but needed to check what sort of premises were available – and what sort of lodgings too.

It might even be better to move right away from Rivenshaw. No, why should she? She loved the moors and the friendly people in the Ellin Valley. The trouble was, everyone knew who she was and if she started looking at places to rent, someone was bound to gossip about it.

Five minutes later her mother tried her bedroom door, then hammered on it and yelled at her to come downstairs *this minute*.

She wouldn't get an apology for the slap, Frankie was sure, so she didn't bother to reply. She'd thought it wise to slide the bolts across the door. When she heard a key in the lock, she watched coldly as her mother found she still couldn't open the door and yelled at her again to come out.

Frankie had fitted the bolts top and bottom herself when her bedroom key had vanished one day last year, because she felt more comfortable sleeping behind a locked door. She'd since found the key that had been pinched hidden in her mother's work basket and had a copy made for herself, replacing it there afterwards.

In the distance the front doorbell sounded and her mother thumped the door one final time. 'You'll be sorry for defying me like this, my girl!' Footsteps moved away and down the stairs.

Frankie waited a few minutes then picked up her outdoor things, holding them over one arm so that they didn't show as obviously. After locking the bedroom door behind her, she slipped quietly down the back stairs, so that she could leave through the kitchen.

Maggie, who'd cooked for them for years, looked up then stared at her. 'Did you bump into something, love? Your cheek's all red.'

'I bumped into a door. It doesn't matter. I need to go and check something at work.'

'Your mother was calling for you. Didn't you hear her?'

'I'm not having tea with *that man*.'

Maggie rolled her eyes, but glanced over her shoulder and then winked at her.

Frankie tied on a headscarf from the hook near the door where she hung her work clothes and walked quickly away along the back lane and into the side streets. She kept her eyes down, hoping the redness in her cheek didn't show with the scarf pulled forward. Sighing in relief she took refuge where she'd always been happiest, in the workshop.

The first thing she did was to get out her personal tools and bring her list up to date. She'd acquired duplicates of some of them over the years so she ticked those. The extra ones would come in useful when she left because she'd have to employ a man and a boy too probably. Her father had given her some tools when she started, but they'd not been good enough. She'd bought most of the ones she now used herself, even going as far as Manchester to buy the finest she could discover. She'd have no hesitation in taking them with her.

She smiled as it occurred to her that her mother might accuse her of stealing them. Well, she still had the receipts, had kept the paperwork on what she did very carefully over the years. It was in her locked box. She even employed an accountant to help her with the taxes she'd needed to pay on her earnings.

It had never occurred to her father to check what she did about that side of things and her mother didn't understand financial details. All she cared about were the final totals and the money that came into her hands.

Old Bill had always said your tools were your biggest friends and he'd left all of his to her when he died, a great honour. She'd stowed them in a separate box, hadn't liked to use them. They were going with her, however. Perhaps there was a trace of his honest kindness still lingering on them and they'd bring her luck.

She would need it.

When the outer door of the workshop opened, she looked up. Her father stood there, looking unsure whether to come in and join her or not. Ah, her heart ached for him. He was a gentle person at heart and they got on well at work. His workmen thought the world of him.

She knew this ongoing discord in his own home was something which had made him spend longer hours than necessary at work over the years. Her mother didn't question that. In her limited view of business, more work equalled more money coming in. But lately, he'd just sat around in the workshop. He might deny it but he looked ill. *Please let him recover!*

'Timson has been told you're not well and he's gone home. Your mother's taken to her bed in hysterics. If you come home and apologise, I'll coax her to calm down.'

'What would I be apologising for, Father?'

He looked at the ground as if he was ashamed. 'Just offer her a simple apology, love, to help us all carry on.'

'She hit me for no reason, Father.' She pointed to her

cheek. 'And you saw her do it, so don't deny it if she claims I walked into a door.'

He swallowed and seemed to be searching for words. 'It'd have made matters worse if I'd interfered. I've spoken to the doctor about her and he says she's having women's troubles and she's to be kept calm at all costs till her body gets used to the change. Some women do get upset easily at that time of life.'

'Most don't have the luxury and she's always had a bad temper, so I doubt her behaviour is due to the change.'

She looked at him, only an inch or so taller than her, balding and thinner than he used to be. He was henpecked at home, a master of his trade at work and kind to everyone, even the beggars in the street sometimes. He'd always been thin, but she took after her mother physically, with a more sturdy build.

He seemed to have grown much older lately and to tire more easily at work. There would clearly be no help for her from him against her mother, because he wasn't master in his own home. 'I can't apologise when I've done nothing wrong, Father.'

His shoulders sagged. 'I'd hoped it wouldn't come to this yet but I knew it'd happen one day. Sit down, love. We need to talk.'

She brought her stool across and sat close to him.

'Your mother's been plotting to make worse trouble for you if you continue to defy her, so I've made some preparations she doesn't know about. Go and see our lawyer tomorrow and he'll explain.'

He fumbled in the drawer of his worktable and pulled out one of his business cards, scribbling something on it. 'Give him this.'

She looked at it. *The time has come. Please help my daughter as we've planned, Henry.*

He pulled her to him and gave her a convulsive hug. 'You can do better in a husband than a liar and cheat like Timson, but you need to find yourself one now, because you'll need someone to protect you legally. Henry will explain that as well.'

Then he shook his head, smeared tears away from his eyes and walked slowly and wearily out, leaving her gaping after him.

What on earth did he mean by 'protect you legally'? What was her mother up to now?

The only other time Frankie had felt as utterly alone as this had been after her twin died.

She didn't go home till it was nearly nine o'clock. She was relieved to find the kitchen door unlocked and knew it was for her, so locked it after her. She didn't switch the light on but cut herself a couple of pieces of bread and put butter and jam on them by the light of the street lamp shining in from the back alley.

After eating them quickly and drinking a glass of water, she tiptoed up the back stairs to her bedroom, finding the door unlocked. Her mother must have been going through her things again. She bolted the door, switched on the light and checked her drawers, seeing at once that they weren't as she'd left them. Well, there was nothing kept here that mattered.

It seemed a long time before Frankie managed to fall asleep. She heard the town hall clock strike the hour twice as she lay there in the darkness.

What preparations had her father made to help her escape? That was how she thought of it now, as escaping. She should have done it years ago, and would have if she hadn't enjoyed working with her father so much.

She would go and see their lawyer first thing in the morning. Why her father couldn't have told her himself what he'd done, she didn't know.

4

Jericho arrived at Tyler's early for his first day at work but others were already starting at the same time and greeted him cheerfully. He was put under the care of the foreman, who gave him a series of small jobs to do, as if testing his skills. Easy jobs, they were, and Ernie nodded as if satisfied when he checked them.

At noon the lad who helped around the place came to summon him to the office, which everyone knew was Mrs Tyler's domain.

'Sit down, Jericho. We work a little differently from some other businesses, especially with our permanent workers. As you will no doubt have realised, we're finding out what you're capable of today. I'm not only in charge of how the details of daily work are organised but I help my husband with other tasks as well.'

'Yes. So I've heard, Mrs Tyler.'

'I'll ask you to do a few jobs for me in here during the next few days so that I can get to know you better and you can gain some idea of how we operate.'

He nodded. Everyone in town knew that she was a clever woman. She was a bit like Frankie Redfern, working at a job usually reserved for men, but that didn't matter to him. He'd answer to the man in the moon to keep a decent job.

She studied him thoughtfully. 'They say you're a clever chap. What are you like at paperwork?'

'I haven't had much chance to deal with that side of things, but I'm good at reading, writing and arithmetic, and I'm a fast learner.'

'Well, we're looking for someone to manage the chaps who give us a day's work here and there, which involves noting down who does what and how much is owed to them daily or weekly, according to the job. That's where we're thinking of starting you off. You'll be doing some work of your own as needed and supervising their work. What that work is will vary, but Wilf says you've done a lot of different jobs and will understand what's needed. How does that sound?'

'More interesting than jobs usually are. I'll enjoy the variety.'

'Good. You'll answer to Ernie as well as me. He says you're a neat worker – which is a rare compliment from him. He's a skilled carpenter, though unlike you he did an official apprenticeship and has the papers to prove it. He'll teach you anything he thinks he can improve on.'

'I'll enjoy that too.'

As she went on, her smile faltered for the first time. 'Our business slowed down last year but we're speeding up again.'

He didn't need to ask what had caused that. Everyone in Birch End knew Roy Tyler had lost his way for a time after his only son died. Who wouldn't be upset by such a loss?

'We're expecting to start work on a big job soon, and will want the best team of men trained and ready to work on it *our way*.'

He could guess what that job would be. He'd seen Mr Tyler and Wilf pacing out the field they'd bought recently, the one next to his new home. And he also knew that Mr Tyler had bought that piece of land from Mrs Morton, snatching it from under the nose of Higgerson, who had tried to trick her into selling it to him for far less than its real value.

'We don't discuss that special job with anyone, not in the pub, not anywhere in the valley.'

'I can understand why. I won't let you down on that.'

'Let's get on then.'

Jericho enjoyed the afternoon's work with her, enjoyed it more than he'd expected. She was a very sharp woman and missed absolutely nothing. And talk about well organised. He ended up admiring her greatly.

In the late afternoon Mrs Tyler said, 'You can drive, can't you?'

He nodded. 'I've mostly driven vans and lorries, not so much fancy cars.'

'Good. We don't use fancy cars here.' She held out a piece of paper. 'I'd like you to use the small van and take this order to our hardware supplier. Wait there and bring back the goods required.'

He beamed as he got into the driver's seat. Everything about his first day had been good. And now a little outing into town.

Frankie walked across town to the lawyer's rooms at nine o'clock sharp, arriving just as the clerk opened the outer front door. Once inside she gave him her father's card.

He turned it over, drawing in a sharp breath at what he saw. 'I won't keep you waiting long, miss. Perhaps it'd be better if you sat in here.' He showed her into a small room at the rear of the building and left her to go and see his employer.

When he came back, he said, 'Mr Lloyd says he'll only be a few minutes. He hopes you won't mind, miss, but it'll be better if you go out the back way afterwards. The fewer people who see you, the fewer to gossip about why you're here today.'

She was left sitting alone, looking at a small table and three upright chairs, still wondering what this was all about and feeling more anxious than ever. Clearly the clerk was involved in these secret arrangements too.

*

Henry Lloyd joined her ten long, slow minutes later according to the small but noisy clock on the mantelpiece. He was carrying a battered cardboard box, which he set down carefully on the table.

'I have a client due in half an hour, so I won't waste time on civilities, Miss Redfern. There must be trouble if you've come to see me with that particular message. Tell me exactly what's going on.'

'I don't know where to start.'

'I already know about your mother's chancy temper and the fears your father has about what she might do to you if anything happened to him, or even if it only came to an open break between you and her.'

'What can she do that worries him so much?'

'This is to go no further. For a while I, together with a few colleagues in various parts of south-east Lancashire, have suspected that certain people have used the services of a small private lunatic asylum to get rid of an inconvenient relative by claiming that the person was insane and getting them locked away. Though we've kept our eyes open, we've been unable to gain proof. The medical profession can act very freely at times and while most of them are to be trusted, some few are most definitely not.'

She was startled by that – and horrified at what it implied. He watched her face carefully and saw the moment when she realised why he was telling her that.

'Even my mother wouldn't do that to me, surely, Mr Lloyd?'

'Your father thinks she would do anything to get what she wants, and if anything happens to him, she'll want you out of the way.'

'How could she have found out about that sort of villainy?'

'Who knows? From Higgerson perhaps. He is, I gather, her closest relative. Though my colleagues haven't traced anyone to him.' He saw her puzzlement and added. 'They've, um, let us say, *retrieved* a couple of clients' relatives from one place but there are others.'

'I don't understand. *Why* would she do that to me?'

'Your father, who is not only worried about his own health, had concerns about her sanity. She is, he feels, becoming increasingly unstable mentally. If anything happened to him and she had you certified, she would be named as your guardian and all your money would be put under her control as well as what is due to her in your father's original agreement.'

'Even so, why would Higgerson risk helping her do that? How would he benefit?'

'If you happened to die in the asylum, after her death everything would pass to Higgerson – and she's several years older than him. She looks it, too.'

'My father hasn't been looking at all well lately, I'm afraid. But even if the worst happens to him, I've given no signs of going mad, surely? How could they possibly prove such a thing about me?'

'You are unconventional and that irks some people. They could force drugs down you, which would leave you seeming stupid and incapable of looking after yourself. She could claim to have been trying to hide your problem for some time.'

He gave her a moment to take this in, then went on, 'Your father and I feel there is only one way of making utterly certain she can't gain power over you if something happens to him. If you were married, your husband would be the one with authority over you should you fall ill, not her.'

Frankie was shocked to the core. 'That's why father made me promise yesterday to consider marriage seriously if a decent man showed an interest in me. Only I'm not courting or . . . or anything like that, Mr Lloyd.'

'That can be remedied by me putting an advertisement in

the *Manchester Guardian* and finding a gentleman prepared to marry you. Such things do happen from time to time. The gentleman would be well reimbursed and would sign a legal agreement about the situation and agree not to, um, consummate the marriage.'

'*Pay someone to marry me!* No, no! I couldn't bear to do that.'

'Not even to save yourself from spending the rest of your life in a lunatic asylum?'

She opened her mouth then shut it again. Could it really come to such an invidious choice?

'You would be well advised to consider this solution seriously, Miss Redfern.'

'I think you must be mistaken. She wouldn't do that.'

He sighed. 'We have proof. The last few times your mother went into Manchester, supposedly shopping, a new thing for her apparently, your father paid someone to follow her. It seems she did very little shopping. Instead, she went to see a doctor in Manchester, the same one who certified one of those wrongly locked away.'

Frankie could only stare at him. The shock of such a horrendous possibility seemed to have deprived her of coherent thought.

'So, Miss Redfern, unless there's a man here in the valley whom you could trust to marry and protect you, I think I ought to place an advertisement quickly.'

She was about to shake her head and say she knew no one when suddenly the image of Jericho Harte crept into her mind. Good heavens! What was she thinking of? She hardly knew the man.

But she'd not know a stranger found by the lawyer at all. And at least she'd liked Jericho – rather too much for her own peace of mind. Could she . . .? Dare she . . .?

She looked at Mr Lloyd, seeing only concern on his face.

He was well respected, not at all the kind of man to jump to foolish conclusions. If he and her father both felt there was something to fear, and her father had made preparations for this eventuality, then she'd be wise to pay heed to them.

'Could I perhaps run away instead, emigrate to Australia or . . . or something?'

'Would you be prepared to do that, leave everything and everyone you know? Would that be preferable to marriage? If so, it can certainly be arranged.'

She thought of yesterday's peaceful hour on the moors. She'd felt so at home there, always did, and had felt comfortable with the man to whom she'd chatted as well. 'I don't really want to move to another country. This valley is the only home I've ever known, or want to know.'

'Then we must find you someone to marry.' He watched her for a moment then glanced at the clock. 'I think from your expression a few moments ago there is someone you might consider.'

'It's ridiculous. I hardly know him.'

'I've seen much stranger things done during my time as a lawyer, and this would be in a good cause. And I've seen respected citizens get away with immoral actions too, much to my disgust. I can assure you that marrying someone quickly for financial reasons is more common than you'd expect.'

'I'll . . . think about it, then.'

'You don't have a lot of time. It's something you must do as quickly as possible. I can deal with arranging the marriage, but even if we get a special licence, the law will still require you to wait a week after that for the actual ceremony to take place. So . . . would you prefer to try to find a husband yourself or shall I do it?'

'I'll see this man first . . . find out if he's interested.'

'Good.' He pushed the box across the table to her. 'There are some other things in here that you should read through.

And there's some money, which is an outright gift from your father for you to use as you wish, not part of what he's been able to leave you in his will. Have you somewhere safe to keep it?'

'Not really. Well, I do have a strong box at the workshop. But that wouldn't hold all this easily and anyway, it could be carried away and then broken open.'

'Then it may be better if you stay and look through this box's contents now. You can come back here at any time – using the rear entrance – and we'll keep the box safe for you, I promise. You may find it useful to take some of the money with you. And finally, there are the deeds to a house in Birch End, which was bought in your name some three months ago.'

'What? Do you mean I own a *house*?'

'Yes. It's near the village centre, not on the Backshaw Moss side, mind, and it has a big shed to one side of it which might serve for a workshop initially.' He handed her a key. 'Number One Marlow Road.'

She was beyond words. Her father must think her in dreadful danger to arrange all this. To have her own house would be a dream come true. But could she do what he and Mr Lloyd thought most crucial of all, ask a man she hardly knew to marry her? She didn't think so.

Even as she was dismissing the idea, the memory came back to her of the look of utter hatred on her mother's face when she'd slapped her. That look showed she'd get no mercy from the woman who'd borne her.

She looked across the table at Mr Lloyd again. He was no fool.

'If I found a husband who would agree not to claim my body, could the marriage be annulled at some later date?'

'Hmm. I have to ask this, I'm afraid: are you a virgin?'

She could feel herself flushing and told him what no one

else knew. 'No. I was engaged and Martin was going off to war. When he was killed I was glad I'd given my body to him, wished I'd been carrying his child.'

Mr Lloyd showed no scorn, merely nodded. 'Then it might be more difficult to annul a marriage. Perhaps you'd be better establishing a proper relationship with this man you know and like. With goodwill on both sides, even living with someone you don't love romantically can be pleasant.'

Pleasant! She'd known deep love, hadn't found anything like it since losing Martin, so had stayed single. But she had liked Jericho Harte and found him attractive too. Would that be enough?

Mr Lloyd glanced at the clock once more and sighed. 'My dear lady, I'm sorry. I don't usually push people into doing things, but I can't spend any more time with you this morning. Can I beg you to do as your father wishes and do it quickly.'

'Very well. I'll ask this man I know first, then. If he says no, I'll trust you to find me someone.'

'Will you please do it today?'

Her stomach lurched with nervousness, but she nodded.

'Then come back tomorrow and let me know what he says. I have a client due now but you can stay in this room for as long as you wish. No one will disturb you as you read through the papers. Let my clerk know when you've finished and he'll put them away safely then see you out.'

When he'd gone, she sat down again, stared at the cardboard box and opened the top flap. Going through its contents showed exactly how her father was trying to help her – and also how deadly serious he was about her being in danger. There was five hundred pounds in an envelope – *five hundred!* – so she took out fifty pounds in crisp five-pound notes and put them in her purse, then put the rest back.

The box's contents only reinforced her acceptance of the need to find a husband.

She must summon up all her courage to ask a man she hardly knew to marry her. How embarrassing that would be!

Her own mother had rejected her.

Would Jericho Harte do the same?

All she knew, was better him than a complete stranger.

5

It was almost midday before Frankie put the papers away and left the lawyer's rooms. She walked across town to the workshop, pausing in the doorway, relieved to see her father.

He was speaking to the boy they'd taken on recently. When he saw her, he gave the boy some money and sent him out to collect the sandwiches they bought every day at lunchtime.

Most men of his status went home for their midday meal, but Frankie realised with her new clarity of vision about their family that this was another way her father managed not only to stay away from his wife but to keep Frankie away from her too.

She waited to speak until he'd finished and the boy had closed the outer door as he left. She'd intended to ask her father whether all this was really necessary, but kept silent when she saw him sway and press one hand to his chest. He was sweating slightly and looked pale.

She swallowed hard. He was looking worse today than she'd ever seen him before. She had to do as he wished, had to, and definitely needed to see Jericho quickly. 'May I borrow the car later this afternoon, father? I, um, wish to visit a friend in Birch End.'

'Of course.' His eyes were asking a question and she could guess what it was.

She didn't want to say the words yet, but his eyes were

pleading, so she nodded and said in a low voice, 'I've just come back from the lawyer's.'

'And?'

'I'll do what you wish.'

'Thank goodness. Do it quickly, my dear.'

He closed his eyes as if in relief and made a keep-back motion with one hand as he fumbled for a lozenge and put it into his mouth. He said the doctor had recommended these for heartburn.

Only it wasn't for heartburn, was it? It had to be something much more serious the way he was urging her to act quickly.

She hoped suddenly that Jericho would agree to do it. He seemed a kind man who clearly loved his family. He couldn't be worse than her mother to live with, surely? Could her impression of him be false? He was good-looking but what she remembered most about his face was the way his eyes had crinkled when he smiled, the kindness. She didn't think she was mistaken about that being an important key to his personality.

If he said yes, would they find enough in common to build a life together?

Something else occurred to her suddenly. Would marrying him keep her safe? Or would she bring danger to him as well?

Neither she nor her father ate all their sandwiches and the boy accepted their leftovers with delight. Afterwards her father said he had to see a customer across town and would enjoy a stroll there and back, since it didn't look like rain.

Frankie spent the afternoon in the office, gathering her own possessions together under the pretence of tidying up. If Mr Lloyd was right, she needed to be ready for a sudden departure and she wasn't leaving her tools behind.

It all felt unreal, though, as if she were living through a nightmare.

Her father seemed to be taking a long time to get back. What was keeping him?

She kept an eye on the clock and sent the boy home early just before four o'clock. Since there was still no sign of her father, she locked up and set off in the car, driving along the main road towards the turn-off that would take her out of town and up the valley to the two other villages.

Jericho had said he was starting work at Tyler's today and she knew where that was in Birch End. She hoped to catch him as he came out of work.

She exclaimed in shock and braked suddenly when she saw him getting out of a van on the main street of Rivenshaw. Another driver hooted his horn at her because she was blocking his way and she pulled over to the side of the street.

It felt as if fate had brought Jericho to her and was nudging her to keep her promise to her father and ask him to marry her. But oh, the thought of actually doing it terrified her.

She took a few deep, shuddering breaths, trying to calm her nerves, then got out of the car and followed him into the hardware shop. No one would be surprised to see her going in here because she was still wearing her work clothes.

That thought made her glance at herself in the glass panel of the door: bruised face, wearing a beret, carrying a workman's satchel and dressed in trousers like a man. He'd complimented her on her appearance yesterday but what would he think of her today?

Inside the shop she watched Jericho hand a piece of paper to the assistant and heard the man say, 'If you'll come back in quarter of an hour, sir, I'll have everything ready for Mr Tyler.'

'I want to buy a couple of things for myself as well so I'll have a look round while I wait.' He turned without seeing her and made his way towards the rear.

She walked briskly through the shop, nodding to the man behind the counter, and stopped beside Jericho. 'Excuse me.'

'Miss Redfern! Good afternoon.'

Since there was no one close enough to overhear, she said in a low voice, 'I need to speak to you privately. It's, um, rather urgent.'

'Is something wrong?'

'Yes. Very wrong. And . . . I'd like your help to deal with it, if you're willing, that is.' She could hear herself stumbling over the explanation.

He studied her face and frowned. 'What happened to your face?'

'My mother hit me.'

He sucked in his breath sharply, clearly shocked. 'I'll do anything I can to help you, Miss Redfern.'

As someone else came into the shop just then, calling a cheery hello, he said equally quietly, 'Perhaps we'd better find somewhere more private than this to talk, though. If you go out into the rear yard and stand looking at the open air displays till there's no one around, you can leave through the back gate and wait for me in the alley behind the shop. It'll be more private there. I'll follow you shortly afterwards.'

'Good idea.'

She walked out, pretending to study some samples of garden railings until another customer, to her relief a complete stranger, had gone back into the shop. Then she slipped out of the gate, leaving it slightly ajar.

Was she really going to ask a man to marry her? Could she do that? What would he say?

She felt quite sick with apprehension.

⋆

Jericho watched her go, upset that the woman who'd seemed in glowing health on the moors yesterday was now looking pale, as if deeply shocked and upset. And her cheek had been bruised. Had her own mother really done that? He would definitely help her if he could. It was a poor lookout if you couldn't lend a hand to a person in trouble.

Only, why had she asked him to help her? They hardly knew one another.

He checked that there were no other customers nearby then slipped quickly outside into the rear laneway.

She was pacing to and fro, but stopped near the next gate when she saw him and waited for him to join her.

In the daylight he saw her face more clearly and was surprised to see how badly bruised it was. He had a vague memory of hearing that Mrs Redfern had a chancy temper but surely it wasn't normal to hit a grown-up daughter. It must have been a vicious blow.

He gestured to one side. 'Let's move a little further along the laneway to have our talk. We don't want anyone in the yard overhearing what we say.'

When they stopped, she swallowed hard, looking nervous. 'It's hard to know how to start.'

'Just tell me straight out what's wrong and how I can help you.'

She closed her eyes for a moment, then started to sum up the situation.

He listened intently until she faltered to a stop, then said, 'What do you want from *me*, though? If your lawyer said you should marry, why have you come to me?' The answer couldn't be – surely she wouldn't be asking him to do that?

'I wanted to ask if you would do it – marry me, I mean?'

He hoped he'd hidden his shock. 'Don't you know someone more, well, suitable? I'm a poor man, and even if

I wanted to, I couldn't afford to support a wife as well as my mother.'

'I . . . well, enjoyed your company on the moors, felt comfortable with you, liked the way you spoke about your family.'

'Nonetheless you could find several men in the valley more suited to marry a lady like you.'

'I've not met a man I felt so comfortable with in all the years since my fiancé was killed in the war. My mother wants to marry me off and is bringing men like that horrible Timson creature to meet me.'

The pieces were all starting to fall into place now. And to his astonishment he didn't even feel the need to think about it. His instinct was to say yes, he would marry her.

The main reason was the same as the one she'd given: he felt comfortable with her too. And it had been a long time since he'd felt that sort of attraction to a woman.

As the silence continued, Frankie almost turned and ran away, she felt so humiliated by the situation. In the end, she stared down at the ground and muttered, 'Please, just say yes or no. I'll understand if you think it's a ridiculous idea. Only, Mr Lloyd thinks it's the best thing to do and he's not a stupid man. He offered to advertise for a husband for me, but I'd rather know who I was marrying.'

'The lawyer said that he'd *advertise* for someone?'

'Yes. He said I must do it as quickly as possible in order to protect myself in case anything happens to my father and my mother becomes my closest relative.'

'Mr Lloyd is well thought of and *he* wouldn't ask you to do something so drastic if it wasn't necessary.' He paused and took her hand. 'If you really mean it, Frankie, then I will marry you.'

She couldn't believe she'd heard him correctly and could only stare at him.

His touch was gentle and his deep voice equally so. 'I'm truly honoured that you've asked me, only—'

'Only what? If you'd rather not do it, just say no, for heaven's sake!'

'I don't want to say no.' His grasp tightened. 'I enjoyed your company yesterday, too, and I believe you've told me the truth today. It's the practicalities that worry me. I have no money, have only just found a permanent job, so how can I support a wife?'

'You wouldn't need to support me. My father left some money for me with Mr Lloyd and I already had some savings, enough to set up a workshop of my own and continue doing the work I love if anything happens to my father.'

'Ah. That's all right, then, though I find it rather embarrassing to think of depending on you.'

'You'd not mind me working? I'm no housewife and I love what I do.'

'I wouldn't mind at all. Women of my class find any sort of work they can to help put bread on the table. And I've heard that you're an excellent cabinetmaker. It'd be a shame to waste skills that take years to learn.'

She believed him, began shaking with the relief of it, but when he didn't continue speaking, she couldn't think what to do or say next. He murmured something and pulled her closer. She gave in to the desire to lean against his warmth and strength, just for a moment or two. She had felt so alone.

He spoke against her hair. 'Ah, Frankie lass, what have your family done to you?'

'It's my mother who's done it, not my father. He's not been well lately and has let her tell him what to do, but I know he loves me and he protects me when he can. I should have left home years ago, not given her the chance to think she could control me as she controls him.'

She looked into his eyes, such beautiful dark eyes, and was

reminded of how she'd reacted when Martin touched her. To her surprise, she was reacting in a similar way now to Jericho's touch.

He moved back a little but kept hold of her hands. She didn't want him to move away, had felt safe when he held her like that. She couldn't work out why he would agree to this, had to know, so she asked him. 'Why did you say yes, then, Jericho, if you can't support a wife?'

'Because yesterday when we parted company, I wished I could get to know you better but knew I had no chance of doing that, given the difference in our backgrounds. Today, I find you beaten and threatened, and I think perhaps I can give you something to make it worthwhile for you to marry me. As you say, my protection.'

He laid one hand on the cheek that wasn't bruised. 'I won't let anyone beat you again, not while there's life in my body. I can promise you that for a start, Frankie.'

She liked the way he said her name. And here was another promise that would change her life. She remembered the one she'd made to her father, hadn't expected to do what he'd asked so soon after that, hadn't expected ever to marry.

She looked at Jericho again and felt tears welling in her eyes at how tenderly he had held her. Could this be really happening? Could she have found the help she so desperately needed? She had felt so very alone and desperate as she set out to find him. Tears overflowed and rolled down her cheeks, hard as she tried to hold them back.

'Ah, come closer again. You need holding. My mother used to take us in her arms when we were little and in distress. It always made things seem better.'

'I can't remember my mother ever hugging me, not once in my whole life.'

His voice was low, his breath warm on her cheek. 'Then I'll have to hug you every day to make up for that.'

And once again he hugged her gently, in such a way that she could have moved away from him if she'd wanted to. Only she didn't want to.

She had to ask again, 'Are you certain, Jericho?'

'I am. It feels right, somehow. I don't know why, it just does. I shall look forward to us getting to know one another better.'

'I shall too.'

'We'll have to deal with a few practicalities, though. We'll need to find somewhere to live and—' He flushed, looking shamefaced. 'I don't have any spare money, not even enough to pay the first week's rent on a single room. My brothers and I have been living from hand to mouth for a while, after looking after our mother when she was ill.'

She hated to see his humiliation. 'We shan't need to pay rent. My father has provided for that and has bought me a house in Birch End, in Marlow Road.'

'Bought it for you!'

'Yes, secretly. I can't imagine how he saved the money for it without my mother knowing. I only saw the deeds for the first time today. I haven't even been inside it.'

'It'll be the one at the end. I walk along that street sometimes. That house has been empty for a while. It'll probably need some work doing to it.'

She saw him brighten, as if there was something good about that.

'I can do a lot of the renovation work, I should think, and that'll also help make up for my lack of money.'

'I have adequate money, so that isn't important to me. I can let you have some, if you need it.'

'No, you keep that to buy furniture. Have you enough to deal with that side of things?'

'Hmm. I've got enough but I'd rather not do it. Someone would see me and wonder why I was buying furniture. So far my mother doesn't know about the house, you see.'

'We could ask my mother to buy the basics for us, just to get us started. She'll be happy to help.' He chuckled suddenly. 'She was nagging me to get married only yesterday. She'll be absolutely delighted at our news.'

'She will?'

'Oh, yes.'

'Can making the arrangements be so straightforward?' she asked in wonderment.

'I doubt it will be at all straightforward, not if Higgerson is helping your mother. But we must trust your lawyer to guide us through the legal aspects, and my brothers and friends will help me to protect you.'

'I think we'd better see Mr Lloyd and make the necessary arrangements as quickly as we can, then. I wonder if he's still at work? There's a back way in and out of his rooms that I've been invited to use.' She wondered if she was being too bossy and held her breath, waiting to see how he responded.

'Let's go and find out. It'd be quicker to go on foot if we use the rear laneways. It won't even take us five minutes to walk there, but I think we should go separately. Do you know the way?'

She nodded.

'Then I'll follow you and keep an eye on you from a distance, as well as making sure we're not being followed. Just let me nip into the shop and tell them I've been called away and can't take the order away yet.'

She wouldn't have been surprised if he had failed to return, still couldn't believe this was really going to happen. But he was back very quickly, his gaze as steady and earnest as ever. She really liked his face. Hoped he didn't mind her appearance today, because she definitely wasn't looking her best.

She turned and set off, feeling more sure now that Jericho

would keep his word and the marriage would happen. But she felt very unsure about what would happen after that.

To her relief no one she passed seemed to pay any attention to her. And the sound of Jericho's steady footsteps behind her made her feel safe.

This was a good start, wasn't it? Far better than she'd expected when she set out to find him.

6

Frankie opened the back gate at Mr Lloyd's and waited just inside for Jericho to follow her. As he closed the gate, the clinking sound of the latch brought someone to an upstairs window. It seemed to be the elderly clerk, so she looked up and waved, hoping Finlay could recognise her in the dimly lit yard.

He waved back, pointing downwards and disappearing from view.

She led the way across to the back door and they waited.

A few seconds later there was the sound of bolts being drawn back and as he opened the door, the clerk kept the chain on the hook, looking at her companion as if assessing whether it was safe to allow him in, then saying in a low voice, 'Come in quickly, please, Miss Redfern.'

When they were inside he locked the door behind them before leading the way upstairs to a small sitting room lit only by a table lamp. Only after he'd drawn the curtains did he switch on the main ceiling light and turn to study them again.

'This is Jericho Harte, who has agreed to—' she began.

Jericho interrupted to correct her. 'Who *wishes* to marry Miss Redfern as soon as can be arranged.'

That statement might be stretching the truth but it was kindly done and tactful, which made her feel that he was already trying to look after her.

Head on one side, the elderly clerk studied Jericho's face

for a second time then nodded as if he'd seen something he approved of. 'I'll telephone Mr Lloyd, who will wish to know about this. He went home at his usual time but I should think he'll want to come back and meet you, Mr Harte, and discuss the arrangements he needs to make with you both.'

Frankie glanced at a clock on the mantelpiece. 'I'm worried that I'm already late home and my mother will make a fuss about it if I'm any later. I don't know where my father got to this afternoon. He went out but didn't say where he was going and he hadn't come back to the workshop when I left, so—'

Jericho again interrupted. 'I don't think you should go to that house on your own, Frankie. You aren't even sure your father will be there and you won't want to be alone with your mother from now on. Is there somewhere else you could stay? I'd rather be with you at your next encounter in case she tries to make trouble. I will *not* allow her to hit you again.'

Finlay stole a glance at her cheek, shaking his head and giving a disapproving hiss. 'Did she do that?'

'Yes.'

'Then I agree with Mr Harte that you shouldn't be alone with her.'

When Mr Lloyd arrived he said the same thing, warning her not to risk going home again but to move elsewhere till after the wedding.

Frankie looked at them in dismay. 'But I have to go home. All my clothes are there. And anyway, there is no one else I can go to. She never made it easy for me to have friends.'

'We'll arrange to have your clothes fetched,' Mr Lloyd said, 'and in the meantime, I'd be happy to offer you the shelter of my own house until you can get married. I've told my wife about you and she agrees that you could stay with us if you need somewhere.'

'You think I really am in that much danger?'

'Yes. You see, something else has happened. My dear, I'm extremely sorry to have to tell you this, but I met a friend on the way home earlier who told me he saw your father collapse in the street this afternoon. Someone called an ambulance and it took him to hospital. I phoned them but they said he was being looked after and couldn't give me any more information at this stage.'

'Oh, no! I have to go to him.'

'They won't let you see him yet. No visitors are allowed. We'll phone again in a little while and I'll take you to see him as soon as it's possible.'

'Thank you.'

'Since I heard about it I've been worrying that if you went home you would be completely at your mother's mercy, only I didn't know where you were. That's why I left Finlay here, in case you came back to see me.'

'It's a relief that you can get my clothes, but there are important things at the workshop too, some business papers and all my tools. They're very good ones and I should hate to lose them. They're just as important to me as my clothes.'

'Your safety is far more important than anything, don't you think? Still, the workshop is nearby and we might just have time to collect your things before she knows what we're doing, so we'll go there first. But I think I'd better phone Sergeant Deemer and ask him to escort us.'

She felt numb as she waited for him to do that.

What was going to happen to her now? It felt as if her whole life had been upended and scattered around in small, disconnected pieces.

She was quite sure her mother would try to prevent her from getting married. There seemed to be nothing but hurdles ahead of her.

She looked at Jericho who was standing quietly beside her,

not pestering her, just there. Ready to defend her? Yes, it felt like that. She returned his half-smile. The more time she spent with him, the better she liked him. Her father would like him too, she was sure.

What a time to find a man she felt attracted to after all these years!

As for her father, all she could do at the moment was hope and pray that he'd be all right.

When they got to the workshop a few minutes later, they found a burly man standing outside the door and he immediately moved to bar their way.

'No one to go inside.'

Sergeant Deemer moved forward, recognising the man as one of Higgerson's employees. 'By whose authority do you say that, Livings?'

He rattled off his reply as if he'd learned it by heart. 'Mrs Redfern sent me to protect her husband's property while he's in hospital.'

'Well, she won't need to protect it against her own daughter, will she? Miss Redfern comes here every day to work, and is presently escorted by a lawyer and a policeman, so she won't be doing anything wrong. And you aren't employed by *Mr* Redfern, whose business this is still. Step aside, please.'

The man hesitated then did so, but as they walked inside they heard his footsteps pounding away down the street.

'Better collect your things quickly, miss,' Deemer said. 'He'll have gone to tell someone and we can all guess who.'

'If you gentlemen will stay with Frankie, I'll go and fetch Mr Tyler's van and we can put her tools in it,' Jericho offered. 'Good thing I've got it handy. I'm sure he won't mind.'

Deemer said immediately, 'Good idea, Harte. My constable will stand guard at the door while I go inside with Miss

Redfern and Mr Lloyd to start collecting her things. Be as quick as you can.'

In the workshop Frankie pulled the box of old Bill's tools out of the storage area, then dragged out the larger box containing her own tools, explaining what they were.

'Best let us see exactly what you're taking,' Mr Lloyd said. He pulled out a small notebook and a small pencil.

Relieved that the locks didn't seem to have been tampered with, she unfastened the lid of each box and showed the contents to the sergeant and lawyer, then turned to get the metal box containing her papers. It was where she'd left it under the desk on which she drew out her designs and the cutting diagrams, as well as dealing with some of the business correspondence for her father.

She brought it across to the other two containers, again opening it to show them what was inside. 'These are all the personal possessions I keep here.'

'You're quite sure there's nothing missing?' Mr Lloyd asked. 'I doubt your mother will allow you back here again if . . . well, the worst happens.'

'Yes, that's everything. I always keep my personal tools locked away when I leave the workshop and pack them in a certain way. I'd know at once if they'd been touched, and they haven't. The men who work here know not to touch them. The tools are quite valuable, you see, because I bought the best I could find.'

'You care greatly about your work, don't you?' the lawyer said.

'Too much perhaps. It's been my main companion and comfort over the years.' She looked sadly into the distance for a few seconds, then went on, 'I got everything ready to take away this afternoon while I was waiting to go and speak to Jericho, but I hadn't expected to have to do that so soon.'

'The difficulty is going to be proving these tools are all yours,' Mr Lloyd said thoughtfully.

'Oh, I can do that easily. I've kept all the receipts from the very beginning. My father always says—' she broke off again then continued, 'He used to tease me that I'd got a tidy clerk's attitude to paper. He's far less tidy and he'd have difficulty proving the other tools are his, but I know which is which.'

There was the sound of a vehicle pulling up outside and they stayed where they were, expecting it to be Jericho returning with the van.

Suddenly the constable yelled, 'Sarge. Come here quickly.'

With a startled glance at the others, Deemer rushed to the front door to find himself confronting Higgerson and Mrs Redfern who had just got out of the car. Two men were standing beside them, one of them Livings.

Mrs Redfern clutched her cousin's arm and stared across at her daughter. 'I told you she'd come and steal things as soon as her father was dead, didn't I, Gareth?'

'You did indeed, my dear cousin.' He looked at the sergeant. 'I call upon you to witness this act of theft.'

The sergeant's voice was chill. 'You'd better come inside, Mrs Redfern. I don't know why you're involved in this, Mr Higgerson.'

'I'm a cousin of Mrs Redfern.'

Deemer frowned as he thought about that. He knew most of the main families in the valley. 'Not a close cousin though.'

'Close enough. I don't know what I'd do without his help,' Mrs Redfern protested.

'Well, come in then. But no one else.'

Before anyone could move, a van drew up behind Higgerson's car. Jericho got out and hurried towards the entrance.

Higgerson glared at him. 'This business is closed until further notice. Go away!'

His two men started to move forward as if to physically prevent Jericho going into the building, but Deemer moved quickly to his side, holding up his hand to stop them. 'On the contrary, this matter very much concerns Mr Harte. We should continue our conversation inside the building, however. Constable, please see that no one else comes in.'

'Yessir.'

Higgerson glared at Jericho but when his men looked at him, as if ready to defy the sergeant, he shook his head and escorted Mrs Redfern inside, leaving the constable and his two men standing in front of the building.

Jericho at once went across to Frankie. 'Are you all right?'

'Yes.' She turned to her mother. 'Did I hear you say my father was *dead*?'

'As good as. The doctor told me he's not expected to last the night.'

Jericho put his arm round her shoulders as she let out a soft whimper of distress.

'Look at her, the hussy!' Mrs Redfern exclaimed loudly. 'That's what she does here, is it? Snuggles up to any man she fancies, probably lifts her skirt for them too. I'll soon stop that.'

'If you make any more such remarks,' Mr Lloyd said in a calm, even voice, 'my client will sue you for slander. Miss Redfern is presently staying with me and my wife, and this man is her fiancé.'

Had the lawyer thrown a grenade at Mrs Redfern, he couldn't have surprised her more and after one loud gasp, she seemed able to do nothing but open and shut her mouth.

Higgerson turned to her. 'You didn't tell me your daughter was engaged.'

'She isn't. Definitely not to him, anyway. I wouldn't think of allowing her to marry such a rough fellow.'

'You're wrong. She is engaged to him,' the lawyer said.

'Your husband knew and approved. He was the one who first told me about it.'

'Well, that still doesn't mean she can take away those tools.' She turned to her daughter. 'Your father isn't even dead and you're trying to steal his possessions, you wretch.'

Frankie felt sick to her soul at this blunt way of telling her the sad news about her father, but she had Jericho's arm round her shoulders and that gave her the courage to say, 'I didn't even know father was in hospital.'

'You must have done. He was taken there three hours ago.'

Mr Lloyd again intervened. 'Miss Redfern went to meet her fiancé in Birch End after she left the workshop at four o'clock and I gather she's been with him from then onwards.' He raised one eyebrow questioningly at Jericho, who nodded.

'When they got back into town they came to see my clerk who telephoned me to join them. She couldn't possibly have known her father had been taken ill.'

'So she says, but I know her and her lies. Now, put those tools back this minute!'

Frankie tried to speak as calmly as the lawyer had done, but it was hard to control her voice. 'The only things I'm taking are my own tools, bought with my own money.'

'*You* can't have bought them!' her mother exclaimed. 'Where would you have got the money? I know how expensive tools are. He's always after buying some fancy bit of metal or other.'

That must have been how her father had taken the money from the business to give to her, Frankie thought. 'I paid for these tools from my wages.'

'You're a liar!' Her mother took a hasty step forward, hand half raised as if to hit her daughter. 'You always were! Your father never said a word to me about those tools being yours, not a single word. I don't believe you.'

'Easy enough to prove,' Mr Lloyd said quietly. 'The

sergeant and I have seen the contents of these boxes and there is a bundle of receipts for everything my client purchased, going back to just after the war. We thought it wiser to check what she was taking, in case anyone tried to cheat Miss Redfern out of what's rightfully hers.'

He gave Mrs Redfern a wolfish smile that was at odds with his quiet tone of voice. 'You're welcome to come to my office and check each and every one of the receipts any time you wish. In the meantime, the tools will be kept at my house and I hope you're not going to suggest I'm stealing them.'

She opened her mouth to protest but Higgerson shushed her then scowled across at Jericho. 'Whether that's true or not, what sort of unnatural daughter are you to be taking away your tools from the business that needs their use, rather than going straight to visit your father in hospital?'

She disliked the man and had avoided having anything to do with him for most of her life, just as he'd avoided her and her father. Her mother had usually visited Cousin Gareth's home rather than inviting him to hers, but not very often until the past few months.

Frankie hated the way Higgerson was acting as if he was in charge here in the place that had always been the nearest thing she had to a home. And judging by what had happened so far, she felt sure she'd better retrieve her clothes this evening, with the help of Sergeant Deemer.

'We'll go on to the hospital after I've fetched my clothes from home. Sergeant, will you please come with me to oversee that as well? I don't want anyone accusing me of stealing.'

'Happy to help you, Miss Redfern, and to act as witness if anything of yours is damaged, too.'

'I won't have her in my house, not ever again,' Jane Redfern said in a harsh voice.

'Then you'll have to have her clothes brought out to her,

won't you? Or I could come inside and collect them for her.' He outstared her until she turned to Higgerson.

'Cousin Gareth, please take me home! And get someone to drive my husband's car home, too. *She* isn't having any further use of it.'

'We'll follow you there,' Deemer said quietly.

Mr Lloyd added, 'Remember, your daughter has a right to her own clothes, Mrs Redfern. If you damage them, she'll be able to sue you for the cost.'

'Why would I want to damage them? They're a sad collection of spinsterish garments and men's trousers, well suited to a stupid unnatural creature like her.'

He shook his head as he watched her lead the way out. 'She's a vicious woman, that one. You'll need to steer well clear of her from now on, Miss Redfern.'

Frankie nodded. She'd been steering clear of her mother for many years now, pretending to go to bed early or to have an extra job to finish in the workshop, whatever she could think of. All with her father's collusion.

If she never saw her again she'd be happy.

By the time they'd got Frankie's boxes loaded into the van and had followed the sergeant's car to her former home, it was raining again and fully dark except for the small islands of light around the gas lamps that lit the street at intervals.

They braked to a halt when they found the drive at Frankie's home blocked by a pile of rubbish.

'What's that?' Ignoring the rain, Frankie got out of the car just as Higgerson came out of the house with his arms full of something. He threw the bundle down, deliberately doing so into a puddle by the side of the drive.

Deemer came forward with a torch and shone it on the rubbish for Frankie to see more clearly.

She waited till Higgerson had gone back into the house to say, 'These are my clothes. They're throwing them all out into the mud.'

'As long as they're not permanently damaged they can be washed and dried. We should save our legal ammunition for something more important, I'm afraid,' Mr Lloyd said.

'I'll pick them up and we'll put them into my van any old how,' Jericho offered.

'What else do you need to get besides clothes?' Deemer asked. 'Do you have any jewellery or other valuables?'

'No jewellery here because I don't wear it. I keep a small box of pieces I inherited from my father's side of the family in the bank vault. There are my books, though. I'd be sorry to lose those.'

'She will also need her books,' Mr Lloyd told Higgerson the next time he brought out a pile of clothing.

Two piles of books were hurled into the muddy flowerbed by the side of the drive shortly afterwards.

Frankie stood in stony silence till Higgerson had taken a step back the second time then she began picking up the clothes from the nearest pile.

He didn't move any further away, saying in a low voice, 'You'll be sorry for doing this to your poor mother. And so will your so-called fiancé.'

'All I'm sorry about is that I'm related to her and you.'

Deemer had moved closer and heard what he'd said to her, but Higgerson's attention was on Frankie and he didn't seem to notice the sergeant.

She felt uncomfortable at him being so close to her. She was a tall woman but he was even taller and running to fat now. As he loomed over her, he edged even closer till she had to take a step backwards.

Still in a low voice, he added, 'Remember what I said and stay away from your mother from now on! Indeed, it'd be best for all concerned if you moved right away from Rivenshaw. And took your so-called fiancé with you.'

'Leave Miss Redfern alone, Higgerson,' the sergeant said in a loud voice right next to him.

He jumped in shock, then shrugged and stepped away. 'With pleasure. I've said what she needed to hear.' He went back into the house, slamming the door behind him.

'What did he say to you at the beginning?' Deemer asked.

'He said I'd be sorry for doing this. And so would Jericho.'

'He's the one who'll be sorry if he hurts you,' Jericho said at once.

'He has men who'll do anything for money, never attacks people himself, which is why it's been so hard to tie the incidents to him. You'll need to be extremely careful from now on, Harte,' the sergeant said. 'One day he'll overreach himself and I'll be waiting.'

'We'll be living in Birch End after we're married. I have friends there who'll help me,' Jericho said. 'My friends have precious little to lose if they upset him.'

Mr Lloyd joined in. 'Nonetheless, you should both take great care. Now, have we got everything?' He looked round but the drive was clear again. 'Do you wish to go and see your father at the hospital before we take you to my house, Miss Redfern?'

'Yes, of course I do.' She wanted quite desperately to kiss his soft, papery cheek one last time before he died.

7

At the hospital they were directed to a long ward containing two rows of beds neatly spaced along the walls, with a small room at either side of its entrance. An orderly was sitting outside the door of the room to the left as if on guard.

The sister in charge of that ward came across from her nearby desk to speak to them, the bottom ends of her starched headdress swaying gently in time to her slow, stately movements.

'I'm here to see my father,' Frankie said. 'Mr Redfern.'

'Ah. He's in that isolation room and I'm sorry, but I can't allow you any closer to him than the doorway.'

'But he's my *father*! My mother has no right to tell you to keep me away from him.'

'It's the doctor who's put the strict order of no visitor to be within touching distance of him, not your mother. Even she isn't allowed into his room.'

So Frankie could only stand in the doorway and look across at her father, who was lying still and flat under the neatly arranged covers, looking more like a wax dummy than a living person. She couldn't even see the covers rising and falling with his breathing. Was he still breathing? How often did they check that?

When she pressed one hand to her mouth to hold in her anguish, Jericho put his arm round her shoulders and kept it there as she watched.

Meanwhile the sergeant had taken the ward sister aside and spoken to her quietly. She kept nodding as if agreeing with what he was saying.

Once their conversation ended she came back to Frankie. 'I'm afraid I must ask you to leave now, Miss Redfern. As you can see, we're doing the best we can for your father. Before you go, however, I have something in my desk that I need to ask you about. Can you come across and look at it, please?'

Frankie went over to where the sergeant was still standing and watched the sister unlock a drawer in the desk and take out what looked like the small tin of the lozenges her father had been taking.

'Do you recognise this?'

'Yes. Father was taking them. He told me the doctor had given them to him to help with the breathlessness. It's definitely the same tin because there's a double scratch down that corner.'

The sister studied it and showed the others the scratch. 'Anything else?'

'I noticed it didn't rattle, so it must be empty now.'

'Do you know what was in the lozenges?'

'No. You'll have to ask the chemist about that. Whatever it was, the lozenges didn't seem to help him much, though. He just kept getting worse.'

'Did your father buy them from the chemist in Rivenshaw?'

'A lad brought them round to the workshop, said the chemist had sent them on the doctor's orders. I remember my father complaining at how horrible they tasted. He was going to ask the doctor to change them but mother told him not to be such a baby.'

'Thank you.' The sister put the tin back in the drawer. 'We need to check everything he's been taking, you see. You may visit your father for a few minutes tomorrow afternoon but until the doctor changes his instructions, no visitors will be allowed past the door.'

Frankie didn't speak as they left the hospital and Jericho didn't say anything either. She got into the van and sat next to him as he set off towards the lawyer's house, still not saying anything.

There was a smell of damp clothing and mud in the van, and her clothes were piled in the rear anyhow on top of and beside her boxes.

She glanced over her shoulder as she pushed a soggy piece of dangling material out of the way. It seemed that her whole life could be crammed into the back of a small van, except for one more bundle of damp garments and the books, which were in the boot of Mr Lloyd's car. By thirty-eight she ought to have much more to show for her time on earth. She had no husband or children and her only legacy would be a few pieces of the furniture she'd made, scattered who knew where.

She realised suddenly that she'd left a couple of small pieces of unfinished furniture that she'd been working on at the workshop. Her mother wouldn't let her have them, she was sure. How stupid of her! But it was too late now to get them.

She felt weary, as if suspended in a bewildering new world waiting for the next unexpected thing to happen to her. She couldn't even guess what that would be.

Jericho shot a quick glance at her. 'Are you all right?'

'Yes, thank you. I'm . . . managing.'

'I'm sorry about your father.'

'Yes.'

She didn't want to talk about what had happened at the hospital, couldn't understand why no one could go near her father. People who collapsed suddenly and died weren't usually infectious, surely?

Thank goodness Jericho seemed to understand her need to think about what she'd seen. He left her in peace and yet it made her feel better to have him nearby. In his quiet way, he had been a tower of strength this evening. Already she was beginning to trust him.

It didn't take long to get to Mr Lloyd's house, a comfortable older-style gentleman's dwelling built of the local stone and situated quite close to the centre of Rivenshaw. While Deemer and the constable helped carry the piles of damp, muddy clothes and the damaged books inside via the kitchen entrance, the lawyer told his wife what had happened.

Irene Lloyd exclaimed in disgust at what Mrs Redfern and her cousin had done, then turned to Frankie. 'My dear, you're very welcome to stay here. I'll get my housekeeper and maid to help us deal with your clothes tomorrow. Dirt is easily removed from most garments. The main thing is that you're safe.'

'Thank you. You're very kind.'

After another searching study of her guest, Mrs Lloyd put an arm round her shoulders. 'Now, you look absolutely exhausted. Say good night to your fiancé and we'll get you into a warm bath. A light supper and a cup of cocoa will help you sleep.'

This motherly concern made Frankie want to weep. Her own mother had never put an arm round her in this way, not even when she was a small child.

When she didn't move, her hostess gave her a gentle push towards Jericho, who was waiting patiently, and Frankie tried to pull herself together. She walked to the front door with him, feeling worried about his safety now. 'Will you be all right tonight, do you think?'

'Oh, yes. I have good friends in Birch End. Higgerson and his bullies are finding it harder and harder to get away with their dirty tricks in our village. They never have tried to cause trouble in the posh northern end of it, of course, and now that Mr Tyler has got his business going properly again, a lot of folk are determined to protect him and the rest of the village.'

'He seems a kind man.'

'He is. And best of all, he'll provide jobs for a good few men once he starts building houses on the land he's bought. Things are going to change and improve in Birch End.'

'Still, you will be extra careful, won't you? Now that Higgerson knows we're engaged, you'll be in more danger than anyone else, I should think.'

He winked. 'You're sounding like a loving wife already.'

That drew a half-smile from her. 'Well, you've been kind to me, extremely kind.'

He seemed surprised. 'You think that's being *extremely* kind?'

She was puzzled by this comment. 'Yes.'

'Wait till you see how us Hartes treat you once you're one of us. You won't just be changing your name, you'll be changing your alliances and finding you have new friends.'

'That will be wonderful.'

As he turned to go, Mr Lloyd stopped him. 'Would you tell Mr Tyler what's been happening as soon as you can, Harte? I'll phone him tomorrow and ask him to give you time off to come and see me in the late morning so that we can book your wedding and plan anything else needed.'

'Yes, I'll do that.'

Jericho surprised Frankie with a quick kiss on the unbruised cheek and left. She could feel the warmth of his lips for a while afterwards and had to resist the temptation to touch the spot.

Mrs Lloyd and her maid cosseted and comforted her and to her surprise, Frankie found that her appetite had returned and ate all of the delicious supper. Afterwards she was more than ready for sleep even though it was still quite early.

It had been the strangest of days.

Irene Lloyd left her guest sinking rapidly towards sleep and went to join her husband in a belated evening meal.

'Is she all right?' he asked.

'Yes. She's worn out by all that's happened to her today, though, poor thing. Who wouldn't be? And I feel angry every time I see that bruise. Are you sure getting engaged to Jericho Harte is the right thing to do?'

'Oh, yes. And they must get married as quickly as possible.'

'He's a bit of a rough diamond.'

'But a strong and honest fellow. And there wasn't much choice. We have to keep her safe from her mother's machinations. You'll stay with her tomorrow, Irene, to help me do that? I promised her father to look after her if anything happened to him and if he's dead that promise is even more sacred to me.'

'Of course I'll help. I would anyway. No one should be treated like that. You know, a few of the ladies I know have noticed that her mother has been acting even more strangely than usual in recent months. And she never was easy to deal with.'

'Yes. I can't stand the woman. But the important thing is to get Frankie married. I'll send someone to fetch her in a car tomorrow when we go to the registry office to get the marriage licence and ceremony sorted out. She's not to walk anywhere or even be left on her own in the house.'

Irene nodded, but gave him one of her wry smiles.

'You're finding some amusement in this?' he asked in surprise.

'A little. It reminds me of those ridiculous Keystone Cops movies you and I used to watch when we were younger. You remember how they were full of people shooting at one another, driving round at top speed barely missing pedestrians or getting into fights and falling over without any blows actually landing. How we laughed.'

That image made him smile reminiscently too.

She sighed. 'It isn't nearly as funny in real life to be chased by bad people, I'm sure.'

'No. Definitely not. I doubt there will be any shooting or car chases in the Ellin Valley, but if Higgerson can, he'll hurt Frankie or at least arrange for someone else to do that. Apart from the fact that he and her mother are up to something, he can't bear to be bested by anyone and has a knack for keeping people afraid of him without ever being caught breaking the law himself.'

After a moment, he added, 'I wish she could marry Jericho tomorrow. He's a strong chap with two brothers guarding his back, and he says he has friends in Birch End who'll help them. I trust him and I don't normally trust people lightly.'

'The law says it has to be a week after notification before you can marry, though, doesn't it? Still, that'll give me time to sort out something pretty for her to wear for the wedding. Those trousers she wears are not . . . well, very flattering. Every bride deserves to look her best on the day and the bruise should have gone by then. Mr Harte might need some help with clothes, too.'

'I'll see to that. Thank you for your help, my dear. I can always rely on you.'

'Oh, I shall enjoy getting ready for a wedding. Do they need to find somewhere to live?'

He explained.

'Does this house contain furniture and necessities like towels and sheets?'

'I don't know. She's never been there and nor have I. That's another thing we need to do tomorrow morning, go and see it. Redfern told me it was old but basically sound, and could be a nice home if someone did the maintenance that's long overdue.'

He helped himself to a second piece of apple pie and poured more custard over it. 'I'm glad you reminded me about the house. They can hardly move into their new home without furniture.'

'Or proper plumbing.'

'Mmm.' He thought about Miss Redfern's future husband as he enjoyed the pie. If the fellow had been given a full-time job by Roy Tyler, he must be a good worker. As for Jericho's family, well, the other Hartes must be all right too because they'd been chosen by Wilf to live next to him and help keep his home and new wife safe. There was bound to be trouble in the area once the building started on the field behind it.

All in all, Henry felt more positive about the situation than he'd expected to this morning, though he felt sad for poor Redfern. He'd have to check first thing the next day whether his client had died or struggled on through the night.

Strange, that sudden collapse. Older people often got a sort of transparent look as their health declined for the last time. Redfern hadn't looked well for a while, but he hadn't had *that look* of seeming close to death, or Henry would have noticed.

That was what life could be like, though, full of abrupt changes. You never knew for certain what was round the next corner.

8

When Jericho got back to Tyler's yard, everyone seemed to have gone home but there was a light showing in one of the offices. There were no other vehicles parked nearby, though. He locked all its doors then left the van in front of the gates and went inside to see if anyone was still there.

He was relieved to find Wilf sitting behind his desk. 'You're working late.'

'Waiting for you. We didn't think you'd have run off with the van but when Mrs Tyler phoned the ironmonger, he said you'd left suddenly without taking the order you'd gone for and he didn't know where you were. Then we got a message from Mr Lloyd's clerk that you'd been delayed by an urgent family matter, but he couldn't, or wouldn't tell us what that was. So Mrs Tyler asked me to wait and find out what's been going on.'

'Oh, hell. I forgot about those things from the ironmonger's. I'll pick them up tomorrow, well, I will if I can. You see . . .' Jericho explained briefly that he'd been getting engaged and why, leaving Wilf gaping at him in amazement.

'You got engaged to Miss Redfern? Just . . . out of the blue?'

'Yes.'

'I didn't think you even knew her and let's face it, you come from rather different backgrounds. It's not the usual sort of match.'

'No, it isn't. But she needs a husband and her father had urged her to find one quickly.' He decided on complete honesty, because Wilf and his wife had been kind to him, as had the Tylers, and he trusted them absolutely. If anyone deserved the full story, they did.

Afterwards he looked at Wilf anxiously. 'I won't lose my job for going off with the van today, will I? Frankie desperately needed my help.'

'That's the least of your worries if you've crossed Higgerson.'

'My job here is a bigger worry because it's even more important now I'm getting married. And I'll still have to help Mam as well.'

Wilf looked at him thoughtfully. 'I reckon we'd better go and tell Mrs Tyler what's happened to you. As you'll find out, she likes to know every detail of what's going on around here, and she often has better ideas than anyone else about how to solve problems. Now you've started working for her, she'll be keeping an eye on you as well. It'll be up to her about the van and the job, but she's usually very fair.'

What did 'fair' mean in these circumstances? Jericho wondered as he followed the other man out to the van. When Wilf got into the passenger seat, he took the driving seat again, worrying now that things might have gone from bad to worse.

Surely he'd not lose his new job because of taking the van and not bringing back the supplies he'd been sent for? They might not starve because of Frankie's money but a fine husband he'd make if he didn't even have a job!

At the Tylers' house, Jericho told his tale again to them both. How many times would he have to go through it? He had got into a tangle of words at one stage and hoped he hadn't left anything out.

His employers were as surprised as Jericho and there was dead silence for a few moments as they took it all in. He didn't interrupt.

Then Mr Tyler said suddenly, 'Well, we don't socialise with the Redferns, but I do know one thing about your fiancée. Old Bill once told me that she was not only a nice lass, but the best cabinetmaker he'd ever trained. He was extremely proud of her.'

'She's going to make an unusual wife,' Mrs Tyler said.

Roy grinned at her. 'You're an unusual wife, too. That suits me just fine and I don't think Jericho will stop her doing what she wants. As for her father, I've done business with him from time to time. Well, Rivenshaw's a small town, isn't it? I've always found him an honest chap who knows his trade and employs good workers. They think the world of him. That says a lot, too.'

Mrs Tyler joined in. 'Well, no one thinks much of that mother of hers. I've met her a few times and to be honest, I can't stand the woman. She's . . . strange.' She tapped her forehead to indicate what she meant by that, then added quietly, 'Her daughter sounds interesting, though. I like to hear of women doing what they want in life, not what men tell them to do.'

Her voice tailed away and she began to stare into the distance, drumming her fingers on the arm of her chair. When Jericho opened his mouth to say something, Wilf stuck one elbow in his companion's ribs and put a finger to his lips.

So they all waited and when Ethel's fingers stilled, she looked up and said, 'We're going to need a good cabinetmaker when we start our new project, Roy.'

Her husband clearly hadn't been expecting this. 'You're thinking of us employing her?'

'Why not? Women can do most things men can given the

chance and let anyone try to tell me different.' She looked round challengingly.

No one would dare contradict her about that, Jericho thought in sudden amusement. And actually, he was more impressed by her every time he spent time with her. She was definitely the power behind the throne here, even though she didn't flaunt it. She turned that penetrating, intelligent stare on him.

'Do you think Frankie would come and work for us, Jericho?'

He nodded. He was fairly sure she would, anyway.

Mr Tyler frowned. 'Eh, I don't know what our other workers would say about having a woman in the workshop, Ethel love.'

'They accept me already and they'll accept her too if she's as skilful as you've been told.'

She turned to their newest employee. 'It's a good thing that house you'll be living in is in Birch End. It'll not only be convenient for your work but safer. I wonder if that's why Mr Redfern chose it, because she'd not be living near her mother when she moved there? How big is it?'

'We haven't even seen it yet. I have no idea what it's like.'

After another brief, thoughtful pause and some more finger tapping, she surprised them again. 'Jericho, I think when you and Frankie go to look at the cottage, Roy and I should go with you to show folk round here that we're on your side. I'm sure Mrs Redfern will be spreading lies about you.'

Another stare into space, then she smiled. 'And it'll fit in nicely with another problem I've been thinking about: we're going to need some night watchmen round the yard and round that field once our big job starts. I'm sure Higgerson will try to damage what we're doing and others will try to steal our building materials. The watchmen can keep an eye on your house as well and help keep you safe.'

Roy nodded. 'You're right about us needing people to keep watch once we start. I've been thinking about that too.'

'We're not letting Higgerson think he can do what he wants here as he does in Backshaw Moss and the poorer parts of Rivenshaw. He's been getting worse since Rathley died because there's been no other villain powerful enough in the valley to fight him for the pickings. Apart from him, most of our problems are just to do with petty crime, the sort you get everywhere, and you can't seem to stop that even when there are plenty of jobs.'

'I was going to hire a night watchman,' Roy said. 'I already told you that.'

'Well, I think we should do a lot more than just keep watch on our building site. It's time to take a stand with Higgerson. If we don't, he'll carry on causing trouble and cheating folk left, right and centre. We should get the people in the village on our side as well and make it clear to him that he won't get away with his nasty tricks anywhere in Birch End.'

'You think we can keep him from playing his nasty tricks in the village?'

'Mostly. If everyone pulls together, that is.'

'That'll take more than one watchman and add a lot more costs to our job,' Roy objected. 'We should just look after our own and let the police tackle the rest. I know the sergeant has been asking for a constable to be put in Birch End.'

'No. If we just hired one man, Higgerson would find a way to get past him and then we'd be repairing damage time after time. You should have seen how he looks at me when he passes me in town. Mark my words, he's still furious that we bought that field instead of him getting it. I think it'll be well worth the extra money we'll have to spend to make him leave our work and our village alone now and in the future.' She leaned back in her chair and waited for her husband to think it over.

Wilf poked Jericho in the ribs again and this time nodded towards Roy, who was clearly thinking hard. He kept chewing on his clenched fist and rocking backwards and forwards. Even Mrs Tyler had fallen silent and was watching him. Suddenly he waved his hand in the air and slapped it down hard on the arm of his chair, uttering a loud, 'We'll do it.'

Jericho, who wasn't used to his ways, was startled by this and jumped visibly. Wilf merely smiled and waited, as did Mrs Tyler.

Another thump of the fist, then, 'By *heck*, Ethel lass, we'll declare *war* on dishonesty and the attacking of hard-working folk. In Birch End at least. We can't help the whole valley, but we *can* help ourselves.'

Wilf nodded. 'I agree with you, Roy, but I doubt we'll manage to keep an eye on Backshaw Moss as well as the village, well, not properly. Eh, that place could do with knocking down. It's as bad a slum as I've ever seen, and I've been all over the north when I was on the tramp. But we can make a start on providing decent homes for hard-working folk with our new houses, eh?'

Roy smiled at them all and nodded vigorously then turned back to his wife. 'You always seem to know when a situation is ripe for one of your clever ideas, my lass. Well done.'

'Your clever ideas too, love.'

He swung round to his newest employee. 'So, Jericho lad, you can go down to Rivenshaw in our van tomorrow to collect your young lady and book your wedding. We'll not let that sod stop you getting wed or slow things down. Afterwards you can bring her back to have a look round your new home. Ethel and I will meet you there.'

'You could maybe get Mr Lloyd's clerk to phone and let

us know when you're on your way,' Ethel added, 'then we shan't waste time hanging around waiting for you.'

Relief surged through Jericho and also amazement at how much these people cared for their community as well as their workers. 'Thank you.'

'Does she know anything about the house?' Mrs Tyler asked.

'No, not a single thing. She only found out she owns it yesterday. She doesn't even know whether there's any furniture been left there, probably not, but if we're inspecting the place openly, perhaps she'll be able to buy it for us. I was going to ask my mother to do that secretly, so that we could get wed without anyone trying to stop us.'

'You'd never have managed to keep it secret in a small town. It has to go in a special book at the registry office once it's booked.' Ethel frowned for a moment, then leaned forward and added, 'I'll go with your lass if you need furniture and we can take your mother too. I love making the insides of houses *right* to live in.'

Jericho looked at her in alarm. The whole situation seemed to be getting out of hand. 'We were only going to buy a few items second hand, just enough to give us a start, like. We have to be careful with money.' He couldn't imagine, even in his wildest dreams, being in a situation where he didn't need to be careful with every farthing, because he'd rarely had any money to spare in his whole life.

'Charlie Willcox has some very nice second-hand pieces in the upstairs of his bigger pawnshop, though some of the bigger items like wardrobes are out in his back shed. You'll get better value and quality from him than you would at the market. Oh, and you'll want to buy some electrical goods from his shop, as well. Harry Makepeace will be able to advise you about that.'

'If they've got electricity on,' her husband pointed out. 'I don't think an old house that's been empty for years will have it installed already.'

'No, I suppose you're right. We'd better check that all the services have been connected.'

As the two men were walking away from the house, Wilf stopped under a nearby street lamp to grin at Jericho. 'Surprised by what they're like?'

'Aye. I was that.'

'When you start working with Roy and Ethel, you find they look after you – sometimes even before you know you need help.'

'I don't know what Frankie will say about all this.'

'You can phone her early tomorrow morning from our house and tell her you'll be down to take her to the town hall with Mr Lloyd.'

He yawned suddenly. 'Eh, I'm proper weary now. Let's get home to our beds. We can still get most of a night's sleep.'

Jericho left Wilf to go in by the front door and went round the back of the house to the separate part where his family lived. When he walked in he found his mother and brothers sitting round the table over cups of cocoa. Now that they had a bit more money coming in, that was a regular treat before they went to bed.

He glanced at the battered clock on the windowsill. Was it still only quarter past ten? So much had happened since he set off to walk to Tyler's this morning it felt more like midnight.

He joined them at the table, sitting down with a weary sigh. 'No, don't get up yet, Mam. I've got news for you.' He saw the worried look appear on her face and said quickly, 'It's all right. It's good news.'

She brightened and they all turned to look at him expectantly but he hesitated for a moment, marshalling his thoughts.

His mother gave him a nudge. 'Well, get on with it.'

'I'm getting married.'

There was dead silence but he saw his mother's mouth drop open and his brothers gape at him in shock.

As the silence continued, he asked, 'Didn't you hear what I said?'

His brothers both looked at their mother, waiting for her to reply.

'Who're you getting married to, son? And why haven't we met her before? How could you have been courting anyone without me finding out?'

'This is to go no further. Family only.'

They all nodded solemnly.

'I'm marrying Frankie Redfern because her father's dying and it seems . . .'

When he'd finished telling his tale yet again, his mother reached out her hand to hold his and his brothers again waited for her.

'Is it what you really want, son? A marriage is for life and you hardly know the woman.'

'I want it very much. I'd already met her and really liked her.' And the more time he spent with her, the more he liked her.

'Well, you've always known your own mind, right from a lad, so whatever reason brought you together, I'm glad for you and hope you'll both be happy.'

His brothers murmured what could have been congratulations and would have got up, but he held out his hand to stop them.

'There's more.'

Tension returned to the room.

'Frankie owns a house in Birch End and we're going to live there. It's the empty one at the end of Marlow Road.'

His mother beamed at that. He didn't have to ask why. To

own your own house was rare for ordinary people but it brought a security that many could only ever dream of. In better times the more skilled workers would have saved their pennies for years to get a house.

'There's going to be trouble from Higgerson about that as well as about your marriage,' Gabriel said suddenly. 'And he'll be causing trouble for Tyler too if he can, so you'll cop a double dose. Everyone knows how furious he was when Mr Tyler bought that land at the back of here.'

'Yes, I know.'

His mother joined in with one of her little lectures. 'Let's not get stuck on the problems; it's always better to look at the bright side. If you own your own house, you'll be set up for life, son. Eh, to think of it.'

'I haven't really taken it in yet.'

'Mind you, I think it's a good thing you're going to be living in Birch End. Let alone you'll be close to your brothers, most folk round here are decent sorts who'd come to your help if anyone tried to cause trouble. Rivenshaw's too big for that. It's better when people know their neighbours.'

Jericho nodded agreement. 'Unfortunately I think we'll need help to keep safe. But we've got Mrs Tyler on our side as well and she has a few plans about the future of our village and their business. She intends to keep Higgerson from damaging either of them if she can.'

Lucas chuckled suddenly. 'We'll be all right then. She's as good as any two men, that one is. Three men, even. Smartest person I ever met.'

They all murmured further agreement. Since Roy Tyler had recovered from the loss of his son and started working properly again, his wife had taken over a lot of what poor Trevor had been doing in the business, abandoning any pretence of only working in the office, going out to inspect jobs and deal with tradesmen. Everyone in the village knew she wasn't nearly as interested in running her own home. She was not only working full time at the business now, she was reorganising it, making one change after another.

'She's a nice lady, always got a pleasant word for you and helps out if she hears someone's in trouble.' Gwynneth stood up. 'Now, if you've nothing else to spring on us, we all need our sleep. And you look bone weary, our Jericho.'

He was exhausted but underneath it all he was excited too. He and his family had been struggling to survive through several years of bad times in the ten years since his father's death. Like many folk, he'd been in and out of work. It was always hard for a family to manage without a steady male breadwinner. His mother had done the best she could, and all of them had snatched at any job, big or small. If it hadn't been for her falling seriously ill, they'd not have been reduced to living in Backshaw Moss, though, and they'd all hated it there.

And now all of a sudden he'd been presented first with a regular full-time job, then with a chance to have a wife and home of his own.

He didn't intend to waste this wonderful opportunity to make a better future for himself and his family. He wasn't going to rely on Frankie's money, either. He intended to make some of his own. He'd do his best to be a good husband and maybe, if he was very lucky, they'd have a child or two. She was older than him, but not too old for that, he hoped.

But he damned well wasn't going to let Higgerson and Mrs Redfern hurt her, or anyone else round here. He'd fight to the last breath in his body to protect the people he loved.

And to protect the new person he was starting to be fond of.

As he slid towards sleep he snuggled down in his narrow

bed, smiling at the thought of what a nice woman Frankie seemed to be. And she'd said she felt comfortable with him. Surely they could build a decent life on that . . .

Mrs Tyler called Jericho into the office soon after he got to work the following morning. 'Mr Lloyd telephoned not long ago to let me know he wants you and Frankie to go with him to book the wedding as soon as the office in the town hall opens.'

'Do you mind if I have the morning off?'

'Of course not. You'd better take the van again, so that you can drive Frankie round in it. That'll be a lot safer than trudging everywhere on foot. Don't bother trying to bring back the hardware supplies today, it's too risky. They can wait. You stay at her side. There's nothing more important than a human life. Never forget that.'

'I'll never forget how kind you're being to me, Mrs Tyler. Nor will my Frankie, I'm sure. One day we'll find a way to pay you back.'

She flushed slightly and flapped one hand at him. 'Get off with you. The best way to pay me back is to work hard and look after that nice young woman. We're going to need her skills as well as yours when we start our big job. Do you think she'll come and work for us?'

'I think she'd love to.'

He was looking forward to the big job. The Tylers were planning to build a whole street of new houses on the piece of land, and from what he'd heard, they'd be really modern houses with indoor bathrooms and proper kitchens. He was sure to learn a great deal from being involved in that.

It wasn't till he was getting into the van that Jericho realised this had been the first time he'd referred to his fiancée as 'my Frankie'. He'd said it as naturally as he'd have said 'our Gabriel' or 'our Mam'.

That made him whistle cheerfully as he drove down to Rivenshaw to pick her up. She *was* his Frankie now, or soon would be, and if it was up to him, she'd never regret marrying him.

Even the sun was shining on him and his valley today.

9

Frankie was waiting for him at Mr Lloyd's house, looking a good deal better than she had the night before, even with the bruised face. She was dressed in a matching skirt and jacket in a brown tweedy material, with a cream blouse and a neat little beret on her head, pulled slightly to one side.

Jericho hid a smile at the sight of the simple beret because he couldn't even imagine her in a fancy hat with feathers sticking out of it like some ladies wore. His fingers itched to twitch that beret off, pull out her hairpins and let her beautiful hair loose, as it had been on the moors.

She was carrying that scuffed brown leather satchel of hers, which she seemed to take everywhere. It looked quite heavy. What on earth did she keep in it?

When she looked at him as if expecting a comment on her appearance after such a long stare, he said, 'You managed to find some clean clothes, then?'

'Mrs Lloyd's maid washed some things for me last night before she went to bed and ironed them this morning.' She touched her blouse self-consciously. 'Wasn't that kind of her?'

'Very kind. You look nice. I wish I had some better clothes. Mine are all rather shabby, I'm afraid.'

'You look fine to me as you are. It's the man I'm marrying not the suit.'

Nice way to put it to spare his feelings, he thought, but he still wished he had some better clothes. What on earth was he going to wear for the wedding?

'I came straight from work and they not only let me have the time off but lent me the van again. By heck, they're well organised at Tyler's. It's going to be a pleasure working there. I can't abide doing a job inefficiently, but them as employ you have the final say in how you work and some of them hardly know which way is up. Now, that's enough about me. Where are we going first?'

'Mr Lloyd says to meet him outside the council offices and to stay in the van till he joins us. He went to his rooms early this morning to get some paperwork done for another client.'

They got into the van but he didn't set off straight away. 'Any news of your father?' It had to be asked but he hated to see sadness send a shimmer of tears into her eyes as she shook her head.

'I telephoned the hospital. Father's alive but barely, the sister told me, and he's still not allowed to have visitors near him. Everyone has to stay in the doorway like we did. They're frightened of other people catching whatever it is from him, you see.'

'Eh, I'm sorry, lass.'

'They're thinking of moving him to a private hospital near Todmorden run by a friend of Dr McDevitt. I shan't be able to visit him at all if they do that.' She blinked furiously. 'I shall always regret it if I don't manage to say a proper goodbye to him.'

'Have you heard from your mother?'

'No. And I don't want to. She's not a good woman, Jericho. Don't believe anything she says about me.'

'I know, lass. I'll be happy to share my mother with you to make up for it. You'll like our Mam and she couldn't tell a lie to save her life. She's really pleased that I'm getting married and I'm to tell you she's looking forward to meeting you.'

Frankie was clearly startled by this. 'She is?'

'Of course she is. She's been nagging me to get married for years because she wants grandchildren. I told her the truth about us, mind. Her and my brothers. I'd not lie to my family. But they'll keep it to themselves.'

'What are your brothers' names?'

'Gabriel and Lucas.'

'Biblical names for all three of you.'

'Yes. Mam has a big family Bible and she found the names in it. All our family have had their names written down in the front of it for over a hundred years – births, marriages and deaths – and yours will be there too once we're wed. That's one thing I can give you, Frankie, a loving family.'

She nodded and swallowed hard, seeming lost for words.

He set off and drove the short distance to the town hall in silence, stopping the van near the entrance. 'No one can sneak up on us here without me seeing them.'

'Good.' She leaned back with a tired sigh.

He turned in his seat so that he could keep watch for anyone approaching the van from the street side, but though there were a few other vehicles nearby, there didn't seem to be any other people around. It was starting to cloud over, but he didn't feel cold. He liked watching Frankie, getting to know her little ways.

'Do you think it'd be safe to go and look at the house afterwards, Jericho? It feels strange to own a house and not even know what it looks like.'

'Eh, I nearly forgot to tell you: we can go up to Birch End openly and have a good look round your house, thanks to the Tylers. If it's all right with you, we'll meet them there and they can come round it with us. They reckon it'll show people in the village that they approve of us getting wed.'

'Oh, good. And . . . do they really approve, do you think?'

'Yes. Actually, everyone I know seems to think it's a good idea. You aren't regretting it, are you?'

'On the contrary. It's a huge relief not to be alone in the world and . . . well, I enjoy your company. Um, *you* aren't regretting it, because if so, you'd better tell me now.'

He saw the worry on her face change to happy relief when he replied without hesitation, 'No, lass. I don't regret it one bit. I don't regret our frankness either. We need to learn to understand one another better and anyway, I hate lying about anything.'

The lawyer drove up just then and stopped his car nearby, which was perhaps as well. Jericho felt he had to tread so carefully with what he said to her. She was like a dog that had been beaten often and as a result flinched away before a human even got close. 'Here's Mr Lloyd. Let's get that first important step taken and book our wedding.'

'Just a minute.' She thrust something into his hand and he looked down to see a five-pound note. 'What's this?'

'To pay for the special licence. I thought it'd look better if you did that.'

He felt his face grow warm with embarrassment. 'I'd forgotten about paying. I don't even know how much that costs.'

'Three pounds.'

He gulped and blurted out, 'It's a good thing you had the money. I don't even have three pounds in the world.'

She closed his fingers round it. 'You do now.'

'Thank you. And it was thoughtful of you to give me the money before we go in.'

'Well, it was thoughtful of you when you told Mr Lloyd you *wished* to marry me.'

'I do wish it. Very much. I shall keep telling you that until you believe me.'

She gave him one of her uncertain smiles.

'I haven't lied to you, lass, and I won't, not ever. I'd have come courting you after we met on the moors if I'd been able to afford it and if you hadn't been from a well-off family. One day I'll make it up to you for me not having any money.'

'You're doing that simply by marrying me.'

But her assurances didn't console him for having to accept money from her. That was not a good thing and left a bad taste in his mouth. The note crackled slightly as his fingers clenched on it and he tried not to show how humiliated he felt. Eh, just as soon as you thought things were going smoothly, something came up to embarrass you.

He hated having to accept that fiver from her, absolutely hated it. But he had no choice. Besides, he'd hate even more not to marry her now.

He wondered how much money she had exactly, then pushed that thought away. If she wanted him to know, she'd tell him. He'd certainly not ask.

He put the note safely in his inside jacket pocket, locked up the van then they walked across to join Mr Lloyd.

The lawyer led the way inside the foyer and along a corridor to the office where you lodged a notice of intent to marry. This was at the back of the town hall next to the room where weddings took place.

The plump young man behind the counter looked up, started to give them a false smile, then looked at them again and gulped audibly. The smile vanished and he began to look nervous.

Jericho frowned. This chap seemed to know who they were and was acting as if there might be trouble. Someone must have told him to expect them and described them, because he certainly couldn't remember ever meeting the fellow. And the glances the clerk was throwing at the lawyer showed that his presence particularly worried him.

'Are you going to stare at us all day or are you going to do your job?' Mr Lloyd asked sharply.

The clerk jerked to attention. 'Oh, ah, sorry, Mr Lloyd.'

'My clients wish to get married by special licence.'

The man got out the marriage notice book and started to go through the necessary steps, but continued to show signs of nervousness.

'That'll be, um, three pounds.'

Jericho got out the five-pound note and held it ready. He wasn't handing it over till the special licence was in his hand.

The clerk knocked the book on to the floor and picked it up again. Why was he sneaking glances towards the door? Who was he expecting?

Jericho exchanged puzzled glances with Frankie and was about to ask him what the matter was when there was the sound of footsteps approaching. A man appeared in the corridor outside the glass-walled office and the door crashed open so violently that it banged off the rubber doorstop fixed into the floor.

He stared at the man. Oh, hell! He knew Livings by sight and by reputation too as a brawler.

At the sight of the lawyer the newcomer hesitated in the doorway then sauntered past him without even a nod. He slowed down to scowl at Jericho, then let out what sounded like a snort of disgust and sat down on one of the line of chairs set against the wall for those waiting to be attended to. He folded his arms, making no attempt to close the door behind himself.

'I'll only be a few more minutes, sir,' the clerk told him.

'Doesn't matter. I can wait as long as I need to.'

There were more footsteps outside and the mayor strolled past the wall of windows, also coming from the front of the building. He stopped when he saw them at the counter, started to smile at Mr Lloyd then frowned as he spotted the roughly dressed man sitting on one of the chairs, legs sticking out, sprawling like a naughty child.

The mayor came over to the lawyer. 'I thought I saw you walk across the foyer a short time ago, Henry. I'm glad I caught you. Would you have a few minutes to discuss something with me before you leave?'

'Yes, of course.'

Jericho studied Reginald Kirby with interest. Like most people, he knew the mayor by sight but he'd never been so close to him before. He wondered if their lawyer was on first-name terms with everyone of importance in the town. He'd heard that Kirby was making a good start as mayor by introducing plans to improve the way their town was run. That were long overdue, if you asked Jericho.

The mayor turned to Frankie next. 'Ah, Miss Redfern. Nice to see you again. My wife absolutely loves that little table you made for us.'

Livings made a disgusted sound in his throat at that compliment, shuffled his feet noisily and scowled at them all.

Frankie ignored him. 'I'm glad your wife's happy with it. Have you met Jericho Harte, Mr Kirby? He and I are going to get married, which is why we're here.'

As the mayor looked at her in surprise, Jericho watched Livings move his chair about again. He ended up with it in nearly the same place but managed to make plenty of noise in the process.

Kirby turned towards him and said sharply, 'What are you doing here, Livings? You're married already. This isn't a public waiting room, you know.'

'It's a free country.' The man stared sullenly at him, folding his arms again.

The mayor stepped closer to him. 'Do you have any actual business here or are you merely intending to live up to your reputation and cause trouble? If so, let me tell you that should you ever put one foot out of line in the town hall while I'm mayor, I'll immediately call in the police. We haven't forgotten the time you broke that vase in the foyer.'

'Wasn't my fault. The stand the vase was on wasn't steady, probably made by a female so-called carpenter.' He threw a sneering glance at Frankie.

The mayor waited and when there was no response to his original question, repeated, 'What *are* you doing here? If you have no valid reason, I'll ask you to leave.'

'I'm here as a member of the public. The law says anyone can see the book that tells when folk are planning to get wed.'

'That doesn't explain why *you* should have come here. What has it got to do with you if these people intend to get married? I doubt you even know them. Get off about your own business.'

'It *is* my business. Mr Higgerson sent me to find out about them for her mother. She's worried about what this one is doing.' He jerked his head in Frankie's direction.

'Then you can jolly well wait somewhere else and come back once they've finished their business. At the moment you're doing nothing but interrupting them and acting discourteously, which is not the way we expect people to behave in public areas of this building.' He held the door open to its full extent and made a sweeping gesture with one hand.

Livings glared at the couple, muttered something and stood up with exaggerated slowness. After he walked out, he went to lean against the opposite wall only a few yards further along with an 'I dare you' look on his face.

Reginald watched him through the glass frontage of the office, shaking his head in annoyance. He moved further away from the counter and beckoned to the lawyer, asking in a low voice, 'Trouble brewing, do you think?'

'I'm afraid so,' Henry said. 'I'll tell you about it in a few minutes. You might want to keep an eye on your clerk, though. He grew nervous once he recognised my client and her fiancé, so must have been expecting something to happen. What's more, it's been his job to deal with the paperwork for years, yet he's working slowly today, fumbling around as if he can't find things.'

The mayor pursed his lips. 'Hmm. I wonder if he's expecting to be promoted to registrar one day? If so, he'll be waiting a long time. Pashley isn't happy with him and is looking for a replacement.'

'Thank goodness this chap isn't the one who'll actually be marrying them. His sour face would blight the day.'

Kirby turned to Jericho, speaking at a normal pitch now. 'I've seen you around the valley, young man. Congratulations on your engagement. I'm pleased for you both and hope you'll be happy. Where are you getting married?'

Henry answered for them. 'Here. This time next week. I'll arrange that with the registrar. Pashley's been a friend of mine for years.'

'If you don't mind, I'll attend the wedding. I like to do that now and then to keep in touch with our younger citizens.' The mayor moved right up to the counter, standing directly in front of the clerk. 'If anyone else gets to hear about me planning to be present at the wedding, *you* will be in big trouble, Tolver.'

'Yes, sir.' The young chap quickly finished making the necessary entries in the book and on a piece of paper, this time without any fumbling.

'Just remember, Tolver,' the mayor went on, 'if Livings comes back in, the law says you're obliged to let him see the book but that's all he can do. If you want to keep your job, you'll tell him nothing else and get rid of him quickly. You understand me?'

'Yes, sir. I mean, no, sir.' He didn't manage to hide his resentfulness as he said that, however.

Mr Lloyd walked out of the office with them, totally ignoring Livings who was still standing nearby watching them. 'I'll just see my clients out and then I'll come back to have that chat with you, Reg.'

'Good.'

He looked back at Livings. 'On second thoughts I'll accompany you all outside. It'll be nice to get a breath of fresh air.'

Near the van they found another rough-looking man lingering but when he saw who was with Jericho and Frankie, he walked rapidly away.

'I don't like the looks of this. Will you two be all right?' Mr Kirby asked.

Jericho was watching the man disappear round a corner so Frankie gave him a nudge. 'The mayor asked us a question.'

'What? Oh, sorry, sir, I was keeping an eye on where that chap went. Could you repeat your question, please?' He listened properly this time. 'Thank you for your concern, Mr Kirby. We'll be safe in the van as we drive up to Birch End and we're meeting the Tylers there. I don't think anyone is likely to annoy *them*, especially in our village.'

He looked at the lawyer. 'Would it be all right if we stop at your rooms on the way, Mr Lloyd, and ask your clerk to phone and let the Tylers know we're coming? They're going to meet us at the house.'

It was the mayor who answered. 'I'll get my secretary to let them know from here. That way you won't have to risk stopping on the way.'

'Thank you very much.'

Jericho would have helped Frankie get into the car but she did that herself before he could get to the door. As he drove off, he felt angry that they had to be so careful, but everyone knew how ruthless Higgerson's men could be.

When they'd thrown his family out of their room in Backshaw Moss only a few weeks previously they'd simply barged in, told them to get out and started chucking everything his family owned into the street. They'd deliberately broken his mother's most treasured possession, a cake stand that had belonged to *her* mother. It had been a good job Wilf and Sergeant Deemer were nearby and had come to their aid.

Well, Higgerson wasn't going to hurt his family again, and that included Frankie now. Not if there was any justice in the world. Not while he was able to stand up and defend her.

The two old friends stood watching till the van was out of sight.

'What's Higgerson after now?' Reg asked.

'He's a cousin of Mrs Redfern. With her husband suddenly taken ill and not expected to last much longer, I bet he'll be trying to get his hands on their business.'

'Ah. I knew he'd not be doing it out of altruism, not even for a relative. He and Mrs Redfern haven't been exactly close over the years.'

'They seem close at the moment.'

He thought for a moment, then said angrily, 'Damn the fellow! He's got his fingers in too many pies around here since Rathley died. Haven't we on the town council enough trouble trying to bring work to our valley and keep our poorer citizens fed without having to worry about him? He doesn't even build decent houses.'

'I think he'll find it harder to keep control of building jobs in the valley as times get better. There will be fewer men then who need to take any nasty little job from him just to feed their families. I hope so anyway.'

'I reckon you're right.' Reg led the way inside the town hall and asked the counter clerk to phone the Tylers, then said, 'I think I'll go and check on that young clerk before we sit down for a chat. It shouldn't have taken him more than a couple of minutes to show the marriage notice book to that rogue but I haven't seen Livings come out.'

'I'll come too.'

They stopped just before the wall of windows and saw the clerk leaning on his elbows on the counter, chatting to Livings and looking as if the two of them were on very friendly terms.

The young man was so intent on what he was saying he didn't even see the mayor come along to the door. When he did, he hastily stood upright but Livings stayed where he was, leaning on one elbow and making no attempt to move.

'You're not paid to chat, Tolver,' the mayor snapped.

'Proper slave drivers they are here. I pity you, lad, I do indeed.' Livings straightened up slowly and strolled out, giving the older men a smug look as he passed them, a look that seemed to say he knew something they didn't.

'I won't forget your behaviour today, Tolver,' Reg snapped.

'I was just showing him the book, Mr Kirby. I have to do that.'

'You were gossiping. Mustn't be enough for you to do here.'

As they walked away, the mayor said quietly, 'I reckon Higgerson and Mrs Redfern are planning something. I hope we can keep Frankie and Jericho safe till they marry.'

'And afterwards. Eh, when will things improve?'

'I've been reading about a new breed of economist, men who're calling this a recession.'

'They can call it what they like. The government should be doing more to help areas like ours.'

'One of these economists, Keynes I think his name is,

reckons the government is dealing with the problem wrongly and should be spending money rather than cutting back.'

Lloyd nodded. 'That sounds more sensible to me than tightening the purse strings still further.'

'Aye, well. You just about need dynamite to get certain members of the council to agree to spend money on our poorer citizens. They seem to believe rates money and government grants are paid to make life easier for themselves and their businesses.'

'Well, we've got a majority on the council now.'

'Only just, Henry, only just. I hope all our new members stay in good health.'

When they got to his office, he shut the door and gestured to a seat. 'Well, that settles one thing. The registrar says Tolver isn't at all satisfactory and anyway he'd prefer to have an older woman as his assistant registrar. I'll see if I can have that young man transferred to somewhere far less pleasant, where he doesn't have time to gossip or even see what goes on here.'

'How about the sewage works?'

Reg chortled. 'Good idea.'

'Trouble is, it'll only get rid of one man. You can't prevent the marriage lists being open to the public, whoever's working in the registry office. It's the law. Just like the marriage itself having to take place where other people can see it if they wish. Pity. We'll have to make sure those two bring some strong friends to their wedding. Now, what did you want to talk about?'

Reg grinned at his friend. 'You'll probably have guessed that I didn't have anything in particular to discuss, just wanted to make my presence felt around the place. I'll order us a pot of tea then you can tell me all about that nice young couple before you go.'

'They're neither of them all that young.'

'Then why are they getting married hastily and not having a proper church wedding? It can't be for the usual reason, surely?'

'Not this time. She needs the protection of a husband, now her father's not there to keep an eye on his wife.'

They both settled down to enjoy a gossip and share all sorts of information.

10

Jericho waited till they were out of town to say, 'I won't let Higgerson hurt you, Frankie.'

'I'm grateful for your care but who's going to stop *you* getting hurt?'

'You don't grow up in the poorer districts without learning how to look after yourself and I have two brothers who'll guard my back. They're both big chaps like me and I've also got friends I can call on for help, if I have to. Us Hartes don't start fights, but we don't let those who try to cause trouble trample all over us, nor do we let them hurt those we care about.'

He gave her a moment or two for this to sink in then tried to turn the conversation to something more cheerful, 'Are you looking forward to seeing the house? I am.'

'You seem more excited than I'd expected.'

'Well, people like me don't usually manage to get a place of their own; somewhere no landlord can throw you out of on a whim. I can hardly believe it's true.'

'I can't believe it's true, either. My father never even hinted at what he was doing. And since spinsters of my age don't usually get a chance at marriage, I've got that to be happy about as well. I'm older than you, though. I wish I weren't.'

He slowed down a little and chose his words carefully. 'You're thirty-eight to my thirty-five. Not much difference. And you don't look anything like your age.'

She sounded hesitant. 'Do you think we can make it work, Jericho? I'm hoping so. I'd like us to have a . . . a proper marriage.'

He hoped she meant what he thought by that, because he had a normal man's desires. 'I'd like that too. I'll do everything I can to make it work, I promise you.'

He shot a quick glance sideways and saw her cheeks were still bright red, so he let go of the steering wheel with his left hand and gave her arm a quick squeeze, then concentrated on his driving again.

As they left town and turned on to the valley road, she said, 'According to Mr Lloyd the house has been standing empty for a while, so it'll probably be in a mess inside. I doubt we'll be living in luxury. I'd guess that it's a small house and even then I don't know how my father found enough money to buy it for me because my mother has always insisted on keeping an eye on his spending.'

'I don't need luxury. Me and my family all had to live in one room for a few months in Backshaw Moss when Mam was ill. It took all our savings to pay for her appendix operation, you see, and then we had to sell most of the furniture when she needed looking after and feeding up afterwards. None of us lads had steady jobs at that time, and of course she lost her work as a day cleaner once she fell ill. But we saved her, that's what mattered.'

'You're good sons.'

'Well, she's been a good mother. Any road, we're living in three rooms now, which is a huge improvement, and she's got a job doing the housework because Mrs Pollard still works in the office at the driving school. So my family will have somewhere to live and money coming in even if I can't contribute much from now on.'

He risked another quick glance and saw her nod. The blush was fading and she was looking more relaxed, so he decided to carry on being frank. 'You and me having a whole house for only the two of us will seem like living in a palace to me, whatever it's like. Well, it will as long as the place isn't falling down round us.'

'It must be reasonably sound or my father wouldn't have bought it. It's one of his rules in life, to make sure that whatever you're buying, selling or making is fit for its purpose.'

'Good rule, that.'

She took a deep breath and spoke in a rush. 'Um, can we visit the hospital later? I'd like to see Dad again . . . if he's still alive.'

'Of course we can. Well, we can if they'll lend us this van.'

'If they can't spare it, I'll phone for a taxi.'

'Please don't go to see him on your own, Frankie. That would be asking for trouble. I can come with you after work and the hospital usually prefers people to visit in the early evening anyway.'

'All right.' She took a deep breath and went on, 'Actually, that's something else I want to talk to you about. I've been wondering if we should buy a car of our own. What do you think? Not a fancy one, mind, just a second-hand one in reasonable condition.'

Since the road was clear he braked to a sudden halt and pulled over to the verge, staring at her in shock. '*Buy a car!* Can you afford it?'

'Yes.' She studied his face as if seeking the answer to a question, then said, 'My father made some special arrangements with Mr Lloyd, you see, in case he died. There was five hundred pounds in an envelope as well as the house.'

He could hardly credit it that she had that much. '*Five – hundred?* That's a fortune.'

'It's a comfortable sum but only covers the main things I might need. If he dies, my mother will inherit the business,

I suppose, since it was expanded from a small one using her money. And she certainly won't employ me, even if I'd work for her, which I wouldn't. So I'll have a business to set up and the equipment and premises for that won't come cheap. Which reminds me, I need to put most of the money in the bank. It's in my satchel at the moment and I worry about someone stealing it.'

That explained why she'd been clutching that bag of hers so tightly. 'Well, for heaven's sake, don't let that satchel out of your sight. And we must get it to the bank as soon as possible.'

She shivered. 'I'll feel better when it's safely locked away, I must admit.'

'You should ask Mrs Tyler's advice about where to buy equipment.'

'Shouldn't I ask *Mr* Tyler about that?'

'No. She's the real boss there when it comes to money and organising the business, and a good one she is too. He's far more interested in what he's building or repairing. Wilf's explained to me how the two of them arrange the work but I'd already guessed. You can't help noticing who's doing what when you work for someone.'

'So I'm not the only woman to do something out of the ordinary.'

He let out a dry huff of laughter. 'Poorer women have been doing so-called men's work, especially in the fields, for hundreds of years, ever since time began, I should think.'

Since it was something she'd always thought unfair, she added, 'Only they don't get paid as much as men. Thanks to my father, I've always been paid at the same rate as male cabinetmakers. He insisted on that when I finished my apprenticeship and went to work for him. My mother didn't want me to be paid at all, said I had no need for money since I lived at home. They quarrelled for weeks about it, but for once he held firm. So I have some more money saved in the bank as well because I didn't have much to spend my wages on.'

'It's a miracle that you got into a skilled trade. You must be really good with wood. I heard what the mayor said about your work and he's no fool.'

That brought another blush. She definitely wasn't used to compliments. He rather liked those blushes. 'Now, let's get back to your idea of buying a car. Todd Selby and Charlie Willcox will see us right if we go to them for one, I'm sure. Everyone says they only sell used cars that are in good working condition.'

'I hope you know more about how to choose one than I do. I might be able to drive, but I'm not sure what to look for when buying a car and I need to spend my money wisely.'

'Well, I know a little about cars. In fact, I know a *little* about many things, but there's not much I know a *lot* about. Like Wilf Pollard, I've done all sorts of work over the years but I haven't as many skills as him. He calls carving little wooden animals his hobby but they're really beautiful things.'

'I know. I bought one at the market, but had to hide it because my mother hated it.'

'Is there anything she does like?'

Her voice was bitter. 'Money. And herself.'

Eh, what a life the poor lass must have led with a mother like that. No use dwelling on that, best to go back to the subject of buying a vehicle. 'It's the engine that counts most, I reckon. It has to be reliable and powerful enough for your purpose. You don't want a vehicle that struggles to chug up steep hills. And the brakes have to be good, of course. They can save your life, good brakes can. We'd not want a car whose bodywork was rusty, either. It'd mean it hadn't been looked after properly.'

'Then if we go to see my father later, perhaps we could nip into the bank and put most of the money in. Afterwards, while we're in Rivenshaw, we can go and see Todd.'

He hoped he'd hidden how astonished he'd been that she could so casually talk about buying a car – and that she had so much money. She'd trusted him enough to tell him the amount, which was a good sign. But it was so much it made him feel even more in her debt!

He hadn't told her that he had less than ten shillings in his pocket and only just over a pound in his savings tin at home, all of it in small value coins. Thinking about that, he fumbled in his pocket. 'Let me give you back the change from your five-pound note before I forget.'

'No, no! You should keep it in case we need anything. It'll look better if you pay for things.'

'Oh. Right. Well, I suppose so. I'll only use it for things *you* need, though, not for myself or my family.'

'I'm sure you won't waste money. And we both might need something, not just me.'

Her smile warmed his heart. Eh, his spirits were going up and down like a child's yo-yo at the moment. Well, his whole life had been turned topsy-turvy, hadn't it? Though not in a bad way. No, definitely not.

And it wasn't just Frankie's money that he cared about. He really liked her – really fancied her too. She didn't shy away when he touched her, either.

Jericho drove through the centre of the village and slowed down to turn along Marlow Road. As he'd thought Number One was at the far end of the short street, which was a dead end. The road now ended at a pair of blank walls marking the end houses of two terraces of dwellings at right angles to it. There were lower walls round their backyards and between them there was a narrow ginnel, a passage not even wide enough for women to peg out their washing.

Eh, they'd built in some daft ways in the rush to provide houses for mill and factory workers coming to mill towns from all over the place a hundred or more years ago. He'd read about that in a book from the library and been fascinated by the thought of how it must have changed little villages into bustling, smoky towns. How must people living there have felt!

Marlow Road wasn't a mill terrace but one of the original village streets, with only ten houses on each side, which had been built in varying styles during different eras. It was slightly curved and the houses seemed to have been dropped here and there along it in a haphazard manner. To his surprise Frankie's house was the largest, much bigger than he'd expected, two storeys high with attics above that.

It had the largest garden, too, a walled area at the end. You'd not even see her house from the village centre. He certainly hadn't noticed it though he'd gone along the road as a lad. But what lad looks at houses closely? Lads were more interested in footballs and making cricket bats out of any likely piece of wood.

He glanced at Frankie and saw that she was as surprised as he was by the size of her house. 'Well, here's Number One. It's only a couple of streets away from where I'm living now, at the back of Wilf's cottage, yet I've never noticed the house before.'

'I don't remember ever coming here.'

Her house seemed to be huddling in the middle of the neglected garden, as if trying to hide from the world. It must be quite old, judging by the local stone used for its walls instead of red bricks, and it had an old-fashioned grey slate roof. It could look much nicer if you bothered to care for it, he was sure.

He saw Frankie staring at it, making no attempt to get out of the car. She didn't look happy.

'It looks . . . tired. Not very pretty.'

'It needs a fair bit of maintenance doing. I'll be able to do quite a lot of that. I wonder what that used to be.' He pointed to a tumbledown outhouse to one side, quite a large one, still with a roof and with a fallen line of bricks from a former wall next to it. 'Could this place once have been a farm, do you think? Not a big one, but not a small one, either.'

She shook her head in bafflement. 'Who knows?'

The house would be quite dark inside at the moment because not only was the front door partly covered by ivy but several of the windows were too. 'That ivy will need cutting back for a start,' he said.

When he turned, he caught her staring apprehensively at him as if trying to gauge his reaction to the shabby-looking house, so he took her hand and told her the simple truth. 'Any house is a miracle to me if it's our own, Frankie. It'll look a lot better once we've smartened it up.'

She relaxed a little and got out of the car. He couldn't help a wry smile at that. This woman didn't even pretend to be helpless and need assistance.

When he was younger, what he now thought of as a mere lad of twenty, he'd seen a lass walk past down in Rivenshaw and thought how lovely she looked. He'd not forgotten her, had even dreamed for a while of finding someone dainty and dark-haired like her to marry, someone he could love and cherish.

He'd never seen that lass again so she must have been a visitor to the town, and he'd never found a woman he actually wanted to marry, even if he'd been earning enough to get wed, which he hadn't. He'd seen other chaps rush into marriage without doing the sums, then the wives got worn down by having a child each year or so and the men by the struggle to provide for their families.

He'd been better off without that dainty dream woman anyway. He'd realised that years ago. When times were hard it was the delicate women who died first.

Frankie was tall and strong, handsome rather than pretty. She'd make a fine wife for any man and she'd chosen him. He'd try not to do anything that made her regret it.

He realised they were both still standing next to the car staring at the house like idiots at a fair, so he took her hand and gave it a little tug. 'Come on, lass. We promised Mr Lloyd not to go inside on our own, but let's open the front door and have a peep through it, eh?'

'Good idea.' She took a large, old-fashioned key out of her satchel and followed him along a path made from pieces of broken flagstones with winter-dead weeds crackling underfoot between them. This was crazy paving gone even crazier. It was so uneven you were better walking on the bare earth beside it or you might trip up, so they both moved off it instinctively.

'I can soon straighten out the flat stones and level the whole path, so that it looks tidy and is safe to walk on.' He had no money to bring to the marriage but he was strong and not afraid of hard work. She'd need that in various ways with a house like this.

'We'll work on the various jobs together,' she said quietly. 'Make it our own. I shall enjoy that.'

The relish in her voice made his spirits rise.

They stopped in front of the entrance, which was under a little porch whose roof sagged to one side. He could fix that fairly easily too, he was sure.

Even the ivy hanging across part of the doorway was

looking weary, as if its spurt of summer growth had exhausted it. The strands now covered a good half of the door and they'd have to lift them aside to get to the keyhole.

On a sudden impulse he grabbed a fistful of ivy and managed to tear off a large clump, dropping it to one side in what might have been a flower bed if the house had been cared for but was now a straggle of dead foliage. 'Get away from our door, you!' he told the ivy in a mocking, growling voice.

She laughed and did the same to a nearby clump of ivy. 'There, we've both set our mark on the house.'

He suddenly felt a prickling in his neck, as if someone was watching them and took heed of it, swinging round rapidly to check the nearby houses.

'Did you feel it as well, Jericho? As if someone is watching us?'

'Yes. But I couldn't see where from. I think we ought to wait for the Tylers before we even open the door. It'll be safer.'

There he went again, having to think of their safety all the time.

A couple of minutes later he heard the sound of a car engine in the distance and soon the Tylers' car came round the slight curve and stopped in front of their house. He kept an eye on the street rather than their car and thought he saw a man's head bob up and then hastily down again in the garden of the third house along on the other side. It was one of the smaller buildings in the street and the shabbiest by far. He'd have to find out who lived there.

Like Frankie, Mrs Tyler didn't wait to be helped from the car but got out as nimbly as a woman half her age and hurried to join them near the front door.

'I've always wondered what this house was like inside,' she announced. 'How exciting it'll be to go round it!'

Her husband followed her, stopping to frown at the facade. 'The place needs a heck of a lot of work doing. It's been let go for a good many years. I can't remember anyone ever living here, can you, Ethel love?'

'I think there was an old man living here around the time we got married. I can't remember his name, though, and he was a recluse, rarely went out.'

'Well, whoever inherited it from him should have taken better care of it. That ivy won't be good for the mortar and it's covering half the windows. I should clear it all off if I were you, Jericho lad.'

Roy and his wife looked at them expectantly and waited.

Frankie put the key in the lock and turned it. It moved easily and she quickly twisted the tarnished brass knob and pushed the door open, stopping on the threshold to stare down at the dusty floor. 'Look at these footprints! Someone's been in here recently.'

Jericho went to stand next to her. 'They've only been made by one person, I reckon, and they're too big for a woman.'

'Perhaps it was my father,' Frankie said. 'I'd like to think he came to look round here before buying it for me.'

They studied the trails of footprints, which criss-crossed the hall between the various doors.

'The house is much bigger than I'd thought from the outside. It goes back a long way.' Her voice rang with delight as she studied the length of the hall.

Jericho let out a long breath and followed her inside, feeling daunted by his first sight of it. 'Yes, much bigger,' was all he could manage. What would he do with himself in a house like this? What did people need so many rooms for anyway? You could only sit in one of them at a time, after all.

Mrs Tyler stayed by the door and made a shooing gesture.

'Why don't you two go ahead and explore your new home? You'll enjoy it more if you go round the first time on your own. Roy and I will take a tour of the outside then join you inside.'

The Tylers stepped back and left the younger couple to go inside.

11

'Let's do this methodically,' Frankie said. 'If we explore all the rooms downstairs quite quickly, then go upstairs, we'll know the layout. We can find out all the details later.'

'Whatever you say. You go first and I'll follow.'

As they stood inside the first room to the right she exclaimed, 'Oh, look, Jericho! They've left some odds and ends of furniture. That'll help. These two armchairs are very old but they're still sound.' She went across to stroke one of the dark wooden arms. 'They must be at least two hundred years old with barley-twist legs like these.'

He stared at them, thinking how ugly and uncomfortable they looked. They were mostly made of wood and covered in dust. The upholstery on the seat and headrest was badly frayed and faded. They'd been pushed crookedly against one wall as if someone had rejected them impatiently when clearing out the house.

He was still feeling overawed by the size of the place but tried to say something good. 'This is, um, a nice big room. And judging by the number of doors lining the hall, the whole house is bigger than I'd expected.'

Then suddenly he couldn't hold in his true feelings any longer and words burst out before he could stop them. 'When I see this, I can't believe that only a few weeks ago all four of us Hartes were sharing one room half this size.'

He looked at her uncertainly, expecting pity. Was he doing the right thing being honest?

Her voice was gentle, her expression kind. 'That must have been hard.'

'Yes, hardest for Mam's modesty and her struggles to keep everything clean.'

'I'm looking forward to meeting her after the kind message she sent.'

'She'll come here too. She'll be happy to have somewhere to visit. She doesn't have many friends round here. She lost touch with most of them when we moved to Backshaw Moss.'

'I've never had many friends. My mother didn't make them welcome.'

The words were so low, it took him a few seconds to realise what she'd said. She obviously didn't want an answer, but he wouldn't forget what she'd said. He had a lot of pals whose help he could call on, some closer friends than others. He watched her walk across the room, run one fingertip along the nearest end of the dusty wooden mantelpiece and bend closer to study the polished surface she'd revealed.

'Nicely crafted. But we'll have to light fires in all the rooms to take the dampness out. Come on.' She walked back, took his hand and pulled him towards the hall again.

He was pleased that she'd taken the initiative in touching him and gave her hand a quick squeeze. They stopped at the next doorway, exchanging tentative smiles as he stopped to let her go through it first.

We're taking one tiny, careful step after another, he thought. Would this lead them into a happy life together? Well, it might – if they could deal with the other problems they were facing. Eh, he hadn't realised how much he'd want a real home and a child or two.

The room on the opposite side of the hall was just as large as the first. Once again, oddments of furniture had been left behind. He whistled softly in surprise as they stopped just inside the door. This time the main piece that had been left was a huge sideboard, at least he thought it was a sideboard but he'd never seen one this big, taking up more than half of one wall.

She went across to examine it, again brushing away the dust at one edge with a gentle sweep of one hand. 'Oh, what beautiful wood! Mahogany. And look at the carved back piece. A master craftsman must have made this.'

When she opened one of the drawers and pulled it out to study how it was made, she frowned and measured it against the surface. 'The drawer should be longer than this. See. It isn't long enough to reach the back. Now why would they make it like that?' She pulled out another drawer. 'This one is the right length.'

She bent to peer along the space the shorter drawer had left and stuck her arm into it to measure it. 'See. It doesn't go right to the back. There's a panel across the back underneath though.'

'Why would they do that?'

'I bet it's a secret hiding place. Some of these very old pieces do have them. Bill taught me about them. I wish he were still alive. He'd have loved to see this piece. I'll get my tools out and have a proper look at that space after we move in. I'll be able to fix up any of the old furniture they've left that needs it.'

It seemed strange to have a woman talking about such practicalities. He loved her enthusiasm about wood.

'We'd better get on.' This time he was the one who held out his hand and she took it with another of those lovely smiles.

There were two smaller rooms behind the front ones, but they were still larger than any room Jericho had ever lived in.

At the back was the kitchen, a huge space, running nearly across the whole width of the house. But it was extremely old-fashioned. She stared at the big kitchen range and searched the scullery to one side for a gas cooker or geyser to heat the water. 'Oh, my goodness! This place can't have been changed for the last hundred years.'

There was only a slopstone in the scullery, sink shaped but shallower than the modern white ceramic sinks. Sandstone this one was made of, with an ancient pump at one rear corner to bring water into the house and various shelves on the walls. Some of the top ones contained oddments of crockery – plates and dishes mainly, by the looks of them.

She turned in a slow circle, frowning. 'I don't think there's any mains water connected, so the pump must come from a well, and there don't seem to be any modern gas or electric connections, either. I shall need to hire a maid who won't mind putting up with this till we can connect to the services. We'll have to add a modern cooker and a hot water geyser to our list of things to buy.'

He was startled. 'You're going to hire a maid?'

'Yes, of course. I can't do my job and look after a house, especially if I'm starting up my own workshop, and I'd much rather work with wood than mop floors, believe me. Besides, we always had servants at home, so I've never learned to do most jobs around the house. Not properly, anyway. And I couldn't cook to save my life.'

He managed not to voice his shock at that. *A maid! Him with a maid!* What next? 'Well, you're right about putting gas and electricity in and we should do that straight away, as well as a proper water supply. If this one comes from a well, it won't be pure, not with all the houses around us. If you can afford it, that is. Otherwise we'll be forever trimming lamps and lighting candles, and they're messy to deal with.'

'I can afford the necessities. We'll need a proper bathroom upstairs as well. We'll have to get Mr Tyler to do all that for us. It needn't be fancy, just functional. Remember, I still have to keep back enough money to set up a workshop.'

'You won't need to if you're working for them as a cabinet-maker.'

She stopped to stare at him. 'Did they say that?'

'Well, it was Mrs Tyler's suggestion, but he agreed with her. I probably shouldn't have mentioned it to you till they say something, though, in case they change their minds.'

'I hope they don't. I'd really like to work with them. Apart from the fact that it's lonely working on your own, I'd feel safer with other people around, I must admit. Would they have enough room for me to do my work, though? I've never been inside their yard.'

'Plenty of room. It's got a large workshop and various sheds, with a very capable foreman to keep watch over the comings and goings. From what I've seen, part of the workshop isn't being used at the moment. I think Mr Tyler let his business slip badly after his son died.'

He could have kicked himself for reminding her of death and therefore her father. She took a few deep breaths and gave him a wobbly look, trying to smile and failing.

'Sorry,' he said.

'I'll have to get used to the thought of losing him, won't I?'

'Sadly, yes. Death comes to us all.'

'Mmm. Death and taxes is what people often say. Well, let's go upstairs. Look, there's a second set of stairs leading up between the scullery and laundry, as well as the stairs near the front door.'

She was climbing up them before he could move, so he hurried after her, hoping there were no nasty surprises up there.

At the top they found themselves at one end of a long

landing that ran from the front to the back of the house over the hall below. It too had rooms neatly arranged on either side, and there was another flight of narrower steps leading up again from the kitchen end to what must be the attics.

They peered into five large bedrooms and one small. There was a large bed frame in one and a small bed frame in another, but there were no mattresses. Curtains drooped at most of the windows, faded and threadbare, some of them little more than rags.

'This small room might make a good bathroom,' he said. 'It's over the kitchen so the water supply would be easy to install.'

He made sure he went up into the attic first. It was dark, with three cell-like rooms to one side.

'These would be for the maids, I suppose,' she said.

There were various piles of lumber and junk in it, as well as trunks and boxes covered in dust and cobwebs.

He caught her arm to stop her going any further. 'We can look at these things later, but what people dump in the attics is usually rubbishy stuff. I've had jobs helping clear out a few attics when I was on the tramp and there wasn't much that was worth a second glance.'

'Well, we'll save this lot till another day but I'm still going to check every single thing before we throw it away, Jericho.'

'Aye, well. You do that. But even then you should get Mam to check them with you. If you don't want them, she'll know whether people still have use for them. One woman's junk can be another woman's treasure.'

'Do you think she'll mind helping me?'

He chuckled. 'Mind? She'll love it.'

As they went back down the attic stairs and towards the front of the house, they heard someone calling 'We're here!' from below, so hurried down to the hall to welcome the Tylers. Then they went through the house again with them.

Jericho let Frankie do most of the talking and Mr Tyler left it to his wife, so the two women led the way, chattering non-stop about what would be needed.

When he could get a word in edgeways, Jericho asked about borrowing the van again and explained about them wanting to buy a vehicle of their own.

'Good idea!' Mrs Tyler said at once. 'Would you trust us with the house key, Frankie, then Roy and I will measure up and plan how to put in your gas and electricity while you go into Rivenshaw? If you're getting married next week, we have to get this place into some sort of shape for you by then, so we can't waste a minute. We saw an old-fashioned lavatory out in that old shed at the back, but you won't want to be going outside to it in this weather. Maybe we should put a lavatory in a corner of the laundry as well as one in the bathroom upstairs.'

'Good idea,' Frankie said without hesitation.

Jericho sucked in air sharply. Two indoor lavatories plus a bathroom! How much was this all going to cost, for heaven's sake?

'There might be a spare key tucked away somewhere,' Mr Tyler said. 'Let's check the lintel above the front door. That's where people often leave one.' He went to do that but couldn't reach high enough, so had to ask Jericho to check it.

'Aha!' He brandished another huge old key at them, testing it on the front door to make sure it worked, then giving it to the Tylers.

'We'll leave you to it,' Frankie said. 'And thank you.'

'I like making houses nicer,' Mr Tyler said. 'This one is soundly built and won't be hard to bring up to scratch.'

As the two of them were settled into the van again, Jericho let out his breath in a big whoosh. What a day!

He set off slowly, telling her to look carefully at the third house along the other side and why. Number Six looked run down, but wasn't nearly as much in need of attention as theirs. 'I wonder who lives here. I may ask Mam to see if she can find out about them without telling people why. She's good at getting people to talk.'

As they left the village Frankie leaned back with a sigh. 'It feels as if I've climbed on a roundabout like the ones you see at fairs, only it's going too fast and whirling me round till I'm dizzy. It's not that things are bad, but they're happening so fast it's hard to take them in.'

'I feel the same.'

'I quite like the house, though. It's got potential. Don't you agree?'

He spoke without considering his words. 'I daresay I will once I've got used to how big it is.'

'Poor Jericho,' she teased. 'I've turned your life upside down.'

'Lucky Jericho,' he corrected. 'And not just to be marrying money, but to be marrying you.'

'Oh. What a lovely thing to say! Well . . . um, I feel lucky to be marrying you as well.'

They smiled at one another and she looked as shy as he felt. So that was all right, then. Another little step forward. He was silly to be so worried about the size of the house. Big or small, it would be their very own. And wasn't that wonderful?

Today had not only shown him that he needn't pretend with her about anything but it had also shown him that she needed someone to care about her now that her father was dying. Care in every way, as her mother didn't seem to have done. Eh, Frankie was lonely apart from him. It must be hard being different from other ladies. Mrs Tyler didn't seem to mind that, but then she had Mr Tyler and the two of them seemed like close friends as well as spouses.

Could he and Frankie become good friends too? He hoped so.

In the meantime they were on their way to the hospital and he had another worry to deal with. He hoped her father was still alive. She was desperate to say a proper goodbye to him.

There was space to park cars near the double front doors of the hospital and only three other cars standing there. He felt reasonably safe leaving the van near them.

When they got to the desk, he held back, intending to let Frankie do the talking to the clerk on duty there, but she just called out to the young man that she knew her way so he followed her upstairs to the ward.

'Oh, no!' She stopped dead and clutched his arm. 'My father was in that little side room and the bed's empty now.'

It wasn't just without an occupant, but had been made up with clean sheets, as if ready for a new patient to occupy it.

As Frankie pressed her hand to her mouth, holding back tears, the ward sister saw them and hurried along the ward to join them, shepherding them into the empty room. 'We can talk more privately in here. It's all right, my dear. Your father isn't dead. Dr McDevitt has done what he said and sent him to his friend's nursing home. He doesn't want anyone visiting him until they're sure what caused the problem in case he's infectious.'

Frankie looked at her in dismay.

'Your father wasn't fully conscious, so I doubt he'd have recognised you even if he were still here.'

'But I'd recognise him.' Frankie was still fighting to control tears. 'Did my mother manage to see him before he left?'

'No. She came in when he was first admitted and asked me to let her know when he died. She also requested that I keep you away from him.' She studied Frankie. 'I wouldn't have done that because you seem a sensible, caring woman to me. And *she* might be his wife but she made no attempt to touch him and she hasn't been to see him since he was admitted. I always notice that sort of thing. So who is she to talk about your supposed faults?'

Her anger at this surprised Jericho but he guessed that Mrs Redfern must have treated the sister scornfully. From what Frankie said, her mother considered herself superior to most other people.

'In my opinion, Miss Redfern, patients can often sense when a member of their family is nearby and it can help them recover – or die more peacefully. But unfortunately this time the doctor didn't feel able to give us the choice. He's sent your father away and an ambulance came to fetch him during the night. The driver told me they were out on another call and thought they might as well take him back with them and save a journey.'

That seemed strange to Jericho. Where else in Rivenshaw could an ambulance from another town have been heading for except this hospital?

'Do you have the address they took him to?' Frankie asked.

'I'm afraid not. They were in such a hurry. But Dr McDevitt will know. Now, how can I contact you if I need to, Miss Redfern?'

'It'd be best to contact me at my lawyer's home. I've moved out of my mother's house and I'm staying with Mr Lloyd and his wife until Jericho and I get married.'

The sister surprised Jericho again by saying, 'Oh, good. You'll be safe with them. Now, I must get on with my work. It's been very busy here today and I haven't finished writing up my notes.'

He watched her go back to her desk, puzzled. Why had the sister used the word *safe*? How did she know that was a problem?

A surprising number of people in the town seemed to know they were in danger.

When the two visitors had left the ward, the sister stopped pretending to go over her notes and hurried along to a small staff room at the rear end of the ward. She closed the door behind her before saying to Dr McDevitt and Sergeant Deemer, 'Mr Redfern's daughter and her fiancé have left now. I'm quite sure they didn't realise you were still here or even how short a time ago her father left.'

'What did you think of Miss Redfern's attitude to him, sister?' the sergeant asked.

'I've seen a good many grieving relatives in my time and quite a few pretending to be upset. In my opinion, gentlemen, Miss Redfern is genuinely upset about her father and truly cares about him. The mother, though – well, if she's upset she didn't show it the one time she was here, nor did she seem to care that he seemed about to die, and she didn't pay any further visits.'

'I'd agree with that analysis,' the doctor said. 'It's a very difficult case, though, which is why I called you in, sergeant. The lozenges are definitely poisoned. I didn't prescribe them, nor did our local chemist make them up. So where did they come from?'

Deemer whistled softly. 'And yet for all her grief, the young lady is planning to get married next week. That puzzles me if she's so grief-stricken.'

The doctor hesitated, looking as if he was about to speak.

The other two looked at him and waited, but he shook his head. 'I'd better not say anything of which I have no proof.'

'I think I'll go and speak to her lawyer about the situation, then,' Deemer said thoughtfully. 'I've worked with Lloyd before and I think we respect one another enough to be honest about the situation.'

'I doubt he'll give you any confidential information about her,' the doctor said. 'He refused point-blank to tell me anything.'

Deemer gave him a wolfish smile. 'No, but he may give me a hint or two – and in return I may drop a little information in his ear. He'll keep it to himself.'

12

It was only a short drive from the hospital to the second-hand car yard and on the way they stopped outside the bank.

'Come in with me,' Frankie begged.

'Are you sure? We're not married yet. I have no right to interfere now and no moral right ever to interfere with your banking.'

'I don't agree. You will have a right, whether you want it or not. Anyway, I want to introduce you to the manager and let him know that we're about to get married.'

Another first, Jericho thought. He'd seen the bank manager in the street, silver-haired and smartly dressed, clearly an important man, but had never spoken to him. Well, he'd never had a proper bank account, had he? Just a Post Office Savings Bank account that had rarely had much in it and now contained only a shilling to keep it open.

Not until Mr Forleigh had taken them into his office and closed the door did Frankie produce the envelope of money.

'Good heavens! You've been carrying this around with you, Miss Redfern! That was so risky! May I ask where you got it from?'

'My father left it with his lawyer in case I ever needed it, as an outright gift, the lawyer called it, not a legacy. I thought my father must have drawn this money out from his bank account here.'

'No. Definitely not. And look! Some of the notes are

quite old, though still legal tender. We get that occasionally when someone brings in their life savings. Excuse me a moment.'

While he was out of his office, she whispered to Jericho, 'That's strange. I wonder how long my father has been saving for and where he managed to hide his money? My mother goes through everyone's cupboards and drawers regularly.'

The manager came back accompanied by a clerk to count the money.

Frankie put out a hand to stop him picking up the whole bundle of money. 'I'll keep back fifty pounds to buy a car and a few other necessities. I wonder if you could change a couple of the five-pound notes into smaller denominations, though?'

'Of course.'

She tucked most of the bundle of mainly big white banknotes back into the envelope and put the ones she was keeping into her purse. 'Oh, and can you please take note of Mr Harte's signature while we're here? Once we're married we'll need a joint account, so that he can draw out money as well, and we may as well arrange that now.'

Mr Forleigh threw a suspicious glance at Jericho and turned back to ask, 'Is that wise, Miss Redfern? Should you not wait to do any of this until after you're married?'

'I think it's wise and nothing is going to stop us getting married.'

As he continued to look worried, she added firmly, 'I trust Mr Harte completely.'

Jericho tried not to show his uneasiness but suspected the bank manager could read it on his face. However, the man had no choice but to do as she'd asked and Jericho wasn't going to contradict her.

When they were outside again, he whispered, 'I won't be taking any of your money, Frankie.'

'It'll not be *taking* but *using* it. We might need to buy something for the house, or materials for your renovations, and I might not be able to get to the bank.'

'How can you trust me so completely when you hardly know me?'

She gave him one of her long, level stares. There was something innately intelligent about her expression. She was no one's fool. And yet here she was trusting him blindly.

'I don't know how I can, Jericho. I just do – trust you, that is. I wouldn't have asked you to marry me in the first place if I didn't feel you were honest and reliable.'

He shook his head and took her hand, raising it to his mouth for a quick kiss. 'Well, thank you for that compliment. I won't let you down.'

'I know. Now, let's go and buy a car. I really need one and it's getting late.'

'And perhaps after that we can fly to the moon.'

He didn't realise he'd spoken his thoughts aloud till she chuckled. 'Yes, let's do that this evening as well.'

As she settled into the van, she smiled at him again as if she understood how he was feeling, so he leaned across and kissed her cheek, which was just as soft as it looked – and had suddenly turned pink again.

He felt pleased by her reaction to his touch. He didn't want to marry a cold fish of a woman. In fact, a lot of things about her pleased him. She had, he felt, an honest soul. The sort of person who would never let those she loved down.

He was already sure she'd get on well with his mother, who was another person who faced the world with absolute honesty and had brought her sons up to do the same.

At Todd Selby's garage Jericho parked in the street in front of the display of vehicles and looked round carefully before getting out. Since there were other people walking past, he felt that the Tylers' van would be safe there, and so would Frankie, who was far more important than a metal box on wheels.

There were ten vehicles lined up in front of the building, which bore a huge sign saying *Willcox and Selby Motor Cars*. As they walked up and down the row, they were unanimous in rejecting five of the vehicles out of hand as too big and expensive.

'Perhaps we should have a look at that little black van next to the far end,' Jericho suggested. 'It's a Ford, which is a good make, and it'd be more practical than a car for us. We're going to have to cart stuff around for the house, after all, and probably for your job too.'

'It's a good little vehicle and not expensive,' a voice said behind them and they turned to see Todd Selby standing nearby. He moved to join them. 'Good afternoon, Miss Redfern. Jericho, I didn't know you were wanting to buy a van.'

'It's Frankie who's buying it.'

'But we'll both be using it after we're married,' she said at once.

Todd nodded to her. 'Of course you will. And congratulations to both of you. I heard the good news only this morning. When's the happy day?'

'Next week.'

He didn't show any surprise at the obvious fact that they must be marrying in a hurry and using a special licence to be able to set such an early wedding date. 'Right then, let me tell you about this van. As you can see, it's a Morris Cowley Light Van and hasn't been over-used. It's only four years old and I've checked it thoroughly. The engine is in excellent condition and there's only one small scratch on the rear paintwork.'

They listened carefully, then walked round the van and sat

in it, after which Todd drove them round the nearby streets. When they came back, Jericho agreed that the motor seemed to run smoothly.

'Why don't you take it for a drive round the town on your own?' Todd suggested.

Jericho glanced at Frankie, who said, 'Good idea. You drive it first, though.'

He moved into the driving seat while Todd held the door on the passenger side open for her to get in, then closed it. When Todd came round to the driver's side, Jericho wound the car window down and said, 'Look, I'd be grateful if you'd keep an eye on the Tylers' van while we're doing that. We're, um, having a bit of trouble with certain people.'

Another knowing stare and Todd said, 'Of course. Give me the key and I'll put your van in front of my workshop. It'll be even safer there than on the street.'

After Jericho had driven the Morris van round the town centre, they changed places and Frankie tried it out. He wasn't surprised to see how smoothly she drove. She seemed to be very capable in everything she did – except housework apparently.

'What do you think?' he asked as they drove back into the yard.

'It seems fine to me.'

'You're a good driver, Frankie.'

'I enjoy driving. It makes me feel – free.'

'I enjoy it too. When I get the chance. Is the price all right for you?'

'It's less than I'd expected to pay, actually.'

They got out and went across to where Todd was standing talking to Nick Howarth outside the latter's new driving school which was on the left side of the building. It had a much smaller sign over the door saying *Rivenshaw Driving*

School. He introduced them then the phone rang and Nick's wife called out that he was wanted, so he nodded goodbye and went inside again.

Jericho gestured to Frankie to take over the negotiations but she shook her head. 'Talking about the mechanics of a car is your job.'

The two men discussed the engine and brakes, then Jericho took a deep breath and said, 'If you'll take a couple more pounds off the price, we'll buy it.'

'Done!' Todd shook hands with him and afterwards did the same with Frankie.

That pleased her because most men didn't include women in business discussions, let alone shake their hands on a deal. 'How soon can we take it?'

'As soon as you sign the paperwork, get it insured and buy some petrol. Today if you bustle round. There's an insurance agency a couple of streets away.'

It was nearly five o'clock and growing dark before they set off again, this time with Frankie driving the new van and Jericho at the wheel of the Tylers' vehicle behind her. He felt pleased that he'd saved her two pounds and relieved that she'd have a vehicle to drive round in.

As they drove through the streets he let out his tension in a couple of whooshes of breath. He'd seen the big dipper at Blackpool on a newsreel once and it had made his stomach clench to think of going on a wild ride like that.

Today he felt as if that was exactly what he'd been doing.

He was rather wary about what might happen next. He doubted her mother would give up control of Frankie easily, and Higgerson would no doubt think it advantageous to be on his cousin's side and try to take over the business. So they had to be careful not to leave themselves vulnerable. Surely after he and Frankie were married the mother would leave her daughter alone, though?

There wasn't much hope of help from her father. The poor man was now helpless to protect either his daughter or his business, but he'd done his best to leave help with his lawyer.

Was Mr Redfern still alive? He hadn't even been conscious when Frankie last saw him.

Strange that he'd collapsed so suddenly. But sadly, that happened sometimes.

Jericho pushed away such worries as they reached the lawyer's house. Thank goodness a half moon was rising in the sky and the gas street lights round here were all functioning, unlike those in Backshaw Moss. He parked so that he could keep his headlights on her and watched from the street as she left her van in the drive and went into the house to explain about the new vehicle.

A couple of minutes later Mr Lloyd came out with her and waved to him. The headlights illuminated the scene clearly and Jericho watched as she moved her van closer to the house. There was no sign of the lawyer's car, which was presumably in a garage round the back.

After locking the gates, the lawyer gave him another cheery wave and disappeared indoors.

Frankie stood hesitating in the doorway, then she blew her fiancé a kiss before following her host inside.

Jericho didn't want to leave her. But at least he knew she'd be well looked after here.

Once again, when he got to Birch End, he found Wilf waiting for him at Tyler's yard.

'Eh, I'm sorry it took all afternoon, but we've bought ourselves a van so I won't have to borrow this one again.'

'Did you get it from Todd?'

'Of course.'

'It'll be a good one, then. Where is it now?'

'At Mr Lloyd's house. Frankie will be better using that

than going about on foot and she's a good driver. It's parked on his drive and there are big iron gates across it, which they lock at night. If it's not safe there, it'll not be safe anywhere.'

'Good. And our van will be safe at the yard. I'll open the gates and you can drive it in, after which I'll walk home with you.' He gave Jericho a very firm glance. 'No walking round on your own after dark from now on, my lad.'

'I can look after myself.'

'Against how many? There were a couple of louts hanging around in the street outside a couple of hours ago till Mr Tyler marched out and told them to clear off or he'd call the police.'

'Has the whole valley suddenly gone mad?' Jericho muttered.

'No, just Higgerson and Mrs Redfern. What mother would treat her daughter like that except one who'd run mad?'

'I reckon Frankie's had a hard life living with a mother like that, poor lass. We Hartes may have been short of money but we've never been short of love.'

As they strode briskly across the village to Wilf's house, Jericho suddenly remembered that it was his companion's wife who'd bought his house and neither Wilf nor anyone else seemed to worry about that, which made him feel a little better about his own situation. 'I'm sorry I've made such a bad start of working at Tyler's. I'll make up for it, I promise you.'

'No one could have expected all that's happened and you had to look after Frankie, so we're not blaming you for the situation.' He chuckled. 'Do you Hartes carry excitement round with you or is that Frankie's fault?'

'I could do without this much excitement, I can tell you. I'm really worried about her safety.'

'Yes, well, it's not excitement you'll be facing next but shopping. Mrs Tyler told me to remind you that you'll need some new clothes to get married in.'

Jericho stopped walking for a few seconds, then carried on, hands thrust deep in his pockets, scowling at the ground. 'I can't afford to buy anything.'

'That's what my Stella reckoned. She says you should go down to Charlie's pawnshop, you and your mother and your brothers. They have some really good second-hand clothes there.'

So he said it again, slowly and clearly. 'I still can't afford to buy any fancy clothes for me or them, however good value the clothes might be.'

'Ah. We did wonder. But Charlie sent a message to say you can pay the money back when convenient.'

'No. I'm *not* getting into debt. Bad enough that I'm not bringing anything to this marriage, but to dump debts on Frankie would not only be wrong but a very poor start and I just won't do it.'

'I have to be honest with you. It'll look bad and people will talk about it if you don't dress better than that for the wedding.'

'Let them. The only ones who matter that day will be Frankie and my family, and they won't care what I'm wearing.' Though his mother had already started worrying about what she could do to smarten up her one half-good dress, he had to admit, and he'd heard her sighing as she looked at his clothes. She'd promised to give his coat a good brushing before the wedding and wash and iron his shirt.

Wilf was silent then shrugged. 'The offer's still there.'

Jericho walked faster. He meant what he said. He was *not* going to bring debts to Frankie as a wedding gift.

*

The trouble with that firm decision was, the following morning at work Mrs Tyler intervened. And Wilf just grinned and said you might as well try to stop an express train going past at top speed as prevent 'the missus' from doing something she thought right.

Only, when Mrs Tyler said she still had some of her son's clothes and they'd probably fit him and his brothers, her voice became choked with tears. He could see how much this offer was costing her and he couldn't, he simply *could not* refuse such selfless generosity.

When she added that she'd also got some of her own clothes from when she was a few years younger and thinner, and his mother could choose an outfit from among them, he looked at her and asked outright, 'Does anyone ever manage to stop you when you've set your mind on doing something, Mrs Tyler?'

That brought a smile back to her sad face. 'Not often, lad. And you won't be one of them. Bring your family round to our house this evening after you've had your tea. Henry Lloyd's going to drive up with Frankie and he'll have a natter to my Roy while we deal with the clothes. It's all right your lass driving herself round during the daytime but we don't want her out on the roads alone after dark, do we?'

He looked at her, humiliation about needing to take charity still making anger simmer inside him, but as he was about to protest, he saw a tear tremble in the corner of her eye and roll down her cheek. *Mrs Tyler crying!* No, he couldn't say anything that might add to her distress, so gave a quick nod.

She sniffed back more tears, patted his hand and gestured to the door, not even trying to speak. He left quickly so that she'd be able to pull herself together in private.

Fate or whatever you called it had clearly got him by the collar and was giving him a good shake-up.

Eh, it was kind of her to do this for them, though. Really kind. She'd touched him to the core.

People like her could make a big difference in a hard world. If he ever had the chance to help people as she was doing, he would. Always.

13

Mr Lloyd phoned the yard to say plans had changed a little. He was bringing Frankie to join Jericho that evening at the cottage so that there would be time for her to meet his family before they all went and collected some new clothes from the Tylers' house in Birch End.

Jericho was a bit late leaving work and was nearly home when he saw a car stop in front of the house, so he ran the last fifty yards. He watched her get out and take a basket off the back seat, admiring her graceful movements.

After she'd waved at Mr Lloyd and called, 'See you later!' she turned towards him.

He moved closer, unable to resist dropping a quick kiss on her cheek. 'Whose idea was it for you to come here first?'

'Mine. I told the Lloyds I'd like to meet your family and then we'd all walk across to the Tylers' house together. He's gone there now to have tea with them. We'll be quite safe walking across the village later, I'm sure. No one's going to attack a group of people with three big chaps like you and your brothers in it.'

'I'm sure they won't. Let me carry that basket for you.'

'It's not heavy.'

'Nonetheless, I do have a few manners.'

'Oh, very well. Be careful how you hold it. It's got a pie and a cake in it, my share of an evening meal for us all. Mrs Lloyd suggested I bring something. It won't upset your mother, will it?'

'Of course not. But don't expect there to be much left once my brothers start eating, and I have a pretty good appetite myself.'

'I like to see a hearty eater. I'm afraid you won't see me picking daintily at my food, either. My mother used to say I had a wagoner's appetite.'

Had her mother ever done anything but criticise her?

'Mrs Lloyd says I can keep the basket and the dishes towards furnishing our new home.'

He chuckled. 'You said you couldn't cook.'

'I can't. The maid we employ will need them, though.'

The mention of them having a maid kept making him feel strange.

As they walked round towards the back of the house, Frankie stopped suddenly and laid one hand on his arm. 'Are you very upset about it?'

'About what?'

'Mrs Tyler and the clothes.'

He shrugged. 'I don't like taking charity, I will admit.'

'I don't care what you wear, surely you know that, but other people will, so she's right to insist on helping you, really. I'd have been happy to lend you the money to buy some clothes, only you'd not have liked that either.'

He stared at her. 'Can you read my mind?'

'No, but I can sometimes hear the frustration in your voice. Anyway, I'd already guessed you'd be upset when Mr Lloyd told me what Mrs Tyler was offering. I feel guilty that I've taken over your life and caused decisions to be made for you. It's just I need your help so much. Can you forgive me?'

Those final words and the anxiety in her voice seemed to melt away his anger, and he stayed where he was at the side of the house, glad of a moment's private chat with her. 'I'm the one who should be apologising, lass. I shouldn't be taking my feelings out on you. Now, let's forget all that. There's something more important than my feelings: is there any news of your father?'

'Mr Lloyd contacted Dr McDevitt to ask and was told that my father was holding his own, but not to build up too much hope.'

'Did he get the address of where your father is?'

'No. The doctor said it was over Halifax way but out on the moors. He could take us to it in his car but didn't know its exact address.'

'Do you believe that?'

'No. But perhaps they're trying to keep it from my mother and they can be certain she'd have hysterics if I knew where my father was and she didn't.'

'You may be right.' He couldn't put his finger on it, but something wasn't quite right about what was happening to her father. Only what? It couldn't be something bad if Dr McDevitt was involved, though.

For the second time that day he was faced with a woman near to tears. But with Frankie he dared do what he wouldn't have risked with Mrs Tyler. He put down the basket, pulled her into his arms and hugged her close, then waited as her body gradually relaxed against his and she let out a long, soft sigh. They stayed close for a few moments before she moved away but she didn't carry on walking.

'Mrs Lloyd wanted to see my new house, so I drove her there this morning in our van. It was very busy there. I couldn't believe it but Mr Tyler has already got his men started on putting in the new plumbing and connecting to the various services.'

'He told me he'd sent men to work there, but he kept me occupied at the yard so I didn't have time to go and look at what they were doing.'

'We could take your mother and brothers for a look at

progress tomorrow if you can all get off work while it's still light. Do you think they'd like to do that?'

'They'd love it. They're dying to see inside it. I can guarantee my mother's already walked past the outside. Well, she was going shopping in the village today and I doubt she'd be able to resist a quick peep.'

'I hope she liked what she saw.'

As he picked up the basket again, Frankie tugged on his sleeve to stop him moving. 'Ought you to go in first and warn your mother that I'm with you? I don't want to take her unawares. She might want to have a quick tidy round first.'

He had to laugh at that. 'Mam keeps our home clean and tidy at all times. Even when we were living in Backshaw Moss and she was ill, she ordered us about to make sure it was as clean as was possible there.'

'Was it very horrible?'

'Have you ever been in any of the slum houses?'

'No. Our workshop is in Rivenshaw, so I always seemed to be going in the opposite direction. And the people we met socially didn't live anywhere near a place like that, obviously.'

'Well, don't go there if you can help it. It's a truly terrible place and it literally stinks, especially at the lower end. The sewers are so bad it's a miracle there hasn't been a big outbreak of illness there, though there have been smaller ones. It's dangerous in other ways too, things you don't always think about and landlords don't care about.'

'What do you mean? Pickpockets?'

'Yes. But fire is the big thing that's always concerned me. I was glad we were living in a first-floor room, not an attic. We'd at least have stood a chance of getting out safely if the building had caught light.'

He didn't elaborate further, hated to remember that place which had reeked of rot and sewage – and hopelessness. It should have been knocked down years ago. Only desperate human beings would put up with such squalor. His family's own desperation had been to make sure their mother received proper care. They'd sold everything to pay for it. That had paid off this time and they'd got away safely, but he wasn't having anyone he cared about going back to live there or even visit it, not if he could help it. He'd do whatever he had to, even ask for money from Frankie, to prevent that.

When he opened the outer door and took her into their part of the house, his mother came forward with a beaming smile. 'Eh, what a lovely surprise!'

The two women studied one another in silence for a few seconds then Frankie held out the basket. 'I hope you don't mind, Mrs Harte, but I brought some food, so that I could eat tea with you.'

'That's kind of you.' Gwynneth took it and peeped inside, nodding approval of what she saw.

He watched them anxiously. Without saying much they both relaxed visibly as they set out the simple meal together.

'Do call me Gwynneth,' his mother said.

'And I'm Frankie.'

How did women do it? he wondered. They seemed so much quicker at deciding how they felt about people than men did.

'I'm glad our Jericho's found someone to marry,' his mother said as she began to cut up the meat pie.

'He didn't find me, I found him. He'll have told you why I need a husband.'

'Yes. But all that means is you've got excellent taste in choosing one, Frankie. My Jericho's a good lad, none better, and he'll make a fine, dependable husband, even if he doesn't have any money at the moment. All my sons are good lads. I'd be dead if it wasn't for them. They gave up everything for me when I was ill.'

His brothers came home just then so that was the

introductions done and they didn't waste any more time but sat down to eat together. Gabriel hardly said a word but Lucas made up for him, and proved to be very witty.

As Jericho had predicted, every single crumb of food vanished from the table.

'That was a good pie,' Lucas said. 'Thank you, Frankie.'

Gabriel merely nodded.

Jericho looked at the battered little clock on the mantelpiece. 'We'd better leave now. We can wash up later, Mam.'

Somehow, Frankie got swept into the midst of them as they walked across the village. He liked to see that. It was as if she'd always been part of the family group and she was soon teasing Gabriel about how monosyllabic his answers were.

'That's our Gabriel for you,' his mother told her. 'He never uses two words when one will do.'

Gabe merely grinned at that.

Lucas chatted away to her, asking about her job. That was his youngest brother for you, always trying to learn about the world. If anyone ought to have gone to the grammar school, it was Lucas. He'd passed to go to it as well and his mother had wept because she couldn't afford to send him.

Then it suddenly occurred to Jericho that it might be possible to help Gabriel into a more interesting job now, at least.

The clothes that Mrs Tyler showed them were the best any of the Hartes had ever possessed. Her son must have been quite tall, Jericho thought, because the trousers were long enough even for him and his brothers. The shirts were a little loose, because they were all thinner than the Tylers' son must have been, especially now. But that would be hidden beneath the three jackets.

Lucas nudged Gabriel. 'Eh, lad, the lasses will be running

round after us. Maybe you'll be following our Jericho down the aisle sooner than we expected.'

Which brought a scowl from Gabriel, who was noted for his shyness with women.

'Lucas will do that,' his fond mother said.

Her youngest son shook his head. 'No, I won't be getting married for a long time, Mam. I want to travel and learn about the world before I settle down.'

Jericho was surprised. Lucas hadn't said anything about that. His clever brother would surely find a way to make something of himself once the others were settled.

Their mother vanished into another room with Mrs Tyler and Frankie to try on clothes. She came out a short time later, beaming all over her face and clutching a parcel wrapped in brown paper.

Afterwards he was sorry to say goodbye to Frankie. He would have liked to spend some more time with her, but they couldn't keep Mr Lloyd waiting too long to take her back.

He watched her drive off then walked back home with his family. It did his heart good to see that his mother hadn't stopped smiling all the way back. She was clutching the parcel close to her chest as if it contained a treasure.

He and his brothers had parcels too. He doubted his brothers would consider them treasures, but it'd be nice to have decent clothes for best.

As they turned on to the garden path, his mother said happily, 'I'm looking forward to the wedding even more now and—' She broke off as Wilf came out of the front door of the main part of the house to meet them before they'd even started to go round to their entrance at the back.

'Can I have a word? With all of you would be best.'

Wondering if they'd done something to upset him, Jericho gestured to his mother to lead the way and they followed their landlord into the main part of the house, leaving their parcels on the hall table.

As they sat down in the living room, where Stella was waiting for them, his heart sank at how grim-faced Wilf was looking. What could have happened now? Wilf hadn't seemed upset about anything at work.

'I'm afraid there's been trouble, an attempt to break into your new house while you were at the Tylers', Jericho. Luckily, I'd spread the word about keeping an eye on it and offered to pay anyone who stopped it getting broken into.'

He was annoyed at himself. He should have thought of that.

'Someone must have been watching the place, though where from, I can't think,' Wilf went on.

Jericho wondered again about Number Six. He didn't like to say anything because he had no real basis for his suspicions, but it made him even more determined to keep his eyes on that house when they went to live in Marlow Road.

'Whoever it was waited till all our workmen had gone home for the day before trying to break in. Luckily for you a couple of young chaps from the village were so desperate to earn a reward they went and hid round the back of the house, intending to spend the night there if necessary.'

He paused before adding, 'They not only chased off the intruders for you but yelled so loudly for help that the neighbours from next door and across the road joined in. You'll have some good folk living near you there. You'd have thought someone from Number Six would have at least come to their door, but they didn't. One of the men said they saw the curtains there move, though.'

'Hmm.' The fact that the neighbour from Number Six hadn't helped fitted in with Jericho's suspicions, but all he said was, 'Thank goodness for you putting the word out and for good neighbours joining in!'

He hated to see his mother looking upset when she'd been so happy bringing her new clothes home. Stella had gone to sit next to her and taken her hand to comfort her. He really liked Wilf's wife. She had come from outside the valley but had soon fitted in. He turned as Wilf continued to speak.

'The same chaps are going to stay at the house overnight but it'd be good if you could go across there and unlock that outhouse to give them somewhere to shelter if it rains. It'll only be fair to pay them a little for their trouble. Do you want me to do that for you?'

'How much did you agree to?'

'Two bob a night for each man.'

Jericho nodded grimly. He could just manage four shillings a night, though it'd use nearly every penny he had. 'I'll see they get paid.' He hated to lose even his meagre savings, only he couldn't keep watch there on his own, not and be rested enough to do his work at Tyler's every day.

His brothers couldn't help because one of the reasons for his family getting the accommodation at the rear of Wilf's house was that they'd be able to keep watch when people were out. They were getting paid to keep an eye on both the house and the nearby piece of land where the houses were going to be built.

It was as if there was a hidden war going on in the valley lately, a war most people in the better areas didn't even know existed, but one for which those living on the edge of starvation could easily be recruited as fighters – on either side. It was a war mainly instigated by one evil man and continued by another. When Rathley had died last year, Higgerson had taken over more swiftly than anyone had expected. He wasn't thought to be quite as violent, but still managed to get round the law at times.

'Who do you think sent men to break in, do you think? Higgerson or Frankie's mother?'

Wilf shrugged. 'I should think both of them were in on it, but it's my guess it'd be some of Higgerson's bullies who were ready to cause havoc so he'd have ordered it done and paid them. Mrs Redfern couldn't have dealt with such as them. She wouldn't have known how to find them even.'

'She's a strange woman.'

'Yes. People who know her say you never know what nasty thing she's going to say next. If she hadn't been married to such a nice man they'd not have invited her to their houses, and they don't do that often even so. And of course Higgerson will be able to prove that he was somewhere else this evening, in the company of respectable people, and he'll appear to be extremely outraged by this shocking attempt to commit a crime.'

'No doubt.'

Wilf turned to Mrs Harte. 'I won't keep you three any longer, but I'd like to have a word with Jericho about something else.'

After they'd picked up their parcels, including Jericho's, and left, Stella said goodnight as well and vanished in the direction of the kitchen. Wilf gestured to a chair.

'I wanted to tell you about something I've heard, then you can decide whether to do anything about it. I'm afraid Frankie's mother is telling everyone that her daughter stole some valuable tools from the workshop and drove her father to his grave with worry about her immoral ways.'

Breath hissed into Jericho's throat. He could guess how this would hurt Frankie. 'It's not true, not a single word of it.'

'You don't have to tell me that. I know which of those two women I'd believe and trust. You can be assured that I'll tell everyone it's lies – if anyone dares mention it when I'm around, that is.'

'So will I.'

Wilf gave his companion a sympathetic look. 'Eh, lad, what have you got yourself into?'

'A big pot of trouble.'

'I'm afraid you're right.'

'But if me and Frankie pull through it, I'll have got myself a good wife and a home of our own. She's a grand lass, you know, even if she is way above me. It's not just the money. I never thought I'd be lucky enough to find a woman like her.'

Wilf looked at him in surprise. 'You sound as if you have feelings for her already.'

'Yes. Actually, I'd already met and liked her before we, um, decided to marry. I like her looks, too, and the fact that she's tall. I'm a big chap and she seems exactly the right size to me. I'd not want to wed a tiny little scrap of a woman.'

'We're going to have to organise ways of keeping you, Frankie and the house safe after you marry, then.'

'I'll sort something out.'

'No, *we* will do it together. You work for me and the Tylers now. We look after our own. And before we do anything else, we need to report this to Sergeant Deemer. I'll do that, if you like. Roy and I have been keeping in touch with him about a few things. You'd better phone and tell Frankie about it tomorrow, even before you go round to the new house to talk to your two guards.'

'Yes, you're right. Eh, I wish I didn't have to upset her. We had such a lovely evening with my family.'

That done, he and Gabriel walked across to the new house to check that the two men were still keeping watch and pay them for the first night.

By that time Jericho felt utterly exhausted and was glad to go straight to bed when he got home.

He felt quite sure there would be further trouble even before they were married.

*

The following morning Wilf phoned Deemer, who listened to his account of the latest incident and promised to send his constable to check on the house a couple of times a day between now and the wedding.

'There's only one good thing going to come of this,' he said.

'A *good* thing!' Wilf exclaimed.

'Yes. I've been asking for an extra constable to be posted in Birch End for a while now. There's far too much mischief in Backshaw Moss for me and my present constable to deal with, and it takes too long for us to go up to the other villages in the valley. So those causing trouble usually get away before we can catch them.'

'It's not easy for you to police a long valley, is it?'

'No. But if we can get Mr Lloyd and a few others on side, and maybe even persuade the mayor to make a formal request for more police, I don't think the district superintendent will be able to avoid doing something about the situation. And things aren't as bad in Ellindale village. Some of the men who're out of work have got together to protect their homes now that they've got somewhere to meet and spend their days.'

'A constable posted in Birch End is going to need lodgings and some sort of small office.'

'Yes. If Frankie and Jericho don't mind, he could perhaps lodge with them till we get a proper police outpost set up. We don't want to put him anywhere in Backshaw Moss itself, though, because one man on his own might be in danger there. But good lodgings aren't always easy to come by in the older part of Birch End. It's too small. And the better-off people in the upper end won't want to take in lodgers.'

'No. You're right.'

'So what do you think Jericho and Frankie will say? A

constable on the spot will kill two birds with one stone: help protect their house and have a policeman handy for problems in Backshaw Moss. Only with them being newly-weds they may not want company.'

'That sort of company would be a big help at the moment. I think they'll be happy to have him lodge there temporarily. They've plenty of room and Jericho says Frankie is going to hire a maid, so she can look after a lodger as well.'

'Right then. I'll continue agitating about it. I'm hoping they'll send me another policeman fairly quickly. It's not just for Jericho and Frankie. Having a constable nearby will also upset a few others in Birch End and Backshaw Moss, folk who deserve upsetting.'

'You seem sure you'll get one.'

'I've been asking for a while, and this time I'm going to make a fuss till I succeed, because this time I've got our new council on my side. Don't say anything about it till I've got it agreed to, though. Our district superintendent doesn't like people taking anything to do with his police force for granted.'

'He's . . . not an easy man to deal with.'

'No. Sticks to the rule book more than is helpful. Looks down his nose at men who're out of work.'

As soon as he got to work that same day, Jericho told Mrs Tyler what had happened and got her permission to phone Frankie and warn her about the intruders. His employer was furiously angry on their behalf.

Frankie was angry too. 'What will my mother do next?'

'You think it's her doing?'

'Who else hates us that much? We'll have to stay watchful. It'd be a lot easier if she didn't have that horrible cousin of hers helping.'

'Yes. Look, I'm sorry but I have to get on with my day's work, Frankie love.'

'Yes, of course. And I have to go shopping.'

'I thought women liked shopping.'

'I don't. I'll see you tonight, won't I?'

'Of course.'

14

Later that morning a woman came to Tyler's yard and asked to speak to 'the missus'. She looked utterly exhausted, hardly able to walk, so the man on the gate helped her into a small room furnished only with a few upright chairs and a rough bench before he hurried to find Mrs Tyler.

The woman sighed in relief at the warmth of the room, holding her hands out to the fire.

Ethel watched her from the doorway for a few moments before making her presence known. She'd been staring out of her office window and had recognised the visitor as she approached the yard, so had started to come across to the small all-purpose waiting room even before the man came to fetch her.

The woman was painfully thin, her eyes seeming huge in a bone-white face and she was a shadow of her former self. What could have happened to her?

Ethel shook her head in dismay. Mattie was, what, about thirty now, if that? Only she looked closer to fifty. 'I didn't think I'd see you here again, lass.'

'Oh! Mrs Tyler.' She tried to get up but couldn't manage it.

'Stay where you are and tell me what brought you back to the valley.'

The woman's voice came in faint spurts of sound as if even to form a whole sentence was too much of an effort. 'Desperation. I didn't think . . . I'd ever be back, Mrs Tyler.'

'What happened to Stan Harris? I gave him money to marry you and pay your fares to his new job in Coventry. And I gave you some money to see you through for a few weeks. So what went wrong?'

'Everything. Not you. You were generous and – you've been in my prayers ever since.' She closed her eyes for a few seconds then continued, 'You were the only one who believed I'd been forced.'

'I did but I never understood why you couldn't tell us anything about your attacker's appearance. I guessed you were afraid to tell us.'

She bent her head, avoiding Mrs Tyler's shrewd gaze. 'Even Stan didn't believe I'd been forced.'

'He's a good actor, then. I thought he had or I'd not have arranged the marriage.'

'Yes. A very good actor.' Another pause. 'When he wants to – he can persuade you – that black is white. He can smell a chance – to make money from a mile away, that one can. Money is all he really loves.'

'Why didn't he marry you?' She waited for her companion to continue, increasingly worried about how breathless Mattie was.

'Stan didn't want to bother with a wedding – just wanted a woman in his bed regularly – someone who'd wait on him hand and foot. I didn't have much choice about that – seeing I was in the family way.'

'Hmm. And how is the baby? Did it survive?'

'Yes. I had a little boy.'

Her expression softened and Ethel suddenly had to fight for control as she remembered feeling the same way about her own lad as a baby. 'What did you call him?'

'I called him Robert – but it turned into Robbie.'

Another stare into the fire, then, 'He's a lovely little lad, my Robbie – though I couldn't feed him for as long as I'd have liked. My milk dried up. Only—' She broke off and took a couple of shaky-sounding breaths before going on in a tight voice, 'Stan didn't like having a child crying and needing attention. He wanted me to be *his* slave not the baby's.'

The bleakness on Mattie's face made Ethel want to hug her, but she held back, letting her companion continue the tale at her own pace.

'He tried to make me give my Robbie away to an orphanage – leave him in the doorway there. In the end I had to run away to keep my own baby. I took the housekeeping money and came back to Rivenshaw. The money got me a train to Manchester. After that I walked, slept rough a couple of nights – cadged lifts, begged for food.'

Her voice broke and she began coughing feebly, had to wait to catch her breath before continuing, 'I need a job. Only I don't want to lose Robbie.'

She burst into tears and continued in sad little spurts of words, which seemed to get weaker by the minute. 'Robbie's all I've got now – I never thought I'd love him so much.'

Ethel had loved her son that much too. 'Where is your baby now?'

'I promised a little lass a ha'penny – to stand outside the yard and hold him. You're my last hope, Mrs Tyler, my very last. You were always so kind to us servants. And to me.' She closed her eyes, looking frail and white as chalk.

Ethel could see that this poor young woman was at the very end of her tether. 'Better go and bring your son into the warmth, then, while we decide what to do with you both.'

'You'll help me?'

'Of course I will. You were the best housemaid I ever had.'

'Thank you.' Mattie tried to stand up but crumpled to the ground in a sudden faint.

Ethel bent over her, shocked at how skeletal she was under

the shawl. She went to the door and yelled at the top of her voice, 'I need help here. Quick!'

Jericho happened to be the nearest person and came running across the yard to the office, staring in surprise to see a young woman lying on the floor.

Ethel gestured. 'Can you lift her on to a chair and hold her there till she comes to properly? I have to go and find her baby. She left him outside.' She was out of the room the minute she'd finished speaking, trusting him to do it.

He knelt down beside the stranger, who was stirring now and struggling to sit up. She couldn't even manage that without his help and her voice was such a feeble thread of sound he had to bend closer to catch what she said.

'Sorry. I don't – don't usually – faint.'

'Don't try to stand up yet. You're all right sitting on the rug till your head clears.'

'Thank you. I'm sorry.'

'No need to keep apologising. No one faints on purpose. Now, let me help you to that chair.' He helped her get up and steadied her as she sat down and leaned her head back with a tired sigh.

'Mrs Tyler's gone to fetch your son.'

That brought tears rolling down her cheeks and a heartfelt whisper, 'Oh, thank heaven! Thank heaven!'

She seemed to have more and more trouble speaking. 'She's going to – help us. My Robbie will be safe – now.'

Her eyes closed again and he had to hold her or she'd have fallen off the chair.

Outside Ethel looked across at the ragged little girls who seemed to be playing some form of hopscotch. Whichever was supposed to be looking after the baby had simply put it down on the cold, damp ground. The two girls should have been in school, but she hadn't time to deal with that now.

She marched across the street. 'Which of you is being paid to look after that baby? He'll catch his death of cold lying there.'

The slightly taller girl took one look at her furious face and ran off at top speed. The other child said, 'It wasn't me.' She edged back a few paces away, staring, poised to run away, curiosity keeping her hovering nearby.

Ethel sighed and bent to pick up the infant. Something twisted inside her heart as he nestled against her, nudging her for food. 'Eh, you could be bonny if you didn't look so hungry.' Cradling the baby against her chest she marched back into the yard and bumped the waiting-room door open with her backside.

As she entered, Mattie stirred, opening her eyes and trying to get up from a chair.

Jericho could see that the stranger was still dizzy, so he put a hand on her shoulder. 'Stay sitting down, lass. You're still woozy.'

Ethel brought the baby across to his mother and watched Mattie cuddle him close, her face lit up by love. She sighed and looked at Jericho. 'Thanks for helping her.'

'I was glad to, Mrs Tyler. Look, I think she's weak for lack of food. I brought a sandwich for my midday piece. She can have that.'

'You're a good man, Jericho Harte, and I won't forget this. But I can feed her. I wonder . . .' She looked at him. 'I can always use another maid. Mattie was the best one I ever had till someone forced himself on her one night and left her with a child. I thought I'd found her a husband, but it seems he took my money and wriggled out of actually marrying her.'

Another thoughtful pause, then, 'I thought at first I'd ask

Frankie to give her a try as a maid, once she recovers, that is, but I think now I'll keep her and the child myself. It'd be good to have a baby in the house again.'

He glanced sideways at the stranger, who was rocking the baby to and fro, not seeming to be taking in what they were saying. 'Is there no end to your kindness?'

She flushed. 'I like to help poorer women, the ones who deserve it, that is. And Mattie was always a good lass. She's not immoral. She was forced by someone, came home battered and bruised after her day off, but she always refused to give his name. Fellows who do that sort of thing should be given a good thumping.'

'Then they should be driven out of the town.' He'd seen some of their victims in Backshaw Moss.

Mrs Tyler looked at her little fob watch. 'You can come with us and do the driving. We'll stop off at your new house and see my husband. Roy said he'd be there this morning so I'll tell him I've taken you away from your work for an hour or two. After that we'll take Mattie to our house and I'll try to nurse her better. I'll ask my cook if she knows a young girl who wants a job looking after a baby. She's got a lot of relatives in the valley.'

So a bemused Jericho found himself driving Mrs Tyler in a car that also contained a wailing baby, and a woman who looked as if she might fall over should a strong wind blow on her.

Mattie had hardly stirred since she got into the back of the car, but she seemed to be holding her baby safe by instinct.

He noticed Mrs Tyler glance at her two or three times, frowning.

Inside her new house Frankie had been enjoying herself, helping Roy measure the windows in the room she intended to use as her and Jericho's bedroom. The wood was rotten and the sash cord must have broken because it didn't hold the window up. There was nothing for it but to put in a whole new window. There wasn't time to replace a couple of others that were also rotten because of a leaking drainpipe, but those rooms weren't needed, so their windows could be replaced later.

Normally, she'd have asked her father to do the carpentry jobs for her. Now, she'd have to rely on Mr Tyler to find someone else. On that thought she closed her eyes for a moment, sending out a wish for her father's recovery, and if not a recovery, then the peaceful death he deserved.

She banished that sad thought because you had to get on with living whatever life threw at you and yours, so turned her thoughts to what she should do with the rest of her day.

Buy some furniture, perhaps. In the afternoon she'd go down to Charlie Willcox's second-hand shop and take a look at his better furniture. She didn't want to use up more money than she had to, but they did need a few items like proper beds and mattresses, and a kitchen table and chairs.

When they heard a car pull up outside, Roy said, 'Can you see who that is, love?'

She peeped out of the window and what she saw made her call out that it was his wife and Jericho, and they looked upset. Without waiting for him, she went running down to find out what had brought them here at this time of day with such worried expressions on their faces.

Surely nothing else could have gone wrong?

She heard Roy's feet clumping down the bare wooden stairs behind her at a slightly slower pace.

Flinging open the front door, she was in time to hear Mrs Tyler say to a woman sitting in the back of the car, 'Will you be all right if we leave you here for a minute or two, Mattie?'

To her surprise she saw a ragged woman clutching a baby,

a woman with that hungry look on her face that said she'd been going hungry for a long time. You couldn't mistake that 'famine look' as people often called it.

Jericho stayed in the driving seat and let Mrs Tyler close the car door herself.

She hurried across to Frankie and her husband, saying in a low voice, 'I'll tell you about it inside.'

When she'd explained, Frankie said at once, 'If the poor thing needs a bed for a few weeks, she can stay here once we've got it fit to move into.'

'No need for that, but thank you anyway. She can come to us, if that's all right with you, Roy love.'

'Of course it is. I remember Mattie. I'd not have recognised her today, though. You do whatever's needed to help her, love.'

Ethel smiled at him. 'I knew you'd agree with me. What I also need from you is for Jericho to drive us round. We'll need to buy a few things for the baby. And Mattie looks to me as if she's not been eating well for a good while so we'll have to feed her up for a few weeks before she'll be strong enough to do any housework.'

They all looked towards the car.

'She hasn't so much as stirred,' Roy said. 'You get off home and take Jericho for as long as you need him.' He frowned and added slowly, 'Don't I remember that you found her somewhere to go, someone to marry?'

'I thought I'd found her a decent husband but it turns out he took my money and didn't marry her as he'd promised. I'll have the police on him for fraud if he ever shows his face in Rivenshaw again, see if I don't.'

She saw Frankie glance involuntarily towards her own husband-to-be and patted her arm. 'You two will be all right, my dear. Now, would you and Jericho please keep an eye on the car while I have a private word with my husband?'

Frankie went to stand beside Jericho, who wound his

window down. 'Don't forget,' she said, 'we're bringing your family to see the house later this afternoon.'

'I won't. Unless Mrs Tyler still needs me.'

Frankie stood watching the car disappear down the street. She'd seen people in a bad way for lack of food, but she thought that poor woman was the worst case she'd ever set eyes on. A walking skeleton, the poor thing was.

When they got to the Tylers' house, Ethel couldn't rouse the young woman and grew even more worried about her. 'If I take the baby into the house, can you carry the mother, Jericho? Look how limp she is and how shallowly she's breathing.'

She took the baby and he picked Mattie up easily.

A maid opened the front door before they got to it, exclaiming in shock as she recognised who the unconscious woman was.

Ethel thrust the baby into her arms and she squeaked in surprise.

'Take little Robbie into the kitchen, Patsy, and lay him down on the rug. I'll show Jericho where the spare bedroom is and we'll put Mattie in there. Fill me a hot water bottle as quickly as you can. She needs to be got warm.'

Jericho followed her up the stairs, wondering how the woman had found the strength to bring the child here from Manchester.

When he laid her on the bed, Mrs Tyler covered her up and stared down at her, frowning. 'I don't like the way she's breathing so shallowly. I'll send Patsy up to keep an eye on her, then you can come down to the kitchen and look after the baby while I phone for the doctor.'

Bemused, he didn't protest that he knew very little about looking after babies but started down towards the kitchen. He heard their voices echoing down the stairwell behind him.

'She doesn't look well, ma'am.'

'No. She's not at all well, Patsy.'

'Do you think she'll get better?'

Silence that went on for so long that he stopped moving, thinking surely not!

'I don't know. We'll have to hope for the best. Now you keep an eye on her.'

Jericho went on downstairs and picked up the baby, cradling it in his arms. It whimpered a little then fell suddenly asleep. It was tiny and looked wizened like a hungry monkey he'd once seen a photo of in the newspaper, poor thing.

He heard Mrs Tyler in the hall, phoning the doctor and insisting he come to see the sick woman immediately.

When she'd finished her call, she popped into the kitchen to see the baby, still in Jericho's arms.

'Let's make him a cradle.' She pulled a drawer out of the dresser, shook most of the tablecloths and napkins it contained out on the end of the table and set the drawer down in front of the fire.

'Put Robbie down carefully and I'll cover him with this shawl. It's the best I can manage for a cradle till I can get to the shops.'

When Dr McDevitt arrived a few minutes later, Patsy came down and took over looking after the baby.

Jericho went back upstairs and waited outside the bedroom in case he was needed to carry Mattie again. He wanted to find out how the poor woman was; he felt so sorry for her and her child.

McDevitt started to examine Mattie but though she moaned slightly, he couldn't get her to respond.

He turned to Mrs Tyler. 'From the looks of her, she's not been eating properly for a good while. How she even stood upright today, I can't think.'

'She did it for her baby.'

'Yes. Women can perform amazing feats when it's to protect their children. The things I've seen! I'd just better check that she's recovered properly from bearing the child.' He lifted her skirts gently. 'Oh, hell, she's still losing blood. How old do you think the baby is?'

'Must be about three months.'

'She shouldn't still be bleeding like this. I don't think she was tended to properly after she gave birth. No wonder she's so pale. I'll arrange for her to be taken into the hospital and the child will have to go to the orphanage.'

Mrs Tyler's voice was fierce. 'No. The child can stay here. It'd help if you could find a wet nurse for him, though. I'll pay for that.'

He looked at her in surprise but all he said was, 'Very well. I do know a woman who may be able to help for a while. Her baby just died, poor thing. This one looks old enough to cope with some bread sops in warm milk as well, just a little at first to see if he keeps it down. May I use your telephone?'

While he was downstairs, Mattie opened her eyes, stared at Mrs Tyler and in a suddenly stronger voice said, 'It was Higgerson who forced me. I was afraid to say before, but I'm dying now and there's nothing he can do to me.'

'You're not dying. But they'll have to take you to hospital to look after you properly.'

She suddenly grasped Ethel's hand. 'It won't do any good. Ah, I can see the light, so bright, so beautiful.' After another moment's silence she said in a faint voice, 'Look after my baby for me, Mrs Tyler. Promise – no orphanage.'

'I promise. I'll raise him as if he were my own.'

'Ah. That's so good. You always keep your promises. I can go in peace now.'

Then her eyes closed and a short time later she stopped breathing altogether.

Ethel Tyler had seen that look too many times to mistake it now. She ran to the door and saw that the doctor was still on the phone in the hall, so shouted, 'Doctor! Come quickly.'

Jericho looked at her as she turned back into the bedroom. 'Is she—?'

'I think she's just died. How could I not realise how bad she was?' She moved back to the bed and bent over the young woman.

The doctor ran in, stared at the still figure, felt for a pulse then took out a small mirror and held it to her lips. He straightened up, looking sad. 'I'm afraid you're right, Mrs Tyler. She's definitely dead. She must have been even weaker than I thought. The child really is an orphan now, sadly.'

Ethel said firmly, 'Well, he's still not going to the orphanage. Her last words to me were to look after him, and I promised her I would, so that's what I'm going to do.'

He gaped at her. 'Adopt him, you mean?'

'Yes. I lost one son. Perhaps fate has brought me another.'

'What will your husband say?'

'He'll agree with me.'

She saw Jericho standing outside. 'Could you telephone Rudman's undertaker and tell them to come for poor Mattie? Their number is in the notebook we keep on the hall table near the telephone. We used them for our son last year and they did a good job. I'm going to the kitchen to look after that child once I've straightened poor Mattie up.'

He was shocked by the sudden death of such a young woman and surprised by Mrs Tyler's reaction and plans. But she and Mr Tyler had been grieving for their own son for over a year. Perhaps fate really had brought them a way to find happiness again.

Eh, fate rarely left anyone alone for long, did it? It was always jerking you in new directions, and money didn't prevent it happening to you.

He went downstairs, told the maid what had happened and patted her shoulder as she burst into great gulping sobs, then he went back to the phone in the hall. He found tears welling in his own eyes as he spoke quietly to the undertaker, explaining what had happened. Eh, that poor lass! What a cruel thing to happen.

A few minutes later Mrs Tyler came down the stairs and turned towards the kitchen, her expression deeply sad.

Jericho followed her to tell her about the undertaker, but didn't say anything straight away. He watched as she picked up the child and sat down, cradling him in her arms. She kissed little Robbie on the forehead and rocked him slightly, her face now fierce with determination and love. 'Cut up some old towels for nappies, Patsy, then get a bowl ready. We need to bathe and change him. The doctor's sending a wet nurse. He knows one who's lost her own child.'

Maybe some good would come out of this sad day for both the baby and that other lass, Jericho thought, watching Mrs Tyler's tender expression as she bathed the infant herself.

You always had to hope for the best at times like this – and sometimes cope with the worst.

15

Once she was sure Mr Tyler didn't need any more help, Frankie set off to drive into Rivenshaw, then changed direction as she had a sudden idea. She stopped at Wilf's house, checking that there was no one suspicious around, then going round the back to see if Jericho's mother was at home.

Gwynneth was sweeping the back step vigorously but stopped when she saw Frankie.

'I hope I'm not disturbing you, Mrs Harte.'

'I like being disturbed by family members. And didn't I ask you to call me Gwynneth? Why don't you come in and I'll make you a cup of tea?'

'I'd like that another time but today I wondered if you were free to come into Rivenshaw with me. I have to buy a few pieces of furniture for the house, just what's essential, and I thought I'd go to Willcox's second-hand shop. Jericho wouldn't want me to go on my own. Would you like to come with me?'

Gwynneth's face lit up. 'I'd love to. I'd better change my clothes first though.'

'Why don't you just take off your pinafore and put on a hat and coat? We'll go straight away. I'm not smartly dressed myself because I've been helping Mr Tyler. Anyway, you and I have to be back to look at the new house with your family later this afternoon, and it'll be a mess in there. It's full of men hammering and sawing at the moment so I got out of their way. I really need some help.'

'Well, if you're sure.'

'I am. If Jericho and I are to move in immediately after our wedding, I'll need to buy some sheets and crockery, as well as furniture. I suppose I'll have to go to the draper's for those. I've never shopped for anything like that before.'

'Sounds as if you need everything, Frankie love.'

'I do. Or rather, *we* do. I only came away from my mother's with my clothes, tools and books, you see.'

'I'll get my outdoor things on straight away then. I love to go for rides in cars.'

The two women didn't say much as they drove down the hill into Rivenshaw but it was a comfortable silence. Frankie glanced sideways at Gwynneth's happy expression, comparing it mentally to how it would have been with her mother, then she cut off that thought, telling herself not to dwell on the past. What had been done couldn't be undone and it was many years since she'd cared what her mother said or did, except when it upset her father or disturbed the peace generally.

Ah, she should have left home years ago, she really should, but it was bad enough her doing a man's job. Living on her own would have made some people highly suspicious of her morals.

Going into Charlie's shop took her thoughts along happier paths. The place was full to bursting with furniture, but with the help of Gwynneth and the man in charge, they found some excellent pieces. Soon there was a pile of items gathered in a back room ready to be delivered as soon as the house was in a better state.

Gwynneth turned to the man, looking thoughtful. 'Do you have any of those baskets of oddments of crockery you sometimes send to be sold at the market? There won't be anything at all in the house, you see, so they'll not only need a nice tea set but all sorts of dishes and bowls for use in the kitchen.'

'If it doesn't matter whether things match or not, Mrs Harte, I can put together a big basket of miscellaneous crockery for five shillings.'

'Could you make up two of them?'

'Yes, of course.'

'Done!' Then Gwynneth covered her mouth with one hand and said, 'Oops, sorry, Frankie. I was forgetting myself.'

'Don't be sorry. You've just done me a favour. I didn't even think about that sort of thing. I'm not very good with domestic details, am I?'

As they drove back, she said thoughtfully, 'I'm going to have to find myself a really good maid, one who can do a bit of cooking, and maybe a daily woman to do the scrubbing and rough cleaning a couple of days a week as well. You don't happen to know how I can best find the help I need?'

'I can ask around, see if anyone knows a good experienced maid and there will be a lot of women who'll jump at two days' cleaning work.'

'Would you do that? I'd be so grateful. It'll have to be someone who knows about getting on with the cooking, shopping and housework without me telling her what to do. I've never learned the practicalities because I was too busy working with my father and staying out of my mother's way.'

'You love your work, don't you?'

'Yes. Very much. I've spent most of my life at the workshop and I'm missing it dreadfully. I keep worrying what my mother will do about it all without my father to run the business.'

'Won't any of the men get word to you?'

'They might.' She didn't say, but Gus had already got word to her that he'd 'rescued' her two current pieces. He was the older of her father's two trusted foremen and if they'd just let him, he could run the business perfectly well. But Mr Lloyd had had the place locked up and no one, not even her mother, was supposed to go in. Had he known about Gus's visit? She wouldn't be surprised.

They drew up outside the cottage just then and as they got out of the van, Gwynneth looked across the road. 'There's Mrs Morton coming back from the shops. Why don't I introduce you? She's a good friend of the Pollards and she and her housekeeper have become my friends too since we moved to Birch End.'

She turned to lead the way across the road, which meant that both women moved in the nick of time. A rock that had been hurled towards them smashed down on the path near where they'd been standing, swiftly followed by a couple more, one of which bounced off Frankie's skirt. She grabbed Gwynneth's hand and they ran across the road to where two ladies were standing gaping in shock.

'Did you see who threw that?' Gwynneth asked.

'Just a lad. No one I know. I don't even think I'd recognise him again because he had his cap pulled down and a scarf wrapped round his face. Come inside quickly.'

They followed Mrs Morton and her maid into the house, where Gwynneth remembered to introduce them to one another.

Mrs Morton was frowning. 'Why would that lad have tried to hurt you, Gwynneth? Have you any idea?'

'I should think it's me he was trying to hit.' Frankie glanced uncertainly at her companion, not sure how frank to be about her situation.

Gwynneth had no hesitation in explaining it all.

Mrs Morton and her maid listened with increasing shock on their faces. The maid seemed more a friend than a servant, Frankie thought, because she'd joined them at the kitchen table for tea and biscuits.

'We'll keep our eyes open for strangers loitering near your house from now on,' Mrs Morton promised.

When it came time to leave, Frankie said, 'I think we'd better run across the road to make ourselves harder to hit. Can you manage it, Gwynneth?'

'Just watch me! I'm completely better now.'

But this time no missiles were thrown and there was no sign of anyone loitering nearby as they ran into the house.

They had to wake Gabriel, who'd been sleeping after keeping watch during the night and he too was shocked that they'd been attacked like that.

Gwynneth glanced at the clock. 'We're supposed to be driving across the village soon to meet Lucas. He got a few hours' work today. Could we go a bit early and stop at the shops on the way? I have to buy something for our tea.'

'Will it be safe to go shopping, do you think?'

'I'll be with you,' Gabriel said. 'I'll stay in the van and keep my eyes open.'

This was a long speech from him, Frankie guessed. 'Surely we'll be all right in the centre of the village?' she asked.

'We must hope so.' Gwynneth snapped her fingers. 'Look, I can introduce you to the shopkeepers and anyone I know while we're at it, Frankie. They might know you by sight, you see, but they won't be sure whether to chat to you or not.'

'Because I'm too posh?' she asked in a teasing voice.

But Gwynneth didn't smile at her. 'No, because of who your mother is. You ought to know that she's not liked by people at all levels. One family is related to a former servant who's whispered a few things and was glad to leave her service because she was so unreasonable.'

Frankie didn't ask who that might be. 'My mother has always found it hard to keep maids for more than a year or two, I must admit. And no wonder, the way she speaks to them and expects them to work all hours of the day.'

'Sorry. I didn't mean to upset you.'

'You don't need to apologise. I think I'm at the top of my mother's list of people she hates.'

'Your own mother?' Gwynneth gave her a big hug. 'Eh, you poor love.'

Frankie suddenly realised that she'd been hugged more often in the past few days than in the whole of her life before – even her father hadn't often done in case his wife saw them.

Frankie watched how Gwynneth did her shopping, selecting the food carefully and chatting cheerfully to the shopkeeper in the little general store, who clearly liked her.

Her mother had most of the food delivered and had probably never done more than toss orders or complaints at a grocer in her life.

'Will you be buying some of your food in the village?' the woman behind the counter at the small grocery store asked. 'If so, I might need to keep a few other items in stock.'

'I'll be buying most of our food here, I should think.'

'Really?' She brightened visibly.

'Or my maid will. When I find one, that is. Where else would we go?'

'I thought you'd want to buy from the posher shops in town.'

'I might buy something there occasionally, if you don't stock it, but it makes sense to use the shops near home, don't you think?'

'If you tell me what else you need, I can try to keep it in stock. If it's not too expensive, that is.'

'I'd appreciate that.'

'Do the other people in Marlow Road buy from you?' Gwynneth asked. 'When Frankie marries Jericho and moves here, my daughter-in-law will want to get to know her neighbours.'

The shopkeeper pursed her lips, looked round as if to check that no one was within hearing even though they were the only customers in the shop, and said, 'You've got some good folk in the street, but there are one or two incomers we don't know much about. They're always changing the tenants at Number Six, it being a men's lodging house. One chap from there tried to run up credit in our shop, but we don't give credit to anyone. Well, we can't afford it, can we?'

Gwynneth made a murmuring sound as if to encourage her to continue.

'The folk at Number Six in your street aren't as bad as some of them in Backshaw Moss, mind, but there are some strange chaps stay there at times. Speak differently to us. Southerners, I think. And there were two Irish a week or so ago. Rough chaps, they were.'

'Ah. Well, it's good to know, so thank you. And you might mention to the other shopkeepers that Mrs Harte will be buying most of her food from the village.'

Gwynneth glanced at the clock behind the counter and stopped gossiping, hurrying up the paying process with an apologetic, 'We have to get going. We're meeting my son at his new house and we don't want to be late.'

She placed her purchases in a well-worn leather shopping bag, saying quietly as they walked out, 'It's very important to everyone that you'll be shopping here in Birch End. They struggle to keep going at times and one more customer who has the money to buy food every day of the week can make a big difference.'

As they drove up Marlow Road, Frankie slowed down to look at Number Six. Like her own house, it didn't seem to be as well cared for as the rest of the small group of slightly larger houses at the upper end of the street, and the garden looked to be in a mess. She wondered who owned it.

Then she saw Jericho and forgot about neighbours, because her heart lifted with pleasure at the mere sight of him.

16

That same day, Henry Lloyd had unexpected visitors at his office.

His chief clerk came in with a wooden expression on his face that said he was annoyed about something. 'Mrs Redfern and Mr Higgerson to see you, sir.'

'*Who?* Good heavens. I don't want *them* as clients. Did they say why?'

'Something to do with Mr Redfern, I gather. He says it's urgent.'

'Better show them in and please stay with us to take notes.' He lowered his voice to add, 'And in case I need a witness as to what happens.'

'Very well, sir.'

Henry stayed behind his desk, not looking forward to this encounter. He didn't give them his usual welcoming smile, couldn't have dredged one up, merely stared across at the doorway as his unwanted visitors arrived and gestured to the chairs standing ready at the other side of the desk. 'Please take a seat.'

He waited impatiently while Mrs Redfern was fussed into place by her cousin then asked, 'How may I help you?'

'It's about my husband's will. I presume you have it here?'

'Yes, of course. I've been his lawyer for many years.'

'Then I'd like a copy so we can set things in motion.'

He looked at her in astonishment. 'But your husband isn't dead yet?'

'The doctor said there was little chance of him recovering. I need to be prepared.'

'I'm afraid I can't release his will until I have a death certificate in my hand.'

Higgerson leaned forward. 'Surely you can see how important it is to deal with the family business. You've closed it down and it's absolutely ridiculous that you won't give my cousin a key. We should be keeping things running.'

'My client gave me strict instructions about what to do if he wasn't able to continue working. For instance, he would be happy for your daughter to run the business with my help.'

'*She* isn't coming near it again.' Mrs Redfern almost spat out the words. 'She's already stolen some tools.'

'I think I've already warned you not to slander your daughter, have I not, Mrs Redfern? Those tools were her own possessions.'

Higgerson reached across to lay one hand on his companion's shoulder. 'Calm down, my dear Jane, and let me handle this.' He turned back to the lawyer. 'If you can't give us a copy of the will then surely you can let us know how things stand, so that we can make preparations for – afterwards?'

Henry shook his head. 'I'm afraid my client particularly asked me to take charge until he was actually dead.'

'I shall bring my own lawyer into this. I'm sure my poor cousin has rights here.'

Henry took a deep breath. 'You can leave the business to me until we hear about Mr Redfern.'

'That's the second reason we're here. Where has Mr Redfern been taken? And why was he taken away without my cousin's permission?'

'It's a public health matter. Since the doctor isn't sure what's wrong with him, he doesn't want to risk it spreading to others in the town.'

'But where is he?' Higgerson thumped the table, his face red and angry.

'He's been taken to a place where he can be quarantined. I don't have the exact address, because I've left the medical details to the doctor. He's already told me he'd rather keep it to himself, so that his patient's relatives won't go there and put their own and other people's lives at risk.'

He had to repeat his refusal a couple of times to persuade them that they'd get no more information from him and even Finlay, whose face was usually expressionless, was looking at the visitors in shock.

The look Higgerson threw at Henry as they left made him wonder whether he too might also be wise to take care how he went after dark. He shook his head sadly as the outer door closed behind them and asked Finlay to type up his notes on the conversation.

He believed in the law, had thought this a mainly law-abiding country, but had found that hard times bred ruthless men. And though Higgerson didn't appear to be breaking the law, he was without morals when it came to dealing with his fellow men and you had to wonder about his motives sometimes.

Jericho arrived at the new house just as the men were stopping work. He went across to chat to Mr Tyler, who was there checking all the work done that day, as usual. 'How are things going?'

'No problems today. We'll be clear of here in a few minutes then you can show your family round. We're hoping the gas and electricity will be connected tomorrow and we're working on preparations for a bathroom.'

'That's marvellous. Frankie will be delighted.'

Since the others hadn't arrived yet, Jericho decided to have a quick walk round the inside of the garden wall to check whether there were any parts of it that needed repairing more urgently than others. Once again, when he got to the wall that bordered Marlow Road, he had the feeling that he was being watched but tried not to show it.

He looked for a good vantage point and stopped behind the outhouse in which his guards would be sheltering again tonight. He piled up some fallen bricks, which let him get high enough to peer across the low roof.

He sucked in his breath when he saw a man at Number Six staring across towards the front of the house, but the fellow hadn't noticed that he was being watched in his turn.

This time Jericho was able to make out the man's features. He was a little older than himself and fleshy, as if he ate too well. He'd recognise the fellow if he saw him again in the village or down in Rivenshaw, by hell he would.

Then the man bobbed back suddenly behind the corner of the house and seconds later two tall men came into view striding up the street. He clambered down from the pile of bricks and went back to meet his brothers, thinking about what he'd seen. He hadn't been mistaken, then. Someone must have been set to watch the house. He'd ask around, see if he could find out more about the watcher, not to mention who owned Number Six.

As he reached the gate and greeted his brothers, Mr Tyler came out, chatting to one of his men, and gestured towards the house. 'It's all yours, Jericho lad. Don't forget to lock up carefully.'

He didn't need telling.

'Better wait for the women before we go inside,' Lucas said. 'Mam won't like it if we get to see the house before her.'

Fortunately it wasn't long before the sound of a vehicle heralded the arrival of the two women in the van. He watched them for a moment or two. His mother was beaming and talking excitedly to Frankie.

He went to put an arm round each of them, something his mother expected but Frankie seemed surprised by. She stiffened slightly, giving him a tentative smile but not pulling away.

As they all went inside, even his mother fell silent. He could see that his family were as surprised as he had been to see how big the house was. His mother recovered quickly, more than making up for their silence by commenting on everything she saw.

The sun had set by the time they'd finished their tour. 'I wish it didn't grow dark so early,' Jericho said. 'I could have done some work on it.'

'You'll need help to mop the place out once they've finished working on it,' Gwynneth said to Frankie.

'Perhaps we could find a couple of women to do that, so that it can be done as soon as Mr Tyler has finished. You said people in the village would appreciate any little jobs I could give them, so if you can help me find someone, I'll pay whatever you think right for their services, Gwynneth.'

'I could find a dozen but two would probably be best. You'll make their families happy and they'll think better of you. Let me find them for you. I know most of the poorer folk round here.'

'Mr Tyler told me the gas and electricity should be connected by tomorrow,' Jericho said. 'That'll make a big difference to getting hot water.'

'We'll need to buy a whole houseful of electric light bulbs.'

'And you'll need buckets, mops and rags for cleaning,' Gwynneth added. 'I've never bought so many things at once in all my life. Isn't it exciting?'

His mother's enthusiasm was infectious as usual, and as

they stopped to chat, she linked her arm in the other woman's automatically. He saw Frankie give her a quick surprised glance, but she didn't pull away.

'What a day it's been,' his mother said.

'There's something else.' Jericho told them about the young woman and baby who'd turned up out of the blue today.

They were all shocked and saddened to hear of such a young woman dying and amazed that Mrs Tyler would be taking the baby in.

'He's a lucky lad,' Lucas said. 'He'll get a good life with the Tylers. I wonder who the father is.'

Jericho shrugged. 'We'll probably never know and he's better off without a father who'd force himself on women.'

He had a quick word with Frankie, then watched her drive away so that she could get home safely while there were still other cars on the roads. He made sure everything was locked up and had a word with the two men who'd be sleeping in the shed and keeping watch, then went home.

Jericho met no one as he strode through the wind and rain. He claimed tiredness, which was true, and went to bed early but had a hard time getting to sleep.

He couldn't stop thinking about the coming changes in his life and the possible problems they'd face. Would Higgerson try to stop the wedding? Surely not? How would that benefit him?

But the mother was so strange he wouldn't put anything past her, so they would all have to take great care not to leave themselves vulnerable to attack.

Thank goodness Frankie was staying with the Lloyds. He doubted anyone would try to get into the lawyer's house.

He'd warned his own family to be careful, and he'd keep his eyes open too.

His fists clenched instinctively. Just let them try to stop him marrying her! He had a few good people on his side – and Sergeant Deemer keeping watch in Rivenshaw. Surely that would be enough to get them through the week?

17

The week of waiting for their wedding seemed to both Jericho and Frankie to crawl past, even though they were busy every single day.

One of the most important jobs to her after buying the furniture was to move her tools inside Tyler's workshop and set up a small area to suit her own needs.

The men often came to watch and lent her a hand when necessary. It wasn't as necessary as they thought and several times she had to say, 'I know how to do that, but thank you anyway.'

They couldn't hide their astonishment at how capable she seemed and when she got out her half-finished pieces of furniture, they came over for a closer look.

'You did that?' one asked.

'Yes, of course.'

'That inlay work is going to be beautiful.' The others nodded agreement looking surprised.

'It's my favourite part of the job.'

It was hard being the only woman cabinetmaker in the district! She ought to be used to it by now, but there you were. Nearly every time a new man saw her work she had to go through similar conversations. And even so, some of them seemed angry rather than admiring. At least these men weren't hostile.

Wherever she went out on her own she was always watchful, and so was Jericho. But there were no further attempts to damage the new house and no one tried to attack her. Whether that was because they were being so careful or because the attempts had now stopped for some unknown reason, who could tell?

'Don't let your guard down,' Jericho told her one day. 'Either Higgerson or your mother could still be planning something.'

'I know. I'm always very careful when I go out, but I'm missing my work. It's been the main part of my life for so long. I'd been about to start work on a sewing table, had even selected the pieces of wood for it.'

'You can get back to it after the wedding.'

'You really don't mind that, do you?'

He shrugged. 'I read about the world outside our valley in the newspapers. Women all have the vote now, so they'll have more of a say in how things are run. And they're doing all sorts of things they didn't before. Look at that Amy Johnson! It's five years now since she flew solo from England to Australia. Just imagine that.'

'I'd love to go up in an aeroplane.'

He pulled a face. 'I'm not sure I'd fancy it, but things will keep on changing so who knows? And the best change for me at the moment will be us getting married.'

She smiled. He'd said that a few times. She was growing more confident that they'd be able to make a happy life together. If only her father was around, it'd be nearly perfect. She missed him so much.

On her wedding day, Frankie looked out of her bedroom window to see a bright day with a cold winter's sun making the world seem more cheerful than the previous dull, showery day. Surely this was a good omen?

She got up, ate a satisfying breakfast and put up with being fussed over by her kind hostess.

When she was ready, she stared at herself in the full-length mirror in the hall. The navy blue suit was flattering, with a pleated calf-length skirt and a matching jacket over a long-sleeved tunic. Mrs Lloyd had offered to lend her a fox fur to drape round her shoulders, but the head looked so realistic it made her shudder.

'I'll take my winter coat in the car, but if it stays fine, I'll not bother to wear it. I'll only be going from the car to the front door of the town hall, after all.'

Not long now and it'd be done. Then surely her mother and Higgerson would leave her alone?

In Birch End Jericho helped his family settle into the new van and set off for the drive down the hill to Rivenshaw.

He knew Frankie wasn't bothered about having a party, but he liked the idea. A wedding should be something special. Mr Lloyd said they would all go back to his house for a glass of sherry. Jericho smiled at the thought. He didn't know why better off people liked sherry so much. He'd rather have a glass of beer any day, though he wasn't much of a drinker.

His mother said they had to go to her house afterwards. She'd invited Wilf and Stella to come in after they all got back from the Lloyds' house and have a piece of a cake she'd made. She'd iced the top, writing their initials on it in untidy pink squiggles. She'd also purchased two bottles of ginger beer from Leah Selby's fizzy drinks factory up in Ellindale. That minor extravagance would have to do for their family celebration.

When he was ready, he stared at himself in their small mirror, which had one cracked corner. He was glad now that Mrs Tyler had given them some better clothes. He'd not looked so smart for years. Frankie deserved that of him.

He hid a smile when his mother insisted on checking all her sons' appearances, lining them up as she used to do when they were children getting ready for school. After straightening Lucas's tie and running a loving hand down the good quality worsted of Gabriel's new jacket, she said, 'You'll do,' and plonked big, loud kisses on each son's cheeks.

She lingered over Jericho, her hands gripping the tops of his arms as she gave him a little shake. 'You're looking your best. I'm glad we don't have to wear shabby clothes. And think on, you'll be getting a good wife in Frankie. I don't need to tell you to treat her well.'

'No, of course not, Ma. You know, I can't believe she'll be waiting for us there, still wanting to marry me,' he confessed suddenly. 'She could have looked a lot higher than me for a husband.'

'Why would she treat you like that? She's obviously fond of you.'

'I don't know why you should say that.'

She gave him another smacking kiss. 'Because she looks at you the same way as you look at her, you great daft lump. Haven't you noticed?'

As he settled into the driving seat, he adjusted the rear-view mirror, which Frankie's van was modern enough to have fitted. They were improving car design all the time and he wondered sometimes what the vehicles of the future would be like. Maybe they'd be able to fly up into the air like little aeroplanes.

His mother was right, though. This mirror told the same tale as the other one. He was definitely looking his best.

'Here we go, then.'

'Drive carefully!' his mother warned.

She always said that – unnecessarily. He did take care how he drove. Life was too short to be careless with it.

*

To Jericho's surprise, when he got to the place where the road from Birch End met the valley road, he saw the police vehicle waiting, with Sergeant Deemer waving cheerfully from the driving seat and the constable sitting beside him. He slowed down instinctively, though he wasn't going fast.

'What's Deemer doing there?' Gwynneth twisted round to stare behind them. 'Has he been waiting for us?'

He could see his brother peering out of the back of the van as well.

Jericho was worried now. Surely Deemer didn't think they were going to be attacked in broad daylight?

'The sergeant's started to pull out. He must be following us,' Lucas said.

Jericho kept his eyes on the road ahead. There was another van parked just round the corner facing outwards from a gate space that gave entry to one of the farm fields with their drystone walls. The van was black with no signs painted on the sides and was much bigger than their small vehicle.

He didn't think anything of it till he got closer and suddenly recognised the face peering out at them. It was the man from Number Six. You couldn't forget that ugly, lumpy face.

If he'd been short-sighted, he might not have acted in time, but he was already braking hard even before the van pulled out suddenly as if trying to run them off the road into the wall opposite the gate.

He was going slowly enough to wrench the steering wheel round and surprise the other driver by veering across to the wrong side of the road, driving on to the grass verge along the very edge of the ditch to get past him.

His mother let out a squeak and he yelled, 'Hold tight!'

As the other van turned after them and speeded up, he accelerated, still going along the verge.

The van just missed ramming them by inches as Sergeant Deemer's police car appeared round the bend behind them.

As he tooted his horn and accelerated towards them, the big van swerved back on to the road, passing Jericho and just failing to clip his rear corner.

The attacker didn't try anything else but speeded off down the hill.

Sergeant Deemer came to a sudden halt and threw his car door open to call across, 'What was that about?'

Jericho wound his window down. 'That chap in the van tried to run us off the road. Good thing I felt suspicious and had slowed down.'

He turned to his mother. 'Are you all right, Mam?'

'Yes. Just – shocked. I banged my elbow, that's all. I can't believe that happened in broad daylight.'

Her voice sounded wobbly so he forced himself to speak calmly. 'We're all right, though, aren't we?'

'We could have been hurt if they'd shoved us into the ditch or against the stone wall,' Lucas said.

She shuddered and pressed one hand to her chest.

Deemer had been listening to their conversation through the open window. 'Good thing I decided to escort you into town.'

'Why did you do that?'

'The mayor suggested it. His registrar told him there have been some people – who didn't seem to be from the town judging by their accents – inspecting the Marriage Notice Book. Fortunately he was there when some of them turned up. He asked his clerk and there had been others but Tolver hadn't mentioned it.'

Jericho's heart sank. Something bad had definitely been planned. Had the van been the only thing? Or would they be facing other attempts to stop the wedding?

'These strangers said they were checking weddings for this coming week but the only one they looked at was yours and there isn't another till this afternoon. Two couples had postponed their weddings, you see, which seemed strange as well.'

'What on earth would they postpone for?'

'I'd guess that they were either warned or paid to stay away. But I'm not having it. Nor is the mayor.' Deemer stared down the road. 'I wonder who those men in the van were? Were there any markings on it, Jericho?'

'No, but I've seen the chap driving it before. I don't know his name but he's living on our street, at Number Six, and I've noticed him keeping watch on our house. I have very good distance eyesight and he couldn't have been expecting that because he made no attempt to cover his face.'

'Well, well. That's very useful information. I'll call round there later and see if there's any sign of him. But I'll see you into town and safely married first.'

'Thank you, sergeant. Forewarned is forearmed, eh? We'd better get going again. We don't want to be late.'

'Don't drive fast and keep your eyes open.'

He didn't need telling.

The sergeant continued to follow them but there were no further incidents.

The next surprise was that there were a lot more cars parked in the space in front of the town hall than usual. Deemer left the police car in a prominent position, where parking wasn't usually allowed, then got out. He stood watching Jericho and his family gather in a group next to their van before moving into the town hall together.

He locked the police car and followed them, with the constable a few paces behind him. Even before they got to the waiting room at the rear of the town hall, they could see through its glass panes that it was full of people and there were no free seats left.

Jericho and his family stopped in the doorway, looking

uncertain what to do. There was no sign of the bride and after a quick glance round, Deemer went up to him and whispered, 'You and your family stay here for the moment, lad.'

Those waiting turned round and glared at them, which made Jericho's mother shrink closer to him. He felt angry. She'd been so happy as they set off, didn't deserve this.

Deemer slipped out again, signalling to the constable to stay and keep watch before hurrying back down the passage towards the reception area.

Jericho stood slightly in front of his mother, ready to protect her if necessary, and studied the crowd. There might be no sign of Frankie but her mother was sitting in the front row of the waiting room and she too turned to scowl at the Harte family.

Beside her sat Higgerson, his expression so smug that Jericho was sure he'd organised this. The crowd wouldn't be able to stop them going into the back room and getting married though, unless that sod had some other nasty trick in store for them.

He turned his attention to the other people. All the seats were full yet he didn't recognise any of their occupants, so why were they there for his wedding? None of the men got up to offer his mother a seat, which was extremely rude and said a lot about the type of blokes they were.

Footsteps made him turn, relieved to see the Tylers walking along the corridor.

They stopped next to Jericho and his family, both looking disgusted at the sight of the crowd.

'Trouble brewing,' Roy muttered. 'Deemer said to wait.'

Since there was nothing else to do, Jericho asked, 'How's the baby?' He hadn't been able to forget the poor little thing.

It was Mrs Tyler who answered. 'Doing well. It's making

a difference already, him having a wet nurse. And Freda's a nice lass. What's going on here? Who are these people?'

'I haven't the faintest idea but I think you might be safer going home again.'

Roy let out a harrumphing noise and said loudly, 'I'm not leaving you to face this alone, lad.'

'Neither am I!' his wife echoed just as loudly.

The door leading to the reception area banged open again and Todd came along the corridor. Like the Tylers, he joined the Hartes to stand at the back of the room.

When Charlie Willcox followed him a couple of minutes later, Jericho realised that plans must have been made to support him and Frankie at the ceremony. That made him feel good until he saw his mother's anxious face and felt her reach for his hand. He stayed slightly in front of her and so did Lucas at her other side.

What was Frankie going to say when she arrived? Were these people going to try to stop her physically from going into the inner room to get married?

The mayor came along the corridor, stared through the glass panels and frowned. He turned and went back without coming inside.

The door at the front of the waiting room opened a few inches and the same clerk who'd been at the counter when Jericho booked the wedding peered out. He gaped at what he saw and when a couple of the strangers immediately stood up as if to move into that room, he shut the door hastily again.

Tramping footsteps had heads turning back towards the corridor and Deemer came in to rejoin them. He moved to stand next to the bridegroom. 'We'll wait for the bride to arrive then I'll stay with you for the ceremony.'

'I'm wondering if they're going to try to stop us going in.'

'They'd better not or I shall be extremely happy to arrest them.'

Except, Jericho thought, even with his brothers and the kind people who'd joined them, they were still outnumbered by at least two to one and Higgerson was continuing to look smug.

What were they planning? Why was Mrs Redfern so keen to prevent the wedding?

Mrs Lloyd was hiding something behind her back and as Frankie moved towards the front door, the older woman brought her hand forward and presented her guest with a small bouquet. The pretty collection of chrysanthemums and foliage was tied with a blue ribbon to match the bride's outfit.

'I think a bride ought to have a bouquet,' she said.

'It's beautiful. It's only going to be a brief, simple affair but I can take the bouquet home with me and put it in a vase.' She actually had a couple from the boxes of oddments they'd bought.

'Well, dear, I have a confession to make. It's not going to be quite as simple as you think. We've organised more than a drink of sherry. We're having a celebration here afterwards and a few of your friends will be coming back with us.'

Which friends? she wondered, and would they make Jericho's family feel uncomfortable?

Mr Lloyd stepped forward and offered her his arm. 'May I escort you to the car, Miss Redfern?'

'Thank you.' She put her arm in his and blinked her eyes to clear them of the tears that would well up every time she wished her father could be with her on this special day. It was his arm she should be holding. She couldn't even go to visit him in hospital because she still didn't know where they'd taken him.

'I'm sure your father's with you in spirit,' Mrs Lloyd said quietly as if she could tell what Frankie was thinking.

She nodded. But how could he be? He probably didn't even know she was getting married.

They drove towards the town hall, and there were far more cars parked outside it than usual. Was there some function taking place? But as she started to get out of the car, a group of men standing at the bottom of the slight slope began walking quickly towards them.

'Get back in and lock your doors,' Mr Lloyd ordered.

As Frankie and his wife did that, he began sounding the horn.

That brought a man in uniform to the door of the town hall, and he produced a whistle and began blowing it.

Immediately two young men came running out to join him, and another man came round the corner from the garden, mud on his boots.

The men who'd been approaching the car stopped and as the commissionaire took out a truncheon and brandished it, and the other men came to stand near him, they backed off and walked away.

'Who the hell were they?' Henry muttered.

The commissionaire came to stand next to their car and tapped on the window. 'I think you'd better bring the young lady inside, sir, while you can. We'll keep an eye on your car.'

Mrs Lloyd clutched her husband's arm. 'What were they intending to do, Henry? And apart from anything else, what are all those cars doing here? There aren't any big meetings taking place today, are there?'

'No. Definitely not. Hurry up. We'd better get inside before those thugs come back.'

'I hadn't thought that even Mrs Redfern would try to spoil her daughter's wedding,' his wife said sadly.

'She'd not hesitate to do it.' Frankie's voice broke as she tried to hold back a sob. 'You'd think she'd be glad to be rid of me.'

'She might be afraid of you inheriting part of the business. And she's always been a snob. She won't like you marrying a man like Jericho who's not a gentleman.'

'Well, if her idea of a gentleman is Timson, I definitely prefer Jericho.' She sighed. 'I wish my father were here with me today. I miss him so.'

'Oh, my dear!' Mrs Lloyd paused to give her a quick hug.

As they entered the building they found the mayor waiting for them in the reception area, looking serious.

'Thank goodness you're all right. I'm afraid there is a crowd of strangers in the waiting area at the rear. They've taken up all the seats and from the looks of them, I'm afraid you might be facing a hostile group. Higgerson and your mother are sitting there too, looking – well, smug.'

Frankie's heart sank. 'She'll be furious that the first attempt to spoil my wedding failed. And she usually has an alternative planned, which is one of the things that makes her so difficult to deal with.'

'Well, she won't stop you today because my registrar will be conducting the ceremony in my parlour instead of in the registry office, which is legally permitted if there is a good reason. I shall be invoking the fire regulations because only a certain number of people are allowed in each public area. If you'll come this way, my secretary will stay with you in the parlour and I'll escort your well-wishers to join you.'

'What about the other people? Won't they try to come too? I thought the law said there must be free access to a wedding.'

He smiled at her. 'Ah, but the same fire regulations don't permit gatherings above a certain number in my parlour either. There are several of your friends waiting and they will be allowed to witness the wedding. There simply won't be room for the others.'

'What about my mother?'

'Do you want her to attend?'

'No. Definitely not. Nor her horrible cousin.'

'Then we'll keep them out. Now, let me get you settled in the mayor's parlour. I've just sent for the fire chief to verify that we're taking the correct steps.'

As she followed the mayor, Frankie found herself flanked by both the Lloyds and though she was as tall as the lawyer and a handspan taller than his wife, their presence was a comfort. She realised she was clutching the bouquet too tightly and forced herself to relax her grip.

She might have known that her mother would try to cause trouble. What had been planned? For those men to drag her into a car and take her somewhere to be classified as mad? This was like living through a nightmare.

She wouldn't put anything past her mother these days. Jane had never been easy to get on with but she seemed increasingly irrational and hostile towards her daughter.

Why? Frankie had racked her brains but couldn't work that out.

The people in the waiting room heard the double doors from the reception area bumping to and fro as someone walked through and left them swinging. Two sets of footsteps seemed to be approaching but they didn't sound like a woman's lighter tread.

Jericho let go of his mother's hand and craned his head to look past his companions. No, it wasn't Frankie; it was the mayor together with the town hall doorman, a burly man used to dealing with trouble. And they both looked very solemn, as if there was trouble.

What was going on here? Whatever it was, he hoped the mayor and his staff could deal with it quickly.

Mr Kirby came only a little way into the room and those standing at the rear shuffled sideways to give him room. He stopped near the door then raised his forefinger and seemed to be counting the number of people there.

When he'd finished, he shook his head as if displeased and turned to the doorman. 'How many do you make it, Ted?'

They both whispered, comparing numbers no doubt, then the doorman left the waiting room and went towards the front of the building.

Higgerson stood up. 'May I ask what's going on, Mr Kirby? Is something wrong with this wedding? It's past the starting time given in the book. Perhaps the bride has changed her mind, which would be a very wise decision, considering who the groom is.' He looked scornfully across the room.

Jericho returned his stare, not allowing himself to show any reaction to this insult let alone respond. He was touched when Mrs Tyler spoke sharply, not letting Higgerson get away with that.

'I can assure you that Frankie hasn't changed her mind at all.'

'She will do if she has any sense.' Mrs Redfern's voice was even harsher than usual. 'Even she must see reason about this. That's no doubt why she's late arriving.'

Higgerson patted Jane's arm and whispered something, his sneering smile suggesting that he was confident the wedding wouldn't take place.

The mayor raised his voice. 'If you'll all kindly wait here, we'll see what we can do to solve the problem of fitting people in. There are definitely too many for the celebrant's room next door.'

'Then keep the bridegroom out,' someone called from the side and the strangers all laughed loudly – false, mocking laughter.

More footsteps approached and the fire chief came in, looked round and immediately frowned. 'You were right to send for me, Mayor. There are definitely too many people in here and that's against fire regulations, which we take very seriously in an old building like this.'

He and the mayor walked outside and stood talking in the hall, then both returned.

The mayor was smiling confidently as he turned to Jericho and whispered. 'Could you please take the wedding party out and wait for me in the reception area, Mr Harte?'

'Yes, of course.' Jericho offered his arm to his mother, leaving Mr Tyler to escort his wife, while Todd and Charlie Willcox fell in behind them. His brothers brought up the tail of the small procession, looking tall and fierce enough to take on anyone who tried to cause trouble.

Once the group of people standing near the door had left, the men occupying the hard wooden chairs stood up and looked towards Higgerson as if for instructions.

He held up one hand to stop them moving, offered his arm to Mrs Redfern and came forward. 'I think the bride's mother would count as part of her wedding party, don't you, Mr Kirby?'

The mayor pulled a piece of paper out of his pocket and stood there as if checking it, still barring their way. 'I'm afraid not. Everyone who has been invited is on this list and—' He looked round the room. 'Yes, they've all left now.'

'Doesn't the law state that there must be free admission to weddings?'

'And there has been – to a certain extent. But we also have to comply with the fire regulations.'

Mrs Redfern cried out, 'This is a trick. Don't let her do this, Gareth. I'm her mother! I have a right to try to make her see sense.'

Higgerson's barely controlled anger showed in his face and the crowd of men had all moved to stand nearer to them.

Before he could say anything else, Mr Kirby said calmly, 'I'm so sorry you've been disappointed, madam. But it's your daughter's wedding and as she's well past the age of needing your permission to marry, it's up to her to select her guests and send out the invitations.'

With that, he left the room. She tried to follow him, shouting, 'Stop! Come back!'

But the doorman and fire chief barred her way and Higgerson grabbed her arm and stopped her from trying to push past them. They once again began to count the number of people left.

'I'm afraid another four people must leave this room to comply with the regulations,' the fire chief said. 'The rest may stay as long as we're open.'

Mrs Redfern burst into loud, angry tears.

Higgerson looked at her in annoyance and made shushing noises.

'Perhaps you'd like to lead the way out, sir?' the fire chief said to him. 'I'm sure the lady will benefit from some fresh air.'

Higgerson gave his cousin a little shake and said something to her in a low, angry voice, then led her forcibly out of the room, followed by two of the men.

In the reception area they hesitated, and Higgerson stared towards the mayor's suite. But its door remained shut and one of the gardeners was now standing in front of it, muscular arms folded, a big hoe in his hand, held as if it were a weapon.

The situation would have been amusing, if there wasn't a threat of violence, the fire chief thought, and waited to see what they'd do next.

Higgerson breathed deeply, then shrugged and tugged his cousin out of the building. She began shrieking and trying to get away from him but he forced her across to his car and pushed her in the back.

The fire chief watched them go, muttering, 'And good riddance to them two! If that's a *lady* give me a washerwoman any day.'

He turned to the two men who had followed them. 'I hope you'll leave quietly, otherwise I'll have to call in some more men to eject you.'

'Nothing to stay for now,' one said.

After they'd left, the fire chief went back to the waiting room and told the doorman to let out the motley collection of people who had been crammed into it.

'There's nothing else going to happen,' he said.

The human tide surged out and paused in the reception area, as if looking for instructions, but Higgerson was already outside in the back of his car, talking to one of his men through the open door.

When he'd finished, the man nodded and the car drove him away.

The group of people all left the building, but the doorman and gardeners continued to watch as they lingered in the parking area, standing in twos and threes.

'Danged if I ever saw anything like it, Ted,' the doorman muttered.

The fire chief smiled grimly. 'No. Neither have I. But we got them two their wedding and stopped Higgerson's shenanigans, for once. I enjoyed doing that. He's caused too much trouble in this town, that one has. And those ramshackle houses of his are going to give me and my men a lot more headaches in future unless we're very lucky. They're ignoring the fire regulations, you know.'

A short time later an older gardener said quietly, 'That Redfern woman puzzles me. Fancy trying to spoil your own daughter's wedding. How mean-spirited can you get?'

'They say that one behaves very strangely at times.'

'Well, she certainly did today. Higgerson had to force her

into his car. Where's her husband gone? No one knows that, either.'

'I don't blame him for leaving her. It'd be like living with the devil, married to her.'

'This mayor isn't like the other one, is he, though? He wasn't afraid to act today and he did the right thing, I reckon. He's starting to make a few improvements in various areas, too, and he's got some good people on the council with him.'

'Yes, but it all takes time. Let's hope nothing happens to him and he stays in office for a good many years.'

18

In the mayor's parlour, eleven members of the public and two officials watched as the registrar gently positioned the two people about to get married in front of the mayor's desk, and Mrs Lloyd took Frankie's bouquet. After that, further gestures brought the rest of the group to stand round them in a semicircle.

While this was being organised, Jericho took Frankie's hand and whispered, 'I'm really sorry your mother acted like that, love.'

'I am too. I half-expected it, though, now my father isn't there to keep her in check a bit. He would have been horrified by her behaviour today.'

'I'm sorry that he isn't here with you today. I know you miss him.'

'Yes. But at least my mother didn't succeed in stopping us getting married.'

Someone said, 'Shhh!' and they looked up at the registrar who was now standing in front of them next to a small table whose contents had been hastily moved to the windowsill.

'Are you ready to begin, Miss Redfern, Mr Harte?'

They both murmured 'Yes' and in a few minutes, and with far less verbiage than a church wedding, the registrar was able to declare, 'You are now man and wife, and you're just as properly married as if you'd held the ceremony in church.'

Frankie found the last statement rather strange since they had deliberately chosen to hold the ceremony in the registry office. As long as they were well and truly married, it didn't matter to her where they held it. In fact she preferred it this way because she was too tall and strongly built to look good in a fancy lace wedding dress.

'You may kiss the bride,' the registrar said.

As she looked at her new husband shyly, she felt as if the rest of the group had suddenly moved further away and she was on her own with Jericho. He was taller than her and she had to look up into his face, which was unusual for her. His height and strength made her feel protected and when he put his arms round her, she leaned into them willingly, feeling as if she'd come into a safe haven.

His lips were warm and lingered on hers so that for a few moments it really did seem as if they'd become one person instead of two.

Then he drew away, put his right arm round her and turned to face their applauding well-wishers who were clearly expecting some sort of speech.

Jericho was smiling as if he was truly happy to have married her. Did she dare hope that was true? She was happy to have married him, far happier than she'd ever have expected.

Jericho was relieved that his mother had warned him something like this might be expected, and had planned with him what to say. '*Mrs Harte—*' He had to pause and wait for their renewed clapping to die down, but it had given him a warm, happy feeling.

He began again, 'Mrs Harte and I are both very happy that you could be here with us on such a special day.'

Then he had to pause again for more applause and a couple of hurrahs. The room seemed full of smiling faces. And when he looked sideways at his bride, she was smiling too. She looked so pretty today he had to plant a quick kiss on her cheek.

After that Mr Lloyd took over and reminded everyone to come back to his house to drink the health of the bride and groom and partake of light refreshments.

Jericho hadn't realised they'd planned to invite so many people and hoped his family wouldn't be too overawed to chat and enjoy it.

Mrs Lloyd handed the bouquet back to Frankie and that seemed to add the final touch to the wedding, turning her well and truly into a newly-wed bride. He offered her his arm and she placed her hand on it with another smile.

As they walked outside, Mr Lloyd moved closer and whispered to him, 'You two sit in the back of my car, Jericho. Your brother Gabriel is going to drive your van back. We need to get you home before our guests. Ignore those louts over there. The mayor has some men ready to intervene if they try to cause trouble.'

Jericho blew out his breath in relief. He'd been keeping an eye on some rough-looking men standing near the bottom end of the car park, but Sergeant Deemer and his constable were watching them from the top end. There were also the doorman and some well-built gardeners pacing to and fro along one side, plus two young men in suits. They were all staring at the men as if itching to pounce on them.

What a thing to happen at a wedding! Maybe he and Frankie would laugh at it one day, but at the moment he couldn't help feeling angry.

In the car Mr Lloyd said in his usual quiet way, 'We sent men to guard Wilf's house and your new home. Some of them will stay nearby all night. I'm truly sorry this is necessary but we hope it won't mar the joy of the day for you.'

A moment later he added, almost as if speaking to himself, 'I must have a word with a few of my friends in county circles. We stand in great need of extra police here in the valley and maybe the time has come to appoint some special constables. They were of enormous help during the war and we seem to have had a miniature war going on in our valley lately.'

Jericho agreed with him. Birch End seemed to be filling up with troublemakers, who'd come in from other places. Was that Higgerson's doing? He reckoned so. Well, just let such louts try to hurt his wife or family!

On that thought he turned to smile at Frankie and let happiness take over again.

When they reached the Lloyds' house Frankie waited for him to help her out of the car and as they walked inside, she whispered, 'I don't like being the centre of attention. It makes me nervous. Does it show?'

'No, it doesn't. I'm nervous too. I'm not used to such fancy houses. For goodness' sake tell me if I do something wrong.'

'We'll stay beside one another for support.'

She took his hand and clutched it tightly. He was getting to like that.

He knew his mother would be terrified to be taking tea with some of the town's more important people, but he thought his brother Lucas might have enough confidence to help her. Lucas usually did cope, whatever the situation. He was quiet but had a knack for doing the right thing and making himself liked.

And Gabriel would be his usual solemn self, seeing much more of what was going on than most people realised and only speaking when he felt he had something worth saying.

Jericho gave Frankie's firm, capable hand a quick squeeze then let go as Mrs Lloyd took over the newly-weds.

'If you two will stand near the door just inside the room, you can greet your guests as they come in.'

They did as she asked but Jericho let Frankie deal with most of the greetings because she was acquainted with the people, if only slightly, while he only knew them by sight. She'd said she felt nervous but it didn't show and when people handed her wedding presents, she said all the right things.

Somehow he hadn't expected that they'd get presents, let alone such pretty things: a little silver bonbon dish (whatever bonbons were), a cut-glass vase, a large, brightly decorated pottery plate (only they called it a 'charger' which puzzled him) and a set of silver teaspoons with fancy tops to the handles.

He joined in her thanks or simply nodded and smiled, then watched how the guests behaved and tried to model his actions on theirs. They spoke quietly, not making any sudden movements or laughing too loudly. It helped a little that he was the tallest man there. That had made him feel more confident somehow.

After everyone who'd been at the town hall for the wedding had arrived and been greeted by the newly-weds, a maid brought in a tray of filled glasses. Mr Lloyd rapped a spoon on a table for attention and called out that everyone should take a glass of wine, or lemonade if preferred, to drink the health of the bride and groom.

The maid offered it to the bride and groom first. When Frankie took a glass of wine, Jericho did too. Eh, it was such a pretty little thing, cut glass that made the wine sparkle. But it only contained a couple of mouthfuls.

Once everyone had been served, Mr Lloyd made a short speech wishing *Mr and Mrs Harte* the very best in their new life. After that he raised his glass and called on the guests to drink the newly-weds' health.

Jericho watched his host, noticed that Mr Lloyd only took a sip, so did the same. He was interested to see what wine tasted like because he'd never had any before. He didn't think much of it, thin pale yellow stuff it was. Ugh. And he didn't like the taste either. He hoped he'd kept his face straight. His mother had taken a glass of lemonade. Lucky her. He wished he'd done the same.

He noted that she'd settled down now, losing her nervousness and watching everything with that bright alert look he loved to see on her face. His brothers, like himself, had chosen wine. Lucas was looking unimpressed by its taste but Gabriel was studying it as if he found it interesting.

The food was fiddly stuff and Jericho found he had to take a small plate first and let the maid put things on it for him. He leaned closer to Frankie and whispered, 'Are we allowed to put the wine glasses down?'

'Yes, of course. I'm going to do it. Oh, look, Mrs Lloyd is doing it now, so we can follow suit. My mother has never allowed wine to be served in our house, though I know she keeps a bottle of port hidden in her wardrobe. I don't really like the taste of it.'

'Goodness! The more you tell me about her the stranger she sounds.'

'I hope I don't bore you.'

'Never. I like to find out everything I can about you.'

The maid was waiting so he accepted another fiddly little pie-like creation. He was enjoying the taste of the food, though it came in such small amounts it didn't satisfy his appetite. Then came a fancy wedding cake. He sidled a couple of steps sideways and whispered to his mother that he'd be looking forward to trying her cake too.

'Isn't this exciting?' she whispered back. 'They've made it all so nice for you.'

It was nice, very, but then to his dismay he found he had to move to the front with Frankie so that they could cut the cake together. It was surprisingly difficult to do that neatly with two hands on one knife. Luckily the maid took the knife from them after one cut and did the real slicing, cutting the cake into tiny pieces, spoiling the fancy pattern on the top of the icing.

Like the other food served, the cake was delicious but the pieces were so small they hardly made three mouthfuls even when you only nibbled.

Still, it was interesting to see how better-off people celebrated a wedding, and this such a modest one, judging from the large groups he'd seen going into church for weddings from time to time. It was a relief, though, when the time came for him and his bride to take their leave. It was exhausting being so watchful all the time.

His brothers and mother had slipped out of the house and got themselves into the back of the van by the time he and Frankie had finished saying their goodbyes and thanking their kind hosts.

He took the driving seat this time and set off slowly and carefully.

'Wasn't it nice of those people to come to the wedding,' Frankie said.

'The kindest thing of all was the way they looked out for you,' Lucas said. 'All except your mother. Frankie, she's very—' He broke off, not wanting to offend her.

Frankie finished off for him. 'Horrible. And getting rather strange. I don't understand why she hates me so much. I never have. It wasn't my fault my brother got killed.'

'There's an old saying: *There's nowt so queer as folk*,' Gwynneth spoke broadly, pronouncing the last word 'fowk' to complete the rhyme. 'Sometimes, when people get older, they start to behave in a strange way. I've seen it happen here and there. Sadly, it can mean they're starting to get forgetful.'

'You think that's what's happening to my mother?'

'I don't know her well enough, dear, so it's hard to judge. It could be. In which case it's not her fault. Some older people just . . . you know, get like that. I think brains wear out just like bodies and some wear out sooner than others. Nothing you can do about it.'

There was a silence, then she added, 'Eh, and what a miserable conversation to have on your wedding day. Let's talk about something nice. What lovely fancy food Mrs Lloyd provided. Imagine going to all that trouble.'

'I'm still hungry, though,' Gabriel said bluntly. 'They didn't give you much.'

'Well, I have some heartier food at home and I've made sure you do as well.'

So Jericho dropped his family in Croft Street, where a man was on watch, then drove round to the new house, looking forward to some peaceful time with his new wife.

'There are two men on watch here,' Frankie said as they drew up. 'Isn't it terrible that we have to do this?'

'Yes. But we managed to get married and that makes me very happy.'

When they got to the front door, he said, 'Stop! Wait there a minute!'

She looked at him in puzzlement. 'What's the matter?'

He turned the key in the lock and chuckled as he swept her up into his arms. 'A new husband has to carry his bride across the threshold. Both my mother and Mrs Tyler made sure I knew that.'

She clutched him tightly. 'I'm too big.'

'No, lass, you're exactly the right size for me.' He carried her inside easily then kicked the door shut with one heel.

He didn't put her down even then and their heads were very close. They stared at one another for a few moments and he couldn't resist kissing her lips. When he pulled his head away, she made a little murmur as if she wished he hadn't stopped and followed that by a glowing smile.

'I think we'll do all right, you and me, Frankie.'

'It won't be my fault if we don't, Jericho. Now for goodness' sake set me down and let's get out of these clothes. I'm terrified of spilling something on them. They'll have to be my best for some time.'

'Mine too.'

Somehow they found themselves again hand in hand as they climbed the stairs and went into their bedroom, which was a large room, with only the bed, a wardrobe and a chest of drawers standing like sentinels around the edges of the bare floorboards.

He had to help her with some fiddly little buttons and somehow that led to him kissing her again – and again – till she lost all sense of inhibition and he dared take things further.

He was delighted that she wanted him to touch her, to love her, to become her husband in every way. He had been hoping for a proper marriage. But he hadn't expected their first coupling to be this good, he thought as he gathered her close afterwards.

'Eh, you're a fine lass, Frankie Harte.'

'And you're a wonderful man, Jericho.' She buried her face in his chest and her voice came out muffled. 'I didn't know it could be like that. I was engaged before and we did make love. But it wasn't very enjoyable. My mother always told me that it would hurt, even if I eventually found myself a man who could stand the sight of me.'

'She was lying to you.'

'Yes. She lies a lot. She'll say and do anything to get her own way.'

'I won't lie to you, my lass. It's not how I face the world.' He didn't try to pull away, was enjoying simply holding her close. 'We match well in bed, you and I, don't you think?'

She flushed as she said quietly, 'I don't know enough to judge that.'

'It was good for me. And you seemed to enjoy it.'

The pink in her cheeks went brighter. 'Yes, I did. Very much. I like cuddling too.'

'Mam has always cuddled us lads. She still does. I think people were made to touch one another. Normal people, anyway.'

'Yes.' She smiled at him then snuggled closer.

He began to stroke her hair and then her soft cheeks, so it was a while before they got dressed again, laughing as they picked up the tangle of fine clothes from the floor near the foot of the bed.

19

The day after the wedding Sergeant Deemer sent his constable round the side of the house to guard the back door, then knocked at the front door of Number Six, Marlow Road.

A frazzled-looking woman answered it, jerking back in obvious dismay at the sight of him.

He smiled. 'Edie Benson! When did you come back to the valley?'

She shrugged, folding her arms across her chest as if to guard herself from him. 'A couple of weeks ago. My cousin offered me a job as housekeeper here.'

'Did he now? I've been told this is a lodging house, only it hasn't got a council permit that I've seen. How long has he owned it and where did he get the money to buy a place like this in a good street?'

She gave him a sulky look. 'He doesn't own it, as you very well know. He's just employed to run it for someone.'

'Who does own it, then?'

'How should I know? Why don't you ask my cousin? He's sitting in the kitchen having his dinner.' She held the door open and gestured to him to come in.

Deemer stayed where he was. 'Which cousin would that be? You've got a lot of relatives.' Too many Bensons round here, he reckoned, always giving him trouble.

'My cousin Nev.'

'Nev what?' But Deemer had already guessed which

of her family's tribe of villains and bullies it was likely to be.

'Nev Carter.'

No surprise, that. The Carters and the Bensons often seemed to marry, or live together as if they were married, anyway. 'Send him out here to speak to me.'

She hesitated then shrugged and went back inside.

But he noticed her quick, furtive glance upstairs as she turned and that suggested there was something or someone hidden up there. She'd never been a clever thief, just a lucky small pilferer who'd got out of the valley a few years ago when the police were close to getting firm evidence against her.

Nev came slouching out from the back of the house and Deemer recognised him as one of the men who'd been sitting in the waiting room at the town hall. He was a small bulldog of a man with the broken nose and battered face of a fighter. The Carters weren't a tall family, but they were tough, you had to give them that.

'Running a public lodging house here, Mr Carter? You need a licence for that.'

'It's not a public lodging house. It's private lodgings.'

'Oh? That's a new one to me. Whatever you call it, the place still needs a licence from the council before it can offer any sort of lodgings. And unless I'm much mistaken, lodging houses aren't allowed in this area, anyway. It's designated for single dwellings only.' The better class of person in Birch End didn't want the troubles of Backshaw Moss coming too close to their own houses and had enough influence with certain council members to see that the slums weren't allowed to encroach any further in this direction.

Nev shrugged. 'Don't ask me, ask the owner. All I know is, I were telled it didn't need a licence.'

'Who is the owner?'

He hesitated, caught the policeman's stern gaze and muttered, 'Mr Higgerson. He only uses this house when he's bringing in extra workers for his building company, not all the time.'

A place to keep men waiting to do little extra jobs on the quiet, men who were best kept out of sight of the law, Deemer thought. Useful information, but it could only be a recent development or he'd have known about it. 'I'll definitely speak to him about a licence then, but in the meantime—'

There was an eruption of shouting and cursing from the back and he recognised his constable's voice calling for his help, so shoved Nev aside and ran through the house. Just outside the kitchen window two men were struggling and he burst out into the back garden in time to help his constable, who was trying to subdue a yelling, kicking man.

Deemer grabbed his handcuffs and quickly snapped one end of a pair on the nearest flailing arm, causing a yell of fury. He used it to tug that arm away from the constable's throat and it didn't take much longer with them both holding the man down, to fit the other handcuff. Thank heavens for strong young constables, because Deemer was nearing sixty now and some days you felt it. He got up, panting, and brushed himself down.

The man subsided, hands behind his back, scowling up at them from the ground. 'I didna do nothin'.'

'Then why did you climb out of the window?' the constable panted. 'And why didn't you stop when I called out that I was the police?'

Deemer clicked his tongue. 'Tut! Tut! Naughty boy.'

'He didna say he were the police,' the man said, pronouncing it 'po-liss'.

'I did too!' the constable insisted indignantly. 'We have to say it whenever we stop anyone. I could say them words in my sleep, I could.'

Deemer was studying the man. 'Now where have I seen you before?'

'Nowhere. I've only just come tae the valley.'

'That's a Scottish accent.' He snapped his fingers as the name came to him suddenly from a couple of fights he'd broken up several years ago. He rarely forgot a name, or a villain. 'Ogilvie, isn't it? Keith. Long time no see. I thought I told you to stay away from Rivenshaw if you couldn't keep the peace.'

'An' I thought you'd be dead by now, old man.'

'Not by a long chalk. I'm in excellent health.'

'Well, I havena done anythin' wrong, so he had nae right to stop me.'

'Then why did you leave the house by the window?'

'Because I knew the poliss would find some lie tae pin on me.'

'Well, let's try these charges for a start, which are not lies but the absolute truth. You'll be charged with dangerous driving, not to mention deliberately threatening lives by causing another driver to run off the road and chasing after him to try to push him into the ditch. I saw you doing that myself so there will be no trouble getting a conviction.'

'It were an accident. I sneezed and it loosened my grip on the steering wheel.'

'One sneeze doesn't make you pursue another vehicle that far along the side of the road. I think I'll make a reliable witness in court.'

That won him a scowl and a muttered curse.

'Add to that the fact that the van you were driving was reported stolen from a street in Manchester yesterday. The notifications of stolen vehicles arrived in the first post today. So either you stole it or you received stolen property. Either will keep you locked up for longer.'

The man would have spoken again, but Deemer held up

one hand. 'We'll do this properly at the station. Constable, arrest him and put him in the back of the car.'

He went back into the house but found no sign of Nev, who had probably nipped off to let Higgerson know what had happened. Edie scowled at him from a seat near the kitchen fire. He let her be. For now.

After he'd made sure Ogilvie was securely locked up in a small cell behind the police station, attached to the sergeant's official house, Deemer went along the street to the nearby town hall and checked the lodging house records. As he'd thought, there was no sign of Number Six ever having been licensed, and also Marlow Road was definitely in the part of Birch End where lodging houses were not allowed under any circumstances.

He'd warn the mayor that Higgerson was trying to sneak one of his ramshackle little businesses into the main part of Birch End. He wasn't having that and the mayor would back him up, he was sure. It was bad enough having unsavoury common lodging houses in Backshaw Moss and in the few poorer streets that counted as a slum on the southern outskirts of Rivenshaw, though its streets weren't nearly as bad as those in the Moss.

He doubted even Higgerson would be allowed to creep into respectable areas. The fellow must have filled up all his houses in the slums. If such dwellings were let by the room and crammed with people, they could be highly profitable. It was how Higgerson had made his fortune in the first place.

He stood for a moment, thinking about the situation.

Redfern's had been a reputable business, but if Mrs Redfern had her way, it looked likely to fall into Higgerson's hands, which would not be good for the town, Deemer was sure.

Unless by some miracle, her husband recovered.

*

Charlie Willcox went back to check on the larger of his two pawnshops, where someone had tried to steal the cash drawer. Vi Cobham, who ran the shop for him, was sporting a big bruise and a scrawny female thief was locked in the cupboard.

'What next?' he muttered. Things were going from bad to worse in this town, and in daylight too. They had to stop it. He knew some people were desperately poor but that didn't make it right to steal others' money. And they didn't have to starve these days, did they? There was a dole to be had, and soup kitchens were being run for those who were desperate for food.

The Methodist Chapel ran a particularly good one, more generous than the Church of England's effort. He contributed to both.

He phoned the mayor and had a quick chat, then went back to phone Sergeant Deemer and tell him about their petty thief.

'I'll send my constable round in a few minutes to bring her in.'

'Good. I wonder if you've got a minute for a chat now I've got you on the phone. I don't want to leave the shop because Vi's a bit shaken up.'

'Always got time for a chat with you, Charlie lad.'

'Oh, good.'

'Do we know this woman?'

'She won't give her name but I reckon she's a Benson, scrawny with that frizzy faded-looking hair. You can't miss them.'

'Not another one! I've just found Edie Benson running a lodging house in Marlow Road for Higgerson. And I've encountered her cousin recently – a certain Nev Carter. He's an unsavoury type, too.'

Charlie let out a disgusted choke of sound. 'Our town could do without families like those.'

'You find that sort everywhere, unfortunately, but lately they've got out of hand.'

'That's what I want to talk to you about. As a council member I think we could and should do something about it. We can do more if we try.'

Deemer didn't hesitate. 'I'm listening.'

'How about enrolling some special constables? I don't know the rules, but they did it during the war, so there must be a way.

'That's a thought. And you're not the first to suggest it, so I'd like to bring Henry Lloyd into it as well. The situation has gone far enough. He's a good citizen, knows his civic duty, and knows the law. Leave it with me to look into it, Charlie.'

It was indeed a good idea.

20

The morning after their wedding both Jericho and Frankie slept late. He woke first, enjoying watching her sleep so peacefully. Then she woke suddenly and blushed as she looked at him. Clearly she was remembering their wedding night.

He smiled at her and since he was no good at fancy compliments, simply said what he felt. 'Ah, you're a grand lass, Frankie.'

She looked relieved and gave him another of her shy half-smiles in return. 'And you're a grand chap, Jericho.'

His stomach gurgled and he chuckled. 'I'm a hungry one, that's for sure.'

'Oh, dear! I didn't think about food for today. And we didn't eat at all last night.'

'I did. I sneaked down and grabbed a couple of slices of bread and butter, but you didn't even stir, so I didn't wake you.'

She threw back the bedcovers. 'I'm ravenous now, though. Let's go and see what there is in the kitchen.'

This brought home what he was beginning to suspect: however clever she might be at cabinetmaking, she didn't have many domestic skills. But, to his relief, there was some food so they breakfasted on boiled eggs and toast – though he had to show her how to time the eggs properly.

She watched it all with brow furrowed as if she'd never been in a kitchen before. 'Ah. I see. It's all in the timing, how long you boil the eggs. I'm a quick learner so I'll remember that one easily enough. Um, Jericho, I was wondering whether I should ask your mother to teach me how to make a few simple dishes. Would she do that, do you think?'

'She'd love to. She's a good cook when she has something to practise her skills on. I can show you a few tricks too. Us lads had to take over when Ma was so ill.'

'She looks well now.'

He beamed at the mere thought of that. 'Yes. For today, why don't you and I stroll to the baker's in the village and buy a couple of loaves, and maybe a meat pie or two for tea? And we'll get some apples from the greengrocer. I'm fond of an apple after a meal. They're not looking their best at this time of year, however carefully they've been stored in people's barns and attics, but they still taste good.'

By that time of day people with jobs had long gone to work so the Hartes didn't meet many other folk as they strolled hand in hand to visit the village baker, grocer, butcher and greengrocer. The owners of these key shops would be pleased to see them patronising the locals, Jericho said.

When he opened the door of the Bibbys' baker's shop and ushered her in, they were greeted with a beaming smile. After they'd made a few purchases, he asked Mrs Bibby if she could spread the word that they needed a maid.

'A fancy lady's maid or a housemaid?'

'A general cook-housekeeper, one with good practical skills who can do a little plain cooking.'

Mrs Bibby glanced doubtfully at Frankie.

'And while you're at it, you'd oblige me by spreading the word that my wife is not at all like her mother to work for,' Jericho added bluntly.

Frankie flushed and so did Mrs Bibby.

He kept quiet, letting his words sink in. He reckoned he'd guessed accurately what the baker's wife had been worrying about from the way she'd been glancing at Frankie as they made their purchases. He hoped his blunt words would help put a stop to such worries.

He managed not to smile as it occurred to him suddenly that however poshly she talked, Frankie wasn't at all arrogant or stand-offish – and it was especially endearing the way she blushed.

Neither of the women seemed to know what to say next, so he continued to share information cheerfully. If you told locals something straight out, they'd pass it on – people always did – but be more likely to get the facts right. He tried to speak as if what he planned to say next was quite ordinary, when actually it was highly unusual.

'My wife is a fully trained cabinetmaker, as you may have heard, and she will be starting work with Mr Tyler now she's living up in Birch End. What we're looking for is a maid who knows what's needed and can be trusted to do it without a mistress peering over her shoulder all the time.'

'And perhaps a young girl to help her, as well as a day cleaner to come in a couple of times a week for the rough work,' Frankie added. 'But I think we may need the cleaner every day at first, because the house is in a dreadful mess from having been left empty for so long.'

He was relieved that she obviously had some knowledge of how to *manage* a larger household, even if she hadn't the faintest idea about how to do the various tasks involved. She'd mentioned this morning that she'd been discouraged from entering the kitchen or chatting to the servants, even as a small child. Eh, it was a wonder no one had wrung the neck of that mother of hers!

It occurred to him, not for the first time, that Frankie's father must have been rather weak when it came to standing up to his shrew of a wife.

Mrs Bibby nodded, still studying her customer as if she

were a strange animal never seen in the village before. 'I'll let folk know you're looking for staff, Mrs Harte. You'll probably find them queuing up for the jobs. Times are hard and good jobs are scarce as hens' teeth round here.'

Frankie nodded. 'I know. Regular jobs are scarce everywhere in the valley.'

Mr Pickup, the butcher, said much the same thing, but went to bring his wife in from the living quarters behind the shop to talk to Frankie about the details of the servants she needed, that being 'women's business'.

He'd had even more trouble than Mrs Bibby hiding his disapproval of Mrs Harte when Jericho spoke of her continuing to work. In fact, he looked sideways at her husband, as if Jericho had suddenly grown two heads for allowing this, since they wouldn't need her wages to make ends meet as poorer people might.

When they were alone Frankie whispered that Jericho would have to get used to people looking at him like that. 'I can't bear to give up my work.'

'I'm not asking you to do that And folk can mind their own business. What you and I do is our own choice.'

'Well, I doubt they'll consider such a big, strong chap as you to be living under petticoat government. Three fine men, you and your brothers are, and your mother is so proud of you all.'

'She's been a good mother.'

'She's always been very kind to me.'

He wouldn't put up with any unkindness towards his wife from anyone, rich or poor.

When Mrs Pickup joined them she was brisk and businesslike. She mostly ignored Jericho after her first greeting, asking Frankie a few pertinent questions about wages and whether it was a live-in job, then saying, 'Well, as it happens, I have a cousin who's seeking work as a cook-housekeeper.

Her name's Hilda Horrocks and she's been doing that sort of job for a while.'

'Has she got good references?'

'No. Not recent ones anyway. She had to leave her last place suddenly because when the mistress turned sickly and took to her bed, the master didn't treat Hilda with respect, if you know what I mean.'

There was a pregnant pause as she let that sink in. 'Hilda's a decent woman who goes to chapel regular and she clouted him good and hard when he tried to force her into sharing his bed. He threw her out of the house late in the evening and she had to seek shelter for the night with the minister at her chapel. Yes, and the minister had to go with her to get her clothes and other stuff back the next day and threaten to bring a charge of theft if the man didn't give them back to her.

'The minister said he'd give her a character reference, and he wrote that down, but his chapel is over in Bury, not here if you need to speak to him about it.'

She paused to wait for a response, staring at Frankie now with a hint of pleading. 'I know ladies usually insist on references, but if you could give our Hilda a chance, Mrs Harte, I'm sure you won't regret it. You only need to meet her to *see* that she's respectable.'

'I'm happy to give her a chance. Send her to see me and we'll have a chat, find out how we get on.'

'Um, just one more question because I don't want to waste your time: do you mind if she's a Methodist?'

'Not at all.'

That seemed to surprise Mrs Pickup and Frankie abruptly remembered her mother refusing to employ servants who didn't attend the Church of England. Her mother was very old-fashioned in many ways and seemed to live her life by all sorts of unwritten 'rules', such as which church the better class of people *and* their servants ought to attend. Perhaps that was why it had upset her so greatly to have a daughter who worked in a man's job. Or had she been jealous of Frankie's freedom?

Ah, what did that matter now? She had to stop thinking about her mother.

'When do you think your cousin can come and have a chat with me? We need someone urgently.'

Mrs Pickup's face brightened. 'Hilda's staying here with us above the shop, so I can go and tell her straight away. She's been doing some house cleaning for me, so she'll want to tidy herself up before she comes to see you, I'm sure, but she won't be long.'

'I shall be happy to see her whenever she's ready. Send her round to our house.'

As they left the shop, Jericho said, 'Just a minute!' and thrust the basket into her hands. He nipped back inside the shop.

'Did we forget something?' Frankie asked as he took the basket and offered her his free arm.

'Yes. I forgot to tell them straight out that you're nothing like your mother, as I did with Mrs Bibby. Best get that out in the open, don't you think? You could see how doubtfully everyone's looked at you when you've said we need a maid.'

'I couldn't miss it. Oh dear! It's as if my mother is casting a shadow over me still.'

'That'll change when people round here get to know you.'

'I hope so.'

'It will, I promise you.' He gave her a quick hug, which had her blushing again and made a woman passing by smile at them and call, 'Congratulations, you two!'

With him carrying the basket again they sauntered home. They were both enjoying the day's holiday Mrs Tyler had insisted he take in order to 'settle into' their new home.

Even the weather was on their side, with a crisp winter sun gilding their small world.

Within twenty minutes of them getting back there was a knock on the front door.

'I'll answer that.' Jericho gestured to Frankie to keep back and reached up to slide back the top bolt. 'Just till we're sure we're going to be safe here, you shouldn't answer the door on your own. And I'd prefer to hire a strong woman, one who can help to defend you, if necessary. What's more, I'm going to put a security chain on the front door so that you can open it slightly without anyone being able to push straight into the house. Those chains don't keep out someone who's determined to batter the door down, but they do slow down any would-be intruders. You be sure to slot it in place before you open the door, mind.'

He called, 'Just a minute!' because he had to wriggle the second bolt to slide it open. 'Needs oiling,' he muttered.

'I'm hoping the annoyances will die down now we're married.'

'I wouldn't count on it, lass, not when we're dealing with Higgerson. I reckon he wants to get his hands on your father's business and maybe you've been named as his heir in your father's will. Ah! There we go.' He got the front door open.

The woman standing there looked as if she'd positively scrubbed her face. She was of medium height and appeared sturdy. She looked very respectable but had a desperate look that made Frankie immediately guess who she was and want to help her.

'I'm Mrs Pickup's cousin Hilda. She said you were looking for a cook-housekeeper. If so, I'd like to apply.'

'Yes, I am. She told us a little about you. Do come in and we'll have a chat.'

Jericho took a step to the side, holding the door wide open. 'I'll leave you two ladies to talk while I oil these bolts. I brought a few things with me to do some work on the house.'

Frankie led the way into the kitchen, her footsteps echoing on the bare boards. 'Please sit down, Hilda. I'm sorry it's all in such a mess. We only moved in yesterday and the house had been standing empty for years. But we've had both electricity and gas put in, as well as two bathrooms—'

'Two!'

'Yes, one for the servants' and downstairs use. Oh, and the phone will be installed tomorrow.'

She hesitated, not knowing how best to start, then decided on complete honesty. That was the way she'd treated her father's workmen and once they'd got used to her, they'd never let her down or been rude to her. 'Not only is the house in a mess, but I've never had much to do with the day-to-day running of a home or managing the servants, because I work as a cabinetmaker.'

'My cousin told me about that. It must be ever so interesting. My last mistress had some lovely furniture and I used to enjoy polishing it.'

'I love making beautiful things, which is why I'm going to carry on working.'

They stared at one another and she had to smile. 'I don't even know what I should ask you, Hilda. Maybe there's just one real question: can you run a house for an ignorant mistress?'

Hilda relaxed visibly and smiled back. 'Oh, yes. I know my job. And I'd enjoy managing the work my own way. I've never had the chance to do that before.' She glanced round with a frown. 'But I have to be honest: this is a big house for one woman.'

'I realise that. I thought you might need the help of a young girl and a scrubbing woman for a day or two a week, maybe. That should be enough for a start, don't you think?'

When this brought an instant nod and smile, she went on, 'We won't be using all the rooms to begin with, anyway, not even half of them, I should think. As for your work, I won't expect the impossible, I promise you, and you can always tell me if you need more help.'

Hilda's expression lost some of its anxiety. 'I know how to organise others to help with running a house, Mrs Harte. I was housekeeper in all but name at my last place and there was other help kept.'

'Well, let's give it a try for a week or so to see if we suit. I feel we shall, though, don't you?'

The other woman looked surprised at such a direct question then nodded her head slowly. 'Yes, I do, if that's not being impertinent.'

'I don't think it is. Look, I don't even know how to find a girl or a scrubbing woman, let alone interview them. Can you do that for me? You can ask around at the shops. After all, you'll be the one who has to oversee them and their work.'

It seemed to take a few seconds for this to sink in and be believed, then Hilda positively beamed at her. 'Oh, yes. I'll get my cousin to help, because she's lived here all her life and will know the hard-working families. I've been working in Bury since before the Great War when I first started as a maid, so I've lost touch with the people round here even though I grew up in the valley. I'm sure my cousin will love to help, though I'll want to talk to people who apply myself before I decide.'

'Good idea. Now, I'll show you round the house and you can choose your own bedroom in the attics, and one for the girl. But we'll have to go out and buy some furniture for you because the few pieces left up there are mostly broken or worn out. I may be able to repair some of them when I have time.'

'I can manage with very little, ma'am.'

'That'd help to start with, anyway. My husband and I have only a bed, wardrobe and chest of drawers, but we need a couple of chairs as well and probably a tallboy, because one chest of drawers isn't enough. You'll probably need something similar.'

'Anything like that would do me just fine.'

'As for wages, I can only offer twenty-five pounds a year, with full board and keep for the first year. I'm sorry. I know that's low, but we'll try not to give you unnecessary work.'

'It'll do just fine.'

'Good. Now, Jericho and I bought our furniture from Charlie Willcox's second-hand shop. He has some quite good pieces there at reasonable prices, and we can get yours there too. At least half the rooms will remain completely unfurnished for the time being because we don't need them.'

Hilda took another pause to digest that information then asked, 'What sort of food will you want cooking, Mrs Harte? I'm a reasonable plain cook, but I don't know how to make anything fancy.'

'I shan't expect you to feed us at all extravagantly, just plain hearty food, the same meal for us all, and we'll have to eat together at first, because there's only the kitchen table so far. I'd better warn you, my husband has a very good appetite and actually, so do I.'

By the time they'd gone upstairs and poked around in the jumble of old furniture, Frankie had decided she liked Hilda, who seemed to be a sensible person with a wry sense of humour peeping out every now and then at the things they found.

After they'd finished looking at the whole house, she supplied Hilda with pencil and paper, leaving her to go round again and make a list of what furniture would be needed for herself and the girl, apart from the oddments they'd found.

That seemed to astonish Hilda.

'Are you sure you want *me* to do that, ma'am?'

'Certain. And your wages will start from today because you're already helping me.'

Hilda sighed in relief. 'Thank you. You won't regret hiring me, I promise you. Is it all right if I nip into the village to let my cousins know? They'll be worrying about me if I'm gone for the rest of the day. Nelly will pack my things and her husband will bring them round when he gets a quiet moment.'

'Ask them if they can start spreading the word about our need for other help as well. There's a lot of mopping needing doing here.'

'I will. We don't want to leave the empty rooms in a mess, even if we don't furnish them.'

Frankie hid a smile. Hilda was already saying 'we' when talking about the house.

It was a relief to have their main helper organised, and the work would be done by someone who'd know what was needed far better than she would.

There was so much to do to set up a new home in a nearly empty old house and she was looking forward to making it into a real home. But at the same time, she was itching to get back to the little bookcase she had been working on, which Gus, one of the workmen, had retrieved for her secretly, along with some other bits and pieces of her work in progress.

He didn't say how he'd managed that and she didn't ask him.

She'd better ask Jericho if it was all right for her to drive herself and Hilda into Rivenshaw later to look for some things at Charlie's shop. No, on second thoughts she'd ask him to go with them. She'd feel safer and anyway she wanted to spend as much time with him as possible on this special day. He'd be back at work tomorrow and she'd miss him and his cheerful smile.

She was hoping to start work next week herself, sooner if she could get the house organised.

21

Henry Lloyd phoned the mayor the day after the wedding and suggested calling at the town hall early that afternoon 'for a further chat about various problems'.

'Good idea. I was going to call you, actually. Deemer wants to discuss it too.'

'I'd value his opinion. I think we should ask Charlie Willcox to join us as well, since what I want to discuss is partly council business, even if it is unofficial. What do you think?'

'Charlie's a good man to have on side when planning something because he knows so many people. I personally think he understands our town better than anyone and he's well liked, deservedly so. He's helped a lot of people. Even his pawnshops don't squeeze the pennies out of people as much as such places usually do.'

'You're right. But his knowledge goes further than Rivenshaw. I think he understands the whole valley better than anyone I know. Don't forget he lives in Birch End and his sister-in-law Leah lives up at the top end of Ellindale.'

Henry put the phone down, then on impulse picked it up again to call Todd Selby and invite him to join them. He'd forgotten to mention Todd to the mayor but was sure Reg would be happy about him being included. Todd was becoming increasingly involved in the affairs of the town and valley, and had a broader experience of life than most people from travelling round the world for a few years after the end of the Great War.

Henry could understand Todd's need to put a distance between himself and the war. He'd had his own painful experiences and still bore a jagged white scar on one leg to prove it, but his main need afterwards had been to come home to live with his wife, who was such a capable and yet peaceful woman.

He'd devoted himself since then to obtaining justice for people or making sure they did things in a proper legal manner, which he found very satisfying after the chaos and horrors of war.

Todd's scars seemed to be in his mind and still occasionally flared. Henry had noticed the way his friend could look suddenly sad when people talked about the war. Presumably that was when something brought his own experiences back to him.

When he arrived at the town hall, Henry was immediately shown into the mayor's parlour, where he and Deemer were chatting. Before they'd done more than exchange civilities, Charlie Willcox arrived, looking like a friendly but shrewd owl in his round horn-rimmed spectacles.

'I invited Todd to join us as well,' Henry said.

'Good idea,' Charlie said at once.

As soon as Todd had been shown in, Henry got down to business. 'I wanted to discuss law and order in the valley. We need at least one more police constable if we're to keep the peace – and we need him quickly. I'd prefer two more, given how quickly things are going downhill.'

'I've tried a few times to get one,' Deemer said with a sigh.

'So have I,' Reg said at once. 'Unfortunately the area superintendent keeps hedging, saying money is too tight and the need here has not been shown to be urgent enough.'

'Not urgent! The place is deteriorating fast,' Charlie said.

'Then I suggest we all go and see my cousin Albert in Manchester. He can be very useful in a crisis.'

'Do you think your cousin will be willing to help, Henry?'

'I hope so. Albert is well connected politically and I'm sure that at the very least he'll be able to advise us on the best way to tackle this. Besides which, he owns a few properties in or near Rivenshaw, so he's got a personal interest in keeping the valley safe and orderly. He was worrying about it last time I saw him.'

'Very well, we'll try that. Um, on another topic, have you come up with any further information about you know who, Deemer? I can't help worrying about his safety.'

Todd looked from one to the other in puzzlement, so Henry explained quickly that they were avoiding using names whenever they discussed this matter, just in case anyone overheard or deliberately eavesdropped on a random conversation.

'Let's say that more pieces are starting to fit into the jigsaw puzzle but none of it is going to be easy to deal with, given who our chief villain may turn out to be – which is not the one I originally expected it to be.'

'Who else is left?'

'Someone very close to our friend.'

There were a few moments of silence as they all considered the situation, shaking heads sadly.

'That is – shocking,' Todd said.

'What can we actually do about it?' Reg asked. 'We can't leave things as they are.'

The lawyer spread his arms wide in a helpless gesture. 'Not much has changed. If we reveal where he's hiding, his life will be in immediate danger, because he's still rather weak. I'm told it'll take him months to recover and it's possible he may never fully regain his strength. We still have no *proof*.'

'Dr McDevitt has proved that the poison was administered through those lozenges.'

'I'm afraid if we don't reveal where he is soon, his wife

will make a huge fuss, guided by her damned cousin, and unfortunately the law will be on her side. She'll be expecting to see a corpse, I'm sure, and sadly, she won't be satisfied with anything less, whatever it takes to complete the job.'

Charlie sighed. 'I'm very tempted to take the law into our own hands on this matter and have *her* locked away. She is still dangerous to other people, especially her daughter.'

'We haven't got proof,' Deemer said.

'Besides, acting outside the law would be to descend to their level.'

'It's tempting, though, Henry.'

'Yes. It's always tempting to get rid of wickedness the quickest way, but justice must be seen to be done in an open and legal manner.'

'In that case, we need to get our friend moved into a better hiding place, and soon. A man was out and about yesterday in a small car checking nearby Pennine villages, because there are one or two small sanatoriums in quiet upland spots, as you know. He called in at one of them, enquiring for a supposed "uncle".'

'Good heavens! Is there no end to their effrontery?' Reg exclaimed.

'We haven't seen any limits yet, sadly. The question is, where else can we keep our friend safe and yet make sure he gets the medical attention he still needs?'

'I've been wondering—' Henry began.

'Wondering what?'

'Wondering whether I can get us the help we need from a relative of mine. She's a doctor and was widowed a year or so ago. Her husband was a junior partner in *his* uncle's medical practice and expected to inherit, and she worked there too. However, when her husband died, the uncle suddenly showed himself not to be as liberal towards female doctors as he'd claimed. In fact, he told Viv outright that he didn't want her working there without her husband to oversee her work, and he even chucked her out of her house as well – in a civilised way, of course.'

'I don't envy women battling such old-fashioned views,' Todd said. 'What's she doing now?'

'She's moved back to the north and is in lodgings at the moment in Rochdale. She helps out occasionally at a women's clinic run by another female doctor, but she doesn't want to settle there and anyway, she needs to earn a living. That town is not *home* to her and Ellindale is. If we can find somewhere near here for her to stay and look after our friend . . . Only how to do it? She'd be seen coming into the district and our friend would probably be noticed if he was moved, however careful we were.'

Charlie cleared his throat to get their attention. 'I can solve one of the problems, at least. It'd be easy to arrange the necessary transport to take our friend wherever we find a place for her to care for him. My men regularly deliver goods round nearby villages and believe me they're loyal to me. No one would think there was anything out of the ordinary about it if I sent one of my bigger vans out for a couple of days, especially if it came back loaded with furniture for the shop.'

They all brightened.

'Are you sure your relative is to be trusted to do what's needed, though, Henry? And I have to ask it: is she a good enough doctor to care for a man whose health has been almost destroyed? If so why did the uncle not want her to stay on where she was?'

'Viv is more than capable. But there's still a lot of unfounded prejudice against women doctors and the uncle is apparently one of the antediluvian dinosaurs who won't accept them as equals. It took her a while to get over the shock of losing Nigel. They were very happy together and he seemed in good health, then he simply dropped dead one day. Aneurism, they called it. He'd barely turned forty. Such a shock.'

'It happens,' Charlie said sadly. 'My brother didn't make old bones but that was because of getting gassed in the war.' He caught Todd's frown and hastily added, 'I'm not unhappy that Leah has since married you, Todd, but I still feel sad that I lost Jonah so young.'

'Your brother was a good man and a good husband. You must be glad he's left a son behind. I love Jonty as if he were my own child.'

Everyone allowed another few moments for Charlie to blow his nose several times till he'd pulled himself together then Henry brought them back to making plans.

'If Viv agrees to do this, I feel it'd be only fair to offer her help in return afterwards. What she wants most of all is to come back to the valley, work as a GP and as part of her duties open a clinic here, one where poorer women can get free treatment for female problems. She's passionate about birth control and the health of women, who usually come last when treatment is needed, as it's more important to the family for the breadwinner to be kept going.'

'A clinic like that would cause a rumpus,' Charlie said. 'Some folk think birth control is immoral and from what I hear there's no truly safe way to do it.'

Henry shrugged. 'It's still a lot better to have three or four children when you're aiming at only two, than ten or twelve, don't you think? My wife and I agree with Viv about that.'

'Would the council agree to pay for a women's clinic?' Charlie asked doubtfully.

'With Higgerson and his cronies on it? Of course not. He'd not even need to persuade some of the men. They'd do anything to keep women *in their place* as they call it.'

Charlie looked thoughtful. 'Hmm. It'd have to be a private

venture, then. Actually, I'd be more than willing to contribute money towards a new clinic, because it's exactly what the valley needs. You're absolutely certain your cousin would want to stay here if there was one? We're a bit out of the way for many folk. It'd be good to have another doctor we could expect to stay long term.'

'I think Viv would love to make her home here again. When she lived in the south, she used to say she missed the moors. It'd be easier if she'd been left more money but her husband made a few unfortunate investments so she can't afford to buy into a medical practice; in fact she can barely support herself at the moment.'

Charlie shuddered visibly at the idea of losing money in investments. Over the years, he'd made one or two impulsive investments and lost money, and had grown far more cautious as a consequence.

'Very well. If she's agreeable, let's set something up.' Henry pulled out his small personal notebook from his jacket pocket and began to write down the steps they'd need to take.

When they'd discussed, argued and put these into the best order of implementation, the notes were carefully memorised and burned in the heart of the coal fire.

As the lawyer put his silver propelling pencil away, he asked with a smile, 'On a happier note, has anyone seen the love-birds today?'

Charlie grinned. 'One of my delivery men reported seeing them in Birch End earlier on. He said they were smiling at one another as if they'd had a good night, and she was tightly linked up with him and chatting away as they walked along the street. They might have married for her convenience and safety but the signs seem to indicate they get on well.'

The mayor nodded. 'Glad to hear that. Jericho's got a lot of promise as an organiser. Roy has been keeping his eyes open for that sort of worker, given the variety of jobs that will have to be supervised and co-ordinated when he starts building his new houses on that land near Croft Street. He's finishing off a few other small jobs and drawing up plans for the big job at the moment.'

'It'll be good to have some more decent housing in the valley,' Charlie said. 'On a big project like that, selecting your supervisors is important. Roy's son used to fill that role for him.'

'Is Frankie still going to carry on working?

'Try to stop her.'

'Some people won't like that.'

'Especially her mother,' Charlie said. 'That woman is pure poison. She's been able to keep that husband of hers on a very tight leash for most of their marriage because of it being her money that gave him a start as a builder.'

'Perhaps not quite as tight a leash as you think,' Henry said.

'What do you mean?' Reg asked at once.

Henry hesitated. 'This is strictly between the four of us, because of client confidentiality, but in view of the current circumstances, you should be aware that he's managed to provide some money and that house for his daughter. It belongs to her outright, you know. He'd found out that if anything happened to him, that odious woman was preparing to have Frankie declared insane and locked away.'

'No one could do that in this day and age, surely?' Todd exclaimed, shocked to the core.

'It's happened already, I'm afraid, and more than once. I have myself helped release another woman from such medical bondage but unfortunately the doctor who arranged it is still free to run his so-called clinic and do it again – if he's paid highly enough.'

After that, the mayor got out a bottle of sherry and they all had a drink to send them on their way.

Henry was very thoughtful on the way home. He hoped Viv would want to take on the job of caring for Sam Redfern, and that they could get him away safely to somewhere secluded.

22

When Charlie left the town hall and parted company with his fellow conspirators, he met no one and began to feel increasingly nervous to be walking on his own through the rustling darkness of the streets. He jumped in shock as a piece of cardboard bumped up against a wall and blew towards him in a sudden gust of wind.

The streets were poorly illuminated by only an occasional gas lamp, some of which weren't working. He'd have to complain about that officially to get something done. Tonight he had no choice but to continue, walking in and out of the patches of light and darkness because he'd parked his car outside his main pawnshop and needed it to get home.

He was relieved to see a light still shining from the windows of his second-hand furniture shop ahead, which meant it had stayed open later than usual. He decided to stop on the pretence of checking that everything was all right, after which he'd get the shop lad to walk with him for the last stretch, then drive the youngster back here. Two people on foot were less likely to be attacked than one, surely?

He was annoyed with himself for not thinking ahead about getting home from the meeting. It got dark so early at this time of year. Remembering tonight's discussion about safety, he decided he'd have to be more careful about where he went after dark.

As he pushed open the shop door he heard voices coming from the rear and went to see who was still there so late in the evening. He liked to keep an eye on any and every detail of his various businesses so they'd not be surprised to see him.

He found his manager speaking earnestly to Jericho and Frankie. Next to them a middle-aged and rather fierce-looking woman he didn't recognise was holding a crumpled piece of paper in her hand and studying it. There were quite a few items piled to one side as if they'd been chosen to buy. Good. He moved forward to join the group.

His manager had turned at the sound of the doorbell and looked relieved to see that it was him. Now why would Glenn be looking so nervous? The shop had stayed open a little longer than usual but the manager wasn't on his own here, after all.

Charlie raised one hand in greeting. 'Evening, everyone. Don't let me interrupt you.'

He listened in satisfaction as they continued going through what was clearly quite a long list of items being bought but didn't interrupt. He had a theory that if you chose your employees well, you should be able to leave them to get on with their work and so far that theory had been mostly proved right, certainly it had with Glenn. If he hadn't felt so unsafe out on the dark streets tonight, Charlie would have left the newly-weds to get on with their buying spree.

'Is it possible to have everything delivered tonight?' Jericho asked. 'I know it's dark, but it's not all that late. I have to go back to work tomorrow, you see.'

Charlie could see the uncertainty on Glenn's face so intervened. 'Send the lad to fetch Barney Cresley. He'll bring his son and come out at any time of day or night if you pay him a bit extra. And with this number of purchases, we'll be happy to pay that extra for you, Mr Harte.'

'Thank you.'

Glenn nodded. 'Good idea, sir.'

'I'll wait here till the lad gets back from Barney's. My meeting at the town hall lasted longer than I'd expected and I'm not enjoying walking the streets. It's not only dark, but there's a raw wind getting up. You were telling me only the other day, Glenn, that there have been a few handbag snatches and attacks in this area lately once the shops have closed.'

'Where are you going next, Mr Willcox?' Jericho asked.

'Just back to my main shop. My car's parked there, you see.'

'It'll only take me a couple of minutes to drive you across to it. I can wait to see you safely on your way then come back here. You'll be all right, Frankie, won't you? You've got Hilda and Glenn to keep you company.'

'We'll be fine.'

He escorted Charlie out and those inside heard the van start up and drive off.

Frankie was surprised to see Glenn still looking round nervously.

'I think I'll just lock the front door before we continue, Mrs Harte. There were a couple of young louts hanging round yesterday evening. Another shopkeeper and I had to chase them away.'

He walked through the long, narrow shop towards the front door but just before he got there, it burst open and three young men rushed in, one brandishing a knife and the others chunks of wood.

'Where's the till?' the one with the knife yelled.

As Glenn tried to grab a nearby stool to protect himself, the youth slashed his lower arm and drew blood, but Glenn managed to swing the stool between himself and further attacks.

Another intruder yelled, 'The till's back there.' He saw the two women and started towards them with a nasty grin on his face, brandishing his chunk of wood. 'Get out of the way, you stupid bitches, or I'll knock you senseless.'

As he got closer to them, he faltered for a moment, looking surprised that Frankie was so much taller than him. Then he stopped to study her, eyes narrowed. 'I know who you are: Mrs Bloody Harte. I've been telled to watch out for you an' make you regret marrying that stupid sod. Bit of luck that you're here! We'll get the shop money *and* an extra payment afterwards. You should move out of Rivenshaw, you should. You've upset some important people.'

Acting on sheer instinct, Frankie grabbed Hilda's arm and pulled her quickly to the other side of the counter, which housed the till. On the wall behind it were shelves of kitchen equipment and standing in one corner a broom. She grabbed the latter and poked it at the youth as he tried to follow her behind the counter.

He tugged at the end of it and she struggled to keep hold, then he yanked it suddenly out of her hand and grabbed her sleeve. As she fought to stop him mauling her, she saw Hilda snatch an iron frying pan from the nearest shelf and run round the other side of the counter hiding the pan behind her skirt.

She screamed for help, hoping to distract him, and he paused briefly in his attack on her to jeer at Hilda, 'Go on, you stupid bitch! Run away. It's this one I want, not you.'

But as he turned his attention back to Frankie, Hilda pulled the pan quickly from behind her skirt and changed direction. She clonked him good and hard on the side of the head before he had realised what she was doing.

He fell to the ground and though she stood over him, ready to hit him again, he didn't stir.

'I'm not too stupid to catch you out, you rascal,' she muttered, then turned to Frankie. 'Are you all right?'

'Yes. He didn't touch me.'

They stared down at him. 'Have I killed him?'

'No, I can see that he's still breathing.'

They both turned to find out what was happening at the front of the shop. Glenn was struggling with the other two intruders near the front door, which was still open, yelling 'Help! Help! Police! Call the police!' at the top of a very powerful voice. But they could see blood dripping down his arm across one of his hands.

'He needs help!' Frankie exclaimed and had just picked up a rolling pin ready to go to his aid when the shop door burst open and a man rushed in.

'Who's that?' Hilda whispered.

'I don't know. Oh, heavens! Are there more of them? We won't be able to fight off a bigger number.'

The newcomer paused to take a quick look round, then whacked one of the men attacking Glenn with the chunky handle of his walking stick, causing him to yell and drop his knife. The newcomer quickly kicked it to one side and went after the youth again, stick raised.

So the new arrival was on their side, Frankie thought. Thank goodness!

Then Jericho erupted into the shop, followed by another man and she let out a groan of sheer relief. He must have seen what was happening from outside.

Her husband's gaze raked the long narrow room and when he saw her, he yelled, 'Stay back, love!' Grabbing Glenn's other attacker, he yanked him backwards and shoved him against a wall, punching him rapidly with one fist then with the other.

She and Hilda stayed close together keeping an eye on the unconscious man and the fighting at the front alternately. If she was as dishevelled as her maid, she must look a mess, she thought.

At that moment, to her further relief, Deemer appeared in the doorway accompanied by his constable. He stopped dead when he saw the signs of a fight but two of the youths were now being securely held and the third was still lying on the floor near the rear of the shop, groaning.

As he looked at Jericho and the other men, the sergeant gave them a mock bow. 'Well done, lads.'

'You should congratulate the ladies as well,' Glenn said, clutching his arm to try to stop the blood. 'They dealt with the third chap or I'd have been done for. That's this one's knife on the floor over there – with my blood on it.'

'Grievous bodily harm,' the sergeant said with satisfaction. 'That'll take him off the streets for a nice long time.'

'Who the hell are they?' Jericho indicated the two surly young men, now handcuffed. The third one, who still seemed to be dizzy, had been yanked to his feet and was being escorted rather forcibly from the rear of the shop by the constable. 'Do you recognise any of them, sergeant? I don't.'

'No. I'd bet they've been brought in from outside the valley to cause trouble. It wouldn't be the first time that's happened in recent months. We'll lock them away for the night and they'll come up before the magistrate tomorrow morning.' Deemer glared at his prisoners. 'And believe me, they'll be in even deeper trouble if they try to give false names and addresses because I'll check everything out carefully before I let them go. *If* I let them go.'

The two shopkeepers who'd come to Glenn's aid went towards the door. 'We'll arrange for a watch to be kept on the street for the rest of the night, sergeant, and if anyone else tries to cause trouble we'll be ready for them. I'm just in the mood to give someone a pasting. I'm still angry about that other pair of sods who broke one of my big shop windows last week.'

'I've kept my eyes open but there's no sign of them. I'll remember your description, though.'

'Damn them for ruining my expensive window. Only good thing is when they tried to grab some of the goods out of it, they didn't get much because, judging by the blood they left behind, at least one of them had cut himself badly on the broken glass.'

He left the shop, still grumbling to the other shopkeeper.

Jericho turned to his wife. 'Are you sure you're all right, love?'

'Yes. Hilda and I make an excellent fighting team.'

'I shouldn't have left you.'

'How could you have known this would happen? Besides, I can't hide in the house all the time or I'd go nowhere and achieve nothing.' She turned to smile at Hilda. 'Well done!'

The older woman shrugged. 'I can't abide thieves, stealing what good people have worked hard to earn.'

'I feel the same.' Frankie explained to Jericho exactly how her new maid had fought beside her.

He gave an approving nod. 'You've more than earned that job with us by what you did today, Hilda. I wanted someone who'd help protect my wife. Where did you learn to fight? Most women don't have a clue.'

'I learned in the streets where I grew up, in Backshaw Moss. It was learn to fight back or get bashed.' She turned to eye Frankie thoughtfully. 'I'd not have expected a lady to even try to fight them off, let alone give a good account of herself.'

'I was taught to defend myself by old Bill when I was first apprenticed to him, in case anyone tried to treat me badly because of being a woman in a man's job. I had to use those skills a couple of times in the early days, but I never needed them as badly as tonight.'

She turned to her husband. 'Jericho, one of the men said

something that surprised me. I think someone must have described me or pointed me out and let it be known that they'd be given a reward if they could hurt me. It's one disadvantage of being so tall, being easy to recognise.' She repeated the exact words of the threat that had been yelled at her.

'Why would anyone pay others to go after you? What does anyone hope to gain by hurting you?'

Frankie shrugged but sadly it had already occurred to her that her mother must be involved. She didn't realise she'd said that aloud until Jericho and Hilda both looked sharply at her.

'Who else but her would want to harm me?' she asked, trying to sound casual, as if used to it. But it hurt. It always did.

He looked grim for a moment then moved along to Glenn who had another shopkeeper with him still. 'Will you be all right if we leave now?'

'Oh, yes. A few of us will take it in turns to keep watch tonight and every night till things settle down. I'll give Mr Willcox time to reach his home then phone and let him know what's happened. Do you still want us to get your furniture up to Birch End tonight, Mr Harte? Barney and his son can be trusted, I promise you.'

'If you can still arrange it, yes.' He turned as if to leave.

'Give me and Hilda a minute to tidy ourselves up,' Frankie called. 'I don't want to go out looking such a mess and I'm sure she doesn't either.'

Barney turned up a short time later just as they were about to leave, a big bear of a man whose son was equally large. He listened incredulously to what had happened and growled angrily. 'If I catch any of them sods near my home or van, I'll make them sorry. Your furniture will be quite safe with me and my Olly, Mr Harte.'

He gestured to the tall youth standing next to him, who said, 'We'll not let anyone touch it.'

'Thank you.' Jericho turned to his wife. 'Frankie, are you ready now?'

On the way back he stopped at a brightly lit chip shop, buying fish and chips for them all. These were wrapped in a sheet of white greaseproof paper, then thick layers of newspaper to keep them warm.

'Give me those, sir,' Hilda said.

He drove them home as quickly as he could and when they went into the cold house, Hilda said, 'Better to eat the fish and chips off the newspaper, sir, madam, because that'll keep them warmer than a cold plate would.'

She worked quickly, putting a warm parcel at each place and getting the kitchen fire drawing up, all without needing to be told. She'd even managed to find the salt and vinegar to sprinkle over them by the time Frankie had got out some knives and forks and Jericho had got them each a glass of water from the new tap.

'You know, this house already feels like home,' Frankie said happily as she broke off a crunchy piece of fish and batter and popped it in her mouth.

Hilda looked round. 'It'll be a lovely, comfortable house given half a chance. I'm going to enjoy working here and helping you make everything nice. You won't regret hiring me, I promise you.'

'I'm already glad of that! You certainly helped me tonight.'

The two women beamed at one another. After that all three of them concentrated on eating quickly, then getting ready for the delivery of their furniture and household goods.

It was nearly midnight before they got to bed but by then all the bigger pieces of furniture were in place and the smaller items could wait till the next day.

*

Hilda went upstairs thankful that electric light had been installed even up here. She was thrilled to have been given the largest of the attic bedrooms. She got out her flannel nightdress and dressing gown, leaving the rest of her clothes for unpacking and hanging in the newly delivered wardrobe the next day.

Kneeling by her new bed she whispered a quick 'thank you' to the Lord for leading her to this job. She also prayed that her new employers would be kept safe. They would if she had any say in it.

Before getting into bed, she set her alarm clock for six the next morning, wanting to have as much ready for the master to start his day as she could. Then she snuggled down under the new bedding, which included a fluffy warm quilt, feeling happier than she had for several weeks. The bedding smelled of mothballs but she'd put it out to air as soon as there was a fine day.

23

The following morning when Jericho got up, he found Hilda already in the kitchen, with a fire blazing in the range and the table set for breakfast. He was back in his shabby working clothes today.

'I'm sorry, sir, but there are only eggs and toast. Oh, and there's a jar of jam.'

'Toast and jam will be fine.'

Frankie came in, also dressed for the day in a woollen suit with a flared, panelled skirt. She wore it for its practicality but it had been sold to her as suitable for golf wear, which had made her smile. As if she had the time or desire to play golf! The suit top had knitted ribbed cuffs and a waistband, which made it more comfortable to move about in, and she was wearing the flat, lace-up black leather shoes which were her usual footwear.

She looked round, pleasantly surprised. 'You've worked wonders here already, Hilda. I don't know exactly what you've done but it *looks* more like a home.'

'Thank you, ma'am.'

She had the bread and a toasting fork ready, so Frankie said, 'I can toast the bread while you attend to the other things. Even I know how to make toast and I promise I won't burn it.'

As she put a plate of toast on the table a few minutes later, she said, 'Do join us, Hilda.'

'It wouldn't be right.'

'There's nowhere else to eat. You ate with us last night and if you think I'm going to have you stand hungry there while we sit and eat, you can think again.'

'I can wait till later. Last night was different. We had to eat in a hurry.'

'Please join us. I'll feel bad if you don't.'

Face slightly flushed, Hilda got a plate and some cutlery and sat down with them.

Jericho winked at his wife and gave her an approving nod.

Frankie began to spread butter and jam on her toast. 'We'll have to do a lot of shopping today, Hilda. I think we'll need one of your lists.'

'I can attend to stocking up on groceries for you, ma'am.'

'I'd rather you stayed with my wife all day,' Jericho said. 'Whatever she does, wherever she goes, you go with her.'

Frankie couldn't hold back a sigh.

He gave her a stern look. 'You know it makes sense after what that lad said to you last night.'

'Unfortunately, yes.'

He left home just before eight and the two women looked at one another. 'We'd better plan our day, then,' Frankie said.

But before they could make a start, there was a knock on the kitchen door and at a nod from her mistress, Hilda opened it.

Her cousin Nelly was there with a lass standing slightly behind her looking nervous.

Guessing what this meant, she held the door open. 'Come in quickly. We don't want to let all our warm air out.'

'It's Mrs Harte we came to see.'

Hilda gestured to the other side of the room. 'Well, there she is.'

Nelly looked across at Frankie. 'Mrs Harte, you were wanting a girl to help in the house and I knew Renie next door was looking for work so I thought I'd bring her round to see you.'

'Why don't you ask the questions, Hilda, since you'll be the one who has to work with whoever gets the job?'

Standing to one side, Frankie listened as Hilda did this, but when the girl kept hesitating and looking towards cousin Nelly for guidance, she stepped in. 'It's kind of you to bring someone so early, Mrs Pickup, but we've agreed to see another girl later, so to be fair to her we can't give you and Renie a decision yet.'

Was that a look of relief on Hilda's face? she wondered as the maid showed the two visitors out.

'Did you guess I didn't want to give her the job?' Hilda asked the minute she'd closed the door on them.

'I did wonder from the expression on your face. Why was that?'

'I've watched her from the bedroom window, shaking the rugs and pegging the washing out for her mother next door, and she doesn't put her back into her work. You have to give rugs a few really good shakes to get the dust out of them, not just flap them around a couple of times, and the washing was always badly hung. It's daft to put more creases into it and then have to iron them out again. I saw her mother telling her off about that a couple of times, but she still did it the lazy way next time. She didn't seem to learn, somehow, or care if she got it right.'

'Well, I thought she had a rather dull expression on her face, so I agree that I'd rather see other girls, though of course appearances can be deceptive. But I do hope someone else will apply for a job today, or I shall be proved a liar. In the meantime, perhaps we should go to the grocer's and put in a big order.'

'That'll make Mrs Parker's day. Her husband does the deliveries and takes orders from a few houses in the posh end of the village while he's at it, but she's the one who minds the shop, with the help of a lad.'

As an afterthought, she added, 'You'll have to pay them cash, Mrs Harte. They simply can't afford to give credit, even to you, and especially with such a big order.'

'Yes, I understand the money side of daily life and shopping at corner stores because of the people I worked with at my father's workshop.' Frankie held up one hand to stop her interrupting. 'That doesn't mean you shouldn't tell me such things, though, Hilda, just in case there's yet another gap in my domestic knowledge.'

'All right, ma'am.'

The shop's doorbell tinkled loudly as they went in and Mrs Parker moved to stand waiting for them behind the counter, gazing at Frankie hopefully.

Once again, Frankie was aware of her utter ignorance about the practical details of everyday life. She gestured towards Hilda. 'My housekeeper is the one with the long list. What we need is just about everything to fill our empty pantry.'

The woman gulped and tears came into her eyes. 'Everything?' she asked in a faint voice. 'Oh, that's wonderful.'

'If there's something you haven't got but can order in for us, we'll make a second list,' Hilda said. 'Now, we'll start with flour and sugar, shall we?'

It was over an hour before they left the shop, with a promise that Mr Parker would deliver the goods the very minute he returned from his rounds.

At the corner of the street they were accosted by another girl. Hilda frowned at the sight of her and even Frankie recognised the pale frizzy hair and lightly freckled complexion as likely to belong to another Benson.

'I heard you were looking for a girl to help out, Mrs Harte. I'd like to apply.'

It was Hilda who answered, her voice sharp. 'Bensons don't usually apply for that sort of job. Your family usually does other . . . work.'

Frankie gestured to her to be quiet and turned back to the girl. 'Why are you applying for a maid's job?'

'Because I want to get away from my family. I want to be *respectable*.' It came out almost as a wail.

'We'll go home and talk about it there,' she said.

Once they were back at the house she went instinctively into the kitchen. 'Let's discuss this before we make a decision, Hilda.' She gestured to a seat and the girl looked at Hilda before she took it.

'Now, tell me all about yourself.'

'I've been waiting for a job to come up. It's not easy for someone like me even to find one to apply for.'

'Take your time. Try to explain it all to us.'

'My mother died a few weeks ago and I promised her on her deathbed that I'd get away from them. She wasn't born a Benson and she didn't like their dishonesty. Only she didn't find out how bad they were till after she'd married my dad.'

'What does your father think of you going after a job as a maid?'

She shrugged. 'He ran away years ago, but she was stuck here because of my little brother who was sickly. At least the other Bensons looked after us and saw we were fed. They boast that they always look after their own and they do. I'll give them that. Only nothing seemed to help my brother and Danny died, then Ma did too, so I'm on my own now. But no one will give me a chance because I look like a Benson.'

From Hilda's expression she didn't fancy giving the girl a chance either but something about this girl's desperate plea had touched Frankie. She wondered how old she was. Not more than fifteen, she'd guess.

'We'll give you a try out for a week. You'll have to live in.'

Hilda gaped at her, looking as if she wanted to protest.

Frankie turned to her. 'Has no one ever given you a chance you didn't expect, Hilda?'

The maid opened her mouth, shut it again, then said quietly. 'You did.'

Frankie turned back to the girl. 'What's your name?'

'Maria.' She pronounced it the old-fashioned way, *Mar-eye-ah*, Frankie noticed. The girl shivered and she realised the young woman wasn't wearing a coat or shawl. 'Do you need to fetch your clothes?'

'I didn't have much and it was mostly ragged stuff. I was going to alter Ma's clothes for myself but *he* sold them, my father's cousin, I mean. It's his family we'd been living with. Ma might have had a pauper's grave but I went with her to it when no one else would, you see. When I got back to Birch End afterwards, nearly everything had gone from our room except a few of my clothes. I have them here in my bag.' She patted a ragged sacking shopping bag. 'That's all there is.'

'Right then, Maria, we'll have to go down to the pawnshop in Rivenshaw later and buy you a few more things to wear.'

The girl burst into tears and Hilda hushed her, looking helplessly at her mistress over the shaking, sobbing young creature, then patted her shoulder and said, 'Hush now, Maria. We need to get on with our day. There's nothing to cry about. You're getting a try-out.'

The girl hiccupped to a halt and blew her nose in Hilda's clean handkerchief, then said in a husky voice, 'You won't never regret it, I promise you, missus. I'll work my fingers to the bone for you. An' I'll be honest, always, just like Ma wanted. I only ever stole when we was too hungry to bear it.'

'See that you keep your promise,' Hilda said sternly.

Frankie didn't know why, but she felt strongly that this

was the right thing to do. People had helped her in several important ways recently and it seemed only fair for her to help others in return.

'We'd better drive into Rivenshaw for some clothes and then I think Maria might like to have a bath before she starts wearing her new things, don't you, Hilda?'

'Definitely, ma'am.'

After he'd eaten his breakfast Jericho walked across Birch End to Tyler's, eager to start work properly for them. They'd been so good to him about his marriage. He had to trust that his wife would be safe, but felt better about leaving her now that Hilda was there to help.

When he got to the workshop, he met Wilf near the gate and followed him inside the yard.

'I heard what happened at the shop last night,' Wilf said. 'Is Frankie all right?'

'Yes. She's a strong lass and so is Hilda. They gave as good as they got. I reckon people will think twice before attacking either of them again.'

He looked round with a possessive air. 'I'm looking forward to working for the same people, not scrabbling for any old job day in, day out. I like working on building things best of all. You see something for your effort, don't you? Now, where do you want me to start today?'

Wilf chuckled. 'By putting the kettle on and brewing a big pot of tea. Whoever gets here first always does that. Then you can walk round the yard and try to memorise where everything is kept.'

'I've a fair idea of most of that already because I've worked here a few times. Have you figured out where Frankie's working space will be? She's itching to start.'

'I thought she'd be more interested in sorting out her new home for a week or two.'

'Nay, not my Frankie. She might know how to *manage* a house, but she's not got much idea about the jobs involved, let alone doing the sorting out. It's a good thing we've got maids to do that now.'

'Well, we haven't sorted out Frankie's area yet. That's one of the things you and I will start to deal with today. What Tyler's is mainly doing at the moment is finishing planning the details and getting everything set up to start work on the new houses in Birch End. It'll be all go once we begin. I'll show you the plans and we'll go through the lists I've got started, see what you can contribute to them. Then we'll see what else is left to do.'

Jericho looked at him in surprise. He'd expected to be set to work on some physical task, not brought into the planning. Eh, but he was going to enjoy this sort of work even more than he'd expected!

24

When Viv Nelson got back from her walk to and from the town centre of Rochdale, she settled down to have a quiet read. Almost immediately she heard light, uneven footsteps coming slowly up the stairs and knowing who it would be, she put her book down with a sigh and got up. By the time the lame young maid knocked on the door of her bedroom she was there to open it.

'Please, Mrs Nelson—'

'Dr Nelson,' she corrected for what must be the hundredth time.

'Sorry, *Dr* Nelson, only Mrs Smales tells me off if I call you doctor when we're in the kitchen, so I forgot.'

'Did you have a message for me?'

'What? Oh yes, sorry. There was a phone call for you while you were out an' Mrs Smales says the man will be ringing back at four o'clock. If you'll kindly wait in the hall, you can take it an' let us get on with our work.'

'Did she say who it was?'

'Yes, miss. Oh!' She clapped one hand across her mouth. 'I've forgot the name. Did it begin with a T? Or was it a D? No, sorry. It's gone.'

It was no use getting annoyed and she didn't want to get the poor maid into trouble by complaining. The lass was distinctly slow witted but a hard worker and always did her best. Who could do more than that?

Viv listened to her going down the stairs and picked up

the book again. But she couldn't concentrate and kept glancing at the small travel clock she kept on the mantelpiece.

A few minutes before four she got out a notebook and pencil in case she had to take a message and ran lightly down into the hall, where she waited impatiently near the table with the telephone on it. There wasn't a chair, probably because Mrs Smales didn't want her lodgers to linger on the phone.

Sunny days in winter were such a treat, Viv thought, admiring the colours from the stained glass streaming across the tiled floor with its narrow strip of carpet down the middle – carpet with beige and orange flowers on a charcoal background, plonked on linoleum which imitated (badly) black and white checked tiles. The landlady boasted that she'd chosen the carpet because it didn't show the dirt but the clashing patterns of the two floor coverings offended Viv's artistic sense and if she ever got a home of her own again, she'd make sure it was furnished with gentler, toning colours.

She turned back to the telephone, studying that in its turn as she willed it to ring. It was a modern Bakelite one, black again, with the hand piece sitting on top of it, so much easier to use than those wobbly candlestick phones she remembered from a decade ago.

At last it began to ring and she picked it up quickly. 'Dr Nelson here.'

'Viv, it's Henry.'

'Oh, hello. What can I do for you, cousin?'

'It's what I can do for you. Look, could we meet at that place we use sometimes? Don't say its name. Someone may be listening in.'

Her reflection in the hall mirror showed her mouth gaping open in surprise. Well, no wonder. What on earth could be going on for a sensible man like Henry to feel it necessary to be so secretive?

'Yes, of course I can meet you there.'

'I'll see you tomorrow then *à neuf heures*.' He said the last three words very quickly, running them together so that it sounded like annoy-vursss.

Everyone knew that telephone operators sometimes eavesdropped on conversations, but that didn't usually make him slip into French or deliberately mangle words. To her annoyance he put the phone down before she could ask any more questions.

How strange! Why didn't he want anyone to know the time and place of their meeting? She was intrigued.

As she put the phone down, Mrs Smales stuck her head out of the door at the back of the hall that led to the kitchen, which proved *she* had been eavesdropping, so maybe Henry was right to be cautious.

'Not bad news, I hope, Mrs Nelson?'

'No. Just an invitation to visit a friend.'

'A male friend?'

She wished Mrs Smales would stop prying into her lodgers' lives and especially stop trying to match-make for Viv. As soon as a year had passed since Leonard died, people had started introducing her to single or widowed men. Not only Mrs Smales but several older women she was acquainted with seemed determined to find her another husband. As if anyone could replace Leonard.

'No. Just a friend. It's out of town so I'll be leaving here at about eight o'clock tomorrow morning. Could I please have an early breakfast? Doesn't matter what.'

'Yes, of course. I'd be ashamed not to give my lodgers a good hearty breakfast in cold weather like this. I'll be up anyway by then so I'll make you something to line your stomach and keep out the cold.'

'One boiled egg and soldiers then, please. No ham.' She was never really hungry first thing in the morning, but you couldn't persuade Mrs Smales of that so she'd have to force down an egg and a few small pieces of toast to keep the peace.

She went back up to her room, wishing she knew what this was about so that she could wear something appropriate. She looked out at the wintry scene. It was going to be cold again. Something warm and practical would be best. And she'd take her medical bag with her, just in case. She always did because you never knew when it'd come in useful.

She sighed. Sadly Leonard's life insurance policy hadn't brought enough for her to live on comfortably. Well, they'd not expected him to die at forty, had they? Once she'd started getting used to life without a husband, she'd begun trying to find herself another job by looking in the newspapers, especially the *Manchester Guardian* because she'd much prefer to stay in the north.

The trouble was, she'd not only lost her husband but her job and home last year and she missed those happy, busy days dreadfully. Leonard would have been furious at his uncle for treating her like this but there had been nothing she could do about it, since he owned the practice and didn't want her as a partner without his nephew. At least she'd been able to keep their car, which meant she could visit friends and get about more easily.

But it had been ridiculous to continue the expense of renting a large house and hiring a maid when she didn't have a job, so she'd stored her favourite bits and pieces in her cousin Henry's cellar, sold the rest of her furniture and gone into lodgings. Not without a pang or two!

She'd make sure next time she found a job with someone who recognised her as a fellow professional, and didn't consider her an inferior sort of doctor who needed supervising strictly and who could be blamed for everything that went wrong.

Unfortunately she didn't have enough money to buy an established practice of her own and she'd failed to find a job so far.

She wasn't going to stop using her medical skills, not after the struggle it'd been to obtain the necessary training in the first place. Leonard would have been the first to encourage her to persist.

The following morning Viv left before it was fully light and drove through the pale winter dawn to the former farm cottage where her old nurse lived. It was in a tiny village called Pelbank near the Lancashire-Yorkshire border and belonged to Betsey's nephew Oscar, who owned the farm.

He'd installed his old aunt there when she grew too old to work as a nanny to small children and what with her savings and the skimpy old age pension paid by the government, Betsey managed quite well. Her kind nephew kept an eye on her, giving her eggs and ham when he killed a pig, as well as bringing her wood and coal to heat her comfortable little dwelling.

Viv didn't have time to send a postcard asking if it was all right to pay a visit but she knew Betsey would be happy to see her any time. Even if her old nanny was out, a rare occurrence, Viv had been shown where the front-door key was hidden and would simply let herself in and wait. Betsey's nephew would recognise her car and not worry about her presence because she'd met her cousin Henry there a few times in the past year, it being halfway between Rivenshaw and her lodgings.

There was still a touch of frost glittering in the shade here and there when she set out but it was melting fast. The roads themselves weren't icy and anyway, she never drove fast. She'd seen the results of motor-car accidents when she was training to be a doctor in London and didn't want to cause or be involved in one.

To her relief, she saw Betsey come to the window and wave as she drove up, so parked the car and went straight in, giving her old nurse a big hug.

'Well, this is a lovely surprise. What brought you here on such a cold day, Viv dear?'

'Henry phoned me last night and asked if I'd meet him here. I didn't think you'd mind. He wants to keep our meeting secret, so could you please not tell anyone about him calling here today?'

'I won't tell anyone except my nephew. Oscar will need to know, so that he and his wife don't say anything.'

'I'll find him and ask him not to mention it before I leave.'

'Would you like a cup of tea? It won't take a minute to boil the kettle.'

'Let's wait till Henry arrives for that.' She sniffed. 'Do I smell drop scones?'

Betsey smiled. 'You do. How lucky that I've just made a batch. And I've still got some of last year's blackberry jam left.'

'Ooh, lovely.'

Henry was a little late and when she heard a car pull up outside, Viv went to peer out of the window. To her surprise he had stopped the car behind hers, out of sight of anyone passing the end of the lane. He even went and stood near the gates to check that it really was hidden.

There was definitely something wrong.

When they were sitting in Betsey's cosy sitting room, which had more ornaments on its crowded shelves than any other room Viv had seen, Henry sighed and stared across the small occasional table at her.

'I won't beat about the bush. Do you want a temporary

job looking after one rather incapacitated patient? It'll pay well and you'll get your keep too, but you'll probably find it quite boring. I know you're trying to save money.'

'What's wrong with him?'

'This is to go no further.'

'Oh? Why?'

'Someone, probably his wife, has been gradually poisoning him. She nearly succeeded, too, and would have done if it hadn't been for our very astute local doctor. Fortunately for this man, our chap had seen a similar case.'

'Good heavens! Is the doctor quite certain of this?'

'Unfortunately yes.'

'Has the woman been arrested?'

'How do we prove it was her doing? Her cousin is a rather powerful figure in the town so we'd not dare do anything without absolute proof.'

'Where would this job be if I accepted it?'

'I don't know yet. I'll have to find somewhere suitable to rent. Are you interested, then?'

'Yes, very.' She'd be able to save some money.

'Thank goodness. I'll go back and start looking for somewhere to rent, probably in Manchester. The trouble is I have to keep it secret, both that I'm involved and who this is for.'

'Hmm.' She looked thoughtful, then said slowly, 'How about him coming here? I think Betsey would appreciate the rent money, and also enjoy helping me with some light nursing duties. We can rely on her nephew to keep quiet if we warn him of the danger and he even has a telephone. It cost him a fortune to get it installed out here but he's a very modern man and considers it a necessity.'

Henry leaned back, beaming at her. 'Looking after him here is a brilliant idea. Trust you to come up with something quickly. Do you think you could go and ask Betsey about it straight away?'

'Yes, of course. I'll bring her back with me if you don't mind. She may have questions for you.'

She returned shortly afterwards accompanied by an elderly woman in old-fashioned clothing with a longer skirt. She favoured one leg slightly when she moved, as old people with arthritis sometimes did, but looked rosy and in good health otherwise.

Henry explained about his friend and the need for secrecy.

'That's easy,' Betsey said. 'We can pretend I had a fall and Viv is looking after me. If I stop going into the village for a while, they'll believe it, and no one except my nephew need know this man is here. He should probably sleep in the attic, though, completely out of sight, and that means a lot of going up and down the stairs for you, Viv love. I'm not so good at stairs now.'

'I won't mind doing that at all.'

Henry beamed at them both. 'That's such a relief. We'll bring him here tonight after dark, Miss Pinner, if that's not too soon for you.'

'I shall look forward to the company. The only problem is, there isn't any furniture up there, only a few old boxes and books. Can you bring a bed and a chair for him as well as bedding?'

'We'll bring them and whatever else you think necessary. Could you show me the space?'

'You do it, Viv love. You're far more agile than I am.'

When they came back down, Henry went to shake Betsey's hand, keeping hold of it and patting it with his left hand. 'I'm extremely grateful for your help, Miss Pinner. We'll pay you rent and make sure you're not out of pocket, but please remember to keep quiet about your visitor. He's in serious danger and you might be too if whoever tried to kill him came after him.'

He looked at his wristwatch. 'I'll leave straight away if you don't mind and get things started. We'll be back after dark.'

When he'd gone, Viv gave Betsey a hug. 'You're a kind woman. I'll leave now as well to collect my things. I'll just nip across and talk to Oscar before I go.'

'I'll do that. But I'm sure my nephew won't tell anyone.'

As she was putting her outdoor clothes on, Viv frowned and said slowly, 'You know what? I don't think I'll go back to those lodgings after this job ends, so I'll bring everything I own here, if you don't mind. It can go up in the attic as well. My landlady is too nosy and she's driving me mad trying to find me another husband. I don't ever intend to remarry.'

Betsey chuckled. 'Famous last words.'

'I mean it.'

The old woman simply smiled. 'They always do. Anyway, you know you're welcome here any time, love, and we'll both appreciate the chance to earn some extra money.'

Viv smiled as she drove away. Betsey would probably spend the extra money helping people or buying presents for her family. She was such a kind person.

When Henry got back, he called on Charlie and explained what he'd arranged. He asked his friend to arrange for the Cresleys to take some furniture out to the cottage after dark and with it the sick man, stressing that the latter's presence and destination must both be kept secret.

Charlie immediately sent word to Barney that he had a job for him and asked him to call in and discuss it. While they were waiting for him, he and Henry quickly sorted out the basic furnishing necessary for the invalid with his manager's help, adding a box of books and a battered but still working wireless for good measure.

Barney turned up with his son and when the job with its need for secrecy was explained to them, he gave Charlie a long, thoughtful stare. 'Best tell me exactly why this secrecy is necessary, Mr Willcox, then I'll know who to keep an eye out for, now and in the future.'

Charlie returned the thoughtful stare then flourished one hand towards Henry, who revealed the full reasons for all the secrecy.

Barney listened open-mouthed to how Mr Redfern had been treated and when the tale ended, he slapped one meaty fist down hard on a nearby table. 'Well, I'm glad you told me because I'm happy to help that man. He's always been kind to ordinary folk like me. I've heard of a few he's got through bad patches. Shame on whoever did this. Shame on them, I say.'

'Good.' Henry looked towards young Olly then back at his father, a question in his eyes.

'No need to look at my boy like that, Mr Lloyd. He'll keep quiet about it too. I'd trust my son with my life any time.'

'We *are* trusting you both with someone's life.'

'Eh, what is the world coming to? You hear that, Olly lad? Not a word to anyone about this. Lives depend on it.'

His son nodded, his expression as grim and steady as his father's.

Salt of the earth, people like them, Henry thought. And there were a lot more like them in the valley, thank goodness.

'Come round to the back door of Mr Willcox's shop tonight as soon as the streets are quiet and we'll load the furniture, then we'll tell you where exactly to go.'

25

Barney and his son waited till the streets were quiet to drive into Rivenshaw and pick up the furniture. Glenn came out to open the back gate for them, then helped them to load the mound of things piled under cover nearby quickly with as little noise as possible.

'Mr Lloyd will be waiting for you in his car at Twobecks Crossroads and he'll lead the way to your destination.'

As the big van started off, Olly peered behind them then grabbed his father's arm. 'Slow down, Da. I think someone's watching us. There's a car parked further down the lane with no lights on, but I'm sure I saw faces pressed against the windscreen inside it, two people. Look, it's set off after us, still without any lights.'

'Well done for keeping watch.' Barney didn't doubt this information because his son's eyesight was far better than his own. 'I'll stop the car just after we've gone round the next corner. You get out the minute we're out of sight and stay near the fence watching them. If they stop and wait, you'll know for sure they're following us, in which case sneak up on them and poke a few holes in their tyres. That'll fettle 'em.'

He added, 'I'll get out and pretend to fiddle with a tyre but I'll keep the engine running.'

The other vehicle did stop, but Olly was able to puncture both its rear tyres, thanks to his wickedly sharp, oversized penknife. Then someone in the other vehicle must have realised what was happening as the deflated tyres caused the car to sink at the back. As he moved forward and jabbed his knife into one of the front tyres, a man jumped out, trying to grab him.

But the lad had been brought up by a father who knew just about every dirty trick to defend himself, from his own youth in Backshaw Moss. Barney had not only passed on his knowledge to his son, but practised with him until Olly was able to do whatever was needed to defend himself from various types of attack, and do it rapidly. Within seconds the man was doubled up and gasping for breath, clutching his groin, unable to call out.

Olly abandoned the task and ran round the corner to the van, hearing a shout behind him. His father was back in it by then and as soon as his son had jumped in, he set off, moving forward even before Olly had closed the door.

The lad grabbed it and pulled it shut. 'I only got three of their tyres, Dad, then someone jumped out of the van. I managed to kick him where it hurts.' He sniggered. 'Should have seen him roll about.'

'Good lad.'

A few seconds later, he said, 'It's a mercy we don't have our name on the side of our van. They'll not be sure whose it is because there are a few old black Fords like this one in town.'

After that they drove for a while in silence until Olly pointed ahead. 'There's Mr Lloyd's car.'

Barney flashed his headlights on and off, then slowed down to let the other vehicle pull out and take the lead. As they drove off after it across the moors, Olly kept an eye out behind them, and also looked sideways at every farm they passed. But there were no signs of any other watchers.

'I reckon we're clear,' Barney said after a while.

'Aye. But I'll still keep my eyes open, Da.'

'You do that, son.'

Mr Lloyd turned off the road and stopped in front of what looked like a large farmhouse. It had no name sign but through the double doors they could see a nurse walking past and realised it must be the small hospital where Mr Redfern was being looked after.

'I never even knew this place was here,' Barney marvelled. 'Open the rear doors of the van, lad.'

As Mr Lloyd got out and went inside, Olly followed his father's orders. They didn't have long to wait.

When Sam Redfern was carried out on a stretcher, Barney joined his son and both of them muttered in shock at the sight of the patient in the light streaming from the open doors. The man who'd been tall and well muscled last time they saw him was now like a living skeleton, so thin he made only a small bump under the blanket.

But Sam's eyes were as alive as ever and he managed to raise one hand in a feeble gesture of thanks as Barney lifted him off the stretcher and with his son's help laid him down very gently on the mattress wedged in the back of the van. One of the stretcher-bearers passed them a letter 'for the doctor' and an earthenware hot water bottle wrapped in a piece of flannel. They tucked that in under the quilt.

Henry came out of the building and gestured to them to close the van's doors, then whispered to Barney where they'd be heading next and got back into his own car.

After that they drove across the moors through windswept darkness, with clouds covering and uncovering a half moon. Even the farms were dark at this hour of the night.

'Can you see Mr Redfern clearly enough to check that he's not in distress?'

'If I twist round.'

'Then do that and keep your eye on him.'

But though the man on the mattress lay still for most of the time, he continued to breathe steadily enough. There was enough moonlight shining intermittently into the van for Olly to see his chest rising and falling.

'Glad we live in the town,' the lad muttered at one stage.

'I am too,' his father replied. 'You can imagine boggarts chasing after you out here in the quiet of the night, can't you?'

'Boggarts!' Olly chuckled. 'No one uses that word now, Da.'

'I do and other older people do too. My ma used to call them that, or bogey-sams, and frighten me with tales of what the creatures would do to naughty boys. I believed in them when I was little, but it was her slaps I believed in most of all if I stepped out of line when I grew bigger. She wouldn't put up with naughtiness or cheek.'

'Nor you don't, neither, Da.'

'Well, why should I? But you're usually a good lad. Now, let's concentrate.'

His father carried on driving in silence, since neither of them was prone to wasting words.

They followed Mr Lloyd's car across some minor roads and eventually reached a village called Pelbank, and beyond it a small farm on the edge of the moors. There were lights on in a cottage to one side of the farmhouse. Henry turned off the road down a rough track that led only to it and switched off his engine.

Barney muttered, 'This must be it and thank goodness. Can't be good for that poor man to be jolted about. 'Bout an hour we've been driving, I reckon.'

'Yes. About that.'

A woman came out of the cottage and Mr Lloyd, who was

now standing waiting near his car, waved her towards the van. By the time she'd got to the rear of it, Olly had opened the doors for her. She didn't wait for Henry to join them but climbed nimbly into the narrow space containing the mattress to one side of the carefully stacked furniture.

Kneeling beside the sick man, she felt his forehead, took his pulse, then got out again and looked at the tall, strong young chap towering over her. 'Can you carry him into the house on your own or do you need help?'

'I'm fine carrying him, missus. I doubt he weighs as much as some of the furniture we lug about.'

'Doctor, not missus, if you don't mind.'

He looked at her in surprise then his father nudged him and he apologised. 'Sorry, doctor.' His father helped him edge the sick man gently to the edge of the mattress, then he scooped Mr Redfern up, shifting him in his arms to get a good balance. 'I've got him. Lead the way, doctor.'

Olly had to bend his head to go through the front door of the cottage, but apart from that he took his time and made sure not to bump the poor invalid on anything in the hall.

'Can you carry him right up to the attic?' she asked.

'Aye.' He started up the narrow stairs, still taking care not to jar the sick man, while his father and Mr Lloyd watched from the hall.

The doctor gestured to her companion. 'Mr Cresley, this is Miss Pinner, whose home this is – and the one carrying Mr Redfern upstairs is his son Olly.'

'Good strong lad, that one,' the old lady said to Barney and Mr Lloyd. 'Now, it won't take me a minute to brew you all a pot of tea. It's a cold night but I've kept the fire burning and a kettle near it.'

'That'd be good,' Henry said. 'Could we use your privy first, do you think?'

By the time he and Barney came back from this outdoor

amenity, Olly had come down and he followed their example. As he came back into the house he brightened at the sight of a pot of tea and a plate of scones set out temptingly on the kitchen table.

'We have to be quick,' Henry told his two helpers. 'We need to get back to Rivenshaw before dawn.'

'We'll do that easy, Mr Lloyd.'

The three men concentrated on their food, but turned as footsteps came down the stairs and the doctor appeared. 'He's fallen asleep quite peacefully. I don't think the outing has harmed him.'

Henry turned to Barney. 'If you two have finished now, I'll just have a word with the doctor, then I'll follow you back to Ellindale.'

As the two Cresleys went outside Viv said, 'Mr Redfern must have been a strong man to have survived if he's been dosed with what we guessed.'

'He used to be physically strong.'

'Well, we'll see what good food and nursing will do for him. I reckon, from the notes Dr McDevitt sent, that there's a fair chance of him recovering and I'll certainly do my best for him.'

Henry left the cottage feeling sad about how weak his client and friend now was, and even more determined to stop that horrible woman from hurting her daughter. As for Mrs Redfern and Higgerson getting hold of the business and money, he'd not let them do that. Higgerson's lawyer was still pressing for the business to be given to Higgerson to look after and Mr Redfern to be returned to his wife's care.

Over his dead body!

Unfortunately, he wouldn't dare tell Frankie anything about her father even though he knew she was fretting about him, not until Sam Redfern was well enough to speak to Deemer and a magistrate anyway.

He just hoped he'd get home this morning without being seen. He yawned. He was going to be tired today, but at least he'd got Sam away safely.

Although he only managed three hours' sleep, Henry got up early and as planned prepared to travel into Manchester with Reg and Sergeant Deemer to consult his cousin Albert.

His wife looked at him in concern as he ate breakfast. 'You're running yourself ragged about this, my dear.'

He shrugged. 'Sometimes things need doing and who else will take a stand if I don't? I'll go to bed early tonight. Besides, Sam is a friend as well as a client. If you'd seen him, you'd not have recognised him.'

He and Reg set off early, using side streets and picking up Sergeant Deemer from the lane at the back of the police station on their way through the town.

The sergeant slid down in the seat, keeping out of sight until they'd left the built-up area and were into the countryside again. They planned to drive into the city rather than taking the train, not wanting to meet anyone they knew on the way.

They visited Albert in his office, leaving the car further down the street and entering the building by a rear entrance. The door was opened without a word by his secretary, a middle-aged lady who had her hair cut short and was dressed more like a man than a woman, even to wearing a tie.

She locked the door behind them and led them to Albert's luxurious office, where he joined them almost immediately.

'I'm afraid I have to be quick about this,' he said.

'I'll summarise for you,' Henry said.

Albert listened intently to a summary of what had been going on in the Ellin Valley recently. He frowned, asking the occasional question and taking notes. A couple of times he tapped his fingers on his desk before writing, as if it helped his concentration.

'Anyway, that's the main outline.' Henry waited for Albert to speak.

'Frankly, my friends, I can't see why the authorities haven't already brought in another constable. They might complain about having to open extra soup kitchens, but they don't usually stint on law and order. I find it rather . . . puzzling. Leave it with me and try to get home without it being known you've been talking to me.'

He stood up. 'I have another appointment shortly and I don't want anyone to see you, so I apologise for not offering you refreshments.'

'But you'll do something?' Henry pressed.

Albert nodded. 'Oh, yes. You can count on that. I'll phone you when I've looked into a couple of matters.' He hesitated, before adding, 'I'd advise you to consult a higher authority about your client, not the local justices of the peace. Why don't we try to involve Judge Peters. He's making a name for himself and I doubt anyone would question what he decreed – nor would he allow them to compromise law and order.'

'If you could have a word with him?'

'Certainly, but I'll need to give him your client's address.'

Henry hesitated. 'You'll keep it to yourself.'

'Of course I will.'

Henry gave it to him, also the name of the doctor caring for Redfern.

'My clerk will phone you once I've spoken to Judge Peters. Now, I really must get on with my day.'

'Do you think we did any good?' Reg asked on the way back.

'I hope so. Albert usually does as he promises. What do you think, Deemer?'

'I'll wait to see what happens. I've had my hopes raised before. But your cousin didn't seem to be all that surprised about the situation, so he probably suspects there's some fiddling going on behind the scenes at upper levels of authority in the county. I've been suspecting the same thing for a while.'

'Well, no one will be able to pull the wool over Albert's eyes if he decides to investigate. He's a sharp chappie, my cousin. Shrewd in other ways too. Has built on his family's money, even in times like these.'

Viv was a light sleeper and since she'd left the bedroom doors open, a faint sound in the attic had her sitting up in bed to listen intently. Yes, that was the bed creaking, so he was moving about. She went up to see how her patient was faring and found him trying to get out of bed.

'I need . . . to relieve myself,' he said in a voice scarcely above a whisper.

'Let me help you.'

He shrank back.

'Don't think of me as a woman. I'm a doctor and I've been hired to care for you. I promise you, nothing that a human being needs to do will offend me.'

She pulled a chamber pot from under the bed and when he'd finished, helped him to get comfortable again. 'It'll be best for you to try to drink as much as you can. I can make you some cocoa for a start. And Betsey, whose cottage this is, has made some broth which I'm going to have for my lunch as well as you, it's so delicious.'

He gave her a faint smile. 'Do my best . . . to force it down.'

'I'll bring you small servings every two hours or so. Easier on the stomach. Now, just let me listen to your heart and chest. If it's any comfort, you must have a strong constitution to have survived so far.'

When she'd finished, he asked, 'How's my daughter? Is she . . . still with her mother?'

'No. She kept her promise to you and got married. She and her husband are living in the house I'm told you bought for her.'

'Ah, good. Who did she marry?'

'Jericho Harte. Your lawyer speaks well of him.'

Sam sagged back on his pillow. 'Thank goodness.'

'Henry was one of those who brought you here and he's hopeful that no one knows where you are now.'

'Where am I?'

'At a farm on the edge of the moors near a tiny village called Pelbank.'

'Never heard of it.'

When she came up with the cocoa, he was asleep, but she woke him up and persuaded him to take a few mouthfuls of the milky drink, before letting him close his eyes again.

She'd wake him in a couple of hours and wash his hands and face as well as giving him some soup. He'd feel fresher and that'd do him good. And patients often seemed to relish the saltiness of soup after they'd been without food because of illness. At the moment, little and often was the watchword, with nourishing liquids and soft food the best, indeed the *only* medicine for him.

As the great Greek physician Hippocrates was supposed to have said: *Let food be thy medicine, and thy medicine be food.*

There was a lot of truth in that. She had seen for herself how those who had been poorly fed suffered compared to those who ate well. What doctor had not? Especially during the last decade or so.

She was thoughtful as she went downstairs. All she could do really was trust Mr Redfern's own body and support its powers with good food. And try to keep up his spirits by being cheerful. If Betsey still had those children's games and a pack of cards, she'd have him playing Ludo and Halma, and even Snap.

When he woke again, Sam didn't know where he was but he saw the woman dozing in a chair next to his bed and something about her reassured him. Ah, yes, he remembered now. She'd said she was a doctor. She was certainly at ease with a person's body.

As he looked, she opened her eyes as if instinctively waking when he stirred.

She smiled and it was such a warm, genuine smile he found himself smiling back.

For the first time he felt he had a real chance of recovering, and after that he would take charge of his life again. This time he'd deal properly with his wife who was, he feared, losing her mind. She'd never been a stable sort of person. Her family had fooled him about her and he'd paid dearly for marrying her. The money didn't make up for the fact that she'd been a poor wife and mother, as well as a liar and cheat.

At the moment, though, he was dependent on others and must concentrate on recovering.

The doctor fed him some soup, praising him for eating a pitiful few spoonfuls. She fluffed up the pillow and seemed to have the ability to make it seem softer. Though the attic wasn't warm, it wasn't cold either.

He caught hold of her hand for a moment, wanting to touch her before he snuggled down. When he glanced up she was smiling down at him again, not attempting to pull away.

'It helps sometimes,' she said.

'What does?'

'Touching someone. Doctors and nurses recognise that some of us have the healing touch more than others.'

'And you're one of them?'

'My late husband used to say I was.' She blinked tears from her eyes.

'Did you lose him recently?'

'It's over a year now but I still turn because I think he's come into a room. Foolish, isn't it?'

'No, normal if you were happy together. I . . . did not have that privilege.'

Sam enjoyed watching her tidy the attic. She had a gentle face and made him feel better just by being there. What would his life have been like if he'd married someone like her? A lot easier. Definitely. But then he wouldn't have his Frankie and his daughter meant the world to him.

He caught her eye again. 'May I ask what your first name is?'

'Viv.'

'Suits you. You know what? I really like you,' he said. At least he thought he said it. But sleepiness kept overtaking him suddenly.

26

Frankie spent two days sorting out the house – or rather, letting Hilda organise things and mostly doing and buying what the older woman suggested. The lass they'd taken on as junior helper was painfully eager to please them and yet woefully unskilled about the actual tasks involved in housekeeping.

'Can you manage to train Maria, do you think, Hilda?' Frankie asked quietly on the afternoon of the second day.

'Oh, yes. She doesn't need telling twice about anything, but no one has ever taught her to care for a house, that's for sure.'

'Even I've noticed that. Well, I'm a bit the same about what's involved in actually *doing* the jobs, aren't I?'

Hilda smiled. 'And like her, you're learning quickly, ma'am, if you don't mind me saying so.'

Frankie chuckled.

'I'm also teaching her to keep herself clean, which is a lot easier with a bathroom that we're free to use. I'm so grateful for that. It's not usually allowed.'

Frankie wasn't surprised at how heartfelt she sounded. It had soon become clear that Hilda was a firm believer in cleanliness being next to godliness in everything.

'The only thing that worries me is her being a Benson. There are a lot of that family living in Backshaw Moss, and that's too close for comfort. I grew up there but managed to get a job elsewhere. I was amazed when I came back to see the building where my parents used to rent two rooms still standing. Most of the streets hardly look to have changed much at all.'

'My father used to say it was a wonder some of those houses hadn't simply fallen down. Perhaps they've been holding one another up.'

'I saw that a couple of places at the end of Primrose Lane have gone but Daisy Street looks as bad as ever, and smells worse.'

'Since Backshaw Moss is close to Birch End, the better-off incomers of the new houses seem to be growing increasingly concerned about the sewers. Some have complained to the council but still nothing gets done, apart from a quick clear-out of the problem section.'

She sighed and added, 'My father used to worry more about the possibility of those houses catching fire. He said it'd spread rapidly and people on the top floors might have trouble getting out to safety. It'd take a while for the fire brigade to get there from Rivenshaw, too.'

'If they even bothered to come,' Hilda said.

'Yes. He wondered why none of the landlords had made any provisions for dealing with house fires, not even to install metal fire escapes, which don't cost a fortune. But there are only a few landlords because most of them own several buildings.'

'Some people seem able to get away with anything.'

'Friends in useful places, my father always said. We all know who owns the most slum dwellings in Backshaw Moss. We seem to run into Higgerson at every turn of our lives.'

They both fell silent for a few moments, then Hilda said, 'Will the Benson family let our Maria go her own way from now on, do you think, or will they try to use her to get information about you and what you're doing for your mother or Higgerson? I'll try to keep my eye on that side of things but I can't promise to do it all the time because I'll have to send her out to the shops for this and that. It's part of her job.'

Frankie thought about that for a minute or so then said quietly, 'I think she was telling the truth about wanting to be respectable. Tell her to let you know if they try to bully her.'

'I will. She won't do anything against you willingly, of that I'm sure. How did you know to believe her that first day, ma'am?'

'Instinct, I suppose. I've met people from all sorts of backgrounds through my work, far more than so-called *ladies* usually encounter. And I've watched my father deal with people at work. He's a good judge of people. It was only my mother he couldn't cope with. She seemed to kill his spirit the minute he walked into the house.' She blinked her eyes furiously at the thought of him.

Hilda's voice grew softer as she asked, 'No word of him yet?'

'No. He seems to have vanished off the face of the earth. I have to trust Mr Lloyd. If anyone knows where Dad is, it'll be him. Look, will you be all right if I go into the yard this afternoon? I'm itching to sort out my tools and get things ready to start work properly next week. Jericho says they've found me a corner all to myself, with a nice big workbench and two windows bringing light to it. He says the other chaps seem to be decent sorts so I hope they'll give me a chance to prove myself capable.'

'As long as I walk there with you. Mr Harte said you were not to go anywhere on your own, remember? If I accompany you there, one of them can escort you home.'

'Oh, very well. Though it's only a short walk away.'

But as they set off Frankie saw the door of Number Six open slightly and that reminded her that she was still being watched. The temptation to disobey Jericho and walk about more freely in Birch End died.

Outside the front door she stopped to ask, 'You did tell Maria not to answer the door to anyone?'

'Of course. But I'll be coming straight back afterwards. There are all sorts of little jobs I'm itching to do around the house.'

'I can see already that you're very good at managing the housework.'

Hilda blinked as if surprised and blushed, clearly not used to receiving compliments, but judging by her smile, she was pleased by it.

That same day Ethel Tyler surprised her husband by coming to find him at work and taking him aside. 'Roy, love, I'm going home for a couple of hours later this morning.'

'Oh? Something wrong?'

'No, but Dr McDevitt is coming to check on Robbie and I want to be there. I think he'll be pleased at the progress that baby is making now he's being properly fed.'

'You're happy with the wet nurse?'

'Very happy. Poor Freda is still tearful about losing her own baby, as is only to be expected, but she's growing fond of Robbie. There's something about a helpless baby that touches people's hearts, normal people's anyway.' She paused. 'There's another thing I want to arrange if you agree. I—'

Surprised at her hesitation, Roy looked at her. 'What?'

'I want to adopt him officially.' She caught her breath, flattening one hand against her throat and staring at him anxiously.

She was desperate for this, he realised suddenly. But why hadn't she raised it at home? 'Don't you think we're too old to raise another child, my dear?'

'No. I love him already, Roy. I can't tell you how much. When I feel his tiny fingers clinging to one of mine, my heart melts.'

'But what if we died? We're over fifty now.'

'We can make legal arrangements for his care in case something happens to us, but we're both sturdy and come from long-lived families.'

'If his mother was right, he's the son of—'

She pressed her hand across his mouth. 'Shh! Don't ever mention that name again. I mean it, *never, ever* say it to anyone!'

He studied her face. He knew that determined look. She'd not change her mind about this adoption and actually, the more he thought about it, the more he liked the idea, too. He had some wonderful memories from when his son was a child, teaching Trevor to use a cricket bat, taking him for walks in the countryside, pointing out the little animals, telling him the names of wildflowers. And as his son grew older, they'd chatted and he'd enjoyed seeing the world through a child's eyes.

'All right, on condition that we tell Henry about it when we arrange the adoption. I insist on that, love. He needs to know in case that man finds out and Robbie needs protecting from him.'

Tears came into her eyes. 'You'll do it, then, Roy love, take him for our own? Adopt him properly?'

'Yes. I'd do just about anything to keep you happy. Really happy, I mean. I hadn't considered it but I think I'd like to raise another child, too.'

She began mopping tears, but couldn't seem to stop crying until he put his arms round her and held her close. When she'd managed to pull herself together she grew practical again. 'You realise this means I'll not be able to spend as much time at the yard, Roy.'

'What? Oh, yes. I suppose so. I'm going to miss your company here as well as your efficient help.'

'I'll still want to *supervise* the business side. I enjoy doing it, so I shall come in part of the time. And if Jericho works out as you think, we may teach him about managing the daily office tasks for me. It would fit in well with what he'll be doing anyway.'

'Don't mention that to him yet, Ethel love. We have to see how he deals with more responsibility first.'

She smiled. 'When have you ever been wrong about a man's potential? Look how you spotted Wilf and how well he's turning out.'

'Nonetheless, let's give Jericho time to settle in and, I hope, time to sort out Frankie's problems.'

Her smile faded. 'You've not heard any whisper about her father?'

'Not a word. I've heard several people wondering where he went, but he seems to have vanished off the face of the earth.'

'Do you think he's dead?'

'No. Dr McDevitt would never have tried to hide that and Mrs Redfern would have trumpeted it all over town and claimed the business for herself if she'd been widowed. Henry told me she'd be the one to inherit. But he's not even letting her into the workshop. He's just closed it up and installed new locks. I did hear that she's hunting high and low for her husband, though.'

'How strange that situation is.'

'I'd bet my life that Henry knows where Sam Redfern is.'

'I hope you're right.'

He nodded confidently. 'I'm sure I am.'

Later that morning Roy watched Ethel leave the yard, seeing the eagerness in her face and the happiness radiating from her. She'd kept her grief about losing their grown son firmly under control during the past year, had managed far better than he had in the early days. Now, in the short time since the baby had come to them, she was looking so much happier he had to wonder how much it had cost her to support him in his own grief.

She was the best wife any man could ever have, the very best. And better at running a business than most of the men in town.

He only prayed that little Robbie would grow up into a decent chap. His mother had been an honest woman and a good worker, but his father – well, the less said about *him*, the better. Any man who forced himself on a woman was the lowest of scoundrels, Roy believed. It was a poor lookout when decent females couldn't walk the streets in safety.

From what he'd heard, it wasn't the first time Higgerson had done that sort of thing, but somehow the fellow had always escaped legal retribution. He always did.

If Mrs Redfern crossed him, she'd be in trouble too, cousin or not. His loyalties only coincided with his self-interest.

Ethel enjoyed driving her own car around but today she was lost in thought, only too aware of the problems little Robbie's parentage might bring them if his real father found out about him. Everyone knew Higgerson wasn't happy with the two sons his wife had borne. One was in his final year at boarding school and though he came home for the holidays, was hardly ever seen out and about. The older son seemed to have vanished completely and was never mentioned by his family.

No, there was nothing to worry about. How would that horrible man find out about the baby being his son? Only she, Roy, and Henry would ever know. She didn't even intend to tell the child. And anyway, if they adopted and raised

Robbie, they'd be the ones who helped form his character. She'd make sure he knew right from wrong.

Just before she turned into their drive, she saw Tam Crawford's car in the distance, going down the hill towards Rivenshaw, and another idea came to her, a more cheerful one this time.

Tam's adopted daughter was a strange lass, rather abrupt and literal in her way of dealing with the world, but she hadn't an ounce of harm in her. Jinna was a skilled artist who earned good money drawing family portraits, especially those of children. Vi, who managed the larger of Charlie Willcox's pawnshops, had shown Ethel the drawing she'd commissioned from Jinna of her nieces and nephews. She'd shown everyone, actually, she was so proud of it, and it was lovely.

It'd be nice to have a portrait of the baby as he was now, right at the beginning, and perhaps other pictures later on. There was something a good artist could catch, almost the soul of the person perhaps, that a camera did less often. And everyone said Jinna had a particular skill for drawing children.

Ethel decided to drive up to Ellindale, perhaps tomorrow, and stop at Skeggs Hill Farm to ask if the lass could do a drawing of Robbie. The very idea of that made her smile. She'd been so much happier in the short time since the dear little baby came into her life, admitted to herself that she'd needed another child to love. She wished she'd been able to bear other children, but her body had let her down in that regard and the doctor had told her there was nothing you could do about cases like hers.

She pulled into her drive and pushed those thoughts away. Only a couple of minutes later, as she was standing by the nursery window cuddling the baby, she saw the doctor's car pull up behind hers in front of the house.

First things first, she told herself and kissed the baby's

cheek. Let's make sure you're all right, my little love, then we'll build a life for you – and with you.

She sent Freda down to bring Dr McDevitt up to the nursery and stared down at the child. 'I think I'd rather call you Robert than Robbie. Do you mind?' She chuckled as he let out a loud burp of approval.

The doctor stopped in the doorway to smile at the sight of the baby sleeping peacefully in its rescuer's arms. 'He's looking a lot rosier, which is a good sign. I'd not have thought he could recover so quickly. He must have a strong constitution. Did the mother tell you who fathered him before she died?'

'That's not important. As far as I'm concerned, my Roy is the father and I'm the mother from now on.'

He looked startled. 'You're going to adopt him?'

'Yes. Why not? We've lost one son and I've never been able to have other children, and I'm too old now, but neither of us feels too old to bring up a child. We shall pray that we keep this one alive into full manhood and that he has children of his own.'

'Well, well. Robbie is a lucky little boy. Mind you, I think it'll be good for you both. You've had a hard year or two.'

'It'll make me very happy to have a son again. We're going to call him Robert from now on, though. It's always been one of my favourite names, and it was my grandfather's name. Robert Tyler. It sounds good, doesn't it?'

'Yes, it does. Robert it is. I'll pop in to check him again in a few days, unless you're worried about anything, in which case don't hesitate to send for me.'

'I won't hesitate, believe me. Thank you.'

As the doctor began to pack things in his bag again, Ethel turned to Freda. 'Remember from now on to call him Robert.'

'Yes, Mrs Tyler. Robert.' Tears filled her eyes.

'What's wrong, dear?'

She let out a hiccupping sob. 'I'd called my son Robert too.'

Ethel patted her shoulder. 'That's good then, isn't it? You've been given a second chance to look after a lad called Robert.'

'But what'll I do when this one doesn't need a wet nurse? You know I don't have a husband to go back to.'

'If you like, you can become our nursery maid and look after Robert and his clothes for many years to come. And if we continue to jog along happily together, you can stay on here as a general maid even after he grows up. Did you think I'd throw you out, Freda, when you've helped us as no one else could have done?'

She freed one arm from the child for a minute to give the poor grieving lass a quick hug. 'Wipe your eyes now and stop blubbing all over him. We want him brought up in a peaceful, happy atmosphere.'

'Yes, Mrs Tyler. And thank you. I'll always do my best, I promise you.'

'No one can do more. Now, take little Robert from me and I'll show the doctor out.'

Outside the bedroom, he stopped to say, 'That was kindly said.'

'I know what it's like to lose a son. She'll be all right with me from now on.'

'You look after a lot of people in a quiet way.'

'Well, let's keep that quiet, eh?'

Downstairs Dr McDevitt stopped again before she could open the front door and said abruptly and in a low voice, 'I have to speak. I hope you're not heading for trouble.'

'What do you mean?'

He hesitated, then said, 'That child resembles another person in this town, something in the way his hair grows in a double crown at the back and the set of his ears. I'm good at noticing resemblances. I've seen photos in his wife's room and that person's other sons had the same look as this child. You can't mistake it. Well, I can't.'

She stared at him in shock. 'Please don't say anything about that to other people. We don't intend to mention it.'

'I won't say a word, for the child's sake as well as yours. It's only conjecture, after all. But what if he looks like his father when he grows up?'

'We'll deal with it if it happens.'

She watched him get into his car then shut the door. There was no fooling this perceptive man when it came to people. He seemed to notice every detail of someone's appearance in one sweep of the eyes, as well as seeing signs of what was wrong with them.

She tried to dismiss what he'd said, telling herself it might never happen. Only, what if it did? What if Robert grew up to resemble his father? Dear Lord, she hoped he wouldn't. Anyway, if they were lucky, Higgerson might be dead by then.

For now, she would continue as she'd planned and see Jinna tomorrow. No, why wait until tomorrow? There would be time to see about having a drawing done this very afternoon. Ellindale was only a couple of miles away. Tam would probably be home by then. He did a little buying and selling at the market and to private buyers, but he also spent a lot of time with his family and he managed Jinna's surprising success as an artist.

She phoned the little general store in Ellindale and asked its owner to get a message to Tam at Skeggs Hill Farm, and ask him if he would come and see her this afternoon and bring Jinna. 'Tell Tam to give the messenger threepence and I'll pay him for it when he comes here.'

Then she waited for him to phone her back. To her relief, he did that half an hour later and agreed to come and see her.

'About a drawing is it, since you've asked for Jinna?'

'Yes.'

'That little baby you've taken in?'

'Yes. You were quick to work that out.'

'Well, Jinna often gets asked for drawings of children and when I heard you'd just taken in a baby, I wondered if you'd want his likeness doing. She's very good at it.'

When she put the phone down, Ethel was smiling grimly. How the latest gossip got round so quickly, she could never figure out. It was as if the wind wafted news up and down the valley.

She went back to give the baby another cuddle or two. It'd work out. She'd *make* it work out. Whatever it took. And the wind wasn't wafting a certain part of her news about.

No, Robert would be safe with them.

When he arrived in Birch End that afternoon, Tam sat in his car studying the Tylers' house. Nice place, but he preferred to live further up the hill in Ellindale, and his farm had views over the moors from nearly every window. That filled him with a sense of freedom and he loved the moors in their every mood.

He got out and headed for the door with his adopted daughter. He knew Mrs Tyler and her husband to say hello to but had never met them socially, let alone visited them at their home.

'This is a nice house.' Jinna followed him to the front door, then stamped her feet up and down to keep them warm.

'Yes, it is.' He knocked on the door and waited, surprised when Mrs Tyler answered it herself.

'Do come in, Mr Crawford, Jinna. Let me take your coats and hats.'

She led the way into a room towards the rear of the house that was part sitting room and part office.

When she gestured to a chair, he sat down. Jinna had gone across to the window where some pretty glass ornaments were set out to catch the light and was twisting them to and fro.

Tam watched indulgently. Although she was in her teens, she didn't seem to be nearing adulthood in some ways. Her late mother had mostly kept her shut in their rented room in Backshaw Moss because she was different from other children. But he liked Jinna's differences, especially her utter honesty about everything she faced in the world. He didn't think she knew how to tell a lie. Which suited him down to the ground. He loathed cheats.

He listened carefully to Mrs Tyler, surprised that she was going to adopt the baby.

'What do you think, Mr Crawford? Would Jinna do me a picture of little Robert as he is now?'

Jinna looked up at the sound of her name. 'I like drawing babies. Can I see him?'

'Yes, of course.' Mrs Tyler rang the bell and a maid answered. 'Could you please ask Freda to bring Robert down to me? And then ask Cook to send us some refreshments.'

They waited and after a while, the sound of footsteps and a baby gurgling happily came from the hall. That heralded the arrival of Master Robert, so pink and rosy in his new clothes that Tam smiled involuntarily.

Jinna got up and went across, holding her arms out to take him.

Freda looked at her mistress for permission and Ethel waved one hand. 'Give him to Jinna, she's used to babies, then go and have a cup of tea with Cook. I'll keep an eye on him.'

'Thank you, ma'am.'

'He's going to be bonny when he's put on some weight,' Jinna said. 'Has he been going hungry?'

'His poor mother found it hard to get food for them.'

'Was that why she died?'

'Yes.'

'He's lucky you've helped him, then. I went hungry a lot till my mother died and Tam took me in. I don't go hungry now and I've got a savings book with money in it if I want to buy something because people pay me to draw their children.'

'That's what I want you to do. And I'd particularly like a picture of Robert just as he is now, looking a bit hungry, so that I'll remember him clearly.'

Jinna looked across at her, frowning slightly, and Tam took it upon himself to explain, to make sure everything was clear. 'Mr and Mrs Tyler are going to make him their son, like I made you my daughter.'

The look the girl gave Tam was full of love. 'Then he's lucky like I've been. I can still see the hunger on his face, so that's how I'll draw him.'

Jinna stared down at the baby for a moment and he seemed to stare back at her, then he panted and began to wave his hands about. She tickled him gently under the chin and looked across at Mrs Tyler. 'I could come here tomorrow, play with him for a bit, then draw him.'

'You can trust her with him absolutely,' Tam said. 'She loves babies and small children, and they seem to love her in return. I could bring her to see him tomorrow afternoon, if that's all right, then come back for her later.'

'Perfect. I may not be here, but it's Robert you'll really need to see.'

Ethel fed him a cup of tea and he ate three little cakes while Jinna shook her head at the refreshments and continued to play with the baby.

When Ethel showed Tam and his adopted daughter out, she felt well satisfied with what they'd arranged, and with Jinna too.

She gave Robert back into Freda's care, plonking a final kiss on each of his soft pink cheeks, then went back to work at the yard. After telling Roy what she'd done, she got on with the paperwork in her office.

Later on, Ethel smiled as she walked round the workshop, stopping to watch Frankie, who was wearing a dark pinafore with paint stains in one bottom corner over what were clearly her working clothes. She was so busy arranging her tools and materials that she didn't notice Ethel stopping nearby.

One of the foremen was helping Frankie put shelves up on the wall behind the workbench, and they seemed to be discussing something about how they should fit it. The friendly look on Gus's face augured well for the others accepting a woman in the workshop.

Fate had been kind to her and Roy lately, Ethel decided. It had brought them a child and their business was starting to flourish again.

She hoped it would be just as kind to Frankie and her new husband.

27

Henry looked up in surprise as the door of his office burst open and his chief clerk came stumbling in, looking outraged and yelling, 'Stop that!'

What on earth was going on?

The clerk was closely followed by Higgerson, who gave him a shove to get him out of the way, and moved quickly past him and across to the very edge of Henry's desk. He planted both hands on it and gave one of his wolfish smiles. 'So sorry but I didn't want to risk being denied the opportunity to speak to you so I came straight through.'

It was rare that words failed Henry, but this was utterly outrageous. 'Look, you—'

'Just a minute.' Higgerson turned and gestured to someone still standing outside to join him.

Colin Jeffers came in and hovered just inside the door, looking embarrassed. He was a lawyer like Henry, fairly new to the town and seeming to deal mainly with the affairs of Higgerson and a few lesser landlords who also specialised in slum properties. Henry hadn't liked the looks of him when first introduced, so only accorded him a nod if he passed him in the street. Judging by his shabby clothes he was less successful than most other lawyers.

Jeffers offered a poor attempt at a conciliatory smile. 'Sorry to disturb you, old chap, but my client is rather anxious about a matter that seems to be of mutual interest to you both and, um, he got carried away.'

His client, far from looking sorry, sniggered.

Henry was still seething at this rude behaviour and felt like walking out on them but decided it might be as well to find out what this was about, and get it over and done with. He doubted he'd agree to whatever Higgerson was after because he rarely approved of anything that fellow did.

Gesturing to two hard wooden chairs and leaving the unwelcome visitors to help themselves to them, he addressed his clerk now standing near the door. 'I apologise for our visitors' rudeness, Finlay. Please join us but fetch your special notebook first. We won't start till you're ready.'

Finlay nodded and left.

He would know exactly what his employer wanted from the words 'special notebook', so Henry turned back to his two unwelcome guests. 'We'll wait for Finlay. He's recently learned Pitman shorthand and has become known for taking notes of conversations. These are so accurate word for word any judge would be able to trust them absolutely. Shorthand is definitely a useful tool of the future.'

He saw Jeffers swallow hard at this, though Higgerson merely gave him another of his sneering looks, leaned back and folded his arms.

Henry went to stand by the window with his back to the room as he waited for his clerk to return. He'd been expecting something to happen to break the impasse about Redfern but had hoped his client would have a little longer to recover before Higgerson made a move.

He was surprised by the way the fellow had pushed his way in here, though, very surprised. Was Higgerson growing over-confident of his position and power in the valley? Any weakness would be welcome in a bully like him.

Not until Finlay returned and settled on a hard chair to one side with his notebook at the ready did Henry sit down again behind his desk. 'Now, how may I help you, Mr Higgerson?'

His visitor leaned forward, speaking emphatically. 'You can put us in touch with Mr Redfern – *if* he's still alive, that is. His wife was told a few days ago that he was dying but somehow he was spirited away from the local hospital and now no one seems to know where he is or whether he's still alive.'

'I can assure you that Mr Redfern is very much alive and recovering, to everyone's delight, though he's still weak. As Mrs Redfern has already been told, the doctors aren't sure exactly what caused him to collapse, so are keeping him isolated for a few days more in case of any lingering infection. We don't want an epidemic after all.'

Well, that was the tale they'd decided on until Redfern could take charge of his own life again. He steepled his fingers and waited.

'You'll need to prove that he's alive.'

'Why should I have to prove anything to you? You're only a distant relative by marriage and can have no legal interest in this case.'

'I'm acting on behalf of his wife, who is my cousin.'

'Second cousin or some such distant connection, I gather.'

'What does that matter? I'm her only relative in the valley and I have the poor woman's full authority to help her out, since she *is* family.'

'And *I*, sir, am acting directly for Mr Redfern. My client wishes to remain apart from his wife until his recovery is complete. Apart from the other risks, his doctors insist he needs peace and quiet to complete his recovery.'

'Not good enough.' Higgerson gestured to his lawyer to take over.

'Should you fail to give us access to Mr Redfern or to

prove to his wife that he is alive, we shall take the matter to a higher legal authority and ask for a binding order that she be allowed to go to him. You clearly know where he is. It's imperative to set the poor woman's mind at rest, or if he's dead, to bury him appropriately.'

Thank goodness for Albert's advice! Henry thought. 'I have already consulted a higher authority, and an official has been sent to see Mr Redfern. They will be happy to confirm to his wife that he is still alive, I'm sure.' He glanced at the clock on the mantelpiece. 'Indeed, that was going to happen an hour ago, so it's probably been confirmed already.'

Breath whistled into Higgerson's mouth. 'I don't believe you. I'd have heard if you'd gone to anyone in the valley about this matter – and who else would do that for you anyway? You're not a relative of the man nor are you acting for anyone who is.'

'I'm his lawyer, acting under his direct instructions. And I didn't go to anyone in the valley for legal advice. I consulted a judge from a nearby area.'

'Who was this judge?' Jeffers asked.

'Dennison Peters.'

There was silence, then, 'I shall check that out for myself.'

Henry didn't allow himself to smile. That particular judge was not in any way corruptible, as everyone in southern Lancashire's legal circles knew. 'Please do, Mr Jeffers. And for the record—' he gestured to Finlay, 'I will add that I myself saw my client only two days ago and he was alive and fully compos mentis.'

He let that sink in then added, 'I'm sure the doctor now caring for him will have been able to bear witness to the judge's emissary that Redfern is in full possession of his faculties.'

'I wish to speak to this doctor to verify that for myself.'

'Not possible, as I've already said. The doctor is in

attendance on my client at all times and there are no visitors allowed.'

'Then you'll have to produce Redfern and let him be *seen* to handle his own affairs, or else appoint his next of kin to do it for him.'

Typical of Higgerson to go over and over what he wanted, like a dog with a bone.

'How many times must I tell you that though Mr Redfern is not yet well physically, he is his normal self mentally, and is recovering steadily. He has appointed me to deal with any other matters that arise in the interim. Kindly tell his wife that.'

The two men locked glances and Higgerson was the first to look away, scowling. 'She'll be pleased to hear that he's alive, but would be more pleased to see it for herself. And there is still the question of Redfern's business. He'll lose his customers completely if he keeps them waiting too long. She's worrying about that too.'

Henry allowed himself to smile slightly as he said, 'Oh, I doubt that will happen. He's very well thought of in the trade and they'll understand if he's slowed down by illness.'

'But with my help, his wife could be keeping the business going. You will not deny that I am a successful businessman.'

'You have a different sort of business. Mr Redfern employs skilled craftsmen and women, and his business's carpentry is acknowledged to be the best in the valley. Besides, my client has told me many a time that Mrs Redfern never goes near the workshop. If anyone needs to keep it going, it should be his daughter, who has worked in it for many years. She would have the help of his foremen, two very capable fellows but—'

'That is not the same. If anything happens to Redfern, it's his wife who will inherit the business since it was her money that gave it an impetus after they married.'

Henry leaned forward. 'Please allow me to finish. Given the unusual circumstances, her father doesn't want his daughter to be put at risk so he's asked me to make sure she stays away from the business for the time being.'

'That's one relief, I suppose. As a woman, Miss Redfern—'

'Mrs Harte now.'

Higgerson ignored the correction. '—doesn't have the necessary skills anyway.'

Henry decided to launch a little attack of his own. 'I admit it surprises me that his wife is so eager to see him, given what we know about the cause of his illness.'

Higgerson froze and studied him for a few moments, his eyes narrowed, a slight frown on his face. 'What do you mean by that?'

'Someone has been trying to poison my client.'

Higgerson looked genuinely puzzled for a few moments, his expression that of someone working through several possibilities in his mind. He was either a far better actor than they'd thought or that woman had plotted to kill her husband entirely by herself. Henry hadn't expected that to be a possibility.

'I don't believe that.'

'I do. The doctor does. And so does Sergeant Deemer.'

When Higgerson still didn't say anything, Henry stood up. 'Now, if that's all, I'd like to get on with my day.'

As Higgerson stood up, Henry added a parting shot. 'Should you push your way into here again, you may be sure I'll not only refuse to speak to you but will call in the police to remove you.'

The look his visitor gave him threatened retribution one day for that.

Jeffers glanced quickly from one to the other, seeming far more nervous now than when he'd come in. Henry was quite sure he hadn't been involved in any attempt on Redfern's life.

At last, with a muttered curse, Higgerson led the way out.

Once they'd left, Henry opened the window of his office, because though it made the room lose its warmth rapidly, it felt as if the visitors had tainted the air within it by their mere presence and it needed to be refreshed.

Had Higgerson really not known what Mrs Redfern had been doing?

No, he must have known. How else could she have obtained the poison?

But what if he hadn't been involved? What if she'd acted on her own? No, she'd have been seen. There would still have to have been someone to help her.

She only saw her servants or the women of her own status with whom she interacted socially. She wasn't known to have any particular friends among them, though. He'd asked his wife to find out about that.

He looked at Finlay. 'Did you get it all down?'

'Indeed I did, sir.'

'What did you think?'

'Given what you've told me, I found Higgerson's reaction . . . well, not what I'd have expected. He didn't seem to be faking surprise. And similarly with Mr Jeffers, who looked, if I may say so, shocked to the core.'

'I wonder if we can find anything else out about Mrs Redfern and who she might have been helped by if not her cousin.'

'Shall I see if I can locate someone to do that?'

Henry didn't answer for a few seconds. He didn't usually spy on people, which he disapproved of, but attempted murder was an extremely serious matter and they had to know the truth if they were to keep his client safe. And his client's daughter.

'Yes, Finlay. Please see if you can discover any other details at all. I shall be glad when this whole situation is resolved.

It's still dangerous for Redfern, who is a good friend as well as a client. But we can do very little until he recovers his strength and is able to return to Rivenshaw.'

His friend must know something or he'd not have made the preparations to help his daughter and keep her safe from her mother's machinations. Or was that simply general distrust of his wife?

Henry took a walk round town at lunchtime and after a while began to feel as if he were being followed. Was it his imagination or was the man wearing a dark cap pulled down low stopping whenever he did? He moved on a few paces and paused to look in a shop window. The same man had also stopped. What puzzled him was that the chap was making no attempt to hide what he was doing. Was this being done to intimidate him?

He didn't need to buy anything but went into Charlie's electrical goods shop and explained what he thought was happening. With the manager's help, he slipped outside again through the backyard, which allowed him to reach the police station without being seen by the person following him.

When he got there, he brought Deemer up to date with the latest happening and the sergeant was also surprised that Higgerson might not have been involved in poisoning Mr Redfern.

'I'd have to be very sure of that to let him off the hook,' he said. 'I'd been counting on it to nab him at last.'

'Well, I will allow myself to bear in mind still the possibility that he was involved in the attempted murder but he'd have to be a brilliant actor to have looked like that. And remember that I've years of experience at judging people's honesty in my professional life.'

Still wondering about it all, Henry returned the same way and before he left the shop, Harry Makepeace, the manager, took him into a side room and pointed out a man who'd been lingering outside ever since Henry came in.

'Is he the one following you?'

'Yes. But I've never seen him before. Do you recognise him?'

'No. I definitely don't. Of course no one can know everyone in the valley by sight, but he's got a memorable face, so I think I'd remember him. He's probably from out of town.'

'I'd better see if I can get a closer look, then I'll recognise him in future.'

Henry strolled out through the front door of the shop and this time he stopped outside a large window in which he managed to get a clear view of the man who'd been following him. He was very heavily built with grey hair and thick eyebrows nearly meeting in the middle of his face. His nose had undoubtedly been broken at least once.

Henry continued on his way and was glad to get back into his rooms, because he'd been feeling unsafe.

When he peeped out of his office window, he saw the man leaning against a lamp post across the street, quite openly keeping an eye on the place. He then pointed the man out to Finlay as well as their typist and the office boy, just in case.

This was one way Higgerson was known to threaten people without saying a word or breaking the law. It was the first time Henry had been the target of it, and it did indeed make him feel threatened and uncomfortable. He picked up the phone and rang Deemer again, but the sergeant had just left, having been summoned to see the area superintendent, the cheerful young constable told him.

Henry hoped this meeting was to arrange the details of when the new police constable was to be transferred to the valley. And even with two constables working for him, Deemer wouldn't be able to keep an eye on everything.

Henry decided to go home before the light failed and tell

Finlay to keep the front door here locked at all times from now on.

When Higgerson got home after his encounter with Redfern's damned starchy lawyer, he was given a message from his cousin. Mrs Redfern had phoned three times apparently and wished to see him *at once.*

He didn't wish to see her, and was only continuing to help her because of the valuable commodity to which she was the key: the company that provided minor building services for Tyler's. It was proving very tedious but he couldn't leave the delicate task of getting his hands on it to anyone else.

Had Lloyd really been hinting that Jane had been trying to murder her husband? He couldn't get that out of his mind.

During the past few months he'd seen Sam Redfern growing thinner and looking ill, had thought he *was* ill. People who got that frail look were often sinking towards death. But what if this wasn't an illness? What if he was being poisoned by his wife?

He whistled softly. He definitely hadn't thought Jane capable of that.

She must have been doing it in a very inept way, though, if they'd found out about it at the hospital. Damn the woman! Was she totally stupid? Whatever she'd been using to poison him might be traced back to her and then he'd be involved. Higgerson wanted no part of anything so blatantly against the law. And the penalty for murder was death by hanging.

That was more than annoying – it might make a difference to his plans, not the long-term ones, just the path he took to get there. He would still prefer to take over Redfern's to prevent them from doing any more work for Tyler, who regularly sent jobs their way. He wanted Tyler to be short of skilled workmen as the first step in putting his company out of business.

Well, accidents could happen once Tyler started building on that land. Not ones which would be traceable to him, even though people might guess he was involved.

He hadn't bothered to do much about the situation before as Tyler's business started to go downhill of its own accord following his son's death. Now that it was beginning to thrive again, he would have to take action. No other building company in the valley was going to grow big enough to challenge his own.

It would look bad to be the only builder, so he allowed small businesses to exist here and there. But he didn't let them grow too big and eat into his profits.

And there were other considerations. If others started to provide *major* building services, people might notice his little economies in materials and the way he always built the houses a little smaller than originally planned.

He was still furious that Tyler had snapped up that piece of land just as Higgerson had done enough to push that stupid old woman who owned it into selling it to him at far less than market value.

The land was perfect for his needs, far more level than was usual in that part of the valley. He could cram a lot of houses on it, well, not exactly houses, but rather tenements like those he'd seen once in Glasgow, with one- and two-room dwellings crammed in like salted herrings in a barrel. The rents would be hugely lucrative, because the dwellings would be slightly better than the ones in Backshaw Moss, yet he'd get almost as many to the acre.

You could never have too much money coming in. One day, in a few years' time, he'd retire to somewhere sunny like the south of France, but not until he was so rich that few of the other wealthy refugees from Britain's damp climate would dare to shun his acquaintance, as they had when he'd gone there for a holiday.

On that thought and with great reluctance, he summoned his car and was driven the short distance across town to see his cousin Jane. He patted the leather upholstery fondly. He loved his Sunbeam. Of course an eighteen-horsepower saloon was more powerful than he needed, and larger too, because he rarely went out of the valley or had passengers in it other than his wife.

He might even buy a smaller car for his wife. She'd been hinting for one and asking if she could learn to drive. That would show people how well he provided for his family – at least, for those members who deserved it.

He still hadn't found out where his elder son had disappeared to, but when things had settled down a bit, he was going to find out.

He realised the car had stopped and with a sigh got out of it. He didn't need a stupid woman messing things up like this.

Inside his cousin's house, Higgerson found Jane sitting in front of a roaring fire in her small private parlour at the rear, staring into the leaping flames. She didn't turn to greet him, didn't even seem aware at first that the maid had announced him as she showed him in. Was Jane pretending or was she really so lost in thought?

'I came as you asked me to, cousin,' he said loudly, impatient to get this over. 'What's the matter?'

She jumped in shock and it was a few moments before she focused on him properly.

That was strange. He studied her closely. Was she beginning to grow senile as well as uglier with age? She was after all, older than him by several years, older than her husband too. 'Are you all right, my dear?'

'No, of course I'm not all right, Gareth. I'm worried about whether my husband is dead – and if he's not dead, what he's up to.' She scowled at him. 'Why did it take you so long to get here?'

'I was out of the office when your message arrived.'

'They must have known where you were. Tell them not to keep me waiting in future.'

He didn't bother to refuse, though he wasn't going to give any of his employees that particular order. He stole another glance at her. She seemed to be in a strange mood today. Very strange. 'What did you wish to see me about?'

'To find out how things went this morning, of course. You were going to see that horrible man, weren't you?'

'What horrible man do you mean?'

'The lawyer, Lloyd. Did you make him prove to you whether my husband is still alive and if so, reveal where he's hiding? I'm going to bring Samuel back if it's the last thing I do, and the first thing I'll do is make him change lawyers. If he's still alive, that is.'

'Lloyd swears he is.'

'Samuel must be ill, though, to have stayed away so long. He needs to be brought back into my care. That lawyer is probably holding him prisoner to keep control of him and his money. You must get rid of him.'

He blinked in shock at that one. What wild accusation was she going to make next? 'Since Lloyd is his lawyer at the moment and is acting on his instructions, I can't get rid of him.'

'Well, hire someone who can do something about it, by force if necessary. I'll pay you back when I get hold of Samuel's money.'

'Apparently Lloyd has consulted a well-known judge in Manchester about the situation and he also claims to have seen your husband himself only two days ago. We cannot therefore make any overt claims about the need to manage the business for him. Not yet, anyway. We must wait until he returns. You said he'd been slowly getting worse, so he's bound to have a relapse.'

He waited a moment to add loudly and clearly, 'And not one so clumsily arranged.'

She shot a quick sideways glance at him, suddenly all attention. 'What do you mean by that?'

'I mean that if you want me to help you, you'll have to leave it to me to do it my own way. I don't think they've got any proof that you've been trying to speed up his death or they'd have arrested you.'

She didn't deny her part in it, merely shrugged. 'I did what I had to.'

'Well, stop doing it now. I *will* deal with him for you – but it has to be later. Neither of us can afford to do anything openly.'

'But Sam *can't* be alive. Not after I—' She broke off and changed what she had been going to say to, 'Not after he was so ill.'

He stared at her, shocked. Lloyd was right, then. She had been poisoning her husband, the stupid bitch. And how the hell had she got hold of whatever she'd been giving him? He'd have to find out and stop her trying to do it again.

Redfern must know by now what she'd done to him. That would be why he was staying away from her.

Did the local doctor know where her husband was as well? He must do, surely? McDevitt had been the first one to treat Redfern when he collapsed. And who was this other doctor who was now apparently looking after him? Higgerson knew the other doctors in the valley and they hadn't gone anywhere. Perhaps one of his men could find something out.

He turned back to study her. She seemed to have lost interest in their conversation and was staring into the fire again, muttering, tapping the palm of one hand with the forefinger of the other, as if counting something off, or memorising it.

He listened carefully. It sounded like, 'Must make sure next time. Very – very – sure.'

He'd heard rumours about her increasingly strange behaviour, but she'd always been rather odd, as well as selfish to the point of obsession when she wanted something. Which was why she'd had so much trouble finding a husband.

Ironic that she'd been planning to have her own daughter locked away as mentally unstable and dangerous to others. He might have to do the same to her to protect himself.

By the time he left, Higgerson had managed to talk her into a better frame of mind and persuade her not to act openly or do anything at all suspicious. At least he hoped he had. She'd agreed to leave everything in his hands but he'd keep a close eye on her to make sure of that.

She didn't come to the door to see him out as usual, but that sour-faced maid of hers came from the rear of the house to hand him his hat and overcoat. The woman had been with Jane most of her life, if he remembered correctly. What was she called? Pearl, that was it.

'Your mistress doesn't seem at all well today, Pearl, I'm afraid. A little delirious, in fact. Perhaps she's caught whatever struck down her husband.'

She darted one worried glance at him then her face became expressionless. But it had been enough to show him that she knew something. He could always tell when people were keeping secrets from him.

'You'd better keep an eye on her. Don't let her do anything else dangerous. Or say anything stupid.'

She caught her breath and it was a minute before she answered, 'Yes, sir. I'll do that.'

'And call me if it's something you can't deal with. Me, not anyone else.'

Her expression wooden now, she nodded. 'Yes, sir.'

How very annoying the whole situation was! No, more than that, infuriating. He'd missed out on the land Tyler had bought and if he didn't take care he'd fail to sort it out. The last thing he needed was a stupid woman creating trouble that would draw attention to him.

He would have to keep a close eye on her. And be prepared to act quickly.

28

That afternoon Higgerson sent men out to spread the word that he would reward anyone bringing him news of the whereabouts of Sam Redfern or of a new doctor who'd suddenly moved to the country near the Ellin Valley. They described Mr Redfern as a poor sick man in need of medical help, with a wife worrying desperately about his safety.

No one who knew Mrs Redfern or her reputation believed her to be upset, but money was money, and people knew Higgerson always paid up if you found out something he wanted to know.

Sure that this would bring results, Higgerson settled down for the evening, pouring himself a glass of his favourite whisky and shaking open the newspaper. Then, on second thoughts, he called his wife in and told her to sit with him but not to disturb him by chattering.

From now on, he wanted witnesses to where he was whenever he was out of the office. No one was going to trap him, not even his own cousin. In fact, he was seriously considering how best to trap her into betraying proof of what she'd done to her husband, if that seemed necessary. He had no intention of being linked to a murder attempt, and such a crude one too.

He wondered what Lloyd would do about the situation. Clever man, Redfern's lawyer. Pity he was so damned honest.

He was going to enjoy these strategic games, however, and come out the winner, or if the outcome he was chasing was not at present possible, he didn't intend to figure as someone who'd broken the law. He always managed to avoid that.

By evening the news had spread that a big reward had been promised to anyone finding out where Redfern was.

The rumours about the reward quickly got back to Roy Tyler with a man knocking on his door late that night because he knew Mr Tyler dealt regularly with Redfern.

Roy paid him then consulted his wife. There was nothing to be done now but first thing the following morning they decided that Ethel would call a meeting with Wilf, Jericho and Frankie to see whether there was anything they could do to help her father. And perhaps they should also ask Henry to join them? Yes, definitely.

Unfortunately the lawyer was in court that morning, so Roy ran the meeting without him.

When they gathered in the office at his yard, he found out as he'd expected that the others already knew about the promised reward.

'The rumour-mongers have been even busier than usual,' he commented.

'This is going to make it more dangerous for Sam, so we need to decide if there's anything we can do to help him stay safe.'

'We should at least find a way to let Redfern's new doctor know the situation,' Wilf said. 'Perhaps Dr McDevitt can get a message to him.'

Roy grimaced. 'I don't think he knows where Sam is now. But at least there's another doctor looking after your father and that's a good sign. Besides, even if we knew where he was, it'd be risky to try to phone him.

And that's assuming he has access to a phone. I'm sure Higgerson will have someone at the local telephone exchange listening in.'

He waited a moment to let that sink in, then continued, 'I'll speak to Deemer about our worries but I didn't invite him to this meeting because someone would have noticed and wondered at his presence. Since we all work together, it won't seem strange that we meet regularly.'

'Yes, but what can we *do* to help my father?' Frankie asked. 'How is it possible for Higgerson to get away with so much anyway? Why doesn't someone stop him?'

Jericho said quietly, 'It's Frankie's mother I'm worried about. She's still free to plot more attacks on her husband if she can find out where he is.'

Roy looked at Frankie sympathetically. 'It must hurt you to know that she's probably the one who poisoned your father.'

'Yes. It does. I didn't even suspect her before and I'm sure my father didn't realise what she was doing to him, either. He told me a few times that he was worried about his health and I could see that he was growing weaker.' She gave Jericho a warm glance. 'That's why he made sure I would have someone who could protect me legally if he died. He said she might try to have me locked away.'

'I'll make sure she doesn't do that,' Jericho said firmly.

Frankie turned back to Roy and Wilf. 'But if my father recovers, and you and Mr Lloyd make it plain to her that we all know what she did – well, surely she won't try it again?'

'How do we know what she'll do? She might think she's got away with it and can get away with finishing the job as well.'

'Perhaps we could force her to leave the valley, make her live apart from my father, in Blackpool or some such place.'

'You know her better than any of us, Frankie. Do you think she'd agree to leave?' Wilf asked.

'I've never been close to her, and she's been growing strange over the past year or two.'

'How do you mean, strange?' Roy asked.

'Erratic behaviour, sudden changes of mood, fits of screaming temper, smashing things.'

'We may be able to get her locked away if we can prove what she's done,' Roy said. 'It might be the only way to keep him safe.'

Frankie stared at him in horror then shook her head vigorously. 'No. That would be going too far. You hear terrible things about lunatic asylums. I don't want to do that to anyone, even her.'

Jericho took hold of her hand. 'Your father's safety is more important than such scruples, love. And your own safety too.'

There was silence, then Roy said, 'Frankie love, you'll have to face it: you and your father will never be safe while she's free to scheme and act.'

'If we pay to have her watched—'

'She still has money of her own, doesn't she? She'll still be able to pay someone else to help her.'

'It's all such a horrible mess.' Frankie rested her head against Jericho's arm for a moment, not even aware she was doing it.

Wilf caught Roy's eye and winked, jerking his head in their direction. He'd noticed how the two of them were looking at one another. It was good to see newly-weds getting on so well, a bright point in dark times. He felt the same way about his own second wife, a wonderful and courageous woman whom he'd married recently.

He didn't interrupt them until Frankie looked up again, seeming more in control of her emotions, then he said thoughtfully, 'There's another thing we might think about. If your mother is related to Higgerson, she might be a weakness for him.'

Wilf waited a moment then went on, 'He causes far more trouble in our valley than she does or ever could. Over the years I've seen how ordinary people are afraid to get on his wrong side. I've heard that some of them are talking about making a stand about it in Birch End.'

Jericho let out a growl of anger. 'I'd help with that. I haven't forgotten how Higgerson had my mother thrown out of our room in Backshaw Moss; how the thugs deliberately trampled on and smashed her possessions.'

'Deemer thinks he brings these thugs in from nearby towns, giving them temporary lodgings in your street, at Number Six and then getting them out of the valley quickly after they've done what he wants. So far the sergeant hasn't been able to prove it well enough to bring it into a court of law.'

Roy frowned. 'Higgerson encourages petty crime, we all know that, but I've been thinking about it and I'd be surprised if he was involved in what happened to Sam. I've never heard that he's had anyone killed. In fact, he doesn't risk doing anything that might get him personally into trouble with the law. Even this latest reward is allegedly being offered for information about your father because Mrs Redfern is worried sick. He's cunning, yes, and unscrupulous, but he's not a killer.'

'Well that's as maybe, but he still needs your mother on his side if he's going to take over your father's business,' Jericho said quietly. 'It's a pity your father isn't well enough to come back and take charge again.'

Harte was showing he had brains as well as brawn, Roy thought with satisfaction. He'd been right about the fellow's abilities, he was sure. 'Well, we've done a lot of talking but not got very far. I'll speak to Henry about your father, Frankie.

It'd help if we had some idea of when Sam is likely to be returning. Surely the doctor who's looking after him will know by now?'

What still worried him was what he would do if Redfern died. It'd give Higgerson an advantage over Roy's business. Oh hell, this was all such a tangle.

'Fine conspirator I am,' Frankie said to Jericho as he walked across the yard to see her to her new work area. 'I hate the thought of locking my mother away in an asylum, even after all she's done.'

'We're neither of us vengeful people and I'm glad of it. I'll still do whatever's needed to protect you, though, even against your mother. And after what's been said today by a group of intelligent men, you must realise that it's even more important for you not to go anywhere on your own.'

'I know, and I won't do. Anyway, for the rest of the morning I'll be here working on my little bookcase. I've only got a few things to do to it now.'

'I'm proud of your skills, love, especially now I've seen the sort of things you create. You put beauty into the world and there can never be too much of that.'

He saw tears well in her eyes, but could recognise happy tears now. She seemed overwhelmed by even the slightest of compliments, didn't even seem to realise what a fine-looking woman she was.

He was lucky to have been given the chance to marry her. She was so easy to love and already he knew he'd give his life's blood to keep her safe.

What no one took into consideration as the next few uneasy days passed was what the men who had worked for Redfern might be doing. They were a small group but close-knit and loyal. They knew and valued their employer and when Higgerson spread this rumour they grew very angry. It wasn't hard to work out that the 'someone' could only be his wife.

One thing they were all agreed on: if Mrs Redfern brought Higgerson in to run the business, they'd leave, it was as simple as that. Even in hard times, they'd not work for someone who encouraged cheap, shoddy work, bullied those who worked for him and cheated his customers whenever he could.

But first and foremost, they weren't going to let anyone hurt 'the boss' again. If he recovered, that was.

His two foremen, Pete and Gus, discussed the situation quietly. Over the past few years they'd noticed him taking money secretly out of the business by falsifying purchases of tools and materials. They'd kept their mouths shut about it. After all, it was his own money to do what he wanted with.

They'd also watched his health go downhill. Eh, that had been painful to see.

A couple of months ago, he'd had a quiet word with them about what they should do if he died – especially if he died suddenly or in strange circumstances. It was typical of him to try to think ahead.

He hadn't died, though – well, not that they knew of. They'd heard rumours that he'd been poisoned then he'd been whisked away by Dr McDevitt.

Mr Lloyd had immediately shut down the business but he'd had a quiet word with them. It seems Mr Redfern had given him some instructions too. So they were still being paid their wages by Mr Lloyd's clerk but were instructed not to tell anyone, to pretend they had savings to live on.

That couldn't be done for the other workers, sadly, or someone might find out, but Henry told them 'the boss' trusted them absolutely to slip money to the other men if they were finding it difficult to put bread on the table. He even gave the two of them money for these and other 'expenses'.

'Use your own judgement if you think something is necessary,' he told them. 'Sam himself may need help to stay safe. Who knows?'

'What about Miss Frankie?' Pete asked.

'She's been provided for, and she's got Jericho by her side.'

'He's a good lad.'

Since then both of them joined other unemployed men on street corners chatting and passing the time, and above all gathering information.

One day they went up to the labour exchange in Ellindale to keep up the pretence of looking for work. They discussed the situation freely as they were walking up the valley, but otherwise took care what they said aloud. Both were keeping their eyes and ears open, hungering for news of Mr Redfern.

'Once the boss comes back, I'm not letting anyone hurt him again,' Gus said grimly. 'Whatever it takes.'

'We can get the lads together at a few minutes' notice, if he needs our help.'

After a few days they decided to go a few steps further and keep an eye on what Mrs Redfern was doing, Higgerson as well. 'We'll get the lads from work to help us, and pay them for it.'

'Will there be enough of them?'

'They'll get help if they need it. Most of their families have lived in Birch End for decades. Folk there look after one another, so they'll know which people to trust.'

Within a few days they had set up their networks, letting the men bring their families into it, as well. And the first people the others pointed fingers at were the Bensons so they were watched particularly carefully. About time they did something about that lot anyway.

If Mr Redfern came back they'd keep him safe, even if it took the whole village to do that.

'I reckon something's going to happen soon,' Gus said suddenly one day. He tapped the side of his nose. 'I can feel it coming. My mother was the same. Psychic.'

His companion looked at him, frowning. 'You sure about that?'

'Yes. You've seen my feelings come true before.'

'Aye. I didn't believe it that last time but it happened just as you said. Eh, I wish we knew where the boss is now, though.'

'If we don't know, I doubt anyone will except that lawyer chap an' he can keep his mouth shut.'

'He's coming back soon, I know he is and we have to be ready to help him. Good thing we can still get into the workshop, eh?'

'Which is more than Higgerson has managed.'

They both let out harsh little chuckles, because they'd stopped a couple of attempts to break into it. That was one thing they'd done for the boss already.

One night, several men came across from Backshaw Moss and approached the Hartes' new home, creeping through the darkness, shivering in the cold wind, but eager to earn a few shillings for giving her a fright and damaging her house.

The place was dark and presumably all its occupants were in bed.

'We'll wake them sods up in a few minutes, eh?' one man whispered.

'Shh!'

All six of them had walked past the house during the

daylight hours and checked the best way to get in, so they split up and turned into the garden from both sides with scarcely a pause.

Suddenly one yelled out as a thin rope strung from one tree branch to the roof of the shed caught his face, scraped his throat and knocked his cap off as he flailed around. Another's shout echoed his almost immediately as he tripped over a rope stretched lower down between nearby bushes and fell headlong into the muddy soil.

A third man yelped loudly as a stone flung by a hand honed by years in the village cricket team hit him hard on the side of his head. It was followed by several other missiles from hidden defenders, most of which hit a target.

It didn't take long to rout the would-be invaders.

'I doubt that lot will be back,' one of the defenders told Jericho with deep satisfaction.

'I'm sure you'll be ready for them if they do return.' He clapped the man on the shoulder. 'Thanks, lad. If you keep watch for the rest of the night, there'll be a hot breakfast waiting for you and if you tell Mrs Bibby I sent you, she'll let you each have a big loaf to take back to your family. Tell the others.'

He wished he and Frankie could afford to pay them properly for their time, but they had to be careful with their money – just in case her father died, because if so, they'd have to leave the valley for good. And take his family with them. Maybe even emigrate to the colonies.

In the attic the young maid shivered as they went upstairs to bed. When Hilda put an arm round her she buried her face in the older woman's shoulder.

'It's all right, love. They've gone now, chased away good and proper.'

'I hate them,' she whispered. 'People like them do

nothing but hurt people or steal things. I wish them Bensons would go away from the village. And I wish it wasn't my name too.'

'Your father's family don't belong in Birch End, that's for sure. They'd fit in better in Backshaw Moss. But though you look like them, you don't act like them an' everyone knows it now. Besides, one day you'll marry a nice chap and change your name from Benson to something else.'

Maria brightened. 'I never thought of that. Any other name would be lovely.'

'Just don't rush into marriage, love. Take your time and choose a good man. A bad husband is worse than none. And before you do think about marriage, learn about running a house properly. That sort of thing makes a difference to a fellow's comfort and keeps him in a better mood.'

'My mum used to say that to me too: don't marry in haste and don't give your body to anyone till you're wed.'

'Then she was a wise woman. Now, let's get some sleep. I doubt those rascals will be back again tonight and if they do return the master will be ready for them. Don't forget, in the morning we've a big meal to cook for the men who were keeping watch.'

Maria went into the next bedroom and snuggled down. It was wonderful to have a proper bed of her own. She'd never had that before.

Her father's family would have been involved in tonight's trouble, she was sure. She wished they'd go and live somewhere else.

She jerked upright in bed as there was the sound of a window being smashed from somewhere in the street. *Not here*, she told herself. *It wasn't here.*

But she lay awake listening for some time to make sure nothing else happened.

*

The man who'd smashed the window at Number Six ran back to the garden shed at Number One, grinning.

'That'll serve those sods right.'

His brother grabbed his shoulder as he slipped into the shed. 'You great daft lump. What did you do that for?'

'Because they're not getting away with their bullying ways, that's why. And because one of the chaps staying at that house tried to grab my daughter the other day – just grabbed her in the street, he did an' tried to touch her where he shouldn't. One of my friends saw it an' punched him in the face. I finished giving him a lesson about leaving my lass when I got him alone later on.'

'You never said.'

His voice was rough with anger. 'She didn't want folk knowing. She said she felt ashamed. As if it was her fault he did that. Eh, I could punch him all over again every time I think of that.'

'If you'd told me I'd have come with you tonight and thrown another brick.'

'Ah well, let's settle down and keep watch. I'm looking forward to that cooked breakfast. An egg, the cook said, and a slice of ham with it. As well as bread and butter. My mouth's watering at the thought.'

'So's mine. It's so long since I've had a good meal, my stomach thinks my throat's been cut.'

'I reckon my wife will cry for happy when I go home with a big crusty loaf.'

'So will mine.'

Word spread out along the valley after that: the Hartes were being watched at night. And anyone in Birch End who tried to hurt them was going to be in trouble.

Jericho chuckled when he heard about the brick hitting Number Six.

The men smiled as they ate their food, chewing it slowly

and with relish. They might not have jobs, but they were doing something useful and filling their bellies too.

The village would be all the better without such out-and-out villains living in it. And without these incomers causing trouble for decent people.

And since no one else had done anything about getting rid of the troublemakers, they'd damned well do it themselves.

29

Sam Redfern woke up at the farm cottage a few days later feeling more his old self than he had done for months. How the hell long had Jane been poisoning him for?

Since he started taking those damned lozenges, that's how long. He'd racked his brain and reckoned the poison could only have been administered in them. His wife had told him Dr McDevitt had prescribed them, but the doctor said he hadn't when Sam was taken to the hospital. It was one thing he remembered clearly, the doctor holding up the tin of lozenges and shaking him to keep him awake as he demanded to know what these were for and where he'd got them from.

Why had he accepted the lozenges when Jane told him they'd been sent for him to take morning and evening? They certainly hadn't been doing him any good because he'd continued to get weaker. You didn't expect your wife to try to poison you, that was why, even a wife as contrary as Jane.

And now he came to think of it, also because he'd begun to feel increasingly dopey and hadn't been thinking as clearly as usual. He'd thought it was old age slowing him down, old age opening the final door to some fatal sickness. Which was why he'd made some very careful plans to have his daughter looked after should he die.

If he could live his life again, he'd not have stayed with Jane so long. She'd been a misery to live with from the start, arrogantly ordering him around. Marrying someone like that for the money wasn't worth it, only when the first lass he'd loved had died, he'd been so upset he'd turned his attention to making money.

His father and grandfather had been in the same trade but had been content to do the work in a small way. He'd been young and ambitious, determined to expand the business.

And he'd done well at that, if not in his marriage.

It was another miracle that Frankie had turned out like his side of the family, calm and sensible, not like her mother's lot. And also that she'd proved so good with her hands from a very early age.

He'd loved his son too, of course he had. Don had been such a happy-natured little boy, but he hadn't been at all interested in the family business and had always been extremely clumsy. At seventeen, he'd not even been a fully grown man when he'd had to go into the army and fight in that dreadful war. He must have made an easy target when the fighting started, always falling over his own feet.

Ah, stop it! he told himself. *You can't change the past, only try for a better future.* He'd get himself dressed today. That would be another small step forward. He smiled. Small step? *Tiny* step more like.

By the time Viv came up to the attic to help him, Sam was dressed and sitting on the bed with his back to the wall, continuing to think hard about his situation and how to resolve it.

She came across to study him and feel his forehead. 'You look a lot better this morning, Sam.'

'I feel it, too. And I'm hungry, really hungry for the first time.'

'Another good sign.'

'Can I come downstairs to eat? I feel like a prisoner stuck up here.'

'I don't think that'd be wise. Anyone could turn up at the door and see you. Better to stay in the attic and be bored, don't you think?'

He sighed. 'I suppose so. But sitting around won't give me my strength back. I'm shockingly weak.'

'I've got some Indian clubs in one of my boxes. I can show you some exercises with them later that will help build up your muscles again.'

He rolled his eyes. 'Those things are for women. I've seen them in the church hall, dancing about and waving those clubs in the air. I'd feel a fool doing that.'

She couldn't hold back a chuckle. 'What does it matter how silly you feel if they help you regain some strength in your limbs? I'll go through a few simple exercises but don't be surprised if you can't do as much as you expect at first.'

He was indeed surprised at how quickly he tired – and angry all over again at what his wife had done to him. He'd always been strong, proud of being a big tough chap, and look at him now! Weak as a newborn lamb.

Thank goodness he'd prepared for what he'd thought of as his coming death. If there was any justice in the world, these preparations would now help him regain control of his life, health and business – and of his wife. He trusted his two foremen absolutely.

He hadn't mentioned anything of what he'd done to the doctor yet, but now might be the time to take Viv into his confidence. He needed to find out how things were going in the valley, and above all, whether Frankie was safe. She was the only one who could help him do that while he was stuck here.

Viv listened to him with her usual serious attention then gave a nod. 'It sounds to me as if your mind hasn't been permanently affected.' She looked thoughtful, then added, 'The last thing they'll expect to find is a woman doctor looking after you, so if necessary I can pretend to be your wife. Mrs Smith or Mrs Jones? Which do you prefer?'

'Either as long as it's you. Eh, I wish you really were my wife!' He felt himself flushing. What a silly thing to say. But he'd so enjoyed their long conversations about anything and everything.

She didn't flinch or grow flustered, just smiled sadly. 'That's a lovely compliment, Sam. I might have enjoyed you courting me. My marriage was a very happy one and I miss sharing my life with a husband. Ah well, there you are. I'd better go and get your breakfast. Good food will help you get stronger, too.'

He heaved a sigh of relief as he listened to her running lightly down the stairs. Thank goodness he hadn't upset her by blurting that out. But he really did wish he had a wife like her. Imagine having one you could chat to easily and joke with. It must be wonderful. It had only taken a few hours for him and Viv to use each other's first names and feel at ease together.

Then he thought of his daughter and another worry hit him. He hoped he hadn't pushed his lass into a loveless marriage.

Oh dear, was there no end to the things he had to worry about?

Let me get my life sorted out and my wife locked away, he thought, then I'll see to anything else that's necessary. Jane's dangerous.

Thank goodness my Frankie's got someone to protect her and fancy it being the chap Roy Tyler told me he was going to employ. He sounds reliable, if nothing else. But if she's unhappy with him as a husband, I'll help her get out of the marriage later, whatever it takes.

One step at a time. That was a very comforting motto at times like this.

*

When Sam had eaten his breakfast the following morning, Viv took his tray away then came back and sat on the end of the bed.

'It's been over a week now, Sam. Perhaps I could go into Rivenshaw to visit my cousin Henry? He'll be able to bring me up to date on what's happened there and maybe help me make plans for your return. I hope you won't even think of trying to go back till we have some way of keeping you safe.'

'Yes. I agree.'

'I think we should find out about your daughter first, though. Her safety is worrying you, isn't it?'

'Is there anything you don't notice?'

'Not much. Now, I'm sure you'll manage all right without me tomorrow so I could go then.'

He thought about that but shook his head. 'Any stranger arriving in Rivenshaw will attract attention. Higgerson was getting on friendlier terms with my wife and I bet he'll have men keeping a watch out for strangers. How about you go into Manchester instead and send a letter to Henry from your hotel? I'd say phone him, but we have an old-fashioned telephone exchange in the valley and there may be an eaves-dropper there.'

'That'd mean me being away for at least one night.'

'I'll manage. If Betsey can leave my trays on the landing, I'll bring them up to the attic – one step at a time if necessary.'

'Very well. If I go really early and post a letter as soon as I get to Manchester, it should get to Rivenshaw by second post. If it doesn't I'll just have to stay an extra day.'

'Good thinking.'

'Henry can come and meet me in Manchester and bring me up to date then we can make a few plans.'

He looked at her challengingly. 'For my return.'

'Are you sure?'

'Oh, yes. I have good men who'll look after me.'

30

Henry's clerk studied the letter suspiciously. Who had been writing to his master from some village near Todmorden? And in such a cheap, nasty envelope too! Then he remembered that Mr Redfern was in hiding. Could this be something to do with him? Mr Lloyd hadn't taken him into his full confidence but he couldn't help noticing a few things that didn't fit with his employer's normal behaviour. And he hadn't forgotten Higgerson's visit and rudeness.

Finlay took the letters in to Mr Lloyd, who waved one hand dismissively. 'I'll look at the mail later.'

'Um, you may wish to see this one straight away, sir.'

Mr Lloyd took the envelope from him, looking at him suspiciously. 'Why do you say that, Finlay?'

'I can't help noticing what goes on here – not that I speak of it to anyone – and it's not hard to put two and two together, what with Mr Redfern disappearing and all.'

'Well, continue keeping your conclusions to yourself. It could mean life or death to my client.'

'Of course I will, sir. And if you need a letter posting, I'll do it myself, instead of sending the office boy.'

'Thank you. Good idea.'

Even so, Henry waited till he was alone before slitting open the envelope. No date or surname inside, just a few words:

Fairview Hotel, Piccadilly. Any time today till late. Or tomorrow. Urgent. Your cousin.

He gasped. Had Sam had a relapse? No, Viv would have risked phoning if it were that. How clever of her to contact him this way, without even giving her name.

He glanced at the clock. If he hurried, he could catch the next train to Manchester, which left in just under twenty minutes.

He called his clerk in again and told him about the message and what he was doing. 'If anyone asks, Finlay, say I'm keeping an appointment with a barrister I deal with regularly.'

He left his rooms and strode across town, trying not to look as if he was in a hurry.

A small man who was calling himself Smith this week followed him unobtrusively, a man who was an expert at tailing someone without them knowing.

Henry bought a first-class ticket to Manchester.

Smith bought a third-class one. He wasn't dressed to look posh and would stand out like a sore thumb if he tried to travel first class, even though Mr Higgerson had given him the money for any expenses and wouldn't have quibbled at the cost.

In Manchester he watched Mr Lloyd take a cab from outside the station, then hailed the next in the line of waiting vehicles. 'Follow that cab. Quick.'

The driver scowled at him. 'Why?'

'Never mind why. I'll pay you double the fare.'

'Find someone else to do your dirty work. I'm taking a break.' He started to drive off.

Smith had been about to open the cab door and had to jump backwards quickly. He looked down the street and grimaced, making no attempt to take the next cab because the first one was already turning the corner into another busy street.

When his cab pulled up at the Fairview Hotel, Henry paid the driver and hurried inside. 'I'm looking for Mrs Nelson. She asked me to meet her here.'

'Your name, sir?'

'Lloyd.'

He consulted a list. 'Ah yes. I'll send someone up to her room. Do you have a business card?'

'Yes.' He fumbled in his pocket and took one out, then paced up and down waiting for his cousin to join him.

The lad came back. 'She'll be down in a minute and will meet you in the cafe. Shall I find you a table, sir?'

'Yes please.' Henry gave him a tip and sat tapping his fingers on the table.

Two minutes later she came in and sat down opposite him. 'Thank goodness you could come today, Henry.'

'Is something wrong? Sam isn't worse, is he?'

'On the contrary, he's a lot better and wants to arrange his return to Rivenshaw.'

'Thank goodness he's better but he shouldn't return yet.'

'He thinks differently. And you may be glad to know you weren't followed here. I didn't join you till I was sure of that.'

'You always were a clever woman.'

'Never mind compliments. Sam's determined to go back and he says his men will protect him.'

That didn't take much thinking about. 'He'd better not go home then. He might be best staying with his daughter in Birch End. Who knows whether all the servants are loyal to him at his own house?'

'He's planning to go to the workshop.'

Henry sucked in air and blew it out slowly. 'We'll need to hire men to guard him then.'

'He insists his own workers will do that. He trusts them absolutely but he needs you to contact Pete and Gus to let them know he's coming. They'll make the necessary arrangements. It's all been planned in advance.'

He looked at her in surprise. 'Planned in advance?'

'To protect Frankie. Only it's Sam they'll be protecting and they'll need to know that. He's made a new will leaving everything to her.' She took an envelope out of her handbag and handed it to him. 'It's very simple but properly witnessed. This is just in case things go wrong.'

He took the single page out and read it quickly. 'Yes. That's all right. That's definitely his signature and with you as a witness as well as this nephew of Betsey's, it'll stand up in court.'

'Good.'

'Their men are devoted to him so I suppose that's all right, but there's still his wife and who knows what she'll do? He does accept that she was the one who poisoned him, doesn't he? I have no doubt about it.'

'Neither does he now. It upset him a lot, not because he cares about her but because he was stupid to trust her after the way her behaviour's gone from bad to worse in the past year or two.'

'You're sure he's fit to return?'

'He hasn't got his old strength back so would be helpless to defend himself physically, but he's fretting and that isn't good for him either. Mentally he's back to normal and I think he *needs* to take his life in hand again. Oh, and he particularly wants to make sure that his daughter isn't unhappy with her new husband. Any chance of reassuring him? Have you noticed how they're getting on together?'

Henry smiled. 'Several of us have noticed how happy she looks with Jericho, and he with her. If I didn't know it was a marriage of convenience, I'd think both of them had married for love.'

She relaxed visibly. 'Good. That'll take one worry off his mind. He doesn't want her to have an unhappy married life like his.'

'Jericho Harte might not be her equal socially but he's a good man, kind and intelligent. He doesn't even mind her working; has a very modern attitude towards women.'

'That's good to know too.'

'Can you come back to Rivenshaw with him, Viv? Just in case Sam needs further medical help. We'll continue to pay you for your services, of course.'

'I'll be happy to do that if he wants me to, but I'm quite sure time will be the best healer now – once he's done something about his wife. It'll take time but it's my guess he'll get most of his strength back. He was a strong, well-fed man, after all. Unfortunately that can't be rushed.'

'Shall I send Cresley to pick you both up again?'

'I have my own car there. We'll probably be better coming back in that. I don't think anyone will recognise it as we drive into town.'

By then it was lunchtime so Henry had a quick meal with her then asked the concierge to summon a taxi to take him back to the station.

He smiled as he got into the vehicle. Things were definitely looking up.

Smith was sitting on a bench outside the station and saw the taxi that had taken Lloyd away return half an hour later. What a bit of luck. No mistaking the driver's large red nose and the small dent in the rear offside wing. Wherever Lloyd had gone couldn't be all that far away. He hurried across to the taxi, which had joined the end of the waiting line and tapped on the driver's window.

'You need to take the taxi at the head of the queue,' the man said.

'I don't want to take a taxi. I saw my employer's cousin drive off with you half an hour or so ago and I know my employer wants to contact him urgently. I thought if I could catch him, I could pass on a message to phone his cousin.' He winked. 'Might earn us both a little bonus.'

The taxi driver looked at him with more interest. 'He went to the Fairview Hotel, if that's any use.'

He slipped a pound note into the man's hand. 'I can't thank you enough. Could you take me there? I'll make it worth your while.'

'Go and wait round the next corner on the left. I'll pick you up there.'

When Smith arrived at the hotel, there was a taxi already waiting there for a fare and the concierge refused to let another taxi hang about at such a slack time of day.

It wasn't a time to make a fuss. Smith slipped the driver an extra pound and asked him to wait round the corner, then went to wait on one of the seats in the lobby.

The concierge frowned and came across to ask what he wanted.

'I'm waiting for a friend. He's going to treat me to lunch in your cafe for a birthday treat.'

The doorman didn't look best pleased but gave him the benefit of the doubt. He went back to his station near the entrance but kept glancing in Smith's direction.

Half an hour later his shift must have ended because another uniformed chap replaced him. The new concierge didn't even glance at the man sitting in the rear corner reading a newspaper. Perhaps the other one had forgotten to tell him to keep an eye on Smith.

To his relief, he was rewarded for his patience by Mr Lloyd leaving the cafe with a lady. She was well dressed but not fashionably so. He folded the newspaper and moved closer, pretending to be checking through the rack for something else to read.

They went across to the desk and he was close enough to hear the conversation.

'How may I help you, Mrs Nelson?'

'My cousin needs a taxi. Could you call one, please?'

'Certainly.' The concierge signalled to the bellboy who ran outside.

Henry gave her a kiss on the cheek. 'You go up to your room now, Viv.'

Smith watched as Lloyd went to wait for his taxi near the outer door and she vanished into the lift.

He hesitated. Which of them should he follow? He decided she'd be more likely to lead him to Redfern.

He watched Lloyd get into the only taxi waiting outside, then heard the commissionaire tell the lad to have Mrs Nelson's car brought round.

As he watched her come down and go to the reception desk to pay her bill, another taxi drove under the portico. He went out to the taxi that was waiting for him and to his relief it was nearby.

Smith hurried across to it.

'Where to now, sir?'

'I have to follow a lady who's about to drive off. Her husband is afraid she's being unfaithful. She'll be out in a minute – yes, there she is. That must be her car. I need to find out where she goes. I'll pay you double the fare to follow her. You'll be doing a favour to a decent gentleman who doesn't deserve such treatment from his wife.'

'Double fare you said? What if she goes out into the country?'

'Doesn't matter. You'll still get double the fare.'

'You're on. It's not a busy time of day so when she sets off it'll be easy to follow her.' He grinned. 'You're in luck. I have my flat cap in the glove compartment. I can change this hat for it and if she notices us following her, she'll think it's another person in another car. Most women can't tell one car from another anyway.'

More likely she wouldn't even check to see whether she was being followed, Smith thought. It was a chance he'd have to take.

They followed Mrs Nelson's car for quite some way, sometimes falling back and risking losing her and at other times staying closer to her vehicle. Smith began to get a bit worried she'd notice them once they'd left the city and the traffic started to thin out a lot more.

When they'd been going over an hour, the driver began to look anxious. 'I might need to buy some more petrol soon.'

'Have you enough to take us a little further?'

'Yes. And I do have a spare can in the boot in case I run out. But I could lose her while I'm filling up by hand.'

'Well, do your best.'

Shortly after this conversation the mysterious Mrs Nelson turned off towards a village called Pelbank.

Smith took a sudden decision. 'Drive past or she'll guess she's being followed.'

It was his guess she'd reached her destination because the small side road she'd taken had a battered sign under its name that said *TO VILLAGE ONLY, NO THROUGH ROAD*. The sign looked old and weary as if it'd been there a long time and the road to it wasn't 'made up' as the taxi driver commented disapprovingly, just a bare earth track.

'They can't afford tarmac for all these small places but it's not good for cars like mine to bump along them.'

Smith ignored him and scanned the surrounding

countryside. He couldn't stand much more of this idiot who'd hardly stopped talking since he set off. Besides, he'd prefer to take over the driving from now on so that he'd have the freedom to react more quickly.

'Could you pull over, please? I need to relieve myself.'

'Good idea, sir. I'm a bit that way myself.'

Smith hid a smile. When the driver turned his back to him and unbuttoned his trousers, he picked up a rock that had fallen off a crumbling drystone wall nearby and walloped him on the head a couple of times. Not hard enough to hurt him seriously but hard enough to knock him dizzy for a few seconds.

By the time the driver had gathered his wits together, his hands were fastened behind his back with his own tie, a good solid piece of material, and his feet were bound together with a handy bit of cord Smith usually carried in his pocket. It'd take some time for him to get free from these.

'What the hell are you doing?'

Smith ignored him and went over to the taxi.

'Hoy! You! Come back! Damn you, come back!'

Smith didn't look round as he drove off. He turned back the way they'd come and then headed up the bumpy dirt road towards the village. A tiny dump of a place it was, too. He slowed down and looked round but there was no sign of the car he'd been following.

Where the hell had she gone? She hadn't come back on to the main road again. He'd have seen her.

31

Long before she reached the turn for the village, Viv became aware that the taxi was following her. The driver might have changed his hat for a flat cap and then back again, but he hadn't bothered to change the yellow chamois gloves.

She couldn't handle this on her own, so slowed down at the village pub and drove her car quickly round to the rear. She ran inside and found the landlord, explaining about being followed and urged him to phone Betsey's nephew to check that she really was a friend and worth helping.

'No need, love. Betsey's told us about you more than once and I've seen you a few times driving out to the farm in that little car of yours. Proper proud of you becoming a doctor, she is.'

Viv managed to squeeze out a few tears and pretended to be terrified as she told him about being followed all the way from Manchester. 'I don't want whoever it is to follow me to Betsey's and hurt her. What am I going to do?'

'What? I'm not having women terrified of being attacked in *our* village, thank you very much. I've got a wife and daughter to think about as well. Anyway, who the hell does he think he is coming here to cause trouble?'

'Do we need to call the police to have him arrested?'

'It'd take them over an hour to get here. No, you leave this to us, little lady.'

The landlord, a chivalrous man, gave her into the care

of his wife and called on a couple of his burly regulars to help him sort out a bit of trouble. The three men waited just inside the doorway and sure enough the taxi that had been following her turned up, slowed right down then parked in front of the pub.

'Is that him, Dr Nelson?' the landlord called.

'Yes, it is.'

'He's going to regret this.' He forced a smile to his face and strolled out to the car. As the man inside started to open the door, he yanked it wide open, grabbed the man and flung him to the ground.

Smith tried to fight back but he was outnumbered and outweighed by his opponents.

Viv and the landlady watched with relish as they shook the man like a rat and one of the men twisted his arm behind his back.

'That'll learn him,' the landlady said.

'Yes, but there's something wrong.' Viv realised what it was and ran out to look in the back of the car.

The landlord turned to her. 'Something wrong?'

'There was another man in the car with him and that man your friends are holding is smaller than the driver and he isn't wearing the yellow gloves. The driver didn't stop anywhere to let the passenger out on the way here, so I wonder . . . does this man own the taxi or has he perhaps stolen it? He must be the one who hired the taxi to follow me.'

The landlord peered inside the vehicle, then opened the boot and pulled out an overcoat. 'This yours?' he asked their prisoner.

'Yes. Of course it is. My car, my overcoat. And if you don't let me go I'll have the law on you.'

The landlord shook out the overcoat and held it against their prisoner. 'This coat can't possibly be yours. It's far too big and you're only a little 'un. It'd fit me, this one would, and I'm a big chap.' He patted his bulging stomach complacently.

'I dropped off my passenger at a farm. He must have forgotten his overcoat.'

'There aren't any farms past here. That road only leads across the moors. Pull the other leg, why don't you? It's got bells on it!' He laughed at his own joke then said, 'Take him inside, lads. It's too cold to do anything here. It may take us a bit of time to beat the truth out of him.'

'But I—'

Just then another customer drove up in a rusty old van and helped out a man with blood trickling from a wound on the side of his forehead. The captive tried to shrink back behind his captors.

'I found this 'un by the side of the road. Had his hands tied behind his back, he did, an' some cord still tied round one leg. Said his car had been stolen.'

The taxi driver pointed to their captive. 'That's him an' that's my car! Call the police! He's a damned thief.'

Viv went across to the injured man. 'They've got him safe. Let me look at that cut. I'm a doctor.'

He reared back. 'A woman doctor? No, thank you. I'll be all right, missus. What I want to do is punch that chap in the face before you call the police.'

The landlord smiled. 'We've got a cold, damp cellar. He might fall down the steps if you give him a bit of a shove. And once he's down there we'll lock him in the coal cellar at the back and he can yell his head off till the police come. No one will hear him.'

They frogmarched their captive across the bar and into the back room. There the landlord opened the cellar door and stepped back, gesturing to the driver. 'Be my guest.'

The taxi driver grinned. 'I'll do it later. He'll have something to look forward to then.'

When they'd taken their captive down, the driver said apologetically, 'I'm still mad at him but I can't hit a bloke who's tied up.'

The landlord chuckled. 'Your choice. He'll be nice and worried about it though. Now, how about I get you a pint of beer?'

The taxi driver's grin grew broader. 'Good idea. That'll set me nicely to rights.' He went across to the bar where the landlady was already drawing the pint.

The landlord turned to Viv. 'What do you want us to do with that sod in the cellar, Dr Nelson?'

'Well, what would help me most would be for you to keep him here till tomorrow afternoon then hand him over to the police. Maybe you could persuade the taxi driver the thief would be the better for a long cold night on bread and water.'

The landlord looked at her in surprise.

'I need to take the man I've got waiting for me at Betsey's away from here. His wife has tried to kill him once and we're about to do something about her. I'm sure her nephew will look after Betsey once we've left. We don't want anyone hurting her.'

He goggled at her.

'It's all true, I promise you. We'll have the police to help us deal with it once we get to Rivenshaw but I need to get my patient there safely and not let his wife get hold of him again.'

'Eh, to think of such things happening in real life! It's better than what you see in the cinema, this is. I enjoyed capturing that sod and I'll enjoy handing him over to the police even more.'

'Tell them Sergeant Deemer in Rivenshaw knows about it all.'

His wife, who'd been listening with great interest, got out a piece of paper and a stubby pencil and wrote that down, then pulled another pint of beer.

The landlord watched her go across to a chair near the fire and give the taxi driver a second glass of beer. 'I reckon he likes his ale, that one, judging by the colour of his nose. Won't be much trouble to get him drunk and keep him here overnight. *Not* in the cellar, in a soft, cosy bed.'

She grinned. 'Perfect. Thank you for trusting me.'

'Someone brought up by Betsey wouldn't lie to us. Anyway, we look after our own in our village. Allus have, allus will.'

Viv drove along the track that led from the village to the farm, allowing herself to sit in her car for a moment or two before she got out. Sheer relief made her shiver and she had to take a few deep breaths to calm down.

They had to plan Sam's return carefully. She didn't want him getting hurt again. His wife was obviously still trying to find him and he hadn't fully recovered yet.

The landlord was right. This was like a film, only she didn't like seeing it happen in real life. She was never going to watch any more whodunit films. Sherlock Holmes and Dr Watson were welcome to the glory of catching wicked criminals. In real life it was terrifying.

What would she have done if she hadn't been near the pub?

The people there might actually have saved her life, just as she intended to save Sam's. Never mind him being her patient, he'd quickly become her friend. He was such a lovely man, so interesting to chat to.

When she went into the cottage Viv found Betsey's nephew sharing a pot of tea and a plate of biscuits with his aunt.

They looked at her, then Betsey stood up and came to

put an arm round her. 'What's happened, love? Something bad. I can tell.'

'Let's bring Sam down then I can tell you all at the same time. Afterwards he and I will have to get our things packed and put them in the car. We're leaving tonight.'

Sam joined them, looking upset as she told them what had happened. 'I didn't mean to put you in danger, Viv.'

'I'm fine. Let's get this horrible situation sorted out. I worry that your wife will go totally insane and hurt someone else. I wonder if she's had a minor seizure or two. Who knows what causes such mental deteriorations? Now, I need to know what your exact plans are and where to drive you.'

'Can you phone someone for me first?' Sam asked.

'Isn't that a bit risky?'

'I'll be careful what I say, believe me. I need to check that my foremen are all set to act. The landlord is Pete's brother. He'll recognise my voice and know if something's going on.'

'Are you sure that's wise?'

'My foremen are good lads and will keep an eye on me. They'll have set in motion some other things we worked out to protect us from my wife.'

'You planned well ahead.'

'I expected something like this to be needed to protect my daughter, not myself. Eh, it'll be good to see them again. The lads and I have been working together for a good many years. I'll feel safer just to have them nearby.'

'So that's where I take you first, to the workshop?'

He looked at her anxiously. 'Yes. I don't really want you involved but I can't see any way round it. I'm too weak still to walk around town. And anyway, I'm intending to take certain people by surprise.'

He seemed to be talking to himself as he added, 'And afterwards there are going to be big changes made. I'm sure

Henry Lloyd will find a way to change my will, for a start. And I'll have the doctor in to check my wife. She's acting so strangely I hardly recognise her any longer.'

Viv said nothing. But she was determined to help protect him if she could. He was a good man, married to a bad wife.

Other plans were under way to take people by surprise. Jane Redfern was furious that Sam had escaped her. If he was still alive, then she might be the one in danger. She had to sit down for a few minutes; the anger about him was so strong it made her dizzy.

The only way to get at him now was through their daughter. He'd do anything to protect Frankie, who'd stolen Jane's husband's affections away from her and was an abomination, a totally unnatural creature who also needed to be prevented from ruining the rest of Jane's life by her wanton behaviour.

She lay awake in bed for most of the night, trying to work out what to do, then fell asleep at last. It was two hours past her usual time when she summoned her maid to attend her the next morning.

Pearl looked at her anxiously. 'Are you all right, ma'am? You look a bit pale and drawn.'

'No, I'm not all right! And you're not going to be all right either unless we stop them. If they find out about the lozenges, they'll lock us both away. And probably hang us.'

Pearl clutched her throat with one hand. 'I only did what you told me. I didn't know what you were doing. It's you they'll charge with attempted murder.'

'And if they lock me away you won't get your money, plus I'll tell them you got the poison for me, which you did.'

'I only picked up a tin of lozenges. And you *promised* you'd pay me, but you still haven't done it.'

'I said I'd pay you when he was dead. And he isn't dead yet, is he? I'll tell them you were involved . . . unless . . .'

'Unless what?'

'Unless you help me get rid of my daughter.'

'You want to kill her as well?'

'We don't have much choice. If we kill her and she leaves a note saying she killed her father and the guilt is weighing her down, that'll take the blame away from us. I can imitate her handwriting.'

Pearl looked at her mistress in disbelief. The stupid old woman had gone completely crazy now and she didn't even seem to be planning to pay what she'd promised. Everything else was ready for Pearl to disappear and go out to Australia as Clarry's wife, the man she'd known secretly for a couple of years. His real wife could be left behind, together with his five brats, and best of all Pearl would never have to see Mrs Redfern again.

Clarry didn't know about the lozenges, though, so she couldn't ask for his help. He thought she was going to steal the money to set them up in the colonies in style. He'd have drawn the line at getting involved with murder. Well, she didn't like it either, but helping her mistress was the only way she'd seen a chance of escaping a miserable life.

She continued to keep her eyes fixed on her mistress as if she was listening carefully, but it was only more of that senseless ranting and raving. The stupid old hag was getting more and more strange by the day. It was a wonder she'd got away with it for so long. Without Pearl here to help her, people would soon realise how bad she was.

Suddenly it occurred to Pearl that all need not be lost. She could do just what she'd told Clarry: steal enough for the pair of them to escape and make a new life for themselves. It'd be more risky to steal the money than be given it, but the state the mistress was in, it'd not be hard to make an opportunity and she'd steal some of her jewellery as well.

Well, Clarry had better be ready to leave at the drop of a hat or Pearl would have to run away on her own. She'd *earned* that money, given what she'd put up with.

Once she had it, she knew how to change her appearance and if Clarry wouldn't come with her, there was another place where she could be safe for a few weeks, till all the fuss had died down.

She prepared a cup of tea for her mistress and one for herself, putting plenty of the stuff that calmed the mistress down into her cup. Then she went up to her attic bedroom to pack her bag quickly. She wasn't staying here a minute longer than she had to.

When she came down, she gulped down her tea, which didn't taste as nice cold, but she was thirsty. Only, the room started spinning and then everything went dark.

Jane waited a few minutes then went to the kitchen, smiling as she saw Pearl lying on the floor, fast asleep, snoring lightly.

The maid hadn't been very clever. The minute she'd taken a sip of the tea, Jane had realised what was in it. Everyone was against her. Everyone. But she was too clever for them. And she was going to make sure they all paid for upsetting her, but she'd start off with her daughter.

She knew one of the men who did jobs for her cousin, knew where he was staying too. She borrowed Pearl's shabby coat and hat, pulling the hat down over her forehead and winding a scarf round her neck.

The man was in and she pretended to be a friend of Pearl's. He agreed to do as she wished for ten shillings, so she went back home to wait in comfort.

As an afterthought she went upstairs and tied Pearl to the bed. There, serve her right! She wished she could see her maid's face when she woke up.

The clock seemed to be moving very slowly tonight, but eventually, the little hand passed midnight and she went out to meet the man who had said he could find a house-breaker to get her into the house her daughter had *stolen* from her, just as she was trying to steal Sam's money.

Everything would rightfully belong to her when he died, everything.

Well, Sam hadn't come back, which he would have done if he'd recovered. He was probably hanging on, so close to death it wouldn't be hard to give him another little push. She even had some of the lozenges in her pocket.

The man she'd found to help her had a friend with him, as arranged, but told her there were men keeping watch near the house, so she had to do exactly as they told her if she wanted to get inside it.

One of them went off to check again that the way they'd found down into the cellar was clear. It was the chute through which coal was delivered. He came back and whispered that the trapdoor was so loosely barred from inside it'd be child's play to free it.

She nodded. It was all coming together. She just had to be patient a short time longer. Once she had her daughter captive, *he* would be brought back to her and have to do exactly as she told him – till the time came for him to die.

She could see her way so very clearly now.

32

It felt good to get out of the cottage. Sam walked slowly but steadily towards the car. He could see that Viv was ready to help him but he didn't need it.

He laughed softly as she got in beside him. 'It makes me feel better just to be *doing* something.'

'You're normally a very active man, I should think.'

'Yes. I don't like to sit around the house doing nothing. Frankie and I worked long hours to keep away from the house and *her*. But also because we loved making things. We used to chat about all sorts of things.'

She drove for half an hour and for most of the time he sat quietly beside her, only speaking occasionally.

As they got closer, she asked, 'Where exactly are we going in Rivenshaw? I don't know where your workshop is.'

'No. I'll tell you exactly where to go when we get near the town. I know ways through the back alleys near shops and businesses, places where we're not likely to meet anyone at this time of a cold winter's night. The lads will be waiting for us at the workshop, I'm sure.'

'I like the way you talk about them and about your daughter.'

'You'll like her too.'

'I'm sure I shall if she's anything like you.'

After a while he said, 'Slow down now and drive as quietly as you can.'

He gave her directions, some of which had them bumping along over uneven surfaces behind people's backyards. As he'd predicted, they met no other vehicles and saw no one out at that hour of the night.

'Pull up in front of that blank wall,' he said. 'This is the rear of our workshop.'

She stopped the vehicle, wishing there was enough light to check the colour of his complexion. 'What do you intend to do now?'

'Wait. One of them will come out soon, I'm sure.'

They seemed to wait a long time then suddenly she jumped in shock and let out a squeak of surprise as a figure loomed beside the car. The man opened the door and squatted to speak to Sam in a low voice. 'Welcome back, boss. We've done what you planned.'

'Good lad. This is my doctor and friend, Viv Nelson.'

Sam nodded. 'Do you need any help to get inside, boss?'

'You could lend me your arm. I'm a bit weak still but not too bad considering.'

The workshop was dark but Sam and his helper moved confidently across it, threading their way past a big piece of machinery and various work stands. He opened a door and they all went inside his office.

Once the door was closed, another man switched on a lamp and came forward to shake his hand. 'Good to have you back, boss.'

'Good to be back, Pete. I need to sit down, though.'

When he'd sunk into his own chair he sighed happily. The men came to stand nearby.

'Eh, we thought we'd lost you, boss.'

'You nearly did. This is Viv, my doctor. Are the others ready?'

'Yes. We didn't put the light on but they're out in the loading bay, waiting. They're raring to go.'

'You'll have to go without me, I'm afraid. I'd only hold you back. The doctor and I will wait for you here. You know what to do. Someone can come and fetch me when you've got Frankie safe, then we can send the police after my wife.'

'Gus is going to stay here with you. We don't expect any trouble but best to be prepared. We made sure no one saw us coming here.'

Sam leaned forward in his chair. 'Have you seen my daughter lately?'

'Aye, boss. Miss Frankie's looking well, and a lot happier than she did when she was living with her mother.'

'And her husband? How does he treat her?'

Viv hid a smile. He must love his daughter very much to be so anxious about her.

'He seems fond of her and she of him. Very protective, he is. I've a neighbour works at Tyler's and he says they both work there happily. It's surprised the men how good she is at her job. There's a couple have had to eat their words about women doing men's work.' He chuckled and patted Sam's arm. 'No need to worry about her, boss.'

'Thank goodness.'

Another man came into the office. 'They're ready.'

'Switch the office light off,' Pete said. He went out first.

Gus whispered, 'I'll just go with them to lock up. Back in a couple of minutes. Don't switch the light on till I'm back.'

The trouble was, Gus didn't come back as quickly as Sam had expected. He heard the big delivery van leave then a door opened and shut at the back, but there was still no sign of Gus.

He turned to Viv. 'It doesn't take this long to get back here from the loading bay. Something's gone wrong. Hide behind that filing cabinet and no heroics if there's trouble. Just try to stay out of sight till you can escape.'

The door opened and a man stood in the doorway, a dark silhouette against the big, dim space outside.

'Don't do anything stupid,' Higgerson said. 'This is not what you think.'

Jericho came awake with a start as someone touched his arm. It took him a minute to recognise the slight figure of their younger maid. He heard his wife stir beside him.

'There are intruders downstairs in the cellar, sir. Hilda sent me to fetch you. She's got a poker to hit 'em with if they try to come up into the house.'

'Hell's fire!' He was out of bed in an instant and Frankie followed suit.

'You stay here,' he said quietly.

She ignored that, grabbed her dressing gown and followed him quietly down the stairs.

As they entered the kitchen they heard a shriek from inside the cellar and he went to the open door that led down into it.

Maria nudged her mistress and passed her the metal bar they used to sharpen knives on, grabbing the rolling pin for herself.

'Good girl.'

There was a curse from the cellar and Jericho roared, 'Someone put the damned light on.' He disappeared down the stairs into the darkness.

Maria switched on the light and Frankie peeped into the cellar, her heart thudding with anxiety when she saw Jericho grappling with a man nearly as tall as him, with another man trying to get behind her husband. Hilda was huddled to one side and the men didn't seem to have noticed her.

'Go to the back door and shout for help,' Frankie told Maria. 'There should be men nearby and they'll come running.'

She paused in shock as she saw her mother appear from

a dark corner of the cellar, also trying to get to Jericho. She had a knife in her hand.

Hilda started throwing jars at her, which distracted her, while Frankie ran down and managed to hit Jericho's second opponent from behind before he'd realised she was there. She sent him stumbling into a pile of coal.

Before she got to her husband she saw another man come down the coal chute and turned to guard herself against him till she recognised Pete's voice.

'It's me, missus. You get back. There are others on their way.' He moved purposefully towards the second man and Hilda continued to hurl jars from the nearby shelves at Mrs Redfern.

It was all over quickly after that but when Frankie moved forward to deal with her mother, she saw Hilda on her knees with blood pouring from her arm and no sign of Jane.

She ran to help Hilda staunch the blood.

'Sorry, Mrs Harte. When she slashed my arm I couldn't think for the pain and she must have got away then. I heard her scrabbling over the coal. She must have got out by the chute.'

It was a few minutes before they had the men secured.

Jericho came across to Frankie. 'Are you all right?'

'Yes. But my mother's got away and Hilda's suffered a bad cut.'

'Can you phone for the police first and then the doctor? I don't want to leave these men till we get handcuffs on them.'

'What do you think they were after? We haven't got anything of value here.'

'Yes we have. Something extremely valuable. You.'

'That must be why my mother was with them. I'll go and phone the police.'

'Did you see Mrs Redfern running away?' he asked one of the men who'd been keeping watch and had now joined them.

'No one ran out of the house. We'd have seen them.'

He frowned. Frankie had sounded so sure that her mother had got up the chute out of the cellar. What if she had run into the house, instead? The cellar was so poorly lit, she might have managed to escape notice.

He turned to the young maid. 'You keep hold of that rolling pin, Maria, and if either of those two men causes any trouble, hit them with it good and hard.' Then he ran up the stairs into the kitchen.

He heard a voice coming from the hall, someone speaking in a strange, almost singsong way.

'I'm going to kill you, Frances. I've always hated you. I never wanted a daughter and you're a bad one. They'll think one of the men got you. They'll never believe a mother could do that.'

She stabbed wildly with the knife and Frankie jumped back, but her mother was between her and any door and she was brandishing the knife.

Mrs Redfern laughed hysterically. 'I'm going to rid the world of you. I made a mistake bearing you, a bad mistake, but I'm going to kill you now.'

In the workshop, Higgerson spread his hands wide. 'I'm not armed and I'm not here to attack you.'

Gus came up behind him in the doorway. 'He let the others go to help Frankie and persuaded me to let him speak to you, but I'm here in case he causes trouble.'

'I'm not here to *cause* trouble but to stop my damned cousin from committing a crime and bringing shame on the family. Just listen to me.'

Sam nodded. 'Go on.'

'I had word tonight that she's got two men who've worked for me to do an extra job for her. She offered them a great deal of money apparently. They've gone to break into your daughter's house but the woman who told me about it doesn't know why. So what your wife expects to do there, I don't know.'

Sam stood up abruptly, felt dizzy and grabbed Viv's arm. 'Was she in a strange mood last time you saw her?'

'Yes. Bit of a wild look in her eyes, that's for sure. That maid had to calm her down when we were talking. That's why I decided not to do anything else for her.'

He saw the incredulity on Sam's face and said harshly, 'Whatever else I've done, I've never murdered anyone and I don't intend to, either. I prefer to act within the law to get what I want, even if that means stretching the law a little.'

Sam looked back at Higgerson. 'If you're telling the truth, she's probably gone after Frankie.'

He swayed dizzily and had to sit down suddenly in the chair. 'I'm not . . . able to walk far without help, let alone run anywhere.'

Gus stepped forward. 'I'll help you, boss.'

'I never thought I'd agree with you, Higgerson, but I do need help to deal with my wife.'

'I can take you to your daughter's house in my car.'

Gus scowled at him and he laughed softly. 'Your master will be quite safe, I assure you. I much prefer to have him alive as a witness to say I wasn't involved with his wife in this. He'd be far more credible than anyone else, don't you think, given the fact that we're not exactly friends?'

Sam stared at him coldly. 'I'd rather you kept out of it but I am still not my usual self, so I'll risk coming with you.'

'I'm coming too,' Viv said.

Higgerson shrugged. 'My car is at the front ready to go. I'll sit in the front with my chauffeur. You three can squash in the back.'

*

Jane was brandishing the knife so wildly as she shrieked out insults and accusations that Jericho had to wait to get it off her. He crept forward slowly, trying to get close enough to intervene successfully because the slightest mistake on his part might let her hurt his wife.

'Don't do this, mother!' Frankie pleaded.

Jericho could tell that she was trying to make her voice soothing and keep her mother's attention on herself not him. Good lass, he thought. Keep it up.

'There are other ways of getting rid of me. Jericho and I can leave Rivenshaw and you'll never see me again.'

'I shall *enjoy* killing you. *You* should have died in the war, not your brother. And your father should be dead too. I don't know why he isn't. He's a fool, too stupid to see you for what you are. Evil!' As she raised the knife, Jericho hurled himself at her.

She was stronger than he'd expected and howled like an animal in pain as she swept the knife wildly to and fro, trying to stab him.

Then the noise stopped abruptly and she sank to her knees, dropping the weapon. He could clearly see the expression of surprise on her face and couldn't for a moment work out what had happened. Then she hit the ground and lay still, eyes open but not seeming to see anything.

Frankie looked across the hall at him. 'Did you knock her out?'

'I didn't touch her. She was waving the knife about and I didn't want to risk getting stabbed. I thought you might have thrown something at her from behind.'

'No. There's nothing to throw on the telephone table.'

'Stay back.' He bent down, saw the knife lying on the floor near Mrs Redfern's outflung hand and kicked it away, then knelt beside the motionless figure. He was surprised at how small she now seemed.

'I think she's had a seizure or something. She's still breathing, but only faintly, more like faint snoring.'

Frankie leaned back against the wall, shuddering with reaction now and with tears running down her face. 'My own mother . . . tried to kill me.'

'Darling, give me another moment to check her. I daren't come across to you yet in case she's faking this collapse, though I don't think she is.'

'She was gloating about killing me.'

He bent over the body hearing a sort of choking sound. The woman hadn't moved at all. He listened but the faint snoring sound had stopped. 'Ah. She's just stopped breathing.'

'My mother's dead?'

'I'm afraid so.' He pulled Frankie into his arms. 'She'd gone mad. She didn't mean what she said.'

'She did, Jericho. She's never loved me.'

'Eh, my darling lass. I'll have to make up for it then.'

She huddled against him, but he kept an eye on the body. Just in case.

After taking a few deep breaths, she moved away. 'You can phone the police now. And the doctor.'

'He'll not be able to help her.'

'No. But he'll have to certify that she's dead, I suppose. I don't even know what the formalities are now.'

Someone hammered on the front door and she heard her father's voice. 'Frankie! Are you there? Someone let us in.'

She ran to unbolt it and turn the key in the lock. 'Dad!' She flung herself into his arms. 'You're alive.'

The woman standing quietly by his side said, 'He needs to sit down.'

Then Frankie noticed Higgerson standing beside them and looked at her father in alarm.

'He was the one who warned us about her coming after you.'

'Oh.'

Her father looked past her at the body on the floor. 'Is that . . . your mother?'

'Yes. Jericho thinks she's dead. She went mad, screeching and shouting that she'd come here to kill me, then she suddenly collapsed.'

'Thank goodness you're safe.'

Jericho came forward. 'Let me help you into the kitchen, sir. I think you'd better sit down. You'll be needed when the police get here.'

Higgerson bowed to them all. 'Since I'm not needed, I'd just as soon go home again now. Deemer knows where to find me.'

Jericho watched him go. 'Why did he fetch you, Mr Redfern? That surprised me.'

'I think he found my wife's mental state too dangerous and murder a step too far. He's always been very careful of his own position in this town, and even he might not have wanted to be caught up in it when it became obvious that she'd stop at nothing.'

Viv was on her knees beside Jane's body. 'She's definitely dead. Probably a seizure.'

Frankie saw her father sway dizzily. 'Come into the kitchen and sit down, Dad. We can wait for Sergeant Deemer there.'

Jericho came forward and picked Sam up before he could protest.

'I'm sorry . . . to be so weak.'

Viv rejoined them. 'I think you'll recover quite quickly now, Sam. She's definitely dead.'

'Yes. I already feel as if a load has been taken off my shoulders, as if a long nightmare has ended. I'm not even sorry for her, and if that sounds harsh, I don't care.'

'It sounds a very reasonable reaction to me,' she said soothingly.

Frankie stared at the two of them. At the moment they seemed to be quite unaware of anyone else's presence, only of each other. Or was she reading too much into the doctor-patient relationship?

Then she felt Jericho's arm go round her shoulders again and leaned her cheek against his hand.

'The police will be here soon, lass. Once they've taken over this mess, everyone can start to sort out their lives.' He looked at the other two people and added in a whisper, 'Have you noticed how well your father and his doctor lady seem to be getting on?'

'I was just thinking about that, wondering if I was imagining it.'

'I don't think so.' He gazed into her eyes. 'And I don't think I'm imagining how well you and I get on together. Or am I? Did you only marry me because of your promise to your father?'

'No. I married you in the first place because I felt safe with you, trusted you. And then—'

'And then what?'

'Then I found out I could love you. As I once loved poor Martin. I didn't expect it to happen twice.'

'It's my first time of loving someone so deeply. Bear with me while I learn how to do it properly and make you happy again.'

'We both need to learn how to make the other happy.'

She was sorry when the police arrived and they had to deal with the unpleasantness.

And by the time they got to bed, she was too tired to do anything but sleep.

Epilogue

The following morning, Sam phoned his daughter and asked if she could come to visit him at her old home. 'Unfortunately, Viv is insisting I have a very quiet day. But I'd still like to see you and talk to you privately.'

'Jericho is going to work shortly. I'll drive to see you in about half an hour. It seems so long since we've had one of our chats.'

She drew up at the comfortable house and the door was opened before she got there.

Viv put one finger to her lips and whispered, 'Don't upset him, if you can help it. He's tired today, but he desperately wants to chat to you. Could you keep your visit to about half an hour then leave him to rest?'

'Has yesterday made him ill?'

'Not at all. It's tired him, yes, but it's also solved a lot of problems for him.'

'I shan't miss her; shan't even pretend to.'

'And why should you? She was in a terrible state of mind, which must have upset you. Oh, and I nearly forgot. We found her maid tied to a bed. She was apparently the one who fetched the lozenges. Sergeant Deemer arrested her and took her away.'

'Good.'

'Anyway, your father's in the sitting room, waiting for you.'

Frankie paused in the doorway, smiling at her father, feeling free to run and give him a hug before she pulled a chair closer to him.

'We're not going to mourn her,' he said. 'We'll attend her funeral, to prevent gossip, but after that we'll get on with our lives.' He took a deep breath and said slowly, 'What I want to talk to you about is—'

'My marriage?'

'Yes. I asked you to promise you'd marry. Did I push too hard? Are you regretting it now? I'd hate you to be in the same position as I was, married to someone you don't love, or indeed, may not even like.'

She took his hand in hers. 'Shh now and listen. I asked Jericho to marry me because I felt safe with him – and comfortable. And I quickly realised what a lovely person he is. I fell in love with him so quickly, I'm still a bit surprised by it. But he loves me too, so that's all right.'

Sam let out a long sigh of relief and reached out to take her hand and pat it a few times. 'Thank goodness. Oh, thank goodness.'

'You look happy but I can see you're tired, so I'm not going to stay long.'

'Yes. A load has been lifted from me. I did my best with your mother but she could never have made any man happy, and the past two years – well, you saw how she changed, got worse and worse. Viv thinks she was having small seizures that were destroying her brain.'

'Viv seems nice.'

'She is. I'm not rushing into anything, but I'd like to get to know her better. Would that upset you?'

'Not at all.'

'When I've recovered, let's invite our friends round and really celebrate your wedding. We want to make everyone aware that I approve of him.'

'Good idea.'

They sat for a while, quietly together, then he fell asleep in mid-sentence. She smiled and blew a kiss in his direction before tiptoeing out. She found Viv sitting reading a newspaper in the hall waiting for her.

'Did you sort everything out?'

'Yes. He's satisfied now that I'm happy to be married to Jericho.'

'I like the look of your husband from how he behaved yesterday, looking after you so carefully. He seems open and honest, and not a stupid man. You'd not be happy with a stupid person.'

'No. I wouldn't.' She looked sideways and rather daringly tossed the words back at her. 'You'd not be happy with a stupid person, either, Viv. Do you like my father?'

The older woman flushed slightly. 'Yes, I do.'

'He's not at all stupid, has learned a few hard lessons in life. Give him time to recover. If the two of you get to know one another even better who knows what will come of it?'

'What's he doing?'

'He fell asleep suddenly.'

'I'll go and sit with him.'

Frankie smiled as she drove home. She thought there was a good chance the rest of her father's life might give him the happiness he deserved.

And she was going home to Jericho. She was so lucky to have met him that day on the moors. It had made her really look at him and talk to him in a way she could never have done in a social setting with other people around and everyone being over-polite.

He was waiting at the front door and came towards her holding out his arms as she got out of the car. When she threw herself into them, he lifted her off the ground and twirled her round.

'Put me down, you fool.'

'Not till you promise to kiss me senseless as a reward.'

So she did. Well, she always kept her promises.

I'M HAVING A GOOD TIME
ON THE (W)HOLE
JWW

CONTACT ANNA

Anna is always delighted to hear from readers and can be contacted via the Internet.

Anna has her own web page, with details of her books, some behind-the-scenes information that is available nowhere else and the first chapters of her books to try out, as well as a picture gallery.

Anna can be contacted by email at
anna@annajacobs.com

You can also find Anna on Facebook at
www.facebook.com/AnnaJacobsBooks

If you'd like to receive an email newsletter about Anna and her books every month or two, you are cordially invited to join her announcements list. Just email her and ask to be added to the list, or follow the link from her web page.

www.annajacobs.com

This book was created by

Hodder & Stoughton

Founded in 1868 by two young men who saw that the rise in literacy would break cultural barriers, the Hodder story is one of visionary publishing and globe-trotting talent-spotting, campaigning journalism and popular understanding, men of influence and pioneering women.

For over 150 years, we have been publishing household names and undiscovered gems, and today we continue to give our readers books that sweep you away or leave you looking at the world with new eyes.